# MACHINE GUN JELLY

MACHINE GUN JELLY

This book is a work of fiction. The characters, places, incidents, and dialogue are the product of the author's imagination and are not to be construed as real, or if real, are used fictitiously. Any resemblance to actual events, locales, or persons, either living or dead, is purely coincidental.

Copyright © 2014 by Shane Norwood

All rights reserved. No part of this book may be used or reproduced in any manner whatsoever without the prior written permission of the publisher, except in the case of brief quotations embodied in critical articles and reviews.

For more information, to inquire about rights to this or other works, or to purchase copies for special educational, business, or sales promotional uses please write to:

Michael Conant, COO
michael@zharmae.com
www.zharmae.com

FIRST EDITION

Printed in the United States of America

Zharmae Publishing, logo, and the TZPP logo are trademarks of The Zharmae Publishing Press, L.L.C.

ISBN:   978-1-937365-39-4 (pbk.)

10  9  8  7  6  5  4  3  2  1

# MACHINE GUN JELLY

### Shane Norwood

This book is dedicated to the memories of "The Big Fella," **Victor George Charles Norwood**, my father, and his wife, **Elizabeth**, my mother.

It is also dedicated to my own wife, **Ximena**, and my children, **Fleur, Cielle, Makai, Kaiko,** and **Koa,** as are my mind, my body, my breath, and every beat of my barbarian British heart.

I would like to publicly express my gratitude to **Travis Grundy**, my publisher, for rolling the dice and for giving me a shot at the title. I hope you roll the Venus Throw, bro.

And finally, an extra-special thank you to **Sara Bangs**, my editor, for taking a clapped out Model T and turning it into a Mustang convertible. The effort and attention to detail that Sara put into this book has been phenomenal and if you enjoy it, which I hope you will, it will be in large part due to her.

# MACHINE GUN JELLY

# Part 1. Vegas. 1999.

The contradictions in Las Vegas begin almost immediately. The Spanish term *las vegas* translates as "the fertile plains" or "the meadows." Another interpretation, used by the people of Patagonia, could be "the water meadows."

Even for a town that prides itself on hyperbole when describing its many and storied attractions, the aforementioned terms seem a bit of a stretch. Las Vegas is set in what is, by and large, a burning, arid, hostile desert filled with wilted cacti, scorpions, and lizard shit. The only water meadow you are likely to encounter anywhere in the region is if some zonked-out greenskeeper forgets to turn the sprinklers off on the golf course. Furthermore, the town would not survive more than three days without irrigation before regressing back into a searing uninhabitable salt pan, and the nearest fertile plain is actually in Kentucky. Of course, this is nowhere near as inappropriate as Los Angeles, the City of Angels, but you get the drift.

In Vegas, they don't wait for the suckers to be born; they make them, and the only thing you are not allowed to do is not have any money. Disneyland on acid, mob playground, corporate meat market...Vegas constantly reinvents itself to stay ahead of the game and, depending on what kind of eyes you have, can be anything you want it to be. Shimmering desert oasis or sleazy skid row burlesque, as radiant as a fairy story princess or as ugly as a two-bit whore in daylight.

Vegas is sugar and cyanide, schmaltz and suicide, soft dreams and hard knocks, where the odds are stacked and so are the cocktail waitresses, and even the fickle finger of fate is on the take. It is the Church of Disillusion with rhinestone icons, where the gods are old fat guys and the only virgin is an airline. The sultan's palace where the harem doors are thrown open, but the tits aren't real, and the eunuchs do requests. The enchanted kingdom where you kiss the frog and take your chances on whether it turns into a handsome prince or a case of herpes. It is The Hard Word Hotel, where the welcome mat is a rental and the long-term residents are required to have their souls surgically removed.

Vegas is a deranged vaudeville, an old-time carnival mutated and gone mad, like one of those old fifties Cold War movies where the innocuous creature gets irradiated by nuclear fallout and assumes gigantic proportions. Las Vegas is a radioactive behemoth, sucking the energy it needs to survive through the I-15 freeway to LA like a giant straw.

In the movies the creature only stomps the shit out of everyone until the jets blow it away or the bespectacled white-coated boffins figure out how to destroy it, although they never tell you what they plan do with the body.

But Vegas just keeps on getting bigger and more voracious, and so do some of its inhabitants. And they never tell you what they plan to do with the body, either.

# Chapter 1

The room went quiet as Handyman Harris prepared to take the shot. The faces of the onlookers appeared ghastly and spectral through the neon-lit haze of cheap stogies and unfiltered cigarettes. They had been playing for six hours straight, and it had come down to this. The eight ball hanging over the top left pocket, the white hard up against the center of the bottom cushion, and Handyman Harris bent over his cue, squinting down its length. Only this. Nothing else in the world but that bright expanse of green baize between the two balls. Between the two balls, and between Handyman Harris and five grand.

His opponent, some rail-thin rube from Chickenshit, Minnesota, leaned his skinny denim ass against the bar, clutching his whisky. He peered from under the rim of his Stetson, using every ounce of his Saturday-matinée-learned cowboy cool to try to disguise the fact that he was shitting his pants. Big time. He had been very good. Much better than Handyman had expected. As a matter of fact, almost too good. But now it had come down to this. A tight angle on the cue, the gentle roll of the white down the table, that soft, sweet, barely audible kiss on the black, the silky roll of the eight ball down the pocket, the white coming softly to rest against the top cushion, and it was five big ones, in cold blood. Handyman closed his eyes for a second and played out the scenario in his mind's eye, mentally rehearsing the shot. He opened his eyes again and slowly drew back the cue, feeling the smooth cool wood sliding between his fingers just right. He started the tip of the cue on its short journey to the surface of the ball.

The phone rang, loud and jarring, in the silent room.

Handyman jerked the cue. The mis-hit shot skewed down the table and smacked into the black with a loud crack, cannoning it off the edge of the pocket and across the table. The white ball rolled, all soft and silky, into the pocket. Handyman stared in disbelief. Nobody spoke. The cowboy took out his finest shit-eating grin and plastered it across his face.

The phone rang again. The bartender lifted it from its receiver, held it briefly to his ear, and looked over to where Handyman was still staring at the hole where the white ball had disappeared. He held it toward him and said, "Handy. It's for you."

Handyman Harris went completely ballistic. "WHOEVER THAT MOTHERFUCKIN' COCKSUCKER IS, TELL HIM I'M COMIN' ROUND THERE, AND SHOVIN' THAT PHONE UP HIS FUCKIN' ASS SIDEWAYS."

"He says it's really important," said the bartender quietly.

"IMPORTANT. I'LL TELL YOU WHAT'S FUCKING IMPORTANT. FIVE GRAND IS FUCKING IMPORTANT. IMPORTANT IS NOT SOME DICKLESS PUKEBAG RINGING THE PHONE WHEN PEOPLE ARE TRYING TO PLAY POOL. WHO THE FUCK IS IT, ANYWAY?"

"It's the Don," said the bartender.

Suddenly the call was very, very important.

At first Crispin thought it was a request, until he looked up and saw the uniform of the bellhop that had handed him the slip of paper. The show was going great, and Crispin was bringing the house down. All the tables were full, all the seats at the bar were full, and people were standing around at the back and sitting on empty blackjack tables. People were screaming with laughter at his jokes and singing along with his songs, and his tip jar was overflowing. They were queuing up and falling over themselves to buy him drinks, and he was already sailing on an uneven keel. It was like the good old days. He was a star again and he adored it, lapping it up like milk and bathing in it like the sun. His fingers were flying over the keys, each intricate run bringing a new crescendo of applause and a new jolt of energy from the audience, and he felt as if he could play and sing 'til the cow jumped over the moon.

He opened the note and stared at it while the bellhop stood by waiting for a reply. The note said: *Urgent, repeat, urgent telephone call for Mr. Crispin Capricorn. Imperative he come to the phone immediately.*

"Oh, for fuck's sake," announced Crispin, forgetting the microphone and sending the room into paroxysms of laughter. Crispin slapped his hand over his mouth, with his eyes wide, mugging for the audience.

"Goodness gracious," he said with a stage giggle. "Did I just say that? Well, wash my mouth out with soap, Mrs. Johnson."

"Say it again," some wag shouted.

"Oh, I couldn't possibly. This is a family show. And besides, I never say 'for fuck's sake' in public."

He mugged again while the audience whistled and howled, before holding up his hands. "Ladies and gentlemen, and those of you who can't make up their minds," —audience howl— "I'm afraid I have to ask you to excuse me for just a teensy-weensy moment. The president is on the phone...probably wants me to do a White House dinner."

Crispin launched into his Marilyn impression: "I wanna be loved by you…"

The audience cracked up again, and Crispin arose to rapturous applause. He boogied through the room, blowing kisses and receiving pats on the back, shouting, "Don't go away, now. I'll be back in five minutes. Stay right where you are."

Holding up five fat fingers he strode toward reception, with the bellhop bouncing at his heels. He grabbed the phone from the bell captain and hissed into it, "Who the fuck is this? What do you want? How dare you? Do you realize I was in the middle of a performance? A professional never, ever…what?"

"You heard what I said. Your friend Nigel is dead. My name is Jordan Young. My friends call me Baby Joe. Your friend Asia asked me to call. Do exactly as I say. Go to your room now. Have them transfer the call. Go now."

Crispin dropped the phone. He blanched, and his lip began to quiver. His heavy face with all its makeup had collapsed like one of those Dalí paintings of the clocks.

"Mr. Capricorn. Are you all right? Not bad news, I hope."

"Would…would you…can you please direct this call to my room?"

"Of course, Mr. Capricorn, right away," the bell captain said, as Crispin turned and walked slowly toward the elevator.

He could hardly get the key into the lock with his palsied fingers, and when he finally managed it he burst into the room and rushed over to the phone.

"Did you close the door?" the voice said.

"Why, no."

"Do it now. Close it, lock it, and put the chain on."

Crispin did as instructed, fiddling with the chain with trembling hands, and picked up the phone again.

"Do you have a mini bar?"

"Yes."

"Get yourself a stiff drink; then sit down and listen."

Robotically, his mind a blank, Crispin shuffled over to the fridge, took out a bottle of gin, and mechanically poured it into a glass. He flopped down onto the bed, picked up the phone, and said, "I'm here," in a small voice.

"Good. Now, Crispin, listen to me. Don't interrupt or ask questions. *Why* doesn't matter for now. There'll be plenty of time for that later. Nigel has been murdered. They were looking for you, and they know where you are. Change into the most inconspicuous clothes that you have. Go down to your car, and drive to Reno. Leave your car there and rent another. Something small that won't draw attention. Drive straight back to Vegas. Do it now! Don't check out, and don't speak to anyone, especially anyone who works for the hotel. Don't get the desk to bring your car. Go get it yourself. Don't use the elevators; use the fire stairs. When you get to Las Vegas, don't go home. Come to this address. Write it down…"

Baby Joe paused to give Crispin time to retrieve the notepad from the bedside table.

"Got it?" he continued. "Good. Now don't call anybody except Asia, on her cell phone. She will be at the address I gave you. Call her when you are on the road, call again when you leave Reno, and call just before you get to Vegas. Don't answer your phone, and drive carefully. Don't risk getting stopped by the police. If you do these things, you will be okay. I know you're in shock, and upset, and probably scared, but everything will be all right if you do exactly as I've told you. I'm going to let you speak to Asia so you'll know I'm on the level. But be brief. Just say hello, and then hit the road. Okay, Crispin?"

"Okay," Crispin said weakly.

"Good man."

Asia came on the phone, trying not to sound upset. "Crispin, I'm so sorry. Are you okay?"

Crispin lost it. "Oh, Asia. I'm so scared. What's happening? That man. That dead man. That was supposed to be me."

"What dead man, Crispin?"

"A man. A man got shot. It was on all the news. A man got shot on the ski slope. He was wearing the same outfit as me. They must have thought it was me. Oh, Asia. Oh dear, oh dear. Nigel. And Oberon. Where's my dog? I want my dog."

"Just hang on, Crispin. I'll give you back to Baby Joe."

"He's losing his grip," she said, as she handed Baby Joe the phone.

"Crispin, what's up?"

Crispin blurted out what he had told Asia.

"Okay. Crispin. Calm down. That's good for you. That means they think you're dead. It'll give you a little more time. But it won't be long before they realize their mistake. You've got to move fast. Hang up now, and do what I told you. Okay?"

"Okay."

Crispin heard the click as the line went dead, and he started to cry.

Back in the bar, the audience was slow-hand clapping and whistling, and shouting, "We want Crispin, we want Crispin," over and over again.

But Crispin wasn't coming back for an encore. Crispin was already on the road to Reno. He changed cars, rented a Ford Fiesta, and drove at a steady seventy all the way back to Vegas.

The next morning, when, as he was pulling into the outskirts of Las Vegas, a big red Mercedes zoomed past him doing almost a hundred miles an hour and the big ugly driver who was drinking from a bottle of Wild Turkey gave him the finger as he went by, he barely paid any attention.

*Rewind three weeks…*

"Are you Tiger Woods?"

It was a question Monsoon Parker was accustomed to hearing, and with his African-American, Asian, and Scandinavian heritage, he did bear more than a passing resemblance to the renowned predator of the fairways. The similarity ended in the appearance, however, and, if Monsoon had ever performed an even remotely sportsmanlike deed, it was purely by accident. Not that he was loathe to take advantage of his features if there was the slightest chance they would benefit him, as the tone in the voice of the fresh-faced and earnest college girl who had just taken the seat next to him suggested they were going to.

Monsoon could sure have used a little luck. A small-time scam artist and pusher — and when things got really desperate, dipper — Monsoon's meager income barely kept him in front of his gambling habit. Just about every cent he managed to scrape together went into his betting. While there were undeniably times of plenty, when the worm occasionally turned, the majority of the time he was firmly in the hole, bobbing and weaving and borrowing from Peter to pay Paul. Actually, borrowing from Eddie the Ear to pay Guillotine McGee would be more accurate.

Monsoon Poontang Eighty-Second Airborne Purple Heart Parker, to give him his full and proper title, had been conceived over a pile of Bud cases, behind the PX in Da Nang, three days before the Tet Offensive. His father could have made it out of there. He nearly did. But he'd rolled the dice one time too many. Five rounds from an M60, including one tracer, came zipping up like spiteful imps from the beach of an island in the Gulf of Thailand. Up through the smoke and fire they came, to where he was crouched in the doorway of a Sikorsky CH-53 smoking a huge spliff and listening to Jimi Hendrix on a cassette player, and extinguished him from all care and fucked up his copy of *Are You Experienced*.

Monsoon still wore his old man's dog tag, which sported the letters P...ker, P., punctuated by a grim and eloquent circle of missing tin. Of the old man's serial number, only the number 5 survived, a number that Monsoon studiously avoided during any kind of wagering proposition, despite any and all omens to the contrary.

From his mother, a petite Vietnamese beauty whose apparent frailty belied the fact that on a good night a full-strength platoon could enter her forbidden city and not come out with enough change between them to tilt a pinball machine, he had inherited an abiding and invincible superstitious belief. A skilled reader of signs, Monsoon could distinguish between the propitious and the ominous in any given situation and, as the girl smiled at him, he smelled the sweet perfume of good fortune waft across his nostrils.

"No, baby, I'm his brother, Black Panther Woods," Monsoon replied, smiling beatifically.

Monsoon Parker could lie with a facility that would put a Texas presidential candidate to shame, a valued ability that he kept polished with constant practice.

The girl beamed, thrilled with her discovery.

Monsoon looked around with theatrical furtiveness and then put a finger to his lips.

"Ssssh," he said, "I'm incognito, man. Family name, see? Don't wanna upset the sponsors."

"Oh, I understand," said the girl. "I won't say anything. This is really exciting. Do you play golf as well as your brother?"

"Well, I really don't like to talk about it, baby, but better, really. I actually taught him to play."

"No?" she said, her eyes wide in her pretty, pale face like two blue marbles. "Do you play professionally, too?"

Monsoon gave a deprecating smile.

"Oh no no, babe," he said, "wouldn't be fair to my baby bro. 'Sides, golf just a little bitty ol' game. I got bigger fish to fry."

"Like what?" said the girl, leaning forward.

Monsoon tapped the side of his nose and assumed a mysterious expression.

"Government biz, baby. Workin' for the man. Can't discuss it."

"Oh," she said, disappointed.

He gave her the full piano-key tooth display. "Let's change the subject, doll face. Which part of Scandinavia you from?"

The girl's eyes widened. "I'm an exchange student from Stockholm. However did you know?"

"I'm trained to notice these things," he said, flashing the Steinway again.

Actually, since she was wearing a sweater with a reindeer pattern, spoke like she had just swallowed a mouthful of gravlax, and had a Scandianvian Airlines hand baggage security tag and a Saab keyring attached to her handbag, Monsoon didn't exactly need to be Hercule Poirot to figure out that she wasn't from Kansas.

"Actually, my grandfolks were from Scandinavia, so we have something in common."

"Were they? From where?"

"My grandfather is a prize-winning elkhound breeder from Norway. Bjørn Eggen Christiansson. Maybe you heard of him."

The girl shook her head, dubiously. Monsoon thought he might have overdone things a bit, which was ironic because the part about his grandfather was actually true.

Bjørn Eggen Christiansson was his paternal grandfather, was from Norway, and did breed elkhounds. Once a year he faithfully visited the grave of his late wife, Maybelline, in Tuscaloosa, Alabama, after which he visited Vegas to tell Monsoon what a useless waste of space he was, how he was nothing like his father, and, if not for the promise that Bjørn Eggen Christiansson had made to his own son, he would not cross the road to piss on Monsoon if he was on fire, before leaving Monsoon a considerable sum of money and going back to Norway, presumably to breed more elkhounds. As a matter of fact, he was due to arrive next week.

Monsoon changed tack, back to safer water.

"Hey, where's my manners at? I'm being rude, baby girl. What's yo' name, and what y'all drinkin'?"

The girl beamed at him. "I am Brita Gudjonssen," she said, extending her hand, "and I would like a Fuzzy Navel."

Monsoon gently took hold of her hand, thinking, *touchdown*. He ordered her drink and a bourbon for himself, and then said to her, "Brita, would you please excuse me for a moment?"

Brita smiled at him. He walked through a doorway into an adjoining room where a basketball game was in progress on a big screen. It was 4:15 to go in the fourth quarter, and the Lakers were leading the Pacers. It was game five in the playoffs, and the Lakers were up three to two in the series. Monsoon wanted them to win by six. In fact, he seriously wanted them to win by six, the reason being that if they didn't win by six the betting slip in his top pocket would be worthless and he wouldn't be able to pay his bar tab. As anyone could tell you, not paying your bar tab in one of Don Imbroglio's joints was not an especially good idea. Furthermore, if the Lakers didn't win by six he would be into the Don for a grand, which, as anyone could tell you, was an even worse idea than not paying your bar tab. Much worse.

Monsoon had always tried to steer clear of borrowing from the Don on account of the Don's easy payment plan, whereby it was easy for the Don to have you turned into salami if you didn't pay up. But lately things had been even tighter than usual, and he was desperate. All his usual sources he either owed money to, or they wouldn't take his action on credit. Getting involved with the Don was like going down a one-way street. There was no turning back. He knew it was a hard road to go down, and he knew he had probably fucked up royally, but his gambling urge had overriden his common sense.

Anyway, he had borrowed a grand from the Don's front man. The first two hundred had gone on a horse that had lost under suspect circumstances. It ran like someone had fed it a pork pie and, if the jockey had pulled any harder, its lips would have fallen off. Then he had lost four hundred in a poker game when some clown who didn't know a full house from a shithouse had filled an inside straight through blind providence and taken the pot.

So he had staked his last four Cs on the game. The Pacers were on the ropes, and the Lakers were at home, and Jack Nicholson was there wearing yellow shorts and brown socks and was ready to step onto the court and straighten things out if anyone got out of line, so it was money in the bank. Monsoon watched a trey go down, making it Lakers by eleven with 3:56 to go, and walked back through to where Brita was sitting, smiling vacantly into the ether like a benign six-foot doll.

"How's yo' drink?" he said.

"Oh, it's delicious, thank you."

"Where are all your friends?"

"I left them, *ja?* Sometimes I think it is better to be alone. More things can happen."

"More things like what?"

"Like meeting Tiger Woods's brother. Can I meet Tiger?"

"Sure."

"Oh, great! When?"

"Tomorrow, if you like. He'll be here."

"You're kidding!"

"No, I ain't. Tomorrow, I promise. Just excuse me again, would you?"

Brita smiled a puzzled smile as he walked back into the other room. She was still smiling when he returned. Monsoon wasn't. One second to go, Lakers by five. O'Neal at the free throw line. He hadn't even bothered to look.

"What's the matter?" she said.

"Nothin', nothin'. Listen, Brita, you wanna go someplace else?"

"Sure."

"Come on, then, this way."

"But what about the drinks?"

"Oh, that's okay. They know me. Let's go."

Brita stood and straightened her skirt. She had a Rubenesque figure and was a good foot taller than Monsoon. He used her size to cover his retreat, hiding behind her as they scuttled toward the fire exit.

Back at Brita's hotel, where they went after Monsoon had explained that it wouldn't be thought proper for them to go to his hotel suite, he being who he was and all, Brita demonstrated her enthusiasm for the fairway, and Monsoon showed her his nine iron and found out what was par for the hole. Afterward, he told her that he really liked her and wanted to see her again, but that he worked for a clandestine government agency and would be going away tomorrow to Uzbekistan on a mission of national importance, but he would visit her in Sweden when he had finished keeping the world safe for democracy.

Brita said that she was disappointed that she wouldn't get to meet Tiger, but that she still liked him anyway, and that she also liked to travel and was training to be a pediatrician and that when she was qualified she wanted to go overseas and devote herself to charity work. Which is just as well, because when she recovered from the mickey that Monsoon had slipped her after he had made full and vigorous use of her various orifices, she realized that she had donated three hundred dollars from her purse.

Private investigation work is glamorous. It is mysterious, veiled ladies wafting tearfully into grim offices in clouds of expensive perfume, and hardened lonely men, men who know the score sitting behind the wheel on rainy deserted streets thinking profound, embittered thoughts in the lamplight. It is all sharp clothes and willing dames not-necessarily-in-distress. It is wisecracks and snappy comebacks to colorful, improbably named villains and hard-boiled cops.

Of course it is. And Sister Theresa wore fishnets and a G-string under her habit, and had a crack pipe hanging from her rosary.

Private investigation work is sifting through the sordid pieces of broken lives like some wino rummaging through the garbage. It is endless hours of tedium, and furtive watching, and shit food and bad coffee. It is ill-kempt, disillusioned men sitting in crappy cars surrounded by cigarette butts and greasy burger wrappings, worrying about money. The only score they know is the score from the baseball game they're listening to on the radio while waiting to drop the dime on some poor hapless bastard scurrying out of somebody else's wife's apartments at four in the morning, where the poor schmuck was only trying to squeeze a drop of joy and comfort from his miserable and meaningless life.

Jordan "Baby Joe" Young ought to know. He had tried it.

Baby Joe was Boston Irish, descended from five generations of cops. His father had been a near-legendary officer of the law. Joseph "Mighty Joe" Young had been the most feared and respected peace officer in Boston. He had been only marginally smaller than his namesake, not nearly so good-natured, but a much better shot. That was why the people that shot him to death had deemed it prudent to shoot him in the back one night as he was rolling out of Bad Bob Boyle's Bar and Grill. Baby Joe had loved and revered his father, who, for all the roughness of his manner, had been a devoted and protective parent.

Mighty Joe was both the reason Baby Joe had become a cop in the first place and the reason that he had ceased to be one.

It is considered perfectly acceptable for Boston police officers to let off a little steam when they get off duty, and if things get a little out of hand every now and then, well, blind eyes can always be turned. However, tracking down the murderers of one's father, one at a time, and decapitating them with a fireman's axe does not fall under the category of letting off a little steam. Due to the universal popularity of Mighty Joe, the investigation into the decapitations was not pursued with especial vigor and, even though everyone from the hot dog vendors at Fenway Park to the secretary of the Genteel Christian Ladies Flower Arranging and Crochet League knew whodunit, Baby Joe was allowed to resign and quietly slip onto the midnight train for all points west.

Which is why, instead of keeping the streets of Boston safe for innocent people, he was now ensconced in the dimmest recesses of Jonah's Whale of a Lounge in Vegas, taking a well-earned respite from a busy day spent watching his telephone steadfastly refusing to ring. Word has always traveled fast, even before the web, which meant that regular police work was out, so Baby Joe had set himself up as a private investigator, knowing from the very first day that it was a mistake.

He began to feel dirty, the kind of dirtiness that won't wash, like that of Lady Macbeth's hands, as if his very soul was being soiled by the sleaziness of the life he had undertaken. He was about to quit when he made an interesting discovery. Even in a town where integrity is looked upon as a severe handicap, he found out you could sell it. He inspired confidence in people. People instinctively trusted him. People who didn't trust their own mothers trusted him. People who would steal from the poor box and not even have the common decency to spit in it afterward trusted him. People who were not even remotely trustworthy themselves, and proud of it, trusted him. Everybody, from the most innocent cherub-faced campus virgin to the most vicious scar-faced scum-sucking douchebag ex-con trusted him. And they were right. Call it quaint, call it naive, call it old-fashioned, call it ill advised…call it what you want, but when Jordan Young gave his word, he kept it. Always.

So he had transformed himself into something different. A go-to guy for hire. Mediator, deliverer, negotiator, protector. And it had worked. He was doing something he could live with, could look himself in the mirror, and was getting by. Most of the time. Recently things had been kind of slow. In fact, if things had been going any slower they would have been going backwards. Of late, the only thing that was going down in his life was the Guinness, and now, as he stared into the brindled foam of a new-poured pint, watching it settle, he was thinking about how far removed he had become from anything that he was before.

In his stillness he seemed to be cast in stone, and the cold blue glow from the bar sign above him flickered on the immobile features of his scarred and weathered face like a scene from an old film noir. More than forty years on a hard road, of tough streets, of hard drinking, of barroom diplomacy, and Vietnam, had left him with a face that appeared to be stitched together from disparate pieces of skin, like a living quilt.

Only the eyes remained untainted, clear, yet distant, as if somehow, when Baby Joe Young looked at the world, he wasn't looking at the same thing as everybody else.

Kneeling on the carpet of a two-grand-a-night suite on the strip, Asia Birdshadow was feeling extremely uncomfortable and becoming more so by the minute. It wasn't the guy's dick that was bothering her, she having seen more pork in a Turkish *mullah*'s lunchbox. Rather, the problem was her neck, which was really hurting from the strain of having to hold still so as not to unbalance the ashtray that the fat, sweaty fuck had placed on the back of her head while he was shafting her. She wouldn't have minded even that so much if the cheap bastard had been smoking a decent cigar, but the stench of the dime-store stinkweed was making her feel sick and it didn't bode well for a tip.

Asia Birdshadow was part Irish, part Louisiana Creole, and all woman. Her given name, as inscribed upon her birth certificate by a somewhat taken-aback cleric, was Euthanasia Birdshadow. The elder Mrs. Birdshadow had not enjoyed much of an education and had named her daughter with the belief that Euthanasia was a Disney cartoon from the thirties. Asia had modified it, for obvious reasons. The youngest of eight children raised on beans and molasses in a chicken shack on the levee near Baton Rouge, she had hitchhiked to Vegas the previous summer. In high school, the other kids called her Isis on the basis that she had the body of a goddess and the brains of a cow, and while she was undeniably possessed of a divine chassis, Asia was nowhere near as dumb as her lack of academic achievement might suggest. It had just been that she had not been able to summon up much interest in how to calculate the surface area of a pyramid, how many atoms were in a helium molecule, or who had broken the Treaty of Versailles. Her failings had more to do with terminal disinterest than inability, however. Since her arrival in Glittersville, she had parlayed her outstanding beauty, her exceptional figure, and her ability to suck the varnish off a Brownsville Slugger into a healthy bank balance and a cozy townhouse in Summerlin, thank you very much.

She was street smart, feisty, wise beyond her years, and spoke French and Spanish fluently. Her interests in life extended no further than getting as far away as possible from the grinding and pestilent poverty she had been born into and ensuring that she would never again have to go without anything she needed or wanted. Ever. And every Monday morning she climbed into her canary-yellow Corvette and drove to the post office on Tenaya, where she bought a money order for one thousand dollars and posted it express delivery to Mrs. Evangeline Birdshadow of Baton Rouge, LA.

Asia felt the guy's thighs start to tremble, so she uttered a few token moans just to help the job along. As he started to come, the man took hold of her long copper-colored hair and pulled her head back, knocking the ashtray to the carpet. He began jerking her hair in time to his thrusts, bringing tears to her eyes.

"Hey, what's with the hair, you fat creep?" she said, somewhat detracting from the romance of the moment as the john fired his little squirt and collapsed onto his back, panting like a hot St. Bernard.

Asia got to her feet, stepped over the spent and prostrate mark, and walked into the bathroom, closing the door behind her. She did the necessary and then carefully redid her makeup and adjusted her clothing. Turning around to check that the seams in her stockings were straight, she noticed the dark spots on the back of her dress where the fat greasy bastard had dripped on her. With a sigh, she turned back to face the mirror and looked long and hard into her own tawny eyes. There were no answers for her there.

Outside, the john had pulled up his pants and was sitting in a chair by the window, sucking on his cheap panatela with a supercilious leer.

"Goddamn, girl. Y'all is really sump'n else. I like to had a fucken heart attack. If'n my folks could only see me now. Sheeit."

Asia smiled with her lips.

"Thank you, hon. Glad y'all had a good time," she said, thinking, *If my folks could only see you now, they'd kick the shit out of you, you lard-ass redneck scumbag.*

Hookers who didn't get the cash up front usually didn't get to drive Corvettes, and Asia already had the man's folding stuff in her purse. She was holding out for the extra, although in this case not holding out much hope.

"Since y'all are so happy with the service, how about a little something extra for my favorite charity?"

"Why, sure, Lindsey baby," he said, Lindsey being the name she was using this evening. "Wouldn't want you to think us good ol' boys from 'Bama got no appreciation."

Shuffling his fat butt forward he reached into his hip pocket, pulled out a wad of bills, and ostentatiously peeled off…a ten.

Asia gave him a look that would have stunned a basilisk. She reached out and snatched the note. "I never realized that the Hasidic community was so big in Birmingham."

In reply, the john exhaled a thick, swirling cloud of stogie smoke into her face.

She spun on her heel and marched out of the room. "Have a pleasant evening, needle dick!" she said, slamming the door.

Crispin Capricorn ruefully regarded the ample nakedness of his reflection in his antique gilt-framed mirror. Still flushed from his bubble bath he turned this way and that, vainly trying to strike a pose that would show his pink portliness to good advantage. The sight of his pendulous butt cheeks, with their deep overhanging creases leering back at him in a maniacal ass-grin, elicited a deep sigh. He peered at his chubby face, floating under the massed blond curls of a bouffant pompadour that made Little Richard look like Bruce Willis, and examined the deepening lines radiating from the corners of his eyes. He poked them with the tips of his pudgy manicured fingers.

"My God," he said aloud, "they're not crow's feet, they're fucking emu feet!"

He considered his eyes, the baby blue irises floating in whites that had turned gray and bloodshot by the excesses of the night before and the night before that, and the heavy darkening bags beneath them that nothing from his comprehensive armory of lotions, potions, powders, preparations, creams, and liniments could keep at bay. His exfoliants and depilatories, mud masks and massages availed him naught. Time had marched on and left its muddy boot prints all over his face.

Crispin narrowed his eyes and scowled at his reflection, now beginning to fade beneath a fine patina of steam, and pursed his Cupid's-bow lips.

"Mirror, mirror on the wall, what the fuck happened, you shiny two-faced bastard?"

Snatching his lilac silk bathrobe from behind the door, he thrust his wobbling arms violently into the sleeves and flounced from the bathroom.

He strode into his boudoir, which, with its pastel pinks and purples, strategically placed mirrors, suitably subdued lighting, and the obligatory baroque chaise longue, would have given a postbellum New Orleans cathouse a run for its money. What was required was solace in the form of a stiff gin and a decent bong full of forgetfulness, and he headed purposefully for his polished eighteenth-century French Bavarian drinks cabinet. As he waded through the apple white carpet, the pile so deep it almost required snow shoes, his bare foot encountered something suspiciously warm and squidgy, and he looked down in horror to see his pedicured toes planted squarely in the middle of an elongated yellow dog turd. The ensuing squeal was very impressive.

"Oberon!" he screeched, his face turning an unbecoming shade of crimson with the effort. Oberon duly appeared, a panting, fluffy white blow-dried fur ball, slightly discolored at one end.

"Oberon. Come," said Crispin, pointing at his encrusted foot. The dog stood, head lowered and ears back, staring at Crispin with a deranged look in his unfocused eyes. The smell of the squashed turd was winning its battle for supremacy against the immense bowl of potpourri on the Japanese lacquered coffee table in the center of the room, and Crispin pulled a face and held his nose. He could feel himself gagging.

"Oberon. Heel," he said, as firmly as he was able through his tightly pinched nostrils.

The dog skipped forward with a peculiar twitching gait, looking like a lamb on smack.

"Bad dog! Bad dog! Just look at this fucking carpet. Come here."

The dog scampered behind the sofa and peered over one arm, panting, his tongue lolling and his eyes rolling about in a most unnerving manner. Further enraged by this act of disobedience, Crispin strode toward the animal, his begrimed foot leaving a trail of brown blotches on the otherwise pristine carpet. Oberon ducked under the settee, and Crispin fell to his knees and tried to grab him. The dog scooched back and, as he did so, Crispin noticed something gleaming, and reached for it. His fingers closed around an empty plastic bag. He struggled to his feet, his face blanching as he stared in disbelief at the torn package, empty save for a minuscule residue of fine white dust collected in the bottom.

"YOU FURRY LITTLE CUNT!" he shrieked.

Crispin's rage revolution counter went off the clock. He grabbed the arm of the chaise longue and upended it, flinging it across the room and exposing the trembling Oberon, who cowered as Crispin raised his meaty fist.

"That was two grand's worth of Colombian, you little fucker!"

Crispin's fist swept toward the dog's snout, not in a slap but in an actual punch. Oberon easily evaded the cumbersome blow, zipped between Crispin's legs, and dashed into a corner where he turned and stood at bay. Crispin whirled in pursuit, and, as he did so, something in the dog's demeanor changed, something Crispin was far too furious to notice. As he advanced, Oberon stiffened and snarled, his fur on end, looking like an enraged carpet slipper. Crispin's eyes went wide in amazement and then narrowed into a look of unadulterated venom.

"What the...? How dare you growl at me, you ungrateful little swine?!"

Like a football player going for the extra point, Crispin swung his foot at the growling dog and, had he connected, Oberon would have been a forty-five yarder at least. But footballs don't generally bite. The dog ducked under the approaching foot, sprang forward, and sank his teeth to the hilt in Crispin's beefy calf.

The Japanese lacquered table had not been constructed with weight support as a major concern, and as Crispin landed squarely upon it all four legs surrendered to gravity simultaneously with the sickening crack of breaking bone. Crispin was too shocked to scream, and he lay stunned, floundering in a state of absolute mortification until the continued snarling and an acute pain in his leg turned his confusion to panic.

"Eeeeeeeee!" he squealed.

His adrenaline-fueled stomach muscles overcame their flaccidity and hauled him upright. Over the wobbling folds of his exposed belly he saw Oberon worrying his calf, like a diminutive wolf worrying a small pig. The dog's pupils had contracted to pinpricks, and the alarmingly exposed whites of his eyes gave him a demonic expression.

Normally the sight of blood would have been an excuse for a good fainting fit, but something about the sight of his own blood pouring from his leg, staining both animal and carpet alike, put Crispin in touch with his Neanderthal side. A large, expensively bound volume of explicit homoerotic photographs lay on the carpet next to Crispin's splayed fingers, having been dislodged from the splintered table by his fall. He grabbed it and, raising it above his head in both hands like Moses with the tablets, brought it down onto the back of Oberon's head with all his might. There was a loud, leaden thud, and Oberon released his grip. He turned his head and looked into his master's face with blank incomprehension, and then his eyes rolled back in their sockets. With a small whimper he collapsed onto his back, his legs sticking rigidly in the air.

Sobbing, panting, and perspiring profusely, Crispin rolled onto his stomach and battled to his feet. He limped over to where an old speakeasy-style phone hung against the wall, leaving alternate red and brown prints on the ruined carpet. He managed to compel his trembling hands to grip the receiver and dial the number. A curiously soft, deep voice answered.

"Hello. Nigel speaking."

Crispin began to sob hysterically into the mouthpiece.

## Chapter 2

Never mind hitting his opponent. Thumper Thyroid was lucky if he could hit the deck. He had chewed more leather than an upholsterer's puppy, and in a boxing career not noteworthy for its integrity only George Patton had seen more tank jobs. Outside of the ring, of course, it was different. His ability to inflict damage in the ring was limited, more or less, by the rules of the Marquess of Queensbury, but outside of it his tactics were closer to those of the Marquis de Sade. Not that he wasn't in favor of the odd gouge, elbow, accidentally deliberate head butt, or hook to the groin when the ref was blindsided, but it just wasn't the same. An artist needs to be unrestricted to do his best work.

In his other profession, as debt collector, mob enforcer, and occasional hit man, Thumper Thyroid was a skilled and dedicated practitioner of the down-and-dirty and knew more tricks than Siegfried and Roy, not to mention his ability to shoot the balls off a running muskrat at three hundred yards in a blizzard with either hand.

He was currently hunched in a neutral corner, patiently enduring a maelstrom of uppercuts and hooks, waiting for the moment when he could reasonably fall over without jeopardizing the interests of his sponsor, Don Ignacio Imbroglio, thereby earning his beer money and enabling him to spend the rest of the night in the relative comfort of his North Vegas fleapit, and not as part of the foundation for the extensive repair work taking place on the interstate just north of Primm.

While waiting, he was speculating on the provenance of the spectacular pair of bosoms on display just below him, priding himself on his ability to be able to distinguish saline from silicone as far back as the fifth row, if the lights were right. At the same time, he was idly calculating that with the feebleness of the blows being rained upon him, he might actually be able to beat this stiff legitimately. But then, why the fuck would he want to go and do something like that?

Thumper turned his attention back to the fight. He saw his opponent setting himself for a long straight right that Mr. Magoo could have seen coming. *Jesus Christ*, he thought, *this clown doesn't telegraph punches, he fucking e-mails them.*

Now was the moment. Being a legitimate bent fighter and a man who had listened to more counts than a Transylvanian heiress, Thumper took pride in his work and was always looking for new and spectacular ways to go down. He was considering, now, the Foreman-Frazier fight, where Big George tagged Smokin' Joe with a nuclear-powered left that actually lifted him off the canvas. Thumper had always wanted to try that. Judging the distance to perfection, he stepped forward with his jaw jutting out at just the right angle for the incoming punch to connect. The glove thudded into his chin with all the force of butterfly's fart.

"For fuck's sake," Thumper mumbled through his gum shield, "my fucking fifth-grade teacher used to hit me harder than that."

He would have to be really on the ball to make this look good. He snapped his head back, making the sweat fly, and leapt backwards onto the ropes, bending the top rope down with his weight and then allowing it to propel him forward. When going down face first, the trick is to not put your hands out like you're trying to protect yourself, so Thumper fell to his knees and made an arch of his spine so that he could roll down without smacking his face too hard on the canvas. He lay still and waited patiently for the ref to count him out.

He was back in the stark, stale, sweat- and liniment-smelling dressing room, having the tapes cut off, when Frankie Merang walked in.

"Yo, Thump, nice dive, man. Fuckin' Greg Louganis, or what? That was Foreman-Frazier, right?"

"You got a good eye, an' a sound knowledge of the profession. So what's up?"

"Don wants to see you right away."

"Okay. No sweat. I'll be out soon as I clean up."

"I'll wait in the bar."

Thumper nodded as Frankie turned to leave, flexing his fingers while the trainer finished cutting. He was in his street clothes and heading toward the door when it opened, and his erstwhile opponent walked in.

"Oh, hello, sweetheart," Thumper said, pleasantly, "come for anotha kiss?"

"Fuck youse!"

"I have to give you credit, pal. That right wudda gave Shirley Temple a nasty jolt."

"Hey! What? You ain't had enough already? You wantin' some more?"

Thumper adopted a cowering pose. "Oh, please, kind sir, don't frighten me. I hate to fucking shit myself when I've just had a shower."

The other fighter swung a looping left at Thumper's head. Thumper ducked under it, stepped in, and slammed his shoulder up under the man's chin, snapping his head back and smacking it into the wall. The lights went out in Georgia, and the pug slid down the wall and sat in a heap in the doorway.

"It's guys like you give boxing a bad name," Thumper said, stepping over him and out into the dingy yellow-lit corridor.

They sat together on the bed in the doctor's office, with Nigel holding Crispin's hand and speaking soothing words to him.

"Ooh, Crispin. I think you are ever so brave. It must hurt terribly. I would be in absolute hysterics if it was me. And what about poor Oberon? Do you think he will be all right? Shall we call the vet?"

"Fuck him," said Crispin. "A fucking taxidermist is what he needs."

Crispin watched the part in the handsome young doctor's hair as he knelt in front of him, examining the wound through a magnifying glass. Crispin looked at Nigel, a tall, slender young man in a tight wetlook T-shirt and a pair of jeans that appeared to have been applied with a trowel. His long blond hair was tied in a ponytail, and he sported a wispy mustache.

Nigel gave Crispin a conspiratorial nudge. "Just what you've always wanted, Crispin. A young doctor on his knees in front of you."

The doctor coughed, without looking up, and Crispin shot Nigel a warning glance. "It's a rather nasty bite, I'm afraid, Mr. Capricorn. Your pet has had all his shots, I presume?"

"The only shot that little fucker needs is one through the back of the head," said Crispin bitterly.

The doctor coughed again. "Er. Yes. Quite. Well, I have to ask, you know. Now, I'm going to have to clean this wound thoroughly before I put in the sutures. It might sting a little."

Crispin made a little muffled whimper, and Nigel leaned closer and put his arm around him. Encircling his right bicep was a tattoo of roses impaled upon barbed wire, although his skinny arm was so entirely devoid of muscle that he should have been entitled to a discount, on the grounds that the tattoo artist had not had to use much ink. Nigel gazed back at Crispin with a look of appropriate concern.

"I'll have to ask you to move," said the doctor to Nigel, as he produced an implement that looked like a brush for cleaning rifle barrels and applied a generous smear of antiseptic to it.

Nigel stood up, and Crispin regarded the implement with horror. "You are not going to stick that thing into me, are you?"

"You don't usually object," said Nigel, with a giggle that was quickly suppressed by Crispin's Medusa stare.

"I can give you a local if you'd like," said the doctor.

"Trust me. I'd like," Crispin replied.

While the doctor busied himself preparing the hypodermic, Crispin addressed Nigel. "Nigel. I don't think these are the proper circumstances for levity, do you? I'm in enough discomfort without having to listen to your feeble attempts at wit."

Nigel's face fell. "Well, I was only trying to cheer you up, Crispin," he said, in an offended tone.

Crispin softened. "I know you were. I'm sorry. This has been such a horrible, terrible experience, and my nerves are in tatters."

"I know it has, you poor pudding," Nigel said, taking hold of Crispin's fat hand.

The doctor advanced, bearing the syringe before him like a weapon. "Just a little prick."

"Ooh, Crispin hates little pricks," said Nigel.

Crispin exploded. "WILL YOU SHUT THE FUCK UP, YOU INFANTILE LITTLE PONCE?!"

Nigel jumped, then released Crispin's hand and stood up with a bleak expression on his face. There was a pregnant and embittered silence as the doctor administered the injection and waited for the anesthetic to take effect. After a pause of some minutes, the doctor approached again and knelt in front of Crispin's leg with the rifle barrel implement at the ready. Nigel stepped forward, bending theatrically at the waist, making sure Crispin knew that he was getting a really good look.

Crispin closed his eyes as the doctor placed the tip of the brush against the lips of the wound and pushed the torn, resisting flesh inward. The edges of the bite had turned blue and, as the doctor drove the implement further in, blood seeped around the brush and began to trickle down the leg. Crispin bit his lip and began to whimper, even though he couldn't actually feel anything. Nigel's eyes widened as he stared at the brush boring relentlessly into the lacerated flesh. The blood drained from his face, cold sweat broke out on his brow, and he stood suddenly upright, raising the back of his hand to his forehead. Then with an almost inaudible sigh, his eyelids fluttered, and he swan-dived forward. The doctor looked up from his work in time to catch a fleeting glimpse of Nigel's forehead just before it crunched into the bridge of his nose, breaking it and knocking him spark out.

Hearing the noise, Crispin opened his eyes and looked in bewildered amazement at the two prostrate men. The doctor lay on his back with blood pouring from his nose, and Nigel was flopped on top him. He looked at the handle of the cleaning brush protruding from his sanguine leg and then back at the two men, lying as if asleep in each other's embrace. His eyes brimmed with tears.

"Oh, shit," he managed to whine through quivering lips.

It was an overcast night, and the reflected lights of the Strip on the bottoms of the clouds made it appear as if dawn was imminent, although it was barely three a.m. Monsoon sat in the ancient Buick in front of the garage, waiting for the door to clank open. As always, it seemed to take longer at night. He drove in and waited for the door to close behind him before he killed the engine and the lights. Inside, he went straight to the freezer, pulled out a bottle of bargain basement bourbon, and took a stiff drink straight from the bottle.

He was fucked! A fucking grand! With the vig, that was twelve hundred by tomorrow night and two grand by the weekend. If he paid the vig from the three hundred he had aced from the Danish pastry, he wouldn't have stake money to try to win the twelve hundred back. But if he lost the three, and couldn't pay the vig…

He was fucked, all right. From asshole to breakfast. He found a glass, wiped it around with his shirttail, poured a stiff one, and sat down in the dark to think it through. Where could he get a stake? Nobody would lend it to him, which is why he had gone to the Don's man in the first place. How fucking smart did that look now? What did he have to pawn or sell? A fucking ten-dollar dink watch and a shitbox car with a dodgy transmission that wasn't worth the price of the gas to get it to the lot.

As he drank and worried, he fiddled idly with his father's dog tag. *A lot of fucking use you are*, he thought. *I don't know why I fucking wear you. If you're so fucking lucky, how come the old man ended up with his entrails splattered over half an acre of rice paddy?*

Wait. That's it! The old man! The box! The fucking medals!

Jumping up, he rushed into the bedroom and, springing onto the mass of tangled bedclothes that hadn't been changed for a week, pulled down an old cardboard suitcase from on top of the dresser. He toted it back into the kitchen, flipped on the light, and set the case on the counter. Mildewed and dusty, it had remained unopened for over a decade, and when Monsoon blew on it the dust made him sneeze. He brushed it with his hand and revealed the faded letters.

*Captain P. Parker. LRRP.*

Monsoon took a slug of bourbon, clicked open the catches, and gingerly lifted the top. *Just my luck*, he thought, *there will be a scorpion in here, or some fucking slope death spider or something.*

It had been so long since he had opened the case that Monsoon could not remember exactly what was in it, but he remembered his mother showing it to him when he was a young boy, just arrived in the country. He remembered staring at the shiny medals and looking, uncomprehending, at the photo of the handsome young Negro in the smart uniform and the stiff white hat. A stale, musty smell came from inside the case, and Monsoon tipped its contents out onto the kitchen counter.

The medals landed on the chipped surface with a loud clank. He grabbed them and held them up to the light, reading them one by one. Purple Heart, Distnguished Service Cross, Legion of Merit, Congressional Medal of Honor.

*Fuck, these gongs must be worth a few hundred bucks, if not more*, he thought. What else? An old dress uniform, a bundle of letters tied up with string, and a pile of faded black and white photographs. He thumbed through them.

Young men in uniform, young men in the jungle, young men on tanks, young men lying on the ground in strange attitudes. White men and black men and Asian men, some smiling, some not. And all with that look in their eyes, that faraway look.

And pictures of the man he knew to have been his father. His father on a beach in Hawaii on R and R, next to a girl with flowers round her neck and a sign that said Honolulu; his father receiving a medal; his father among low smoking hills with choppers in the background; his father in a bar surrounded by other men and smiling Asian girls; his father in the doorway of a Huey, with the jungle far below him; his father holding a beer; his father holding an M14; his father holding a baby. He looked closely at that one, then tossed the pictures aside and went back to rummaging. There were clothes, and a bayonet in a steel scabbard, and an old Russian camera with Cyrillic script around the lens. And nothing else.

*Fuck it*, he thought. *Is this what I've been keeping all these fucking years? A shit, Stone-Age commie camera and the memories of some bastard I never even knew?* He grabbed the case, angrily, to throw it. And something moved. He tipped the case, and it moved again. There was something square and heavy inside the lining. He grabbed the bayonet and tried to pull it from its scabbard, but it was corroded fast. Snatching a knife from the kitchen drawer, he punctured the lining and made a long diagonal cut through its center. An oblong package, a foot long by six inches wide by an inch deep, fell onto the counter. It was hard and heavy and covered in very thick foil.

*Jesus H. fucking Christ*, he thought, leaping back in a sudden panic. *Plastic explosive.*

He stared at the package glistening in the light from the bare bulb. It did nothing. Approaching cautiously, like a dog approaching a stranger, he studied it. There was printing on the foil, and what appeared to be a motif, or decal, but so badly faded as to be illegible. Over the top, somebody had scratched something into the foil with a nail or a screwdriver, and these words were just about readable. He moved around the table so that he could examine the writing without touching the thing.

It read: *Machine Gun Jelly. Good on yer mate. Woolloomooloo Wal.*

*What the fuck is machine gun jelly? And what the hell is a Woolloomooloo supposed to be?* Monsoon considered the packet for a long moment. Shit to it. If it was going to explode, it would have gone off when he dropped it. Picking it up, he very carefully made a small triangular incision in the foil and raised the flap. Inside was a dark waxy substance. He poked it with his finger, and it made a very slight indentation. He smelled it, and his eyes widened.

"Sweet Mary's Ass!" he said out loud. It was dope. Definitely some kind of dope. Precisely what kind he had no idea, but if it was dope he could sell it, and if he didn't know what it was, then chances were nobody else would either. And if they didn't, so much the better. That way he could charge the suckers what he wanted.

With exaggerated care, he sliced a one-inch strip from the wad. Taking a roll of tin foil from the drawer where he kept his paraphernalia, he resealed the package, wrapped it in a plastic sandwich bag, and put it into his fridge. The one-inch strip he cut into twelve more or less equal chunks, then wrapped them in foil and stashed them in his cket pocket. Downing his drink, he killed the kitchen light and headed for the garage. Minutes later, the old Buick was clattering and coughing down the empty street, heading for the lights of the Strip.

The claws were out, and the fur was flying thick and fast.

"Get her. I wouldn't wear that to a fucking dog fight."

"I didn't know there was a Salvation Army shop in Henderson."

"Two-faced? She's got more faces than Rod Stewart."

Crispin and Nigel were sitting together on a plush tiger-stripe sofa in a penthouse just off Tropicana. Crispin was purposely wearing a pair of paisley-pattern Bermuda shorts that would allow him to show off his wound and elicit the proper amount of sympathy, but thus far the reaction had been less than satisfactory. The French doors to the balcony were open, and a gentle breeze ruffled the lace curtains. On the stereo, Rod was singing "The Killing of Georgie," and a maudlin crew of inebriate stagehands was singing along with their arms around each other's shoulders. Behind them the lights of the planes and helicopters zoomed to and from the airport, floating through the night sky like slow meteors.

It was an after-hours show biz affair, and some of the boys and girls of the chorus were still in their paint, a gaudy cocktail of fruits with barely a cherry between them. One of the leading lights from the new show at the Bellagio was holding court in the center of the room, and the younger queens were fluttering around him like hot moths. A rumor was circulating that Aerosmith was coming to the party, and a frisson of excitement passed through the room every time the doorbell rang.

The hostess, an aging English dowager named Dorothy Deviche (pronounced like *ceviche*), a fast-fading bloom with the demeanor of a ded parrot, had locked herself into the bathroom and was refusing to come out, claiming that someone had taken advantage of her after she had had just a teensy-weensy bit too much coke and passed out on her bed.

"She should be so lucky," whispered Crispin to Nigel. "It would have had to have been fucking Ray Charles!"

Nigel snickered behind his hand and said, "Crispin, shush."

The bell rang, and as the door was opened eager heads turned, hoping to see Steven coming in. But they were all disappointed. What they saw instead was a slight man with dark skin and large almond eyes, wearing frightful clothes, walk across the room, fix himself a drink, move into a corner, and stand there looking nonchalantly around. After an initial flurry of curiosity and catty remarks, the gathering went back to preening and bitching.

Crispin sipped his gin. "Who on earth is that pleb?"

"It's not that golfer fellow, is it?" said Nigel.

"Heavens, no. You don't think a famous golf player would be parading round in those rags, do you? Does look a bit like him, though."

Ten minutes later, the hostess had been coaxed out of the bathroom and was standing in front of Crispin and Nigel, allowing herself to be consoled. She was pushing sixty, had more lifts than Lake Tahoe, and was wearing a bizarre sequined creation that flashed and winked like a defective Christmas tree. Crispin hailed her with a little grasping motion of his chubby fingers.

"I say, Dorothy. Lovely party, my dear. Simply lovely. And you look ravishing as always."

"Oh, thank you, darling. Those Bermudas are simply divine. But my God, what happened to your leg?"

"Oh, don't ask," said Crispin, happy to have been asked at last. "It was Oberon. He ate some stuff that I had left lying around and he turned into some kind of ravening wild beast. It was dreadful."

Crispin went on to recount the whole sorry tale, with Dorothy making the right oohing and aahing noises in the appropriate places, and Nigel chiming in when it got to the part where he had rescued Crispin's leg by driving him to the doctor.

"My God. You poor dear," said Dorothy at the conclusion to the tale. "And where is he now?"

"We left him at home, sedated, with an ice pack on his head. I'm taking him to the vet tomorrow to make sure he hasn't got a concussion."

"Well, my advice to you, darling, is to have a stiff gin, and take lots of drugs."

"The gin is no problemo, sweetie," Crispin said, displaying his half-filled glass, "but as for the drugs, I'm afraid my entire stash is inside poor Oberon. We haven't had time to get more. I don't suppose…"

"Well, I'm a bit low myself, luvvie, but you might just have dropped in lucky. You see that little man over there, looks a bit like that handsome golfer what's-'is-face?"

"Yes, we were just talking about him."

Dorothy started to giggle, making her dewlaps wobble. "Well, you're not going to believe this, but his name is Monsoon Parker."

Crispin, who was just taking a sip of gin, blew like a spouting dolphin, soaking Nigel.

"Oh, thanks very much," said Nigel, pouting, looking at the wet spots on his blue satin pants.

"You have got to be shitting me," said Crispin, raising his eyebrows.

Dorothy scooched in between Crispin and the sulking Nigel, and put her hand on Crispin's thigh. "No. Really, that's his name."

"So who is he? Don't tell me he's a friend."

"Good God, no. What do you take me for? No. He's a tradesman."

"What do you mean?" asked Nigel, too curious now to continue his snit.

"Oh, don't be dense, Nigel," said Dorothy. "He supplies me sometimes."

Nigel went back to sulking.

"How very interesting," said Crispin. "You must introduce us."

"I'll fetch him," said Dorothy, shuffling up and stepping across the room, smoothing her dress.

When she came back with Monsoon in tow he was wearing his best ingratiating smile, which, it has to be admitted, was pretty good as far as ingratiating smiles go.

"Crispin, Nigel, allow me to introduce you. This is my friend, Monsoon Parker."

Only Nigel was unable to suppress a giggle. Monsoon's smile never wavered.

*Fuck these shirt lifters,* he was thinking. *They'll be laughing on the other side of their faces after they've paid five Cs for what is probably compressed bat shit.*

"*Enchanté*, brother," he said, offering his hand. "Definitely pleased to make yo' acquaintance, my man. Seen yo' act couple of times. Yeah. It's a scream, baby, an absolute scream."

Crispin gave a nod of appreciation, royalty acknowledging the admiration of a peasant. "Dorothy tells us that you may have something to sell us, Mr. Parker."

"Call me Monsoon. I sure do, but it's very special merchandise. Unique, you might say."

"Well, what is it?"

"Shouldn't we go somewhere a little more private?"

"Oh, nonsense," said Crispin, tut-tutting. "We are all friends here. What is it? Show us."

With a theatrical flourish that he thought appropriate for the company, Monsoon pulled out one of the little packets and unwrapped it before them.

"Looks like hash. Is it?"

"Well, not exactly, bro. More of an...opium derivative. But I promise you, it will be like nothing you ever smoked before."

"So you smoke it?" said Nigel.

"Yeah. Melt it a little and spread it on paper, just like oil."

Monsoon had to suppress a laugh at the picture that jumped into his head. What if the stuff really was plastic explosive? He imagined this little cocksucker blowing his head off trying to light a Semtex reefer. He bit his lip and continued.

"Now, there is only one source for this shit, baby. A small region in Southeast Asia. It is very, very potent. You got to be careful, amigo, an' only use it in very small amounts, at least until you get used to it. *Comprende?*"

"Sounds wonderful," said Dorothy. "How much?"

"Five hundred dollars an ounce."

"WHAT?" blurted Crispin, spraying Nigel with gin again. "Five hundred fucking dollars an ounce. I could get a ticket to Cartagena for that. What part of Israel did you say you came from?"

"For fuck's sake, Crispin," said Nigel, fussing with his newly spotted pants.

Crispin's outburst had raised a few eyebrows, and caused a few heads to turn in their direction. Monsoon looked nervously around, and made a calming motion with his hands.

"Easy, brother. I know it seems a shade high, my man, but once you've tried it you will realize it's worth every cent. And as I said, you only need yea much to get higher than Yuri fucking Gagarin." Monsoon held his pinched fingers together, to indicate the miniscule quantity required.

"Who the fuck is Yuri Gagarin?" Nigel said.

"The first Soviet cosmonaut, you ignoramus," said Crispin, still looking at the little brown wad in Monsoons hand.

"I don't know," he said. "What do you think, Dorothy?"

"Oh, you know me, dearie. Anything goes."

"Nigel?"

Nigel studiously examined his fingernails. How could he be expected to know anything about Soviet cosmonauts?

Monsoon played his ace. "If you ain't sure you can afford it, that's cool. I know plenty folks that can."

Crispin fixed him with a glacial stare and pulled out his billfold, making sure that Monsoon could see how fat it was. He peeled off five hundreds and handed them to Monsoon as if he were handing him a used tissue.

"This shit had better be as good as you say it is, young man, or there will be repercussions. I am very well connected in this town."

*Your bum buddy's butt cheeks are the only thing you're connected to, you fat turd,* Monsoon thought as he took the green, saying, "Don't worry, Crispy baby. This stuff will have yo' jockeys inside out in no time. And if it doesn't, Dorothy knows where to find me. What about you, Dorothy?"

"Well, yes," she said. "Never let it be said that Dorothy Deviche was afraid of a new experience. Crispin, be a dear and lend me five till I fetch my purse, would you?"

Crispin handed the notes to her, who in turn handed them to Monsoon, who passed one of the packets to Dorothy.

"A distinct pleasure doin' business with y'all. See you around, ladies. And don't forget, there's plenty more where that came from."

"What an objectionable, smelly little object," said Crispin disdainfully, as he watched Monsoon hot-footing it across the room and out the door.

"Not the most pleasant of people, I agree," said Dorothy. "But he comes in handy from time to time. Now, what say we repair to my chambers and give this stuff a try?"

The three swanned across the increasingly crowded room, exchanging smiles and pleasantries and air kisses as they went. Entering Dorothy's master bedroom, they locked the door behind them.

Monsoon Parker was a happy man as he tripped down the stairs to the underground car park. He hoped the shit was legit because Dorothy was a steady customer, and he couldn't afford to close any more doors. On the other hand, it would be sweet to lay a burn on those other two Nancy boys. Whichever way it panned out, he wasn't going to worry about it. If it was good stuff, so much the better. If not, fuck 'em. He had more important things to concern himself with. Like the grand nestled snugly in his inside pocket, just itching to get out and into the action.

# Chapter 3

Where most people have eyes, Don Ignacio Imbroglio had stones. Cold, coal-black stones. Shark's eyes. Eyes that you almost expected to roll back in his head when he took a bite of his food. There were several reasons for this. One was that he was Sicilian and shared the olive complexion and dark eyes of his race, and another was that he was the most ruthless, cold-hearted, merciless, murdering son of a bitch since Attila the Hun.

Another reason was that he was totally blind.

Of course, this condition was not general knowledge and Don Imbroglio went to very great lengths to ensure that it remained so. After all, Stevie Wonder is loved and admired by millions, but not many people are afraid of him. The Don had not always been sightless, and while clawing his way to supremacy over the bloody remains of his rivals he had had sharper vision than most. He would have thought it ironic, if he thought in such terms, that he could live through Korea, several gang wars, innumerable assassination attempts, and a close brush with the Big C, only to be blinded by an inept chef and a spectacularly botched attempt at a bombe surprise. The chef quickly ended up being surprised by a real bombe, and the Don went into seclusion for a year to recuperate. Such was his indomitable will that he had not only survived but had also overcome his disability, kept it a secret, and maintained his hold on one of the most powerful organizations in the west for twenty years.

Only his most trusted people and his immediate family, who were installed behind the high walls of a villa in the hills above Palermo and who saw almost as little of the world as he did, knew. Since the accident the Don very rarely left his apartments, and when he was compelled by extreme circumstances to do so, it was always under conditions that would absolutely preclude anyone from discovering his affliction. In his apartments, everything he used and needed was kept in precisely the same place so that, with his practiced movements, he could disguise his condition from his occasional visitor. The lighting was always subdued, visits were always kept brief, and most visitors were usually too intimidated to notice anything but how slowly the time seemed to be passing.

The Don had the most fearsome of reputations, and it was entirely deserved. He had the instincts of a barracuda, the intellect of a summa cum laude, the manners of an English gentleman, and all the compassion of a Waffen-SS tank commander with a sore ass in a winter shitstorm in a Polish ghetto.

And if he had been a cruel and ruthless man before his blinding, since the accident he had become worse. Much, much worse. As if the extinguishing of the light from his eyes had caused the extinguishing of any remaining vestiges of humanity in his black and bitter soul. Life, suffering, and human dignity had become concepts as meaningless to him as the sun that he would never see again, and his own mortality would be just an extension of the darkness in which he already existed.

Small, slight, and always impeccably dressed, the Don had perfected a faux British accent to such an extent that few people could tell he was not English. He had used this to great effect over the years, causing many to underestimate him who would later live to regret it. Or rather, wouldn't. He'd begun his love affair with all things British while seconded to an English artillery regiment in Korea, in the frozen windswept hills above the parallel. He was a forward observer, another fact he would have viewed with some irony if he had recognized such a thing, given his current circumstances. The English officers had impressed him with their poise, their style, and particularly their stoicism and sangfroid in the face of the uncountable hordes of the People's Republican Army that came pouring through the valleys and over the hills. After the war, he bought recordings of recitals by Noel Coward and Gilbert and Sullivan, listened to the BBC world service, watched endless movies, and practiced and practiced, until only the most practiced ear could discover him.

The Don—or plain old Ignacio Imbroglio, as he had been then—had never risen above the rank of corporal, although his records miraculously showed him receiving an honorable discharge with the rank of colonel and a whole lapel full of gongs. His proper name was not even Imbroglio. It was Lo Vuolo, and he was descended not from the proud and imperious lords of Palermo, but from a fishmonger in Taormina. But as the Soviets were well aware, and Ignacio Lo Vuolo soon learned, history can be anything that you want it to be and, in fact, the only genuine thing about Don Ignacio Imbroglio was his Patek Philippe wristwatch. And his power.

Don Ignacio lived for power. It was a current that ran through him. A living, pulsating thing, a thing that he could feel, spreading its tentacles into the avenues of the city, into the corridors of power, into hotels and homes and boardrooms, reaching with an icy and pervasive grip into people's hearts and minds and souls. The Don could feel the city the way other people could hear it and see it, and he sat in its epicenter like a chill, sinister spider in his web, leeching life from the life around him, projecting images onto the black screen of his eyes, always thinking, always calculating, always waiting.

People came to the Don with information, with knowledge as gift and supplication, as sacrament, and the Don used that knowledge to fasten his teeth ever tighter into the jugular, into the arteries. And now, word had come to him of a drug, some new exotic drug, and drugs meant dependence and control and money. And power.

"I can't believe you fucked Dorothy!" Crispin was saying. "Incredible. What a fucking sight."

"Well," said Nigel, "you never told me she was a real woman, until it was too late. How the fuck was I supposed to know?"

"Jesus, Nigel, you're not blind. And even if she wasn't, how could you? I mean, how on earth did you know where to stick it, with all those wrinkles?"

Crispin and Nigel were lying in each other's arms on Crispin's massive four-poster, with the morning sun coming through the opened window. What they were feeling was somewhere between euphoria and incredulity. What the fuck had they smoked? The world had become a many-splendored thing, the bubbles in their champagne had turned to angel's kisses, Barry Manilow had turned into Luciano Pavarotti on the stereo. And while Nigel usually bore more resemblance to the old gray mare than the Italian Stallion, last night he had looked like Tom Cruise, Omar Sharif, and Clark Gable all rolled into one, and had kicked the stable door in all night long. Oh, and he had fucked Dorothy — albeit by mistake. The three of them had rocked and rolled and writhed on Dorothy's antique heirloom bed in a bewildering variety of positions and configurations while nuclear butterflies exploded around them and the mirror in the ceiling turned to undulating golden honey, dripping down to form great glistening globes that floated around the room. At one point, as Crispin had been hunched over preparing to penetrate the nearest orifice that presented itself, he had looked down and had actually done a double take. He was prepared to swear to Christ, Congress, and Chuck E. fucking Cheese that it had actually gotten bigger. He had been a ram, a mandrake, an incubus, a Roman legion,

Adonis, Antony and Cleopatra, Leda and the Swan, and Snow White and the seven bastard dwarfs.

Crispin had experienced an unprecedented series of orgasms that felt as if his soul were being pulled out of his stomach, his fading libido had made a better comeback than Frank Sinatra, and he had performed with such astounding vigor that his member had resembled a boiled wiener when he had finally run out of steam. It was going to be red-raw for a week. It had been like popping amyl nitrite and Viagra, with a mouthful of shrooms, a noseful of uncut Colombian, and a jalapeño suppository, all at the same time. What the fuck was in that shit? And, more important, when could they get some more?

Finding drugs in Las Vegas was about as difficult as finding a hot dog at Wrigley Fields, but they weren't talking about just any run-of-the-mill drug. And right now, they needed Monsoon Parker.

"I wish I had got his number," said Crispin.

"Who?"

"Mel Tormé, who do you fucking think? Monsoon Parker, you dildo."

"Well, Dorothy will know."

"Dorothy will be unconscious for a week, after you turned her pussy into a shopping basket. She'll be pissing blood and rubber for a month!"

"Well, call her anyway."

"Okay. Give me the phone, put some coffee on, and see if Oberon is awake."

Surprisingly, Dorothy answered on the second ring.

"Crispin, I was just going to call you. What on earth was that? I feel like the fucking Jersey Tunnel."

"Tell me about it. My dick looks like something you'd find in a longshoreman's sandwich. We have *got* to get some more of that shit. Have you got Monsoon's number?"

"I haven't, unfortunately. He's not really on my guest list. Or at least he wasn't. He fucking is from now on. But I think I know where he lives. He slipped me an address last night."

"Right. Give me the address, and I'll get round there right away, before he sells it all to somebody else."

"Right-ho. Give me a second."

Crispin waited while Dorothy rooted around in her purse.

"Here we are, darling. Oh, dear. Not in a very nice area, I'm afraid. Are you sure you want to go there?"

"If it meant getting hold of that stuff, I'd go to Baker on a fucking bicycle."

"Yes, well, I know you've always enjoyed a Bun Boy, dearie. Anyway, it's 2694 Wampum Vista, all the way round the 95, off Lake Mead. Maybe you should take Nigel."

"Nigel!" Crispin snorted. "Nigel couldn't frighten Winnie-the-fucking-Pooh. I'll take Oberon. At least he's got all his own teeth. I'll call you later."

Crispin hung up, rolled off the bed, and opened the door to his walk-in closet, shouting to Nigel as he entered, "Ho. Where's that coffee, you dilatory ckoff?"


"Jesus, Joseph, and Mary's holy fuckin' pissflaps!"

The daylight screamed at Baby Joe as he drew back the curtains, and he squinted his eyes against the piercing light. Outside his kitchen window the grass appeared a flickering stroboscope, sunflower-yellow. The kettle began to howl like a banshee and he staggered across the kitchen, killed the flame, and attempted to spoon some coffee into his cup, but the palsied trembling of his hand kept dumping the grains back into the jar and he had to resort to pouring coffee directly from it. The resulting brew looked as if it had been dredged from a Hoboken sewer and tasted about the same way. Inside his skull, a crew of fugitive mining engineers were attempting to drill their way out, while in the pit of his stomach the National Association for the Advancement of Swamp Eels was holding its annual convention. Parking it on a stool, Baby Joe surveyed the aftermath of the night before.

Strewn around two empty John Powers bottles was an uncountable legion of empty Guinness cans, and rising from the center of the wreckage like a queen among her subjects was a slender, elegant, and empty bottle of Galliano.

*Where the fuck did that slime come from?* he thought, momentarily uncomprehending.

And then he remembered the girl. Indistinct images began to hover at the periphery of his memory. A wild careening car ride, a bar somewhere, some loud Sly Stone rhythms, a party, a tall black girl. The images started to come into focus. He had been in the Whale, and the band had forced him to go with them to some new club that had opened. There had been a group on. A soul group. And they in turn had compelled him to go to this party. And this one girl, a backup singer, had forced him to bring her home.

Relieved to discover that none of this had been his fault, he shuffled into the bathroom. Some debauched gargoyle leered back at him from the mirror, with red swollen eyes entrenched in sandbags. He leaned forward, with his hands on the sink, and peered at himself.

"You've got to stop fucking doing this to yourself," he said aloud.

The debauched gargoyle said nothing.

"Okay, pal. You asked for it."

Baby Joe stepped into the shower, and steeled himself for the icy blast that came rushing out to take his breath away. He stood there for five minutes, trying to let the fierce jets batter the fog from his brain and the nausea from his stomach. Shutting off the glacier, he padded still-wet into the kitchen, took up his coffee, went out into his small garden, and sat on the grass against a wall to let the morning sun dry him off.

Baby Joe was in his forty-fourth year, beyond the age of reason and into the age of regret. He was the quintessential survivor, but had recently come to the conclusion that that was all he was and that survival was the rhyme and the reason. Nothing more, nothing less. A hard man in a hard game, he was just hanging fire, going on one day at a time, and waiting for it to be over, one way or another. Not happy, not unhappy, just there; halfway down the street of broken bones, hearts, homes, and promises, but not yet broken in spirit.

Inside him, the dragon still coiled and uncoiled in the darkness, waiting for some circumstance to release it. Tired? Hell yes. He was tired. He was entitled to be tired. But he was in much better condition, physically, than he was entitled to be in at his age, considering the way he lived. He worked out, ran some, but counterbalanced that with an almost continuous supply of Guinness. It sometimes seemed to him that he spent half his time trying to stay in shape, and the other half fucking himself up.

He had his share of ghosts, but had not been in love—or what he recognized as love—for many years now. He did okay, though. Women liked him for some reason. Here, late in the eighth round, he wasn't handsome or distinguished-looking, as he had once been before the bell rang. But he had charisma and a certain bad-dog charm, and despite the anger that smoldered in him, despite what he had seen, something of the boy still remained in Baby Joe Young's soul, to shine out on the world through his ice blue eyes.

He took a sip of his coffee and grimaced.

"Fuck that shit," he said, tossing the brew onto the lawn.

He stood and, with grass imprinted on his ass, headed for the fridge. A solitary black can formed the entire inventory of its contents.

"Hallelujah, brother," he said, cracking it with a sharp hiss.

As he was heading back out to the garden a tall, willowy shape emerged from the bedroom, rubbing its eyes, and said, "Hi."

The girl was naked except for one of his shirts, which she wore hanging open, with the tips of her breasts exposed. Baby Joe stared, momentarily taken aback. Last night she had looked like Halle Berry, but this morning she looked more like fucking Chuck Berry.

"Morning," he said, wittily.

He had absolutely no idea what her name was but she had a very good body, with long legs, high, tight breasts, and a look on her face that said he ought to remember more than he did.

"Can I offer you some coffee?" Baby Joe said, struggling with his recalcitrant memory.

"I'd love some," she replied. "You lose your pamas?"

"They don't make them in my size."

"Ain't that the truth, baby," she said, easing her long legs behind the counter.

Baby Joe handed her a steaming cup. "I hope you like it strong. I was having a bit of trouble with my spoon control this morning."

"I can see you're having trouble controlling your spoon," she said.

Baby Joe grinned. He liked her, whoever she was, and he was sorry for his uncharitable thoughts.

"Listen," he said, "you'll have to excuse me, but I'm afraid I can't remember your name."

She smiled, graciously.

"I'm Miriam. Don't worry, baby. The state you were in, I'm surprised you can remember your own."

"I think it's Dickhead, isn't it?"

"Something like that."

Miriam stood and slinked over to where he was perched on his stool, his member at half-mast as if waiting to hear how the conversation was going to turn out. She leaned forward and kissed him, gently, and put one hand on his dick. His dick immediately made up its mind as to which way the wind was blowing.

"Mmm," she purred.

She reached down and touched her own wetness, and put her long, cool, slender fingers to his lips. Baby Joe breathed deeply, and reached behind him to put his can on the table.

"Do you feel bad this morning, baby?" Miriam said.

"I've felt better," Baby Joe croaked.

Miriam lifted one long leg over him, placed him with her cool fingers, and slowly slid herself down onto him.

"Don't you worry, baby," she whispered. "Mama will take care of you."

And Miriam put her hands on Baby Joe's muscular back and began to gyrate, ever so slowly.

Monsoon peered through the spy hole in his front door and was dismayed to see the colorful, distorted figure of Crispin Capricorn in the silver circle, looking like the Easter Bunny trapped in a bubble. He cursed under his breath. *What is that fat, perfumed ponce doing here? And how did he find the place? Dorothy! That shit must have been no good, and he wants his money back. Well, I'm sure if he asks the pit boss at Arizona Charlie's nicely, they'll give it to him. Anyway, fuck him. Money back, my Asiatic ass. Full refund of price of purchase if not completely satisfied? Who does he think he's dealing with, fucking Walmart?*

What Monsoon definitely didn't need, after waking up with a hangover of biblical proportions to the realization that the Don's grand had gone down the drop box, plus the three from Brita the Buxom, putting him right back where he started, only worse—and before he had the chance for a cup of coffee, even—was to have to listen to the breathless twittering of this fat prick. Well, what was the limp-wristed douchebag going to do?

Monsoon went into what passed for a sitting room, took out a snub-nosed Police .38 Special from under the sofa cushion and stuffed it down his waistband, just in case he was required to explain the situation a little more clearly.

He systematically opened the battery of locks, deadbolts, and chains that afforded him at least the illusion of safety—although nothing short of living inside a Sherman tank was any guarantee in this neck of the woods—and forced himself to smile a big hello to the beaming Crispin. As soon as he opened the door, Monsoon realized it was worse than he had thought. A manic bounding fur ball attached itself to his shin and began a vigorous attempt at sexual congress with the hem of his jeans.

"Crispin, my man," he said, "what a pleasant surprise. Where'd you get the sheep?"

Assigning it to his indelible mental book of scores to settle, Crispin let the knock on Oberon slide. Smiling relentlessly, he bent down to Monsoon and air kissed him in the vicinity of each cheek, starting back involuntarily when a whiff of rancid breath hit him like a slap in the face. Monsoon stepped aside and ushered Crispin in, following behind with one hand on the butt of the .38 and dragging the tirelessly humping Oberon with him.

"Hey, amigo, what's with the mutton?" he said, indicating the dog with a nod of his head.

"Oh, he's just such a playful thing," said Crispin, detaching Oberon by main force, and holding him up to his face.

"Oh, isn't he just daddy's adorable little bunny-wunny," he said, burying his face into the animal's fur and making a series of peculiar asthmatic snuffling noises.

Monsoon gritted his teeth and set about resetting his defenses.

Wrinkling his nose against the unmistakable smell of penury, Crispin surveyed the room with a mixture of distaste and contempt, eyeing the cheap furniture and tasteless trimmings, noting the cigarette burns in the carpet and the glass rings on the chipped veneer table. Oberon struggled to be free, so Crispin set him down and restrained him on his short pink leash, making a mental note to give him a bath as soon as they got home.

Monsoon lived in a single-story, low-frame house set in a big, bare lot in an area of North Vegas so poor that pigeons were afraid to land there. The good news was that the rent was so low even he could afford it. You can't get much lower than free. He had found the joint empty and moved in. He'd had the utilities secretly hot-wired to the guy that lived in back. Everything he owned would fit into the back of his shit-heap car and he could be out of there in five minutes, so if the real owners ever showed up it was no big deal. He kind of doubted they would. It had been six months, and nobody had pitched. On that side of the tracks, it was anybody's guess what the story with the owners was. In the slammer, maybe? Croaked? Who knew? It was such a derelict shithole that the insurance money wouldn't be worth the cost of the gasoline to torch the joint.

His neighbors were transients and illegals, welfare cases, and a host of other unfortunates who had been sucker-punched by life, who had either never gotten a fair deal from the big croupier in the sky, or who had drawn to twelve, with the dealer showing a six, and gotten a ten. Everywhere windows were barred and steel grates covered doors. On every wall, arcane graffiti ciphers proclaimed their grim and colorful warnings. Empty bottles, tin cans, and Styrofoam cups rolled in the streets, the byproducts of an unforgiving consumerism, just like the people who had left them there. Sirens and helicopters, breaking glass, and the occasional gunshot filled the bleak nights with their unchained melody.

It was the perfect environment for Monsoon's small-time pushing business. The majority of his neighbors were also his customers, and only the needy, desperate, or foolhardy ever went down there. Normally the only vehicles in the neighborhood newer than ten years old were squad cars, and Crispin's pink Lexus was about as inconspicuous as a crocodile turd on a pool table. Crispin would never have come to such a place after dark, and even in the sweltering brightness of afternoon he was jittery. He would not have come at all except under these exceptional circumstances.

As soon as he had pulled up to the curb, the car had been surrounded by a crew of sinister children adopting bizarre gangsta poses, hooded and capped and draped in ill-fitting sports clothing, like a race of malevolent basketball-playing dwarfs. As he climbed from the car, rocking the suspension and holding Oberon in front of him like a weapon, the leader stepped forward, his Lakers shirt down to his knees and his shorts down to his ankles, like Sammy Davis Junior in Kobe's uniform. Oberon growled, a sound calculated to strike terror into the heart of the most hardened gang member. The crew burst into gales of laughter, their flinty juvenile eyes watching Crispin melting in the heat and the fear.

"Yo, Mistah," said baby Kobe, "You wan' we should watch yo' ride? Hate to see anythin' happen to nice wheels like these."

"Why, er…yes. That is very kind of you. I won't be very long. I'll give you something when I come out."

"We know," said baby Kobe, and again laughter riffled through the pack, laughter that had pushed Crispin all the way to the door.

Inside, Monsoon was saying, "What can I do for you Crispin? I suppose you are here about the stuff I sold you?"

"Yes, Monsoon, I most certainly am."

The words "Fuck off" were already forming on Monsoon's lips when Crispin said, "Yes. I need some more."

"You do?"

"Monsoon, that was absolutely the best shit I've ever smoked."

In his head, Monsoon heard the loud joyous ringing of a cash register. The price went up to a six hundred an ounce.

"I told you it was some serious shit, bro."

"Mr. Parker, I've never smoked anything even remotely like it. I just have to have some more."

Seven-fifty an ounce, and counting.

"Tell me more, my man."

"Well. Dorothy had some, too. And if Radio Dorothy knows, Las Vegas knows. She's a more reliable source of information than the Revue Journal. So I wanted to get round here, before they start knocking down your door."

*Crispin, my man,* Monsoon thought, *an entertainer you are. A businessman you ain't. A straight grand an ounce, sucker.*

"Well, Crispy baby, I'd like to help you, but see, the shit sellin', man, and I've only got a couple ounces left. An' see, the thing is, I don't know when I can get any more."

"Shit. Okay, I'll take those two."

"They yours, baby, but it's goin' to cost you two grand, my man. Simple case of supply and demand."

"Jesus Christ," said Crispin.

"No, sir, you dealing with Monsoon Parker. Jesus couldn't make it. Two grand, yes or no? C'mon, Crispy, you know you goin' to sell half."

"Oh, no, I'm not. This is going to be all mine. You are a shameless bandit, Monsoon, but all right."

"Okay. Sit tight. I'll be a minute. Have a chair."

Monsoon went through a door at the back, and Crispin looked in disgust at the grimy sofa. Taking his handkerchief from his top pocket, he carefully spread it on the discolored cushion, and lowered himself down. Momentarily, Monsoon returned with a package and a bottle.

"Drink?" he said.

"No thanks. I really must get along. Here's your money."

Monsoon took the proffered bills, flicked through them like a deck of cards, stuffed them into his pocket, and handed Crispin the packet. Crispin grabbed Oberon, and waited while all the locks and bolts were clicked and clunked. He said a hasty goodbye, dispensing with the air kiss on hygiene grounds, and bustled out to where the basketball dwarfs were arrayed around his car. He managed to get away with only giving them twenty dollars, and was soon speeding gratefully back down the freeway to his pad.

Behind his locked door, Monsoon was dancing a little jig. Taking his drink into the kitchen, he took out a set of scales, and weighed the remainder of his stash. Two pounds, three ounces. Thirty-five grand! *Halle-fucking-lujah. Thirty-five thousand motherfucking dollars. Maybe more. Maybe a lot more. Got to put this stuff someplace safer.*

He swallowed his bourbon, took down his threadbare cket from a hook behind the door, put the .38 in the side pocket, and headed for the garage.

When the late, late crowd spilled out of other bars, the Black Tarantula Cocktail Corner was where they spilled into. In the kind of place where creeps go to socialize with other creeps, you were guaranteed to meet a better class of lowlife. It never closed; you could acquire, or arrange to have acquired for you, just about anything that anyone could possibly wish to acquire—and short of actual murder on the premises, all forms of human interaction were tolerated. The Black Tarantula used to have a real tarantula in a big glass jar on the bar, but someone had eaten it. The light in the Black Tarantula was baby-shit yellow, and twisted skeins of smoke writhed slowly upwards towards the cupola ceiling like midnight spirits in a Celtic graveyard. Cigarettes and joints winked at each other from dark corners, and the jukebox reflected its voodoo colors from the sleeve-polished bar. From a back room, a vicious swamp guitar whined with evil intent and a raw, angry female voice bit off jagged pieces from the night. From a deep shadow in the corner, under dead neon, a ragged butterfly wafted her wings at no one in particular and softly sang to herself, sad songs of better days.

Bugle Buchanan was sitting at the bar, ostensibly minding his own business as he sipped his gin, but actually closely earwigging a conversation that was taking place at a nearby table between a couple of none-too-convincing transvestites and some weird, Chinese-looking spade that Bugle recognized.

Nobody knew for sure if Bugle was called Bugle on account of the massive, hooked schnoz that cast a permanent shadow over his feet or the fact that he had ratted out enough people to populate a decent-sized, Midwestern town. His livelihood was knowing other people's business and making it his own business by selling info to whoever might be interested. In fact, it was more than a livelihood. If it weren't for his carefully stashed collection of other people's dirty laundry — laundry that might be aired at any minute — where his next meal was coming from would have been a moot point.

The chink was waving a big cigar about, voice too loud, eyes a bit too shiny, being expansive in the way that people are when they think they are holding all the aces. Apart from the hooter, Bugle was all ears.

"This town thinks it has seen it all," the weird-looking geezer was saying, "but wait till they get a load of what ol' Monsoon is bringing to the party. This shit make cocaine look like chocolate mousse. Give you the biggest high and the biggest hard-on of yo' entire natch, baby. And ain't but one source. Yessir, boys — er, excuse me, ladies — Mr. Parker in the house. But you gotta act fast. When word start gettin' around, sheeeit, they gonna be buildin' a new fuckin' freeway right to my front door."

A short while later, Bugle Buchanan was whispering into the reeking receiver of the public phone next to the restroom at the Black Tarantula Cocktail Corner.

"That's right," he was saying, "Parker. Monsoon Parker. Some kinda wigged-out jig. Looks like a Chinese coal miner. We all seen him around.

And hey, numbnuts, jus' remember to make sure that the Don knows where the information comin' from. Otherwise...!"

Bugle smiled to himself as the line went dead.

Handyman Harris was not a religious man. In fact, to the best of his recollection, the last time he had been near a church was the time he and his buddies stole the lead off the roof of the Chapel of Our Lady of Redemption, in Chicago, on a freezing Christmas Eve night the year "She Loves You" got to number one on the Billboard charts. But as he waited for the elevator in the richly appointed lobby of Don Imbroglio's apartment building, he was praying fervently. He was praying fervently that the Don had not made the call himself, and had therefore not overheard his outburst. Five lousy grand. What good would five *hundred* grand do if you were at the bottom of Lake Mead covered in bass shit? He felt the cold sweat on his forehead, and brushed it off.

Across the lobby, the cadaverous superintendent leered at him. That fucking vulture! He could smell fear as unerringly as a junkyard mutt. The elevator arrived and Handyman dragged himself inside and punched in the code, without which the elevator would not go to the penthouse. He saw the second floor light blink on and off, wishing he were getting off there. Handyman had taken an apartment on the second floor, which the Don let him have cheap in return for the occasional service rendered, which had seemed a good idea at the time. Still was, if you didn't mind living like a circus tightrope walker. They don't pay rent either, but one false move and...!

The ride seemed to take an eternity. He hoped it would seem as long coming down. He had heard of guys coming down from the Don's crib very quickly indeed.

The car jerked to a halt on the third floor, and a pretty brunette climbed in. She was wearing a tight-fitting business suit, and she smiled at him openly. Handyman did his best to compel his tight facial muscles into a smile, while simultaneously checking her waistline for bulges. Well, you can't be too careful.

"Seven, please," said the woman, brightly.

Handyman crabbed towards the buttons and pressed seven without turning his back to her.

The elevator bumped to a stop at the penthouse, the bell rang with a portentous clang, and the doors slid open. The man standing in front of Handyman, who was smaller than the Statue of Liberty but only just, grabbed him by the lapels and spun him around. His companion, who was only as big as the stratosphere, dragged his wrists above his head and patted him down. Satisfied, he indicated a large, polished double door with a nod of his head, and as Handyman headed for it the two men walked close enough behind him to be able to read the label on his shirt. A discreet brass plaque by the side of the door read: *Don Ignacio Imbroglio. Investments.*

Stratosphere opened the door, while the Statue of Liberty pushed him inside. The room was dimly lit by lamps of Italian glass, and through the open window Handyman could see the spotlight at the top of the Luxor dividing the night in two. Walking on the carpet was like walking on dollar bills. In a deep leather armchair, behind a low black marble coffee table upon which stood a decanter, a single crystal glass, and a brass ashtray, a slight, immaculately dressed figure was smoking a cigar. Handyman could not make out the man in the chair clearly because of the two bright lights, one next to each arm rest, that were pointed towards him at eye level. All he could see was the soft glow of the cigar tip and a small plume of smoke drifting towards the open window. Handyman stood, feeling the cold sweat trickle between his shoulder blades, waiting for the Don to speak. The cigar tip glowed brightly, and dimmed.

"Hello, Mr. Harris. Good of you to come."

The voice was like a bad impression of Lee Marvin, but the diction was pure Oxford English.

"Good of you to ask me, Don Imbroglio. How can I help you?"

"Please, please. Let's not be hasty. Plenty of time to discuss business. Let's be sociable. Have a seat."

Handyman looked around. There was no seat. He was wondering whether he should sit on the floor when the Don snapped his fingers, and Stratosphere lumbered over with a leather chair and set it behind him. Sitting on it was like sitting on a cloud.

"Drink?"

"Yes, please…"

The cigar glowed and the fingers snapped. Stratosphere's hand appeared over his shoulder with the kind of glass that you are not sure whether to drink from or wear, and put it on the table. It made a slight screeching noise on the marble.

The Don himself leaned forward to pour Handyman a generous measure. The effect was dramatic. "Cognac is all right?"

"Yes. Good."

The fine liquid glowed yellow in the lights as the Don poured, whirling around the glass in a tiny cascade. He handed it to Handyman. Handyman had spoken to the Don many times, and seen him on a few occasions, but never like this. This was different. This was Dracula in his castle. The Don sat back, and the cigar glowed.

"I know why they call you Handyman, Mr. Harris."

"You do? I mean, do you?"

"Yes, indeed, Mr. Harris. I know they call you Handyman because you fix things. You fix things like boxing matches, and horse races, and the like." The cigar glowed.

"Well, yes, Don Imbroglio, but I never interfere…"

The cigar tip waved in a small circle. "Nobody is accusing you of anything, Mr. Harris. The fact is, I need a little repair work done myself. I was wondering if you might help me."

"Of course, Don Imbroglio. Anything at all. I'd be happy to."

"Very kind of you, Mr. Harris. Do you, perchance, know a fellow who goes by the rather quaint name of Monsoon Parker?"

"Yes, Don Imbroglio. You might even say he is a client of mine."

"Good. Good. All right, then. Listen very carefully, Mr. Harris. Here's what I want you to do."

The Don leaned forward.

Handyman's mind was racing as the elevator descended towards the lobby. He had a bad feeling about all this. It seemed simple enough, but what was he getting involved in? What was the English-sounding Guinea creep playing at? Lord fucking Grease Ball. He's about as English as a fucking lasagna. But what choice did he have? The French have an expression: "He who says no to Champagne, says no to life." Saying no to the Don was very similar.

The elevator landed and Handyman stepped into the lobby, seeing the vulpine old superintendent leering at him as he walked towards the door. He gave him the finger, and pushed out into the street.

# Chapter 4.

Asia was standing under the sun-bright lights of a casino sign, negotiating with a prospective client through the rolled-down window of an out-of-town Chevy. She was looking at him the way princess Leia looked at Jabba the Hutt.

"How much for a blow job?" the guy was asking. Asia couldn't place the accent, but he was from the north somewhere, maybe over the border. The state of his wheels told her that however much it was, it would be too much.

"Sorry, I can't," she said. "I'm Muslim."

"What? Muslims don't suck dick?"

"No. They don't eat pork. Now fuck off!"

The guy gave her the finger and gunned the engine.

Asia straightened up as he accelerated away. She looked up and down the stream of traffic in both directions, looking for the cops and looking for guys that were driving like they were watching something other than the road. She wasn't too concerned about the cops and had it mostly covered, but she was still relatively new in town and didn't need any unnecessary hassle. In the center lane she watched a big black Cadillac slide over and slow down. A colored girl, with whom she was quite friendly and sometimes went partying, strutted her stuff over to the tinted window as it rolled down. The girl put her head to the window, and then looked over to where Asia was standing and waved to her.

"Guess this one don't eat dark meat," she said, as Asia stepped up to the car. "He wants to speak to you. Good luck, hon."

Asia smiled at her friend and bent to the window. A most unsightly man, with dark glasses and halitosis that could have stunned a hyena, looked her up and down with slow contempt. She had seen better complexions on a bubonic plague victim.

"Get in," the man said.

"Listen, Dracula, only if you promise not to bite me in the neck."

The man leered at her. "Don't worry, sweet cheeks. It ain't for me. I'm careful where I put mine. Now get in."

"The only place you put yours is your hand. Fuck you!"

The man removed his shades. "If I have to come out there and get you, you ain't gonna like it."

Asia took a step back from the car. She bumped into something hard and turned around. While she had been talking, the other passenger had gotten out and come around behind her. Looking up at him towering above her she was suddenly frightened, but she didn't show it.

"They must be feedin' 'em good in Joliet these days," she said. "What do you want, Lurch?"

"Lurch" slapped her hard. A mean, backhand slap that she hadn't seen coming. He grabbed her arm, twisted it, and, as the door opened, bundled her roughly inside and climbed in after her, still holding her wrist. She tried to pull away, but the grip tightened.

"Ow. You creep! You're hurting me."

"Baby," the man said, in a soft, nasty voice, "you don't even know what the word means. Now, you just sit tight. We goin' for a little ride. You get paid, don't worry."

The man released her arm and sat back as the big car pulled away from the curb.

For twenty anxious minutes Asia tried to look through the darkened windows as the car wound through the back streets. She knew they were headed in a southerly direction, but could not be certain exactly where they were. Just as she became concerned that they were headed out of town altogether the car pulled up in front of a tall building, which she calculated to be a couple of blocks back from the Strip, about level with the Mandalay Bay. None too gently, she was hustled out of the Caddie, through the foyer, and into an elevator. No one had spoken to her since the first exchange. The elevator stopped at the penthouse, and she was handed over to two enormous men. They escorted her through large wooden doors and into the presence of a small, dapper man, with slicked-back white hair and dark glasses, who was sitting in a deep leather chair behind a low table, smoking a cigar.


Monsoon Parker had dollar signs in his eyes, and for the first time in as long as he could remember he was looking beyond his next score. He had the old man's case opened on the table in front of him and was gazing lovingly at it, deep in thought. The dog was having his day, everything had come to he who had waited, and the meek were definitely going to inherit the fucking earth. He had opened a safe deposit box in a downtown bank, and had stashed the Machine Gun Jelly and all but two hundred dollars of the money from Crispin. This time it was going to be different. This was his big break, and he was going to be smart and not piss all his money away at the book and the tables. He was moving upscale, uptown, and up the fucking ladder. No more days and nights of worrying, sweating over nickel-and-dime bets, and looking over his shoulder for the crew of some sadistic shyster loan shark to put the arm on him. From now on, the only close shaves he was going to have were going to be with his Gillette, and his only nighttime worries would be whether he should have fucked the redhead instead of the brunette. He was looking at thirty-five, forty grand by the end of the week, and he would stash twenty, leaving twenty or so for investment. Make way for Monsoon Parker, fucking entrepreneur! It was time to think big.

There had to be more of this stuff somewhere. The way the fat faggot had gushed about it, it was obviously big news to him, and if there was any consciousness-altering chemical substance that was not widespread and generally available in Vegas, then it would have to be fucking Kryptonite. Something that was not already on sale in every high school can in America had to be either very new or old and forgotten. And since it had come out of a case that had been brought from Vietnam thirty years ago, it had to be from that era, and from a generation who would all be old farts by now.

The first thing was to find out exactly what it was and where it came from. He needed to get it analyzed, to take a small sample down to the lab at UNLV and lay a few bucks on some spotty-faced nerd to buy himself a new PlayStation with and get him to check it out. And he was going to go through this old case like Philip fucking Marlowe, and see if he could come up with a clue.

The old man's case. It had to be fate. Some karma shit. His mother had brought it with her when she came to America, just after the last chopper had been ditched into the South China Sea. She had put her childlike Asiatic looks to good use in the world's oldest profession in the days when Vegas was still Vegas. When family entertainment meant one of the five families entertaining themselves by burying somebody in the desert. When you listened to Sinatra and Elvis, or, if you wanted to see some imbecile in a mouse outfit waving at you, you had to go to California. She had beavered away, literally and figuratively, and religiously saved her money, so that by the time Monsoon was fifteen she had accumulated a stash big enough to open her own joint and decided to split. Before lighting out for Bangkok, she made an important decision concerning her son. She decided that she didn't like him very much and dumped him with her cousin in Seattle.

Young Monsoon very quickly decided that dissecting stray cats in the cold room of a waterfront chop house for a bowl of rice every day and a bug-ridden mattress in an attic full of refugees was not his interpretation of the American Dream, and his Seattle residency was short-lived. The years that followed were years of rough living, of wandering from one rat-infested fleapit to another, always on the lam, always one step ahead of the flashing blue lights or the vigilante retribution for whatever burn he had put on somebody. It had been all moonlight flits, and early mornings climbing out of windows, and midnight train rides, floating around like a piece of flotsam in the scum of low-tide America, until he finally washed back up on the dark side of the brightest city in the land.

The case had been left with one of his mother's friends, another Vietnamese girl who had married a GI. It was only a battered old army-issue case, containing a few tarnished artifacts from a war that everyone wanted to forget, the only thing that remained of a man he never knew and rarely thought about. But he had kept it nevertheless. It had been as if some vague and ill-comprehended sense of security had been attached to it — as if it were a charm or a talisman, some essential prop, some relic of a forgotten past, or a faint trail leading back to something that might have been if things had been different. As if it contained not the dusty clothes and fading photographs of a man long dead, but the essence of the boy, the secret of who Monsoon Parker really was. As if it encapsulated the childhood he never had.

Ah, fuck it! Something like that. In truth, he didn't really know why he had kept the damn thing. What he did know now, however, was that while he had schlepped through every West Coast city, burg, and hayseed Hicksville between San Diego and the Canadian border for the best part of fifteen years, most of the time without a pot to piss in or a window to throw it out of, he had been sitting on forty fucking grand every step of the way. The irony was almost too much to bear.

He grabbed the case and tipped the contents out. Nothing had changed. Medals, Russki camera, photographs, a regimental tie, a dress uniform, clothes, some old letters. Not much of a fucking inheritance. Monsoon flicked through the photos again, turning them over to read the handwritten inscriptions on the back.

*The Ia Drang. Hue. A ride on the big bird. Eddie goes home. Zonker, Grisbo, and No Nuts. Zipperhead firelight party. Ooh lah lah. R and R on Waikiki. Back to the shit. C'mon baby Light my fire. Pissing on the peninsula.*

He tossed them back into the case, and picked up the letters. They had weird stamps, some from places Monsoon had never heard of, and were dry and flaky, and some of the writing was illegible. He set them aside. He would read them all later. Maybe there would be something in them, some sign, some message from a hand long stilled, to point him in the right direction. He took the dress uniform jacket out and shook it. The dust made him cough again. Sweat marks had discolored the lining under the armpits. On a whim, he slipped it on. It was at least three sizes too big for him, and the sleeves reached past his fingertips. There was something heavy in the side pocket, and his fingers closed around the cold metal of a Zippo. There were words engraved on it. Monsoon held them up to the light, and read: *If you find this, I am dead, so shove it up your ass, and light it. Phil Parker.*

Monsoon grinned. At least the old bastard had had a sense of humor. He felt through the other pockets, and in the breast pocket found small canvas bag with a zipper. Inside was an envelope. On it was written, *To my son, Monsoon Poontang Eighty-Second Airborne Purple Heart Parker.*

Monsoon's jaw dropped open. He turned cold. With shaking hands, he thumbed open the envelope. Inside was a photograph and, on yellowed paper, a single typewritten sheet—faded, but just about readable.

```
Dear Son,

    I am planning on being around to see you grow up,
and teaching you all the things I know. Charlie has
got other plans for me. Charlie has got other plans
for all of us. If you are old enough to read this and
I'm not there, reading it right along with you, then
Charlie's plan probably worked. If this is so, don't
hate Charlie, son. Don't hate nobody. There is enough
pain and shit in the world as it is. Charlie sees it
his way, we see it ours. You're half Charlie
yourself, son. Half Charlie, half nigger. Shit, son,
you sure as hell drew the short straw. People are
going to despise you for it, son. Charlie because you
ain't yellow enough, the brothers because you ain't
black enough, an ol' honky because he just hates
everybody who ain't a honky and most of them that is.
Maybe bringing you into the world is a way of making
up for all the other little Charlies who ain't never
going to be here, because of what I did. Because of
what we all did. I don't know. This is a bad
business, son, and I hope you never have to go
through it. I hope a lot of things. But hope don't
mean shit out here. Before I go, I want to say sorry
about the name, kid. At the ass end of a three-day
furlough, looking through the bottom of an empty JD
bottle, it seemed like a pretty cool name. One more
thing, son. Keep this picture and take care of it.
The one on the left with all his teeth is me. The
other one is the finest human being I have ever met.
His name is Woolloomooloo Wally, and he is from
Australia. If it wasn't for him, I wouldn't be here,
```

*and neither would you. I don't know how, but I just know that he is going to make it out of here. If you ever get in trouble, son, baaaad trouble, so you don't know what to do, look for this man, at the address on the back of the photo. Well, so long, son. I'd like to say I love you, but how can you love what you don't know? I would have, if there had been time.*

*Stay Frosty, son,*

*Your father,*

*Phil Parker. (Cap.)*

Monsoon's hand shook as he read through the letter three times. His eyes brimmed with tears. He placed it almost reverently on the table, and picked up the photograph. It was of two men sitting in a bar somewhere, under a bamboo roof. On the table in front of them was a platoon of empty beer bottles and a half-full bottle of bourbon. The two men had their arms around each other's shoulders and they were smiling broadly and holding glasses towards the camera. The man on the left, the handsome light-skinned Negro, he recognized as his father. The other seemed older and was much darker. He had wild bushy hair, and his eyes glittered from wrinkled sockets. His front teeth were missing, and he had broad white lines smeared on his face. He looked like an inebriate and unhinged clown. Monsoon flipped the picture over and read, *With Wal. Saigon. 68.*

And beneath those words, *Woolloomooloo Wally. Care of the proprietor. Big Blue Billabong Hotel. N. Queensland. Australia.*

Woolloomooloo Wally! The same dude whose name had been on the MGJ package. Monsoon picked up the letter, carefully folded it, and slipped it, together with the photo, back into the envelope. Going to the refrigerator he took out a bottle of Wild Turkey and a Corona, and went over to where a tattered chair stood by the window. He topped the beer bottle, killed the light, and sat in the chair, sipping the bourbon from the bottle and chasing it with Corona, illuminated only by the occasional flashing lights from the squad cars passing on the street outside.

An undefined ache gripped him. A sense of longing for something forever out of reach, an embrace he had never had and never would. These were completely alien sensations to Monsoon Parker. For a while he sat, not knowing how to handle them. Then the old anger and resentment came flooding back.

*Fuck it*, he thought. *Get your head out of your ass and back into the real world.*

He had made a pretty good score, but there had to be more where that came from. There just had to. And since it was in the old man's case, it was a cinch that it had to have come from the 'Nam. Since nobody seemed to have heard of it, it had to be either very rare or some shit they cooked up during the war that had been forgotten. And this character, Woolloomooloo Wally, had something to do with it. Anybody with a mouthful of handle like that had to be into something. But could the jungle-looking fucker still be alive? In the photo he looked a good bit older than the old man, and the old man had been in his late twenties when he'd bought the farm. That was close to thirty years ago. So even if the old man was right, and the old bastard had survived the war, there was no guarantee that he hadn't croaked since.

Monsoon decided to have a good look at Woolloomooloo Wally. He switched the light back on, went back to the case and took up the pictures, and sat back down. He sorted the photos as one sorts out a deck of cards, turning them all face up and the right way around. He then sifted through them one by one, placing the ones that depicted Wally on the arm of the chair, and flicking the others onto the floor. When he had finished, he had a stack of about twenty pictures. He examined them carefully, one at a time. The first thing he noticed was that in each and every picture, Woolloomooloo Wally had a beer in his fist and an indefatigable grin on his face. Except for one. In this one, Wally had a beer in his fist, but you could not tell if he had an indefatigable grin on his face or not—although the chances are he did. The reason being he was in flagrante delicto with a young Asian girl, against the wall of what appeared to be an outhouse. She definitely had an indefatigable grin on her face, but all you could see of Wally was his bushel of hedgehog hair and his narrow black ass.

Monsoon allowed himself a grin, and went back to studying the photos. You could tell from the way the other people in the pictures looked at Wally that there was something special about him, something that set him apart, as if he was there but not there. Not there in the same sense that the others were there. There was something else. In the pictures with Wally the others, the young soldiers, did not look so lost and afraid as they did in the pictures without him. Monsoon went through the pictures again, and selected those that showed only Wally and his father. There were just three. One was taken in a clearing in a jungle, by a tank. On the front of the turret was written "Waltzing Matilda" in big red letters. In the photo, his father and Wally were pissing against the treads of the tank. In another, they were in a paddy field with a buffalo. Wally was pretending to hump the buffalo. The buffalo was pretending to enjoy it. In the third they were sitting in bamboo chairs outside a bar. Wally's grin was more than usually indefatigable as he pointed at a crude, hand-painted sign above his head that read, "Wal's Outback."

Monsoon looked again at the images, each in turn, searching for something, anything, that might help him. The photos told him nothing. He threw them to the floor in disgust. The one of Wally and the girl in the outhouse fluttered down and landed, face up, on his shoe. He bent down idly to retrieve it, and looked at it again. He smirked again, took a belt from his bourbon, and was just about to fling the picture away, when he saw something…or thought he did. He stood up abruptly, knocking over the bottle. Dashing into the kitchen, he wrenched open a drawer and grabbed the chipped magnifying glass with no frame that he kept there. He stood directly under the light and peered at the photo through the lens. He moved the lens backwards and forwards, trying to make the image as big as possible. He froze. He stared. He dropped the lens, shattering it on the bare floor.

"Holy shit!" he exclaimed. "Holy fucking shit!"

Behind the girl that Wally was holding against the outhouse, and behind the indefatigable grin on her face, the wall was built with bricks of Machine Gun Jelly.

Monsoon righted the bourbon where it had fallen and quaffed a serious portion of the remaining contents. He sat down until he had recovered himself somewhat, and then reached for his phone and dialed Information. He put on his best please-help-me-kind-sir voice.

"Excuse me, but you wouldn't perhaps be able to get me a number in Australia. Yes, that is correct. Queensland, in fact. It is called the Big Blue Billabong Hotel."

"Please repeat, sir," said a weary voice.

"The Big Blue Billabong Hotel."

"Please hold."

Monsoon held.


When Asia emerged from the apartment several hours later, in a state of considerable disarray and on wobbly legs, she had been fucked from midnight to Washington. Not to mention being borderline amazed by what had just happened to her. She hadn't thought the old fucker had it in him. At first she had been scared, but she had been reassured to find the man beautifully spoken and impeccably well mannered—until they got into the bedroom, at least. He had given her a glass of champagne and, when she had complained, apologized for the rough handling she had received from his men, promising to remonstrate with them. He had complimented her on her looks, had allowed her to draw a hot bath in his huge marble-tiled bedroom, and had let her take the bottle of champagne with her.

When she had emerged from the bath he was standing naked at the foot of the bed with what, if she hadn't known better, she would have said was a giant spliff smoking in his hand. He looked so pale and thin and frail, as if a quick glance at the centerfold of Playboy would be enough to kill him stone dead. If you discounted the fact that he had an erection so proud that he looked like he could hit a home run with it, that is. So stiff it seemed to vibrate — it was huge and made to seem even bigger by the diminutive stature of its owner.

And the man had been transformed. Instead of the suave, debonair sophisticate, he had become some kind of leering, grinning satyr, an insane priapic gargoyle from the roof of an ancient gothic cathedral. His eyeballs were flicking backwards and forwards erratically, like he was trying to watch two jai alai matches at the same time, and he began to giggle, a soft bubbling that swelled and grew until it became a high hysterical cackle. Crabbing over the deep carpet with a disjointed gait he went to a drinks cabinet, from which he pulled a bottle of Moët and opened it, firing the cork at her like an actual weapon. He scuttled over to a stereo in a corner, and turned up the music to an earsplitting volume. Asia recognized "The Flight of the Valkyries."

And then, drinking from the bottle, the man advanced, purposeful but ungainly, like a rampant zombie, with his threatening member poised and presented as if he intended to impale her upon it. The only problem was, he was headed the wrong way. Confused and nervous again, Asia giggled, and the man instantly turned towards the sound. His hands waved like antennae in front of him, as if he were playing some perverted form of blindman's bluff. When his hand brushed against her breast, he howled like a banshee and leapt at her like a corsair.

Three hours later her twat felt like the bottom of a birdcage, her rectum as if she had shit an anvil, and her mouth as if she had stopped a left hook from Iron Mike. She felt as if she had been keelhauled, so fervently and unremittingly had the man pursued her around the room, stabbing her in every aperture, from every conceivable angle, an entirely unfeasible number of times. Finally, he had gone abruptly rigid, and then convulsed and keeled over backwards onto the bed, with his tongue hanging out and his eyes staring fixed and vacant into space, as limp as a defrosted squid. For a dreadful second she feared that his ticker had given out.

She checked his pulse and it seemed strong and regular, and his chest was rising and falling steadily, so she dressed and walked out into the room where the two titans were waiting. She explained what had happened, and one of them detained her while the other went to check. He came back moments later and nodded to the other, who had escorted her to the lobby, given her an envelope with one thousand dollars in it, called her a cab, and waited with her on the street until it arrived.

Back at her flat, she fixed herself a stiff drink and got into a hot bath. She soaked for an hour and went to bed, but her racing mind would not let her sleep. She got up again an hour later and made coffee, fidgeted for another hour, and finally reached for the phone.

It hadn't been a very good fight. Nothing broken except for a couple of glasses. The two protagonists, one with a bleeding lip and the other with a gashed knuckle, were sitting at the bar with their arms around each other's shoulders and tears in their eyes, professing undying love and fealty to one another. Stavros "Big Bazouki" Papastopalotovus, having mopped up the blood, keeping a sharp eye out for gold teeth but finding none, sighed as he righted the chairs. He looked down the long length of the bright bar. Every chair was occupied, and the floor space filled. The jukebox was blasting and some of the girls, at least those who could still stand, were dancing. The clientele were mostly aboriginal—a few pure of blood, many more mixed — and a scattering of whites, rough-looking men with big muscles and big bellies, dressed in vests and wearing hats to a man.

*A lot different than when I first moved here*, he thought. The girls behind the bar were working full-on, trying to keep up with the constant demand. *Saturday afternoons are always good*, Stavros was thinking happily, when a voice hailed him from the office door. He looked over to see his wife, a full-figured black woman, holding the phone. Stavros lumbered over and grasped the receiver in his hairy grip.

"Yeah, Stavros."

The voice on the other end sounded far away, and foreign. "Can I speak to Woolloomooloo Wally?"

"Not unless yer got a fucken loud voice, mate. Who are ya?"

"Wally was a friend of my father. In Vietnam. I've got some things for him. I'm trying to find him. I'm calling from the States."

"Well, you won't find 'im 'ere, mate, 'e's gone."

"You mean he's dead?"

"Nah, don't be a bladdy drongo. 'E's gone walkabout."

"Oh, he's gone for a walk. When will he be back?"

"Jesus. Are you dense or what? I didn't say walk, I said walkabout."

"I'm sorry. I don't understand."

"'E's gone away. 'E doesn't live 'ere anymore."

"Well…do you know where he is?"

"Yeah, course I bladdy know. 'E's me mate."

"Well, will you tell me?"

"'Ow do I know who yer are, or why you want 'im?"

"I got the address of your hotel from my old man. He and Wally were good friends."

"Is that right? What was yer old man's name?"

"Parker. Captain Philip Parker."

"Ah, yeah. Fair dinkum, mate. I 'eard Wal talk about 'im. Sorry, but you 'ave to be careful."

"I understand."

"Yeah. Well, Wal's in Vietnam. 'E's got a bar in Ho Chi Minh City called Wal's Outback. 'E…"

The line went dead. Stavros looked at the receiver in his hand with some puzzlement, until the sound of breaking glass informed him that another fight had broken out. He dropped the receiver back into the cradle.

"Strewth," he muttered, reaching for his mop.


Of course, Crispin Capricorn's right name was not really Crispin Capricorn. Even in a country whose greatest icon of rugged masculinity was actually called Marion, and where parents can actually saddle their own kids with names like Shaquille, nobody could really be called Crispin Capricorn. Crispin had been christened Alvin Hardware, and might have continued quite happily as Alvin Hardware had it not been for two circumstances, which you may or may not consider unfortunate depending upon your sexual persuasion, but which were undoubtedly consequential.

The first was the problem he developed with his feet—the problem being that he couldn't keep them out of Burger King, thereby ensuring that by his thirteenth birthday he was already the wrong side of two hundred pounds.

The second, and most significant, was his tendency after the onset of puberty to develop spontaneous erections at inappropriate moments, such as the time he developed a full-on boner while reaching for the soap in the shower after a school football practice, having found his face at butt-level of the well-scrubbed cheeks of his classmates.

By the time he got out of hospital, and by the time, upon advice from the principal, Mr. and Mrs. Hardware had removed him to a different school district, Alvin had come to the conclusion that he was "different." However, unlike the thousands of young men who make the same discovery every year and go through the tortures of the damned—wracked by guilt, daily hiding, and denying their secret desires—Alvin threw himself into his new lifestyle with gay abandon, no pun intended. And while he was experimenting with handjobs and blowjobs in the company of likeminded young men and deciding whether or not it is truly better to give than to receive, he found that many of his clandestine paramours were employed in the so-called "performing arts." When, at a particularly riotous New Year's bash in his seventeenth year, memorable for some old queen losing a testicle to an improperly adjusted vacuum cleaner, he discovered that he had a halfway-decent singing voice, the die was cast. Naturally outgoing and with a good talent for mimicry, he was on his way to diva-dom, and the only looking back from that point on was to see who was coming up behind him.

A good stage name being essential to any aspiring *artiste*—especially one of his calling—he struggled initially to come up with anything suitable, trying and discarding Jacob Sladder, Madame Buttockfly, Bobby Helmet, Melissa Missionary, Patricia Pudenda, and Gloria Euphoria. He seriously considered Crispin Cornucopia for a while, picturing his cup ever full as it were, before being inspired by a close encounter of the weird kind with a very well-endowed, but not especially hygienic, astronomer and goat enthusiast, the details of which need not concern us here. So Crispin Capricorn it became, and Crispin Capricorn it remained, although he did flirt briefly with the idea of Dick Ramsbottom. As his fame grew, and he sank more and more comfortably into the fluffy pink pillow of the life he had made for himself, and as Alvin Hardware became nothing more than the fading and vaguely discomforting reminiscence of gin-induced nostalgia, Crispin changed his name officially and Alvin became a yellowing photograph in a dusty yearbook that nobody ever opened, half a continent away.

As with any self-respecting moth, Crispin was inevitably attracted to the brightest flame. He headed for the scintillating lights of Vegas, where he became—by virtue of his talent, his wit, his industry, and the occasional blowjob in the right quarter—quite a gaudy flower even in that outrageous garden.

Alas, as it goes with seasons, so it goes with the affairs of men. Public tastes changed, regimes changed, and his star waned, until by his fiftieth birthday Crispin was reduced to the matinée performance in a low-watt fleapit on the wrong side of town, pretending to be Bette Midler six days a week amid the clang of slot machines for a bunch of blue-rinse geriatrics who didn't know an E-flat from a heart bypass. But though there was more life in a Haitian cemetery than at one of his gigs these days, Crispin was not complaining. He had prospered while it lasted, was well-respected and well-liked in his circle, had a nice comfortable apartment in the right part of town which was all paid for, and had enough in the bank to see that he wouldn't have to go without for whatever time he had left. In fact, he didn't even really have to keep working but, old trooper that he was, he clung to the dimming vestiges of his former glory while he still could. And anyway, he liked pretending to be Bette Midler.

He was currently—and had been for a couple of years—seeing his boyfriend Nigel, who, while not the brightest match in the box, at least had the advantages of being loyal, half Crispin's age, and only moderately annoying. Crispin was becoming attached to him, in more ways than one.

Other than Nigel, the person he spent the most time with these days was Asia Birdshadow, a young woman who he liked to think of as his protégé, whom he had taken under his wing when she had just gotten off the bus from some fetid, mosquito-ridden swamp south of the line. She was currently prospering as an up-market sperm receptacle, but Crispin could tell that her heart wasn't in it, and he hoped that she would have the sense to quit before the light went out of her eyes. She was feisty and fierce and independent, more the pro with the balls of steel than the proverbial hooker with the heart of gold, but he knew that she didn't have the necessary flint in her soul to swim unscathed in these waters for very long.

He thought of her very fondly, almost paternally, as the daughter he never would have, since the product of his ejaculations invariably took a wrong turn at the first bend. In fact, he was thinking of her fondly when she rang his mobile.

"Asia. I was just thinking about you. How's the traffic?"

"Pedestrian. Listen, we have to meet. The most bizarre thing has just happened to me. I want your opinion."

"Well, you know where I live, dearie."

"Right. Don't move. I'll be round in an hour."

"Okay, Sweetie." Crispin blew a kiss down the phone and wandered into his walk-in wardrobe to find something appropriate to wear.

Monsoon was on hot bricks and had not slept or eaten for over forty-eight hours, such was his state of high excitement. He was existing on coffee, bourbon, amphetamines, and nervous energy. He had an acquaintance called Weeds. He had given Weeds a couple of bucks to call Wal's Outback and ask how long they had been open. Weeds had told him they had been open since ten o'clock. Monsoon had called Weeds an absolute cretin and explained that he had meant since what year had they been open. Weeds had called back and asked if Wally was around and if there was any Machine Gun Jelly — for sale. Someone had asked Weeds what the fuck he was talking about, called him a drongo — whatever that was — made reference to his mother's genital region, and told him to fuck off. So much for the direct route. It didn't necessarily mean that Wally wasn't around or that there was no Jelly. It just meant that Weeds was a drongo.

A day later he called Wal's Outback himself. Woolloomooloo Wally had not been able to speak, but the person who he had spoken to, who sounded like a child, had confirmed that Wally was alive and well and would be able to speak in about eight hours, by which time he would have more or less recovered from the effects of the twenty-eight bottles of beer which he had just finished drinking. The boy also confirmed that the bar had been opened during the war, but had closed when the Americans left, then opened again about ten years ago, and yes, it was in the same place that it had been before. He also confirmed that Monsoon was himself a drongo and told him to fuck off.

Monsoon had made some calculations, the results and implications of which had almost sent him around the bend completely. He had replaced the broken magnifying glass with a more powerful one, and examined the photo minutely. There was no question that the walls of the shithouse were lined with MGJ. Of crucial importance, also, was the fact that the shirt that Wally was wearing as he was rogering the girl in the outhouse was the same as the one he was wearing in the picture of him and Monsoon's father outside the bar. This led Monsoon to conclude that either Woolloomooloo Wally only had one shirt, or that the pictures were taken in the same place on the same day. Almost too conveniently, and in keeping with the ever-swelling wave of good fortune upon which Monsoon now found himself riding, the latter fact was confirmed by the date and location written on the back of the photos, together with the legends, *Wal opens his bar* and *Wal opens his pants,* respectively.

His now-unshakeable belief in the inviolable preordination of his lucky break, coupled with the fact that he now knew the bar to be in its original location, led him to conclude that the chances were astoundingly good that, due to its construction material, the real estate value of Woolloomooloo Wally's shithouse was approximately the same as Bill Gates's townhouse. Extrapolating from what he could see, there were no fewer than a thousand packets in the walls, resulting in an erection-inducing equation, which—although mathematics, and in particular multiplication, had never been Monsoon's strong point—appeared to resolve itself at an extremely significant amount of money. Or, in simple terms, THIRTY-EIGHT MILLION MOTHERFUCKIN' DOLLARS, AND CHANGE. Monsoon began to hyperventilate, and his brain began to throb with an almost audible hum, as if it could not accommodate the enormity of the consequences of the calculation it had just made.

The thought of thirty-eight million motherfuckin' dollars and change, and what he could do with it, sent his already-agitated mind into overdrive, which, combined with lack of sleep and drug and alcohol abuse, allowed him to think with a clarity that would not otherwise have been possible. It was in this almost nirvana-like state of lucidity that the curtains in his brain parted to reveal an idea of unparalleled brilliance.

What if he went to Vietnam and ingratiated himself with this Wally? What if he showed him the letter? What if he said that he had come to find out all about the father he never knew, from Wally? What if he told this Wally character that there was a missing piece in his life that only Wally could give him back? That only by knowing about his father would he be able to know who he himself really was. Nobody could fail to fall for a sob story like that, coming from the son of his late, lamented best friend. This was when the curtains parted yet further, and an idea of unprecedented sophistication exploded into his fevered sconce.

What if he took his grandfather? What if he took Philip Parker's father? He would have Woolloomooloo Wally's heart on a platter. Wally would welcome them with open arms into the bosom of his family. The old man would be here in a week. All he had to do was bullshit the old bastard into going with him. And he knew exactly how to play that hand. After that, it was just a matter of demolishing the shithouse and getting a shitload of illicit dope out of Vietnam and into the good ol' US of A undetected. Of course, it didn't necessarily follow that Machine Gun Jelly had to be illegal, just as heroin was once perfectly legal, but why take the chance? Having his grandfather with him had the added advantage of being able to stash some in the old man's suitcase, just in case.

It was as he was appreciating the irony of the fact that he might not actually be breaking the law that the idea of Machiavellian complexity flew into his brain like a jeweled bird. He grabbed the phone and dialed, sucking from the bourbon bottle while he waited impatiently for a response. After what seemed to him an interminable number of rings, a high falsetto voice answered.

"Yo, Chicken Man," Monsoon said.

"Don't call me that. What do you want?"

"I need a favor."

"No you don't, you need a kick in the balls," replied Chicken Man, not sounding entirely thrilled to be talking to Monsoon Parker.

"Least I got some."

"Fuck you."

"I need a coffin."

"A what?"

"A coffin. I need a coffin."

"For you, I hope."

"Very funny. I mean it. I need a coffin."

"Well, go and fucking buy one."

"No, you don't understand. I need a used one."

"I don't think there is a real big trade in second-hand coffins."

"Listen, dipshit. I need a coffin with bones in it. I need you to dig one up."

"You got to be shittin' me."

"No, I'm serious. And it has to be full of bones. I don't want to open it and find some ripe fucker who's only been dead for a week."

"Hey, in case you ain't aware, grave robbing is a felony."

"So is armed robbery, I believe."

"Meaning what?"

"Meaning maybe the cops might like some information about the jewelry store job last week. You know, the one where the guy got shot?"

"You shit bird asshole," the voice said, hanging up.

Monsoon grinned and took another shot from the bottle. He went into the kitchen, took a pen and legal pad from a drawer, picked up the receiver again, and dialed Information.

"LA. California. Yeah. Gimme the number for Singapore Airlines."


Crispin had been wrong. Dorothy wasn't a more reliable source of information than the Las Vegas Revue Journal. Dorothy was a more reliable source of information than CNN! Within two days the buzz was in the streets, and Monsoon had set himself up with a mobile and was sliding around some very up-market real estate and making frequent trips to his safety deposit box. Apart from a couple of minor losing propositions, he hadn't even had time to really gamble, and even after his repayment to the Don he still had twenty grand and half the MGJ.

On the fourth day, he got a call from Handyman Harris.

"Handyman, my man. How's it hangin'? Are you getting any?"

"More than a candle in a fucking convent. Listen. I hear you got some serious merchandise on offer."

"Serious ain't the word, amigo. Try spectacular. You want?"

"Not me, bro. A friend of mine. A real cool dude."

"Oh yeah? Well, you better tell him this shit ain't cheap."

"Money is no object to this guy. He's loaded for bear."

"So when do we meet?"

"How about three o'clock? The Shell on Sahara."

"You got it," said Monsoon, hanging up with a grin.

Monsoon was surprised when Handyman's buddy climbed out of the car. The guy looked to be about seven feet tall, and looked as if he had never indulged in anything stronger than an aspirin. Handyman introduced him as Frankie Merang, out of Chicago.

"Jehesus Christ," said Monsoon, watching his hand disappear into Frankie's massive paw, "who the fuck do you play for, the Bulls or the fucking Bears?"

Frankie's grip tightened. "I play for the chapter eighty-six, ass kicker's society," he said, with a grin that had all the warmth of a T-Rex's in December, and was about the same size.

Monsoon decided to conduct business without further pleasantries. Frankie bought two ounces and took Monsoon's number, saying he would call him tomorrow if the shit was anything like as good as he'd heard it was. Monsoon assured him that it most definitely was.

Monsoon was even more surprised the next time he met Frankie, which was the following day, after Frankie had called and arranged another meet, this time in the long-term parking at McCarran. He was surprised when Frankie punched him in the mouth with a fist the size of a pork knuckle, and cold-cocked him.

When Monsoon came to, he was sitting in the back of a stretch Caddie with blacked-out windows between two guys wearing dark glasses who made Godzilla look like Barney. Frankie was driving, and when he noticed that Monsoon had recovered he turned around and smiled his saurian grin.

"Hi, Monsoon," he said, pleasantly. "Where's the box?"

Monsoon rubbed his jaw. He looked up at the massive figures on either side of him, and then at Frankie. "Which part of Jurassic Park did you find these two in? What fucking box are you talking about?"

Frankie smiled indulgently. "Monsoon. C'mon, man. You know the score. Tell him, Thumper."

The man on Monsoon's right removed his shades and grinned. Monsoon had once had a boil on his ass that looked more pleasant. His blood ran cold as he recognized Thumper Thyroid…the Don's man. End of charade.

"Okay, Frankie," he said, "I'll show you."

They made him walk inside the bank and empty the box, and then they took him back to the car and drove him to the apartment building of Don Ignacio Imbroglio.

# Chapter 5.

Milton "Eyeballs" Gonski was finding it difficult to concentrate. He wasn't supposed to be in here for one thing, and if someone snitched to the Prof he'd be in deep doodoo. Again. He'd been warned several times about using the Uni lab after hours, and he'd had to fork out five bucks to the security guy for the key. Furthermore, tonight was the weekly meeting of his discussion group CWESTYAN ('Cos WE're SmarT, & You Are Not), and they were in the middle of a really interesting debate about the effects of water pressure on the reproductive cycle of pre-Cambrian arthropods, and he had a really unique perspective that he wanted to introduce, at which point Lily Blauengel would undoubtedly recognize him for the genius he was and agree to accompany him to the next lab tech expo at the Convention Center. But that weird little Asian-looking guy had given him a hundred bucks up front to analyze this resin, with another hundred when it was done. And with two hundred bucks he could get a shitload of extra RAM for his PC and some really cool new software.

He was called "Eyeballs" because he could sit at a microscope longer than anyone else without getting tired. Or so he thought. The real reason was that he wore glasses with lenses like the bottom of fruit jar, which made his eyes goggle like a dying tuna and which made Lily Blauengel think he was an absolute dork.

Eyeballs eyeballed the big white clock on the wall. If he left now, he could still get to the meeting in time to make a dramatic entrance and impress Lily, and anyway he was getting seriously nervous about getting caught. Weighed against his growing anxiety was the fact the Asian guy had been adamant on the point of absolute secrecy, and had hinted at more money to come. The erotic image of a softly glowing state-of-the-art flat screen materialized in Eyeballs's mind. He decided to take a quick look.

The sample he had been given was miniscule, so small that he had to hold it in a pair of tweezers in order to pare off a scope-sized slice with his scalpel. He spread it onto a glass slide, slid it under the lens, flicked the switch, and pushed his eye sockets down onto the cool, comforting, familiar lenses of the microscope.

"Holy shit!"

Eyeballs sat back in surprise, and quickly leaned forward again. What the hell was this stuff? In his hand it appeared a dull, lifeless gray, but magnified a thousand times it looked like a bad acid trip. Purple and lurid green, lava red, with sinister-looking black veins running through it like an evil cheese. Eyeballs prided himself on the encyclopedic gallery of chemical compounds he was able to recognize from memory, but he had never seen anything remotely like this and had absolutely no idea what he was looking at. Images of the smiling Lily Blauengel in her holey-kneed baggy grunge jeans, and the wrathful figure of Professor Medes bursting through the swinging doors of the lab, and even a pulsating bank of chips giving his PC mega brain power to the max faded from his mind as his intellectual curiosity kicked in.

Eyeballs took a hard copy and ran it through to mainframe, but not only did he not come up with a match, he didn't come up with anything even marginally similar. He was going to have to break it down. Man, this was a real turn-on. He was into it, man. Eyeballs Gonski, chemistry ace, hot on the trail, and Professor Medes could go and fuck himself. And when word of this got around campus he would be famous, and Lily Blauengel would not have to fuck herself, 'cause Eyeballs would be in the chair.

Eyeballs went through into the lab next door and came back with a glass-stoppered bottle and a pipette. He got himself a hot chocolate from the machine in the corridor and turned on the small radio next to the microscope. It was tuned to an oldies station, but he left it. He wasn't interested in music anyway. It was just white noise, to take the static off his brain and help him concentrate. He took a sip of his chocolate and got down to it. He slipped on a pair of white gloves and then, with extreme care, transferred a tiny droplet of liquid from the bottle and dropped it onto the smear of compound on the slide. Letting it settle for a couple of seconds, he leaned forward and turned the volume dial on the radio up a notch. He vaguely recognized the tune as some song his old man listened to all the time. Some Stone-Age group. The Beatles, maybe.

Eyeballs leaned into his scope and his goggle eyes goggled even wider. The sample was changing color, and it was fucking moving! He saw the vivid colors on the slide all swirling together, becoming a flat brown, and then beginning to glow at the center—orange at first, brightening to an angry red, and then to hot white. Eyeballs Gonski was fascinated. Mesmerized, in fact. So mesmerized that he didn't hear the banging of the lab door as the irate professor of chemistry charged into the room and strode towards him. Nor did he hear the explosion that immolated the bench, torched Professor Medes's new hairpiece, and turned Milton "Eyeballs" Gonski into the most spectacular chemical reaction that he would never see.

Fear comes in many degrees. If mild alarm is one and trouser-shitting, hair-raising, spine-chilling, abject ice-cold nervous system shutdown comatose petrification is ten, then Monsoon was an eight-and-a-half climbing out of the limo, rising to nine as they stepped into the elevator. The sight of Stratosphere and Liberty put him up to nine-point-five. From there it leveled off a little, and it wasn't until the Don spoke to him that he actually reached eleven.

"Mr. Parker. Good of you to join us."

Monsoon really, really wanted to speak. But some things are just not to be.

"It's perfectly all right. I fully understand your reticence, Mr. Parker. Permit me to speak on your behalf. Could I offer you a drink?"

The realization that he was not about to die anytime soon—at least not in the next few minutes—allowed Monsoon's rigor mortis to relax enough for him to nod his head. The fingers snapped, and the chair and drink arrived.

"Drink up, Mr. Parker. Drink up. Now, to business. We understand that you have had a little windfall, shall we say. Las Vegas really is such a small town, Mr. Parker. Nobody keeps their secrets for very long here. Especially from me. When we got wind of your new merchandise, and the excitement it was causing in certain circles, we decided to see for ourselves. The results were quite…surprising. Now, I'm sure you will agree, something this good should be made available for all to enjoy."

The fingers clicked, and the box was handed to the Don. He removed the contents and placed them on table in front of him, without looking at them. He gave a stage whistle.

"One thousand dollars an ounce. Remarkable. Where is the rest of it?"

The bourbon had restored some of Monsoon's circulation, and he was thinking as fast as he could, under the circumstances. He could tell the truth, but the truth seemed so unlikely that the Don might assume he was lying and put him to the test. And the test was liable to be somewhat less than pleasant, what with the Don working on the assumption that being suspended by the testicles from a twelfth-floor penthouse window staring at the pointy bit on the Luxor is a fairly convincing argument that honesty is the best policy. A simple lie might be the less stressful alternative, in the short term. He could lie, and buy time, but sooner or later the Don would find out, and then leaving town, the country, and, if at all possible, the solar system, would be the advisable option. And whatever he said, it was unlikely that the Don would leave him unwatched, so giving him the slip was probably unfeasible.

So, at the risk of having a blowtorch pedicure, the truth seemed to be the wisest course of action. Or, at least, as much of it as would see him out of the room in one piece and not qualified to stand outside the door of a harem with a tea towel wrapped around his head.

"Don Imbroglio," he began, his voice growing stronger after a weak start, "I realize what I am about to tell ya will seem incredible, but I am gonna tell ya everything, exactly as it happened."

"Pray continue, Mr. Parker. You have our undivided attention."

*It's like listening to Shere Khan in the fucking Jungle Book*, Monsoon thought as he prepared to continue.

"Well, Don Imbroglio, I have to admit I was in dire straits. I was into ya for a grand up front, plus two for the vig, and I didn't have the green. Fucking O'Neal! Anyway, I'm looking round for something I can sell for a stake to maybe get the money back, when I remember my old man's suitcase. My old man got greased in Vietnam, and this case has been with me ever since I was a boy. I'm thinkin' maybe I can sell the medals or somethin'. Anyway, I find this shit, Machine Gun Jelly. I have absolutely no idea what it is. It looks like dope, and smells like dope, but it could be fucking C4 for all I know. Anyway, like I said, I'm so desperate that I don't give a rat's ass what it is. I know this old Brit society broad is having a party, so I go round there and sell this stuff to her and a couple of fags for five hundred a pop. The next day, this fairy is knockin' my door down. I figure the stuff is a dud, and he wants his dough back, so I have the old insurance policy handy when I open the door. But it turns out the shit really lit his candle. That's when I know I'm onto something, so I up the price to a grand a shout, and the rest you know."

"So you are telling us that what is here is all that there is left?"

"Don Imbroglio, I swear by my mother's ovaries."

"And you really don't know where to get any more?"

"Don, I only wish I did."

The fingers clicked, and two things happened. First, from over Monsoon's shoulder, an envelope with Singapore Airlines printed on the front flew into sight and landed in his lap. And second, a hard, heavy object—which later turned out to be a monkey wrench—slugged him hard in the back of the head, lifting a piece of his scalp. He fell forward onto his face, and a boot came down on the back of his neck, pinioning him to the carpet.

"So. We must assume, then, that your ticket to Ho Chi Minh City is merely a celebratory vacation, to enjoy some of your newfound wealth."

Monsoon attempted to speak, but the neck-breaking pressure prevented him from doing much more than breathing.

"Tell me, Mr. Parker. Have you suffered a bereavement in the family recently?"

The fingers clicked, and Thumper relieved the pressure on Monsoon's neck just enough for him to be able to reply.

"Don Imbroglio, I..."

Before he could finish, the fingers clicked and the boot came down again.

"Mr. Parker. While you have been our guest, my associates paid a visit to your apartment. In addition to these tickets, they found a coffin. It was occupied. We all have skeletons in our closets, do we not, but in your case the skeleton is real. A man's hobbies are his own business, of course, but if you do not tell me for what exact purpose you have acquired a coffin and a skeleton, and tell me quickly—let's say in the next three seconds, for example—your closet will shortly have two skeletons in it."

The fingers and Thumper's boot did their little routine again, and Monsoon was grabbed by the collar, hauled to his feet, and shoved into his chair. Thumper punched him in the face, and then handed him his drink. Monsoon drained his glass, coughed, and started to speak.

"Don Imbroglio. Please. I'm not holdin' out on you. It's just a long shot. An idea. It's probably bullshit."

"Well, indulge us."

"It's a guess, for chrissake. I swear. It's a big maybe. You gotta believe me. It's a what-if. The fucking Yellow Brick Road. What do I have to lose? How can it be worse than here? I go. I look around. I ask questions. I come home rich or I get to fly business class, get drunk, and get laid. That's all there is. Believe it or don't. I can't tell ya nothin' else."

"And the coffin?"

"Well, that's part of my plan, see? And not bad, for a joker like me, even if I do say so myself. I ask myself this: If I do find a supply of this shit, how do I get it into the country, first without the Feds finding out, and second, without some mob muscling in on the action. No offense meant, Don Imbroglio. Then I get my idea. My old man's remains were never recovered. But he was a big-time war hero. More gongs than a

Buddhist temple. So, what if I go over there, say I have discovered the stiff, and inform the military and the media. I still got the dog tags, see?"

Monsoon opened the top button of his shirt and pulled out the dog tags and held them towards the Don. The Don remained impassive.

"Big splash in the paper," Monsoon continued. "The USAF'll fly the bones back with full military honors, and a big fucking band. Except it ain't the old man in the box. It's the dope. The beauty of it is, not only do I get the shit flown back and into the country without being inspected, but I get it flown in for free by the fucking Air Force. I had someone bring me the coffin, so I could experiment with the weights. I was going to put it back when I was finished."

It went very quiet, and stayed like that for a good two minutes. Monsoon started to sweat. And then the Don clapped his hands, slowly, three times. The fingers clicked, and a hand came over Monsoon's shoulder with another drink.

"Mr. Parker. I'm impressed. Congratulations. A scheme like that deserves to succeed."

Monsoon relaxed and smiled. He grabbed the drink, glanced triumphantly and contemptuously at Stratosphere, took a large gulp, and faced the Don.

"Break both his arms and throw him down the garbage disposal," the Don said.

Monsoon knew the routine by now. Fingers, punch in the face, boot on the neck, etc. etc. He tried to forestall the impending.

"Okay, okay, okay. There's more. Lots more. I got contacts. I can get more. I can get more."

Something surprising happened. Nothing. Nothing happened. No fists, no boots, no nothing.

"You see, Mr. Parker, confession is good for the soul after all. How much more?"

"I reckon about thirty-eight mill. Thirty-eight million dollars' worth."

The Don gave an ever-so-slight whistle of appreciation. "I see. Thirty-eight million dollars, you say. A sum not to be sneezed at. At the current selling price, I imagine. Hmm. Perhaps that could be increased. It would appear that cooperation would be to our mutual benefit. I could always persuade you to reveal your contacts, could I not? An industrial compressor inserted into the lower bowel generally does the trick. But I admire your plan, and I can use your local knowledge, and you need my financial backing. I would like to offer you our assistance. You have no objections, I presume."

"No. No, Don Imbroglio, none whatsoever."

"Very good. Now, I couldn't help but notice that there are two tickets. One for yourself and one for a Mr. Bjørn Eggen Christiansson. Who is he?"

"He's my grandfather. My father's father. He's part of the plan. To make the whole thing seem more legit. Only he don't know it's a scam, see. He comes over here once a year. To see me and to visit my grandma's grave. He's arriving on Wednesday. I suckered the old bast...I mean, I convinced him to go with me."

"Excellent, Mr. Parker. Ever more impressive. In that case you will proceed as you have described, except for one detail. I see your grandfather has a reservation at the Mirage. He will not be needing it. Your grandfather will remain with us, as our guest, until such time as you have contacted your business partners. We'll arrange a...shall we say...courtesy car, to meet him at the airport, and the new arrangements will be explained to him. My associate, Mr. Merang, and his assistant will accompany you. Arrangements will be made for the provision of funds sufficient for any transaction once we have your assurance that everything is…"kosher," I believe is the term used these days. Your grandfather will accompany my financiers. Later, you and I can come to some arrangement as to how you are to benefit. Do we have an understanding, Mr. Parker?"

"Yes, Don Imbroglio. Yes we do."

"Very good. Now, I notice that you have purchased an open return ticket. How much time are you expecting to need to conduct your transaction with your contacts?"

"Well, quite a while. A coupla weeks at least. The shit…er, that is the, er, merchandise…has to be brought in from the jungle."

"I see. Very well. But before you leave, you must know that if our arrangement fails to come to fruition, for any reason, I shall be very disappointed. I have several ways of expressing my disappointment, none of which you will find very amusing, I fear. I rather doubt that your grandfather would enjoy them either, I'm afraid. Furthermore, you must also be aware that anything you may be able to think of, I shall have anticipated you. So if you were thinking of any… deviation, shall we say… from your stated path, I strongly advise you to think again."

"Don Imbroglio, I would nev—"

The Don stopped him with a motion of his hand. "One final question, Mr. Parker. If one were to throw a chicken from an airplane, how long would you expect it to survive?"

"I, er…I don't know."

"Neither do I, but an interesting question, don't you think?"

Monsoon said nothing.

The Don permitted the silence to work for a few moments before saying, "All right then. Mr. Thyroid will escort you out and see that you are driven wherever you wish to go. Stick to your travel arrangements.

Mr. Merang will rendezvous with you at the airport. We will hold onto your ticket and your money for the time being, if you don't mind. They will be returned to you at the airport. Well. Goodnight, Mr. Parker, and bon voyage, as they say. I shall be monitoring your progress with great interest."

"Yes. Goodnight, Don Imbroglio, and thank—"

The fingers clicked, and Thumper Thyroid grabbed Monsoon by the collar and dragged him towards the door.

Asia was sitting in the passenger seat of Crispin's Lexus as they headed down the freeway towards Monsoon Parker's house. Elton John was blasting out of the stereo, and Crispin was singing falsetto harmony parts to "Crocodile Rock."

Oberon was cringing in the back, with his paws over his ears.

"Turn that shit down and listen," said Asia.

Crispin sighed as his pudgy fingers turned the knob.

"I still can't get over it," Asia continued. "That guy had to be seventy. He had to be helped out of his chair, for fuck's sake. I would have laughed if I hadn't been so scared. Anyway, one minute he's this wheezing old geezer, then he takes a couple of tokes on this spliff and the next thing he's all over me like a dog with two dicks, giggling like a schoolgirl and drooling like some cretin. I'll bet that's the first hard-on he's had since he was jerking off in the back row of *The Seven Year Itch*, watching Marilyn Monroe's knickers gusset."

"You're probably right. Usually the only stiffs he sees are in coffins."

"But don't you think this is a coincidence? And why didn't you tell me about this stuff before?"

"Well, I never had the chance, luvvie, did I? But like I said, I've never experienced anything even remotely as good as this stuff. It was worth the money just to watch Nigel fucking Dorothy." Crispin erupted into squeals of laughter at the thought.

"Well, what if he hasn't got any left?"

"Well, pumpkin, if he hasn't, he hasn't. We'll just have to wait and see. The little bastard lied to me the last time and said he only had two ounces left, and the next thing it's all over town. Anyway, we're nearly there now."

Minutes later, they pulled up in front of Monsoon's house. Crispin was mildly surprised when the expected reception committee of hoop-playing midgets failed to materialize, and he kept looking over his shoulder as he led Oberon up to the front door. Asia rang the bell, while Oberon pissed against the portal. No reply.

"Maybe the bell's broken," Crispin said.

He balled his beefy fist and rapped on the front panel. The door swung open a couple of inches, and they could see the splintered wood and hanging fittings where the door had been jimmied.

"Shit. Look at this," Asia said. "Something is definitely upside down here. C'mon. Let's go."

She turned to walk away. Oberon decided to piss on the other portal for the sake of symmetry.

"No. Wait," Crispin said. "Let's look inside."

"Crispin. Come on. You were the one who told me that in Vegas, the smart play is to mind your own business. The best thing to do is just turn around and get the fuck out of here!"

In reply, Crispin pushed the door open and stepped inside.

"Oh, fuck," said Asia, following him inside. "I just know I'm going to regret this."

The house looked as if a herd of bison had celebrated the Fourth of July in it. Cushions, mattresses, upholstery, pillows—anything that could potentially conceal anything had been shredded. The fridge had been emptied out onto the floor, a fact that did not go unnoticed by Oberon, who immediately seized upon a moldy, half-chewed enchilada that looked as if it should have been in the Smithsonian, and began chomping on it.

They went into the bedroom. All the drawers had been pulled out, there were clothes everywhere, and on the floor next to an ancient suitcase with the lining ripped out, an old military uniform lay in a pile of photographs and letters.

"Jesus Christ," said Asia, really nervous now, "somebody really did the job on this place. C'mon."

"Wait, there might be something in here," Crispin said, heading into the bathroom and stepping gingerly over broken bottles and squeezed-out tubes. Oberon, meanwhile, who had never fully recovered from the episode with the coke and had been looking and behaving like a disturbed angora sweater ever since, had finished his impromptu Mexican dinner and had begun to take an interest in the door to the garage, sniffing at it and scratching.

Crispin came out of the bathroom and said, "What's with the fur bag?"

"I don't know. He wants to go into the garage."

"Let's look, then."

"What if someone's in there?"

"Asia, for fuck's sake! Stop being such a big blouse. Come on."

With Asia close behind him, Crispin pushed open the door. Inside, the garage was dark, with just a thin streak of light coming in under the shutter. Crispin felt around for a light switch and flicked it on. He let out a high, thin wail.

"Oh my God. That's it. Asia. Come. On. We're out of here. Oberon. Come here."

"No, no, wait, wait," she said, her curiosity suddenly overcoming her trepidation. "You were the one that insisted on coming in. I'm going to open it."

Crispin was barely in control of himself or his sphincter. "Are you insane?" he gasped. "Are you completely out of your tiny Confederate mind?"

"No, I'm not. And who's being a big blouse now? I bet that's where he keeps the stuff. It's better than a safe. Nobody would touch it."

"Leave it and let's go, you stupid cow. You don't know what disgusting incurable disease you could…"

Crispin never got to finish the sentence. Asia strode purposefully towards the soiled black coffin that leaned against the back wall, grabbed the unscrewed lid, and yanked. A white skeletal forearm rattled out from behind the door and shook back and forth, the thin bleached bones of the hand moving in a macabre but strangely good-natured wave. Asia screamed. An astoundingly loud noise erupted from Crispin's nether regions, accompanied by a noxious odor. He sprinted for the door, dragging Oberon, with Asia close on his heels. Crispin speed-walked to the car with a strange shuffling gait and, wrenching the door open, swung Oberon in like a bolas. As soon as Asia was inside, without waiting for her to close her door, he started the engine, and with a squeal of tires circled round in the road and headed for the freeway.

Such had been their haste that neither he nor Asia had noticed the car pulled up on the other side of the street a little way down the road, with the engine running. Nor had they noticed, sitting in the passenger seat and watching them with great interest, Monsoon Parker, and beside him, behind the wheel, watching with even greater interest, Thumper Thyroid.

They were heading down the freeway, going only marginally faster than ninety-five, when Thumper said, "Know what it's about?"

"Nah. Somethin' to do with some fruit, an' that spook-lookin' slope we dragged in."

"Oh yeah? Listen, Francis. Pull over, man. I gotta take a leak."

"For fuck's sake, Thump. You're worse than a dame."

"C'mon, stop the fucking car unless you want me to piss on the leather."

Frankie pulled the Caddie up under an overpass, and Thumper climbed out. He was standing in the shadows with his meat in his hand, enjoying a long luxurious piss, when he was suddenly illuminated by a flashing blue light, which turned the arching urine stream an interesting shade of night-purple. He heard the squad car doors bang and saw two flashlights approaching. He finished pissing and turned to face the cops, leaving his dingus hanging in the breeze.

"What the fuck do you think you are doing?"

"I was playing with it, but my magazine blew away in the wind."

"Hey, Marve," said the cop to his partner, "this guy is so funny, I think we musta pulled Jay Leno over. Gee, Mr. Leno, can I get your autograph?"

"C'mon, officers. What's the beef?"

"The beef is what's in your hand, pal. Firstly, this is a sixty-five stretch, an' we clocked you at ninety-seven miles an hour. Secondly, urinating in a public place is an offense. And thirdly, if we really want to dance, public exposure of genitalia is a serious misdemeanor."

Thumper took a deep breath. "Gentlemen," he said, "if you can see my wang from thirty yards away, through the windows of a squad car doing seventy miles an hour, in the middle of the fucking night, then either you've got eyes like a shithouse rat, or I'm a better man than I thought I fucking was!"

"Right, that's it! You're comin' in. Spread em'. Cuff him, Al."

Thumper heard the unmistakable sound of blued steel sliding from leather as the cops approached. Then they suddenly stopped and spun around, aiming their torches at the sound of the voice behind them.

"You boys must be new in town."

"Jeez, Frankie. You almost made me shit in my pants," said the first cop.

"Marve. Al. What's the deal?"

The cops holstered their weapons.

"This guy with you?"

"No, he was fucking hitchhiking, what do ya think? This is Thumper Thyroid, the fighter, you assholes."

"Shit. Didn't recognize ya, Mr. Thyroid. Sorry 'bout that."

"Ah, no sweat, fellas."

The two cops turned off their flashlights and started walking back to their car.

"G'night, Frankie. G'night, Mr. Thyroid. Tell the Don we said hello. And Frankie, try'n keep it down, hey? You'll make us look bad."

"Yeah, yeah, yeah," said Frankie, waving at the departing boys in blue, and then to Thumper. "C'mon. Put that skunk back in its cage and get in the fucking car. The Don's waiting."

The doors slammed shut, and the sleek black Cadillac slid back onto the tarmac and headed towards the distant lights of the big hotels blazing in the night sky, more brilliant than the heavens themselves.

# Chapter 6.

Bjørn Eggen Christiansson was a contented man. Not necessarily a happy man, but contented. He was two summers and a winter away from his eightieth birthday and still had a thick head of hair and most of his own teeth. The sky-blue eyes were still keen and observant, and twinkled out from under snow-white eyebrows that resembled small furry animals. The gnarled, blue-veined hands that curled around the shaft of his fishing rod were still strong, and his slender, bowed legs and knobbly knees could still carry him a day's march across the ice. A lifetime of drinking and smoking had dulled neither his wits nor his wit. He had outlived his wife and his only son and most of his friends. His only living relative was a worthless and improvident grandson with a ridiculous name who lived in far-off America, whom he visited once a year to tell him what a useless waste of space he was, how he was nothing like his father, and, if not for the promise that Bjørn Eggen had made to his own son, he would not cross the road to piss on him if he was on fire, before leaving a him considerable sum of money and returning to Norway, where he no longer kept elkhounds.

Bjørn Eggen did not fear death, as he had not feared life, and, although he carried his grief with him every waking moment, he was not defeated by it and it did not detract from the beauty of his memories.

Often he dreamed of his wife, as she had been when he had first brought her north, after the war, smiling from under her sealskin bonnet, her beautiful young face very black against the snow.

Bjørn Eggen had arrived at a simple acceptance of things the way they were. He had had a good life, and now he fished and drank and waited for God to summon him with all the stoicism and fatalism of his Viking ancestors. His beloved dogs had passed on one by one, and were buried in his yard beneath neat rows of white crosses, each with a name inscribed upon it and a collar hung from it, and now he no longer kept a dog for fear that he should predecease it and leave it friendless and alone in a bitter world. He lived on the edge of a lake in a wooden cabin that he had built with his own hands fifty years earlier, on the edge of the small village of Gjudbumsenningbjerg, and the Arctic Circle actually passed through his outhouse.

He was now sitting on a small wooden stool inside a reindeer-skin tent, drinking periodically from a bottle of aquavit and watching the point where his line disappeared into the frigid water in the small neat circle he had cut through the ice. His pale blue eyes watered, like melting ice, his nose was Santa-Claus red, and his white breath mingled with the smoke from the ancient, thin-stemmed pipe that was stuffed into the corner of his mouth. He was humming an ABBA song to himself and tapping his booted foot on the ice in time to his humming.

Suddenly the tip of his rod dipped, and he struck fast and hard and began reeling in. Presently he hauled out a large Arctic char, flapping and struggling, through the hole, sprinkling his face with icy water from its frantically flailing tail. He unhooked the fish and deftly broke its spine. He stuffed it into the pocket of his fur coat and picked up his bottle of aquavit. He stooped and pushed through the flap on the tent and began trudging through the translucent light, across the thin layer of snow atop the ice and back towards his cabin, singing in time to his crunching footsteps.

"So I say thank you for the music…"

When he reached his front door, two lines of footprints informed him of a visitor, and he entered to find an envelope on his hall table and an empty glass beside it. The postman had delivered a message, and helped himself to an aquavit for his trouble. Bjørn Eggen picked up the envelope and carried it through to the kitchen, where a log fire flickered in a stone grate. Taking the fish from his pocket, he slapped it on the sink top, and then went to sit on the aged tree stump that he kept next to the fire. He took a long pull from his bottle and examined the envelope. "From USA" was written on it. From his boot he pulled a knife with a worn, shiny blade and a deer horn handle, and neatly slit the envelope open. Inside was a printout from a computer and a newspaper clipping. Bjørn Eggen had no use for a computer. The few people that he was in communciation with knew that they could send a mail to the postman.

It was from his waste-of-space useless bastard grandson.

*Dear Grandfather,*

*I hope you are well. I am just writing you a short message to tell you that I am looking forward to your visit as usual. Plus, I have great news. I know you will be happy to learn that my father's remains have been found at last, and I am going to Vietnam to bring him home. He will be buried with full military honors, and the United States Air Force will be flying him home. I have sent a copy of what they said about it in the newspaper.*

*I would really like you to go with me, so that we can spend some time together before you die, and so we can bring my papa back home together. I will pay all your expenses. I know you are very old and feeble, and, if you think it will be too much for you, I will understand.*

*Your loving grandson,*

*Monsoon.*

The cutting was from the Las Vegas Review Journal and read:

### HERO TO RETURN HOME AT LAST

The remains of Captain Philip Parker, the father of local entrepreneur, Mr. Monsoon P.E.S.A.P.H. Parker, are to come home at last. Captain Parker is a war hero, and one of America's most decorated soldiers, who fell in defense of his country in Vietnam. Lost for all these years, his body has been discovered by Vietnamese villagers and identified by the military. His father is to go to Vietnam to accompany his son's remains on their voyage home. Mr. Parker's body will be repatriated by the USAF and buried with full military honors.

The old man read through the mail and the cutting, each twice, then folded them and put them in his coat pocket. Taking a brand from the fire, he re-lit his pipe, took another long drink from his aquavit, and stared into the flickering, crackling flames, with the rising blue smoke from his pipe swirling slowly around his head.

Tears attempted to come into his eyes, but he fought them, just as he fought the pain of an old wound re-opened as he thought of his son, who he had not protected. Even though his son had been a grown man and had volunteered to go to the war, and there was absolutely nothing that Bjørn Eggen could have done, he felt guilty and grieved for his son. He was afraid of the pain that he would feel, but he knew that he must go, and that he would go.

He also thought that perhaps his useless grandson was not quite as useless as he had imagined, and that his English and grammar had improved dramatically. He also thought that when he saw him he was going to kick his ass for calling him a feeble, old man.

It was one of Crispin's favorite times of year. He loved everything about it. The long drive from Vegas though the desert and the hills, with his music playing and a jigger of gin on the seat beside him. The final approach across the winding road over the mountain and the magnificent blue lake surrounded by those majestic white peaks and towering trees. Every year at this time he did a two-week booking at Harrah's, in Tahoe, and every year he looked forward to it. He wasn't a great skier, but he could manage to navigate the moderate-intermediate slopes on his skis and not on the crack of his ass most of the time. And he just adored those après ski parties. All those fit and tanned young men in their ski gear. Some of the tight lycra-clad butts and muscled thighs that he got to see on the pistes were worth the drive, just for that. This year he had treated himself and bought a new Italian ski suit in flamingo pink, and a yellow mask that made the world look like those summer days that he remembered from his boyhood.

He had arrived the previous evening and checked into the suite that management always gave him. He had ordered a bottle of Moët from room service, drank it as he settled down in the tub for a long luxurious soak, and afterwards slept like a baby. In the morning, he had walked down to the corner for coffee and bagels with cream cheese and blueberry jelly and had watched the colorful people entering and leaving the gondola station, and the little cars climbing over the treetops, glistening in the morning sun. And now he was back in the hotel calling

Nigel, who had stayed in Vegas to dog-sit Oberon. Crispin pretended that he was sorry Nigel couldn't be with him, but secretly he was glad of a little time on his own, and you never knew, a guy in a hot-pink Italian ski suit just might get lucky.

"Hey, Nigel. How's it going?" he said.

"I'm fine. How was your drive?"

"Oh, it was an absolute delight. Just like a picture postcard. How's my baby?"

"Oh, he really misses you already. Like me. I had ever such a job to get him to settle. I had to give him a glass of wine in the end. That did the trick."

"Oh, my. I swear that dog is an alcoholic. Well, must dash. I just wanted to let you know I got here all right. I'll call you tonight, after my show. Ciao." Crispin blew a kiss down the receiver, pressed the button, and called the bell captain to have someone come up and carry his ski gear downstairs.

"Black queen takes vhite knight," Bjørn Eggen said.

A black family was standing next to him. The lady looked at him and pulled the child closer. The man stepped forward. The father and the son were wearing the same red t-shirts and caps. "Roll Tide" was written on them.

"Come again, pops?"

Bjørn Eggen looked up from the grave absentmindedly. He smiled at the man. "Oh. Please excuse me. I am old, *ja*. Talk to meself sometimes."

"Are you okay?" the lady said.

"Ja, ja. For sure. I am fine. Thank you for asking." Bjørn Eggen turned his gaze back to the grave. "Was me wife," he said.

The lady looked at the headstone. It read,

*Maybelline Celeste Christiansson née Parker.*

*Loving Mother of Capt. Philip Parker, US Airborne.*

*Loving wife of Bjørn Eggen Christiansson.*

*September 13th, 1925 to September 13th, 1979*

*Finis vitae sed non amoris.*

"What does it mean?" she said.

"The end of life, but not of love."

"That is very beautiful."

"Ja. So vas she. Vind took her. Vas her birthday."

The man motioned to the woman. She touched Bjørn Eggen on the shoulder, and walked away. Bjørn Eggen smiled as he heard the boy say something about his clothes to the father, and the mother tell him to shush. He looked at the roses he had brought, red against the white marble. As red as blood. He closed his eyes. He could hear the birds. The sun was warm on his face.

He felt anew the pull in the pit of his stomach that he'd felt all those years ago, when she'd walked into the restaurant to meet him. She'd been so beautiful he felt that he could not breathe. He had not known what to say. It was in Naples, in 1946. The floor was black and white marble, like the marble that now marked where she lay. It had been in huge squares, like a chessboard. She'd been very dark. He was very white, except for where the sun had burned his face and arms. Later, she laughed when he she saw him naked, with his bronzed face and his lily-white ass. That's what she had said.

"That there is the whitest ass I ever seen, boy. Why, it's as white as a lily."

Bjørn Eggen smiled at the memory. He remembered standing there, not knowing what to say.

Finally she'd said, "Damn, boy. Don't you ever hush up?"

He had smiled then and said, "Ve are looking like the chess pieces on the board, you and me, *ja?*"

He had felt foolish saying it, but she'd laughed, and the ice was melted, and the warmth that came flooding in to replace it stayed with them until the day she died, and held them together even when the war took Philip from them.

He had not been there, when the wind came and took her from him, just as he had not been there when the war took Philip, and, even though he knew it was not his fault, and there was nothing he could have done, he felt ashamed and guilty because he had not protected her.

Maybelline Celeste had become pregnant with baby Philip and, given the ruinous and austere state that Europe was in, they decided to live in the States. They moved to Alaska at her suggestion, so that Bjørn Eggen could continue to work with dogs. She couldn't expect Bjørn Eggen to fully comprehend that, given an alternative, no woman in her right mind would voluntarily choose to raise a mixed-race child in 1950s 'Bama. She also thought it advisable to avoid the distinct possibility of her and Bjørn Eggen, as a mixed-race couple, having the shit kicked out of them on a biweekly basis. Philip was already three months old when they were married in Kodiak, and he cried all through the wedding. As if he knew something. With all the shit that was going on after the war, it took a while for Bjørn Eggen's paperwork to come through, by which time Philip already had his mother's maiden name on his birth certificate. They kept meaning to change it, but time went by and they were busy being happy, and somehow they just never got around to it.

Her father died in '79, and she flew home for the funeral. She never came back. Hurricane Frederic only killed five people in Alabama, but she was one of them, taken by the sea from the bridge to Dauphin Island when the hurricane tore it into pieces and hurled it into the ocean.

Bjørn Eggen did not attempt to fight the tears as he knelt down and put his lips to the cold stone. He had fought enough in his life. If the tears wanted to come, let them. He stayed like that for a long time, and the shadows had moved across the grass to touch him on the face before he said softly, "Black queen takes vhite knight. Checkmate."

He struggled to his feet, and walked slowly to the gate of the cemetery. As he approached the road, he could hear the tooting of car horns and singing, and, as he rounded the final bend he saw a throng of young people parading past the gate, laughing and dancing. They were mostly wearing red.

He could not cross the street because of the people, and he stood watching. A group of young men stopped in front of him.

"Shit, dude, where'd ya get them crazy threads?"

The boys were obviously on the wrong side of some serious alcohol abuse.

"Threads. Vat is threads?"

"Your clothes, man," another one said. "Far out, like in the movies. You foreign?"

"I am from Norway."

"Man, we kicked LSU's sorry butts, man," another young man explained.

"There is no need to be sorry."

"Say what, now?"

"Sometimes the butts are having to be kicked, *ja*."

"Shit, man. This old dude is cool. Let's take him with us."

"Hey, old timer. You want to come with us?"

"Vhere are you going?"

"For beer. We handed LSU their asses, big time. We're going to get shit-faced."

"You said beer, *ja*."

"Yeah, bro, beer."

"You said the magic focken word. Let's go."

The boys were laughing and singing as they put their arms around Bjørn Eggen's shoulders and led him down the road.

And that was how Bjørn Eggen came to miss his flight to Las Vegas.

Don Ignacio Imbroglio leaned his head back and blew a cloud of gray smoke towards the ceiling. Behind him, through the opened window, the lights of the Strip were chasing the last vestiges of twilight from the sky. The Don looked at Thumper, sitting across from him, nursing a glass.

"So, who did you say these clowns were?"

"According to the slope, the one fat guy is some fruit lounge act goes by the name of Crispin Capricorn."

"Oh, yes. I know him. He used to be quite big, back in the old days. Not a bad tenor, as it happens."

"Well, he's still pretty big. Two-fifty, easy."

"Yes. And the lady in question?"

"That weren't no lady, boss. That was a hooker. The reason I know is because it was the same one that me and Frankie brung ya, yesterday."

If the Don was surprised, he didn't show it. "What did Mr. Parker have to say about it?"

"He sez he knows Capricorn and he sold him a coupla ounces, but he don't know the girl, an' he don't know how come they come to be inside his house."

"Do you think he was telling the truth?"

"I think so, boss."

"So what do you suggest we do?"

"I dunno, boss. Sumtin like this drug could turn out to be a big deal. Don't want a coupla fuckheads screwing thing up. If they was in the house, they seen the joint turned over, and they musta seen the coffin. Plus, the bitch was here, and she seen ya...well, like, she seen ya, ya know?"

"There is no need to be more explicit. I understand. Continue."

"Well, ya know how people talk. I say we waste 'em. Just in case."

"I think your assessment of the situation is correct, Thumper. We are talking about potentially a very great deal of money. The streets of Las Vegas will not be noticeably poorer for being minus one hooker and a has-been lounge act. Pity, though. He was a good singer. Well, never mind. Take care of it. Do it yourself. The fewer people involved in this thing, the better."

"Okay, boss. Consider it done. Just one thing. They had a dog with them?"

"What kind of a dog?"

"I dunno, boss. Little fluffy thing. Kinda like a sheep."

"I see. Well. Take care of the dog as well."

"Okay, boss."

"And one other thing. I want to know everything there is to know about Mr. Monsoon Parker."

"Sure thing, Don Imbroglio."

Thumper walked out of the room. The Don got to his feet and walked through the open French windows to the balcony and stood feeling the cool breeze, listening to the faint honking of horns below and the occasional roar of a jet overhead, blowing smoke into the gathering night. And thinking.

Monsoon was nervous. The kind of nervous that three vodka and tonics would not dispel. He kept looking from the TV screen behind the bar to his watch, then to the elevator, and back to the screen. He looked at his watch now. It said eight fifty-one, twenty-nine seconds later than the last time he had looked. There was a fight on the TV—two junior middleweights going at it pretty good—but Monsoon could not concentrate. His eyes were locked into an uninterruptible rhythm. Screen, watch, elevator, screen, watch, elevator, over and over. He signaled the barkeep to set 'em up.

He had been wracking his brains ever since the Don had pulled him in, turning the shit over and over and over again in his mind, examining the situation like an Amsterdam jeweler looking at a diamond. Testing every facet. Every angle. What the fuck was he doing? He should have known better. Vegas is too small a place. He should have taken the stuff someplace else to unload it once he realized what it was. He had known he was making a mistake borrowing a lousy grand from the Don, and now look at the shit he was in. There was no going back with these people. No "thank you, nice doing business with you." Their shadow was everywhere, and their hand in everything, and even if, by the remotest possibility, you came out of it with two of everything that you went in with, you could never again walk down any street in America without looking over your shoulder. Right from the very beginning, when there had been nothing out here but sand and scorpion shit, every inch of Vegas—every trash can emptied, every bed sheet laundered, every drink sold, every chip cashed, every burger eaten, every pair of whore's knickers hitting the carpet from Freemont Street to fucking Parhump—had had "mob" written all over it. These people did not forget, and they did not go away. And that fucking Don. That creepy wop undertaker could kill you just by looking at you.

Monsoon pulled his folded Revue Journal out of his jacket pocket, and looked for the hundredth time at the article.

### UNLV STUDENT KILLED IN FREAK ACCIDENT

*Professor Archie Medes, long time head of the Chemistry department at UNLV, walked into his lab early yesterday evening on a routine checkup and walked straight into a tragedy. Milton Gonski, star chemistry student, was killed right in front of Dean Medes when an experiment he was working on exploded. There was extensive damage to the lab, and Dean Medes's new ten-thousand-dollar hair replacement*

> treatment was ruined. Fire department officials are today continuing their investigation into the cause of the explosion. Dean Medes was quoted as saying he was shocked by the tragic loss, but that he would be getting another hair replacement as soon as possible.
>
> Milton Gonski, 19, was an extremely promising and popular student, and everyone... etc. etc.

Monsoon stuffed the paper back into his pocket. The cause of the explosion. The cause of the fucking explosion had been some psycho greaseball with a fucking grenade or some shit. And this is what he was talking about. Their eyes were every-fucking-where. He had spoken to the kid once, for ten minutes, and now he was a cinder. And what had the kid found out, before they got to him? What had he told them? What did the Don know now about MGJ that he didn't? And if they would flambé some innocent punk kid, who had probably never even had it out of his pants, then he was going to last about as long as a bar of chocolate in a crack den if he didn't get out of this.

Monsoon's drink arrived and he slugged the vodka straight down, ordered another, and continued his eye routine. Screen, watch, elevator, screen, watch, elevator. He knew what he had to do, and he knew it was his only chance. He had told the Don there was more stuff. Thirty-eight million's worth. Why the fuck had he had to say thirty-eight million? What if he had second-guessed himself? All of a sudden his absolute conviction that Woolloomooloo Wally's crapper was built of bricks of MGJ was not so absolute. In fact, the only Absolut was the fucking vodka he was drinking. What the fuck had he been thinking? Fifteen years, and nobody renovates the shitter? Not to mention the odd NVA shell landing here and there. And if there was no thirty-eight million dollars' worth of MGJ, the Don was just going to pat him on the back, and say, "Nice try, Monsoon, thanks for your trouble." Sure he was. And if he did get lucky, the Don was going to say, "Hey, Monsoon, look what we got. Let's share." Yeah, right. Good ol' loveable Uncle Don Imbroglio, friend to the poor. Either way, that evil son of a bitch was planning to have him end up in a bin liner in the Mojave Desert, with the roots of a fucking Joshua tree growing through his eye sockets.

There was only one thing to do, and hope that the Don didn't have him figured for enough moxie to try it. Maybe, if he could just pull it off, this could turn out to be an even bigger break than finding the stuff in the first place. Maybe he had been pushed into something that would be bigger than anything he had ever imagined. And maybe what he had in mind was so unthinkable, so unexpected, so beyond the Don's reckoning, that a nobody like himself would try to put a burn on him, that it might give him just the edge that he needed.

Vegas was fucked for him now. Whatever happened, there would be no going back. MGJ might be a fucking pipe dream, but if he could set things up so that the Don thought he had scored some, and sent the money over, there might be a way to get his hands on it. Somehow, he was going to have to give Frankie and his man the slip and figure a way to get the money away from them. And the others. If he did find the stuff, he would have to figure a way to get his hands on that, too. The money, the drugs, the whole nine yards.

But what about his grandfather? Where the fuck was the silly old fart? At least that missing-link-looking fucker Merang had been with him at the airport and could confirm to the Don that the senile, old bastard hadn't shown up, and it was a legitimate snafu and not some con. The Don had decided not to delay the trip, but that would make it worse for the old man, if and when he did rock up. He would freak out when the Don's men snatched him from the hotel or the apartment. He had gotten his grandfather involved. He was responsible! What would they do with him? What would they do *to* him? Would the Don still send him over with the moneymen? What could he do about it, either way? There had to be a way. There had to be a way to make this come out right.

He had one thing. He had managed to get away without telling the Don about Woolloomooloo Wally, whoever the fuck he was. The way this thing was panning out, anything that might prove to be an ace up the sleeve was worth hanging on to. This whole fiasco might balance on something so small.

Things were going to get tight. As tight as a crab's ass at fifty fathoms. But he didn't see that he had a choice. And when they got to the 'Nam, he would be on home turf. Even though he hadn't lived there since he was a boy he knew the lingo a little, and the customs, and enough people to maybe be able to call on some backup. If he played it cool and close to his chest, then maybe…Close to his chest! He put his fingers through the top buttons of his shirt and felt the old man's dog tag. Maybe this was the old man talking to him. Maybe this had all been written a long time ago.

When he looked from his watch to the elevator and saw Frankie Merang—accompanied by an orangutan in a cheap suit—walking towards him, he realized that he would know soon enough.

"Hey, Frankie. You been to the zoo?"

"You get smart with me, you little slant fucker, and you be goin' to the fucking chiropractor," the orangutan said.

"Hey, I was jokin', man. Have a drink. What say? We got time."

The orangutan shrugged. "Scotch," it said. "Rocks."

"Me too," said Frankie. "So how ya bin, pal? Lookin' forward to your vacation?"

"Sure," Monsoon replied. "Got my ticket?"

"Right here," Frankie said, handing him a fat envelope. "Dough's there, too."

Monsoon opened the envelope and saw his ticket and two thousand dollars in hundred-dollar bills.

"What's the deal here, Frankie?" he said. "A little light, ain't she?"

Frankie grinned his great prehistoric grin. "Yeah. Well. The Don didn't want you to get distracted by all that slope pussy they got over there. Don' worry, you get the rest when we get home."

Monsoon said nothing. So. The stakes had just gotten a little higher. He ordered the drinks and then turned to Frankie. "The Don say anything 'bout those characters back at my house?"

"Nothin' that concerns you. This here's Joe, by the way. Belly Joe."

"Nice to meet you, Joe. No offense meant with the zoo crack."

"None taken," Belly Joe said, looking at Monsoon as if he would just as soon eat him as drink with him.

Frankie downed his drink, and said, "Okay. Let's hit it. We got to go and check in."

When Frankie started to walk across the airport, with Monsoon next to him, Belly Joe slipped in behind them at just the right distance. *This might be even tighter than I figured*, Monsoon was thinking, as they approached the gate.

A scratching noise woke Nigel from a deep and contented sleep. He sat up and stared at the bold ray of light that lay across the baby-blue satin sheets, coming from a gap between the curtains. He looked at his watch. 2:25 p.m. The scratching continued. Fucking Oberon! Nigel sighed and dragged himself out of bed. Outside the bedroom door Oberon was skipping up and down, and as Nigel stepped outside he leaped up and shoved his snout into Nigel's crotch. Nigel shoved him away irritably.

"It's too early for your antics, my furry friend. Come," he said.

He let Oberon out through the French doors that led onto the little roof garden so that he could do his business, and then wandered into the kitchen and turned on the coffee machine. A chirping sound came from the living room, and Nigel went through and removed the hood from a large gilt cage in the corner. A disheveled African gray parrot peered at him with rheumy eyes, stepping from one foot to the other.

"Morning, Liberace," Nigel said. "Sleep well, did you?"

The parrot said nothing.

Nigel put his lips to the cage, and made coochy-coo noises. Liberace looked at him blankly and continued to say nothing.

"Useless fucking bird," said Nigel in disgust, turning back to the kitchen. He made himself a big cup, with three sugars, picked up the Journal from underneath the mail slot, and went into the bathroom. He set his coffee next to the commode, undid the drawstring of his red silk pajamas, sat down, and opened the entertainment section.

The doorbell rang.

"Oh, for Christ's sake," he said, struggling up, "if it's not dogs, it's the fucking door. Can't a man have a minute's fucking peace around here?"

Nigel tried to keep the irritation out of his voice as he said, "Yes? Who is it?"

"Delivery for Mr. Capricorn."

"Okay. Just leave it by the door, would you?"

"I need a signature."

Nigel peered through the spy hole but couldn't see anyone. He opened the door anyway.

Nigel immediately felt as if he had been punched in the mouth, very hard, by a man with an enormous fist, the reason being that he had been punched in the mouth, very hard, by a man with an enormous fist. He flew backwards into the room and landed on top of the recently repaired Japanese lacquered table, whose legs once again gave way with their customary bone-breaking sound. Nigel lay unconscious on the wreckage, with blood streaming from his ruined mouth and his breath making small whistling noises in the gap where his front teeth had been.

Thumper stepped into the room, closed the door behind him, and walked over to the prone Nigel. He lifted one eyelid, examined the pupil, and let go. Perhaps he had overdone it. He hadn't realized the long fuck was so skinny. Bit too much shoulder. He pulled his piece from under his arm and strode into the bedroom. Empty. Likewise the bathroom. Stepping out onto the roof garden, he saw nothing but a little fluffy white dog who came scampering over to him.

"Take care of the dog as well," the Don had said.

Thumper knelt down and, as Oberon planted his paws on his knees and started to lick his face, grabbed him by his jeweled collar and stuck the muzzle of the .38 against his fuzzy head. Oberon looked up at Thumper with his tongue lolling and his little tail wagging furiously. Thumper thumbed back the hammer. Click! Oberon squirmed round and began licking the barrel of the gun. Thumper increased the pressure on the trigger, hesitated, and then he pulled the gun away, let the hammer drop, and slid it back into its holster.

"What the fuck," he said aloud. "'Take care of' could mean take care of, not just 'take care of', right? Hey, little guy, c'mere."

The big man took up the animal, tiny in his huge hands, and began to scratch it behind the ear. Oberon squirmed in delight, and a pale green bubble appeared at the end of his penis. Just then a loud groan came from inside the apartment. Thumper set the dog down, took out his piece again, and went inside with Oberon frisking happily at his heels.

Nigel was stirring, but still out. Thumper looked around and spotted Liberace, still stepping from one foot to the other. He walked over, opened the cage, and grabbed the bird, which made no attempt to resist. A single blue feather floated in the air. Thumper carried Liberace into the kitchen, popped the door of the microwave, shoved the bird inside, and slammed it shut. Liberace did not appear unduly alarmed, but peered out through the darkened glass with every appearance of avian equanimity.

Thumper went to the kitchen drawer and examined its contents, finally deciding upon a shiny steel sushi knife. He tested its edge with his thumb. Leaving the blade next to the microwave he filled a large saucepan, carried it through to the lounge, and poured its contents onto the face of the prostrate Nigel. Nigel spluttered and coughed and opened his eyes, and Thumper grabbed him by the front of his pajamas, dragged him into the kitchen, thrust him into a chair, and stood over him for a moment, staring down at him, watching him begin to dissolve.

Finally he said, in a voice like dragging chains, "What's the dog's name?"

Nigel's mouth was swollen, and he had bitten his tongue. He attempted to speak. "Ob…Ober…Oberon," he managed.

"Ober what?"

"Oberon."

"What the fuck is an Oberon?"

"He was…"

"Can it, fruit. Where's your boyfriend?"

"He's…he's out. He's not in. He's not here. He's…"

Thumper stepped forward and slapped Nigel across the face, being careful not to hit him too hard on account of the fact that he now knew the guy had a glass jaw. Nigel's head jerked back and blood welled again in his cut mouth.

"Lemme show you sumtin," Thumper rasped, stepping back and pointing to the imprisoned Liberace. Nigel's eyes went wide with horror and disbelief as Thumper pressed the button. The microwave illuminated for a couple of seconds, during which time Liberace became more animated than Nigel had ever seen him, and then Thumper clicked it off.

Nigel, close to hysteria, began to hyperventilate.

"Okay, sweetheart, I ask one more time. You don't tell me. The bird here is KFP. Get it?"

Nigel was in turmoil. Loyalty and abject terror were battling inside him, but right now loyalty wasn't putting up much of a fight. "Tahoe," he blurted. "He's in Lake Tahoe. He'll be there a week."

"You ain't shittin' me, are ya? 'Cause if you are…"

"No. No. I swear. You can call."

"That's okay. I trust you. Come on."

"Wh-where?"

"The big room. You an' me gonna have a little drink together. A little chat."

On trembling legs, Nigel staggered through the door with Thumper right behind him. Liberace, meanwhile, was becoming agitated and was scratching at the glass door of the microwave. The scratching excited Oberon and he began to jump up at the appliance, scrabbling at the glass, which in turn freaked out Liberace, whose scratching became more frantic, which spurred Oberon to even wilder leaping.

"You got bourbon?"

"Yes."

"Good boy. Gimme."

As Nigel went to the drinks cabinet, Thumper shifted his weight. The sushi knife, which he had slipped into his pocket, was threatening to stick him. Nigel came back with two massive slugs of whiskey and set one in front of Thumper. The other he half-drained, gasping for breath when he had finished.

Thumper took a mouthful of his, wondering whether he could get away with not smoking the pansy. He decided to see how the frighteners worked. Slowly, theatrically, he slid the blade from his pocket and fixed Nigel with his most intimidating stare. Nosferatu would have shit himself, never mind a poor little faggot who got alarmed watching the WWF. Nigel was within a hair's-breadth of fainting when Thumper said, "There's nothing that you can do to help fatso. You can only help yourself. There's nowhere you can hide from us. If you try to leave town, if you talk to anybody, if the fat fuck ain't there for any reason—if he gets any phone calls, any messages, even if it ain't you—you gone, baby. Unnerstan'?"

Nigel buried his face in his hands and began to sob.

"Got any beer in this perfumed shit pile?"

"I think there might be one in the fridge," replied Nigel, in a muffled voice.

"Fetch."

Nigel shuffled off, sniffling. Thumper was weighing the options. He was thinking maybe just to leave the fag be. Maybe he should call the Don. Or maybe off him, just to be safe.

Then, things got seriously weird.

Nigel walked into the kitchen just in time to see Liberace explode in a spectacular display of blood and feathers. Oberon, who, in his breathless bounding, had accidentally hit the button on the microwave, was skipping up and down, wagging his tail. Nigel screamed and dropped his glass, and the sound of its shattering was the last mortal sound he ever heard because, hearing the bang and thinking "gun," Thumper Thyroid rolled forward off the couch instinctively and, with surprising speed, came up onto his knees with the .38 in his hands and put five slugs into Nigel's back where he stood in the kitchen doorway.

Walking up to the body Thumper stopped in amazement, and then began to laugh as the scenario replayed itself in his mind's eye. Nigel lay face down with blood pooling around him like a small, sinister lake. There was smoke coming from the microwave, and the inside of the glass was spattered with parrot à la grenade. The fucking dog! Oh well, at least that saved a phone call to the Don. But he hadn't intended so much gunplay. One shot you could get away with, but cars don't backfire five times straight.

Time to exit stage left. He stepped back into the lounge, drained the bourbon, and hurled the glass out onto the rooftop, shattering it. He hadn't touched anything else except for the sushi knife, which he pocketed. Then, stepping over Nigel, taking care not to step in the blood, he took up the wiggling Oberon and hit the stairs. As he walked out of the ground floor fire escape, Oberon was licking his face.


Morris Albright was just an ordinary joe. A poor, working schlub from Asswipe, Kansas, or some place. Nice guy, kind of shy. Lived alone with his two Persian cats. Had a couple of friends, but kept himself to himself most of the time. Heavy-set guy, maybe two-forty, two-fifty. Never hurt anybody, except for perhaps a couple of gerbils. Liked to dress up in stockings and a bra and parade in front of the bathroom mirror some nights, but so what? Liked skiing. Liked it a lot. Wasn't very good, but really enjoyed it. Had been saving up to buy himself some new gear for the winter. He had bought himself a flamingo-pink Italian ski suit and couldn't wait to get it back to his hotel and try it on. It was outrageous, hot pink, and he would never dare wear anything like that near home. But in Tahoe, what the hell? Who was going to know?

He had no way of knowing, when he bought his flamingo-pink Italian ski suit with the money that he had saved up, that he was making the biggest mistake of his life.

# Chapter 7.

Thumper Thyroid hated snow. He hated snow, skiing, and skiers. Anybody who dressed up like some European pansy and thought it was fun to slide down a big, white hill on two pieces of plastic, freezing your balls off, had to have something radically wrong with him. And he hated scenery. To him, "picturesque" was a nice, big ass in a leopard-skin leotard and a massive pair of wobbling jugs. This was just a load of fucking trees and a big fucking duck pond. Big deal. Outdoors was for assholes. And how the fuck could he be expected to shoot straight with fucking gloves on?

Davy Dupree was a happy man as he leaned on the bar, alternately switching his gaze between the beautiful, coral light of the setting sun on the snow-blanketed upper slopes and the emerald-green sheen of the lycra ski pants stretched tight across the bodacious ass of the waitress as she fixed his drink. It had been a great day and, no mistake, it was showing every promise of becoming a great evening. Yessir-fucking-ree! He had spent a brilliant day at the chairs joshing with his buddies, watching the ski babes, helping folks onto the lifts, and had scored a cool two-twenty in tips, his second best result for the whole season. And best of all, when he had helped that cute little doll from down in the Keys someplace to her feet, something in the way that she looked at him had prompted him to ask her out, and she had said yes! Fucking A!

The waitress set his piña colada in front of him, and flashing his best sun-tanned ski instructor schoolboy-cute seductive smile, he peeled a ten-spot from his roll and said, "Keep the change, baby."

The waitress shone her light on him and rang the big brass bell behind the bar, and Davy picked up his glass and strolled over to a table by the window, where he could look down into the street. Darkness was gathering in the valley, and the lights were coming on, and colorful people were emerging from the hotels and laughing in the streets. And here was ol' Davy, sitting on two-ten with his first drink of the night, waiting for his bayou babe and looking so cool in the new Wranglers that he had bought to celebrate. This was the fucking gravy, man! Davy smiled to himself as he raised his glass to his lips, anticipating that first sweet taste.

What he didn't anticipate was the hand, the size of a polar bear claw and only marginally hairier, that closed around his forearm with a hydraulic grip and caused him to drop his drink, which crashed onto the table and splattered over his new jeans. Davy looked up in shock, into a mug that could have curdled goat's milk.

Over the top of his pounding heart, Davy heard a voice like a grating gearbox say, "Aw, jeez. You spilled your drink, miss."

By way of a witty retort, Davy made a hard, painful swallow.

"Ya work the ski lift. I seen ya."

Davy managed to compel his neck muscles into an approximation of a nod. A waitress was passing, and Thumper reached out and grabbed her.

"Hey, baby, we need a bourbon an' back over here, an' another milkshake."

Davy was encouraged by the fact that they were now apparently drinking buddies and summoned up the vocal resources to ask, "Who are you?"

"What's it to ya?"

"I was just…"

"Well, don't. Shut the fuck up an' lissen. You work the same place every day, yeah?"

"Yeah."

"Good, tha's real good. You remember seein' a big, fat guy, kinda wobbly-looking, in a pink suit?"

Just then the waitress came over with the drinks, and Thumper put his finger to his lips. Davy averted his eyes and massaged his forearm. Thumper leered at the girl as she wiped the spilled piña colada from the table, studiously avoiding eye contact with him.

"Betcha get plenty, working here, huh?" Thumper said, staring at the retreating waitress's butt.

"Yeah, some. In fact, I…"

"Shut up. Can this fat fuck ski?"

"Er, not really. I mean, he don't fall over or nothing, but…"

"So he uses the easy routes?"

"Yeah."

Thumper chugged his bourbon, swallowed half the beer, belched, and pulled a map from his coat pocket.

"Show me," he said, tossing the map to Davy.

Davy opened the map, and turned it the right way up.

"Okay. The gondola lets off here. Yesterday, the guy was all afternoon on these slopes here." Davy pointed to a series of yellow lines radiating from a central hub, like a rudimentary spider's web.

Thumper put his chewed thumbnail onto a point at the highest elevation. "So, from here, I can see down all these slopes, right?"

"The upper slopes, yeah. From there you have a good view of the top sections of all of those."

"An' what's this?" Thumper indicted a dotted line leading horizontally across the mountain.

"That's the cross-country trail. It's a different discipline. It involves…"

"Who cares? Can you walk on it?"

"Well, you're not supposed to, but if you had to you probably could."

Thumper grabbed the map, skulled his beer, leaned over so his brewery breath was right in Davy's face, and stared hard into his frightened eyes. Davy felt he was looking into the eyes of a rabid dog.

"I know what you look like. I know where you work. I can find you, anywhere, anytime."

Thumper Thyroid strode from the room in which the temperature seemed to have suddenly dropped by several degrees.

When the girl from Florida showed up later in her war paint, she was disappointed that Davy wasn't there. She gave him the benefit of the doubt and waited for a whole hour and a half before going back to her hotel with a basketball player from Des Moines.

The following morning the ski lifts set off as usual, at six sharp. But Davy Dupree wasn't at his station. Davy was asleep in the backseat of a Greyhound bus, heading north.

Crispin looked out at the sunlight on the lake and felt like it was shining just for him, and just to demonstrate this fact he sang, "It's for people like me that they keep it turned on…"

He felt absolutely marvelous. The mountain air was so invigorating, the hotel people were treating him like the queen he was, and his audience—far less jaded than those Philistines back in Vegas—had been very appreciative, almost like the good old days. Some weirdo had even asked him for his autograph, a huge, scary-looking guy with breath like a warthog. Well, what the fuck, a fan was a fan. And, best of all, his hot-pink ski suit was turning heads everywhere he went.

Even his skiing was improving, which was something at his time of life. His last couple of runs yesterday had been quite impressive, and he was almost considering moving onto one of the more difficult slopes this afternoon, except that the advantage of going at a more sedate pace was that it gave people the opportunity to admire his ski suit, and anyway there was another set of curves that he wanted to negotiate first. He was certain that one of the instructors at the first lift had been giving him the eye, so he had one of his cards in his pocket to slip him at an opportune moment. And, if the kiddy happened to turn up at the show, maybe he could slip him something else at an opportune moment. Hey, you never know. For a guy in a flamingo-pink ski suit, anything could happen!

Thumper held up his finger and growled at the barman. Except for an elderly couple in matching his-and-hers plaid spandex leisure suits and plastic cowboy hats bent over a slot machine opposite, the bar was empty. The room had a sour, stale-beer smell, the light was gray and greasy, and the pall of last night's smoke still lingered, as if the bar itself had a hangover. Thumper looked at the shiny, black piano and the poster on the wall behind it with a glossy photo of Crispin, his fat cheeks grinning from under his pompadour like a manic cherub. He had caught the act last night and the Don was right, the guy was pretty good. He had even gotten his autograph. Frankie would get a big rise out of that one.

The barkeep silently handed Thumper a bourbon and back, his third, and took the money from the pile of dollar bills on the counter. Thumper did not acknowledge him. He looked at his watch. Nearly time to go. He looked and felt ridiculous in his ski outfit, but he had to admit that it was a perfect disguise. Inside all these hoods and balaclavas and goggles, it could be Ming the fucking Merciless, and nobody would know. Plus the boots were pretty cool, although not really much good for getting the boot in, there not being enough flexibility in the ankle for the proper range of movement. And his ski bag looked exactly like everybody else's ski bag, the only difference being that the majority of ski bags contained skis, and Thumper's contained a precision-milled .375 Remington rifle with a silencer and a scope.

He went over his plan once again as he finished his drink: Wait in the lobby of the hotel until the fat prick came out, just in case the fruit had a whole wardrobe of rainbow-colored outfits. Once he made sure he was wearing the same gear, give him a half-hour start and then wander down to the lift and ride it up to the vantage point that that little ski-lift shithead had showed him on the map. Stake out a spot in the shadow of some tree. Nobody would pay any attention to him shuffling around in the snow. Just another clown who couldn't handle the ice, picking his way down on foot.

Then the easy part. Pick his shot. Head shot, if possible; if not, one wing shot to drop him, and one placed shot to close down the store. He figured that, depending on how much blood there was, it would be a while before anybody took any notice of the stiff, the sight of somebody lying on their ass on a ski slope not being exactly noteworthy. When someone finally paid attention, the hill would be crawling with blue lights and badges, by which time he would have skedaddled along the cross-country trail marked on the map and down into the California side where he had left his wheels gassed and ready. He'd be having a breakfast of beaver and bourbon in some ranch house before the police quack had even prised the slugs out.

On his way out Thumper overheard the old lady saying to her husband, "I hear this fella's real funny, hon. What say we stop by tonight?"

Thumper smirked to himself. *The only place you goin' to see that fat fuck is on the six o'clock news*, he thought, as he headed towards the lobby.

Morris just loved these ribs. So juicy, and the meat just falling right off the bone, and if this wasn't the best damn barbecue sauce he'd had his chops 'round in a coon's age, then he didn't know shit from Shinola. And all washed down with this good Mexican beer. He could go another plate, but he didn't want to feel too heavy on the slopes. He could always come back tonight. Morris licked his chubby fingers and carefully wiped his mouth. Taking up his beer he tilted his chair back against the wall, took a deep, satisfying swallow, and grinned to himself.

In the coffee shop immediately adjoining the rib shack where Morris was enjoying his lunch, Crispin was enjoying his third blueberry muffin and his second café latte. He knew he should feel guilty about the third muffin, and he knew he should feel guilty about not calling Nigel and not really missing him, but he actually didn't give a flying fart. He did miss little Oberon, of course, but that was only natural. Anyway, he was going to have a great day. He took up his cup, with his pinky finger extended like some English maid at tea, and tilted his chair back against the wall. This was the same wall against which Morris was leaning on the opposite side, so that, but for the thickness of some bricks and insulation, they would have been leaning against each other, back to back.

Morris finished his beer, left a handsome tip, smiled at the waitress, collected his skis from the rack outside, and headed towards the gondola.

Crispin finished his café latte, left a handsome tip, smiled at the waitress, collected his skis from the rack outside, and headed towards the gondola, then froze in his tracks, dropped his skis, and exclaimed out loud.

He just couldn't believe it. Some fat-ass crud was wearing the same ski suit as he was. Exactly the fucking same. Stitch for fucking stitch. Crispin's eyes narrowed into slits, and his glare could have drilled holes in Morris's back.

*This is fucking outrageous*, he thought. *Outrageous. Just look at the size of that butt. What the fuck does he think he looks like? The last time I saw an ass that size it had fucking fins on it. The fucking cheeky cunt. You have to have style to be able to pull off something like this, a natural grace. That lumpy fucker. About as graceful as a camel humping a cactus. That sack of shit. Of course my day is ruined now. Ruined. I shall have to go to the California side. I can't possibly be seen on the same slopes as this schmuck. Not only will I not get to see my little instructor with the buffed buns, but if I don't want to walk all the way back to the hotel for my car, I shall be compelled to ride on the bus with these peasants. Oh, the fucking humiliation. If there is any justice in the world, that fat turd will break his neck on the first bend.*

Crispin spat venomously in the direction of the diminishing figure of Morris Albright and, still seething, stomped across the road to the bus station, ignoring the traffic and flipping the bird to a housewife in a station wagon full of kids, who had the audacity to honk her horn at him.

*I hope the next time the Don sends me to waste somebody, it's in fucking Miami,* Thumper was thinking as he lay in a two-foot snowdrift under the low-hanging branches of a fir tree. *Fuck this for a game of soldiers.* He was going to have to take the next decent shot, otherwise he was going to be too cold to shoot. He had followed the ass bandit from the hotel, but he had passed the gondola and gone into some coffee shop a bit further down the street, so Thumper had had to sit in the bar across the road and wait. He knew the fat bastard wouldn't waddle very far, so he was either going to take the bus or he was coming back after his coffee. An hour later, Thumper saw him enter the gondola station and moved in.

As he reached the top, Thumper had seen this pink speck meandering slowly down the slope and, after eating a lot of snow, had finally made his way to what seemed the prime spot. He had a really good view of two slopes and a reasonable view of the third. Pink pants had made one run down the third slope, and Thumper had tracked him through the scope. Not an easy shot, although he could have made it, but he decided to wait. For one thing, the later it got, the better. Also, he figured that the guy was bound to use one of the two easier slopes before long and, hey, why make things more difficult than they had to be? But the bitter chill creeping through his bones was rapidly changing his thinking.

Thumper was reaching into his pocket for his hip flask when he saw a flash of pink ascending slowly on the lift. It disappeared over the crest of the hill, and Thumper let go of the flask and picked up the rifle. After a couple of minutes he saw the pink-clad figure slither down the slope immediately in front of him, slowly and somewhat unsteadily, like the Michelin Man on mescal. This was going to be almost too easy. He was going to have to add a couple of hundred yards to the range and some speed to the skier when he started bragging about this shot. There was a flat spot in front of him, about a hundred yards out, where he had noticed people swinging out wide to make the turn. The nearest skier was fifty yards away when the target hit the flat and steered towards him. Thumper held his breath and took up the slack in the trigger, making sure to allow for the resilience in the material of his gloves. He waited until the bright-yellow goggles filled the lens of the scope, with the cross hairs meeting at the bridge of the nose, and squeezed.

The yellow mask exploded in a cloud of red mist. The body snapped backwards onto the snow and slid in a slow circle with the ski poles swinging on their strings at the end of arms outstretched like a broken puppet, leaving a thin red trail in its wake before coming to rest in a deep drift at the foot of a tree.

As Thumper Thyroid was clambering through the trees towards the cross-county trail, he heard a woman's voice screaming.

Morris was really, really enjoying himself. He was on his third run and had only fallen down once, and that hadn't been his fault. Somebody had bumped into him and they had helped each other up, laughing. The slopes were incandescent in the late-afternoon sun and below the lake sparkled, a majestic, cobalt blue. He had time for a few more runs and then he would have a few beers and watch all the beautiful, young people enjoying themselves, and then go for a big plateful of those ribs. Mm-mm-mmm.

He had not been down this slope before, but looking ahead he could see that it leveled off and then went into a steep left-hand turn. His confidence was building and he was thinking that, when he got around this bend, he was going to try to go really fast. It was going to be really exciting, and if he fell over, so what? He would just get right back up again, and carry on.

And that was the last thing that Morris Albright ever thought.

Crispin's mood had improved immeasurably and, once he had got over his snit, the day had been a great success. He had had several great runs and when, after a surreptitious wander through the changing rooms—taking the scenic route, so to speak—he had gone into the bar for a quick après or two, there had been a band playing, and the singer had recognized him and asked him to sing with them. After a not-too-convincing show of reluctance and some feeble protestations he had allowed himself to be cajoled onto the stage, and had done "I Will Survive" to great applause. Then some cute guy in his thirties had bought him a drink and said he was coming to the show, and you just knew what that meant.

And as Crispin was sitting on the bus, glowing with pride, gin, and anticipation, he looked down into the car park and saw a huge man shoving things hastily into the trunk of a big red Mercedes. The bus's headlight fell momentarily on the man's face, and Crispin recognized him. *That's that big smelly creep who asked me for my autograph,* he thought.

Crispin's hand was shaking as he gripped the receiver, with a combination of shock and increasing agitation. Why didn't the little shit answer, and where the fuck was he at this time of night? This was bizarre. A horrible, morbid coincidence, and he was just dying to tell somebody, and the sneaky little bastard was probably getting his tiny cock sucked in a public toilet somewhere.

He still couldn't believe it. Those awful pictures on the news. It had almost been as if he himself had been lying there, in all that frozen blood, looking so black against the snow in the darkness. It made him shiver just to think about it. And what he had said? How he had hoped that the guy would break his neck. What if…? No, that was ridiculous. *And this is fucking ridiculous. Where is he? He'd better have a good excuse, or he'll be looking for another meal ticket. In fact, he'd better be fucking dead!*

Crispin slammed the receiver down. He drained his G and T and fixed himself another, examining his face in the mirror behind the bar as he tinkled the ice in the glass. He looked pale beneath his tan. He took a piece of ice, pressed it to his eyelids, and tried to breathe deeply. Taking his gin into the bathroom he bustled about getting ready for the show, trying to concentrate, trying to keep those horrible pictures from his mind. Before he left for the gig, he called Asia and left a message asking her to pop round and check on Oberon when she had a moment.

# Chapter 8.

A transcontinental flight gives people a long time to think, and Frankie Merang was doing just that. He'd had a hard ride in his thirty-four years. It hadn't been the School of Hard Knocks; it had been the University of Fucking Adversity. He'd been shot, stabbed, slapped down, shit on, and reamed from asshole to breakfast. And then he left school, and things got really tough. He looked around at the darkened cabin, most people asleep except for a few isolated lights where people were reading. Next to him Belly Joe was snoring, squeezed inside against the window. The slope was out for the count. Frankie got up and stretched his legs, heading back to where the stewardesses were playing with their crotches behind the red curtain, or whatever it is they do on long trips. He pulled the drape aside and a pretty, sleepy girl raised a smile.

"Got a bourbon layin' around, baby?"

"Sure."

Frankie watched the material of her skirt stretch over her buttocks as she bent to get his drink. She handed him two miniatures, smiling. He nodded and went to stand by the emergency exit. He peered out of the window. Far below some river meandered along, shining silver in the moonlight. He cracked one of the tiny bottles, poured it into his plastic glass, and drained half of it.

Yup. Hard slaps, all right, and plenty of 'em. And how long was it gonna be before his luck ran out, or he made a mistake, or he got in the ring with the wrong guy and got his slate wiped clean…permanently? Workin' for the Don had its perks, and paid good, but there wasn't much of a retirement plan. So far, the Don was treatin' him good. But that could change. The Don didn't get to be the Don because of his full social calendar. And here he was, headed for the asshole of the world, an' maybeez a shot at the title.

He looked back down the plane, wondering who the Don would have sent to watch them. Or was he already there? How far was the Don's reach? If he did what he was thinking about doing, the Don would have to believe he was dead. That was the only way it could happen. It didn't matter how much dough you had if you had to spend every second of every day for the rest of your natch looking over your shoulder and shitting yourself every time somebody dropped a glass, or a car backfired, or the doorbell rang when you weren't expecting anybody. And a fat Geneva account would be cold comfort if you were sitting in some alley with your cojones in your mouth, wearing a Colombian necktie. With this deal, baby, when you said you were puttin' your balls on the line, you weren't fuckin' kiddin'.

Frankie opened his second miniature and looked at the soft benign clouds floating past the window, like the innocent dreams that he had never had. He imagined what they would look like from the deck of his yacht, moored in the harbor of some European hotspot, with a bottle of Moët in one hand, a cigar the size of a mule's wang in the other, and some French courtesan on her knees with her cherry lips round his dingus. Fuck the Don. Shit or get off the pan. *All I need is a bulletproof plan and a bit of luck, and I'm away. At least I'm lucky the Don sent Belly Joe. That wasn't very smart. Belly Joe couldn't find his asshole in a diarrhea epidemic.*

Frankie went back to his seat, where his two companions were still soundly sleeping. *You be sleepin' even better soon, boys,* he thought, sitting down to rehearse his plan.

Asia was concerned. She had just gotten back from Crispin's apartment, after getting his message, and found it locked and strangely quiet. The hairball usually freaked out when anyone knocked, but not this time. And it was much too late for Nigel to have taken him out for a walk. If Nigel had gone away somewhere, surely he would have told Crispin. And there had been something else. A smell. A weird, sweet, sickly smell. Something definitely didn't feel right. She would have to go back and break in. But she knew enough not to go alone and she knew she needed some backup, preferably some backup with muscles. She called up her friend, the colored girl she knew from the streets. Rhonda would know the score.

"Hey, Rhonda," she said.

"Hey. What's up, girl?"

"Nothin', babe. Listen. I need some muscle. Not for anything heavy. Just in case. You know anyone? You know I'm still kinda new around here."

"Sure, baby girl. No sweat. I'll send you a guy over. How soon?"

"ASAFP."

"Okay, hon, jus' hang tight. I'll call you back."

Rhonda called back fifteen minutes later and said the guy was on his way. She said his name was Baby Joe Young and that you couldn't bang nails into him.

The heat slapped Bjørn Eggen Christiansson in the teeth as he stepped off the plane at McCarran International. He was not accustomed to it, and even though Tuscaloosa had been humid it was nothing like this. He was feeling faint by the time he had negotiated customs and was standing in line for a taxi, especially as he was nursing a hangover of biblical proportions. He was pale and sweating, and the young woman in front of him in the queue asked him if he was all right.

"*Ja, ja*. I'm very gud, thank you very much. I'm not very much used to the weather."

The lady smiled understandingly and, when it was her turn, she attempted to let Bjørn Eggen go ahead of her.

He tipped his hat with the reindeer band, and graciously refused. "No, no. Women and children first into the boats, *ja*," he said.

When the next cab pulled up, a wiry woman in her forties with a rose tattoo on her shoulder was driving, and she got out to open the door for him. Since she had been a Vegas cabbie, she had seen humanity in all its bizarre and colorful splendor. If a sumo wrestler in a tutu had gotten into the back of her ride, she wouldn't have been surprised, so she hardly paid any attention to this frail old man with his skinny white legs sticking out from the bottom of his leather shorts, with long socks pulled right up to his knees and leather braces that crisscrossed over the front of his embroidered shirt. She smiled a little when the old fart refused to let her lift his case into the back.

"Where to, hon?" she asked him brightly when he was installed in the backseat. Bjørn Eggen handed her a piece of paper with 2694 Wampum Vista written on it.

"Please, I need to go here. This is the house of me grandson. But first I need to stop somewhere for a beer. I am haffing the very bad overhang."

The woman smiled at him through her mirror. "You mean hangover?"

"*Ja*. This also. I am in need off thee hair off thee dog vhich has been biting me, no?"

"You got it, pops. Sit tight."

She hit the meter and pulled out into the traffic, muscling in front of a minibus full of Hare Krishnas, who smiled at her and chanted a blessing in unison. She flipped them the bird.

Bjørn Eggen stared out of the window at the huge hotels marching down the strip, examining every structure, every billboard that they passed. They made the short journey to the Tropicana, where the cabbie pulled up outside the Crown and Anchor.

"Vould you care to join me for something, maybe? You can leave the meter."

The woman smiled again. She was beginning to like this old dude. What the fuck, why not? She had been at it for six hours, and her dogs were biting. She killed the engine, and the meter.

"Hey, why not, pops. Let's go."

She smiled again as Bjørn Eggen opened the door for her and ushered her inside with a small bow.

Inside it was cool and dark, the air stirred by the slow fan sweeping overhead. A strange glow emanated from the slot machines set into the bar. There were few other customers, and they took a seat at a high, shiny table underneath a flickering TV screen with the volume turned down.

"Vat vill you haf to drink?" Bjørn Eggen asked.

"Oh, just a Coke, thanks. I still gotta work a coupla hours on my shift."

"I am Bjørn Eggen," said the old man, extending his hand.

"Maggie," replied the woman, taking his hand. She was surprised by the strength of the grip. "Pleased to meet you. Are you on vacation?"

"Not really. I haf my grandson here, he sent me this from newspaper, *ja*."

Bjørn Eggen took Monsoon's letter from the back pocket of his shorts and handed it to Maggie. While she was reading a waiter came, and Bjørn Eggen ordered a Coke and a pint of lager.

"Wery cold, if you don't mind, *ja*."

Maggie handed back the letter and the clipping, looking quizzically at the old man.

"Ya, so you see I vant to go vith him on the trip."

"Is he at work?"

"Vork? Him? Ha. This idiot don't know even vat means this word."

"So why didn't he come to meet you?"

"Ah. This is maybe my fault. I vas supposed to be here yesterday. I meet some very fonny boys from ball game. I get very much dronk, and miss me flight. This is vy I am having the overhang."

Maggie smiled vaguely and shook her head. The drinks arrived. "To Las Vegas in all its splendor," she said, raising her glass.

She watched the old man grasp his glass in his horny claw, say "Skoll," and drain it in one go.

"Damn, you were thirsty," she said.

"*Ja*. The beers on the plane very small and varm. This is very much better, *ja*. If ve haf time, I would like another, *ja*."

"Go for it, baby," Maggie replied, considering him closely.

The newspaper clipping was a fake. Every souvenir shop from Downtown to the Strip could knock you one up in two minutes. Any child could see that. Couldn't they?

Asia peeked through her spy hole when somebody knocked on her door. Usually people rang the bell. She saw a man standing with his back to her, and punched the intercom.

"Yes, who is it?"

A static voice came back. "Young. Baby Joe. I believe you're expecting me."

She opened the door and looked into Baby Joe's steady blue eyes. She was wearing a green gym leotard with a black silk blouse hanging loose over the top of it, and her long red hair framed her face and hung over her shoulders. She smiled.

"Jaysus," Baby Joe offered, involuntarily.

"Excuse me?" Asia said.

It was Baby Joe's turn to smile. "Sorry," he said. "I wasn't expecting…"

"You weren't expecting what?"

"Listen, can we start this conversation again? Hello. I'm Baby Joe Young. I understand you're in need of a little assistance."

Asia held out her hand. "Asia Birdshadow. Yes. Yes I am. Thanks for coming at such short notice. Please come inside."

She stepped back to let him pass, and Baby Joe stepped into and out of her warm, heady fragrance.

"Have a seat," she said. "Can I offer you some coffee?"

"Asia, I don't want to give you the wrong impression, but you wouldn't happen to have something a little stronger, would you? I had a rough night."

Asia smiled again. "Sure. What?"

"Bourbon?"

"Done. How?"

"Straight, no ice."

"Coming up."

"Louisiana, if I'm not mistaken," Baby Joe said as she set his drink in front of him.

"You've got good ears. What about you?"

"Boston. Fifth-generation Mick."

"You don't sound Irish."

"Wait till I'm drunk."

"What happens then?"

"I sing."

"I'd like to hear that."

Baby Joe grinned. "No you wouldn't," he said. "I have a musician friend who says my ears are only painted on."

Asia laughed. It was like water trickling over stones.

"So. What's the deal?"

Asia explained the situation to him, and Baby Joe listened as much to her voice as to what she was saying. It was honey and smoke. When she had finished he said, "Well, it's probably nothing, but you were right to call me. You never know. This is Vegas. Things are rarely what they seem."

"Tell me about it," she said, and the water ran over the stones again.

Baby Joe downed his bourbon. "Shall we?" he said, standing.

"Should we take two cars? If everything is okay, you won't have to bother driving me home."

"No. We'll take my car. I'll bring you back."

"Okay. I'll just get my purse."

"You won't need it. Come on."

Asia shrugged and headed towards the door. She wasn't accustomed to acquiescing so easily, but there was just something about Baby Joe's manner that she was comfortable with. There was actually no good reason for going in one car, except that Baby Joe wanted to be in his car with her. Baby Joe's white '72 Mustang convertible was parked across the street, and Asia curtsied as he opened her door for her.

"This is a beautiful car," she said when they were pulling away.

"It's like its owner. Old and tired, but it still goes if you give it a bit of attention."

Baby Joe smiled without looking at her, and Asia smiled at the side of his face and turned to look out of the windscreen.

"Take Rampart, and the Summerlin expressway to the freeway, then get off on Jones, and I'll tell you from there."

Baby Joe nodded. "Do you like music?"

"What have you got?"

"There's a CD case behind you."

Asia opened the case, and flicked through it. A lot of jazz and bebop, Sinatra, Bennett, some blues. The Stones, the Beatles, Hendrix. Zappa. Steely Dan. Some Irish bands.

"Haven't you got anything by anybody who's still alive?" Asia asked.

Baby Joe grinned. "I think there's some Prince in there somewhere."

Right at the back Asia found *Around the World in a Day* and slotted it into the machine. They were listening to "Raspberry Beret" as they pulled up outside Crispin's apartment.

Baby Joe knew something was wrong before they even got to the top of the stairs. It was a just a feeling that you got, a way of knowing without knowing. He turned to Asia, who, at his request, was just behind him.

"Listen. Asia. I don't want you to be alarmed, but I want you to go and wait in the car. Here's the key. Use it if you need to."

Asia gave him a questioning look, but did not argue, and wordlessly turned and went back down the stairs.

As he turned the key, the smell confirmed Baby Joe's sense of unease. There was only one thing that smelled like that, and once you smelled it you never forgot it. He opened the door, and the stench washed over him. He could hear the buzzing of flies. He doubted anybody would be inside — anybody still capable of shooting, anyway — but without turning on the light he stepped into the room, letting the light from the open doorway guide him. Between that and the dim light coming through the windows, he could see the feet of the body in the doorway of what appeared to be the kitchen. Approaching more closely, he could see a telling, dark shape around the corpse. Stepping over it, he opened the refrigerator door. Its light revealed a ghastly scene. Nigel, bloated and pale, lay in a corona of congealed blood, his swollen features frozen into an expression of pain and terror. As Baby Joe looked, a fat bluebottle crawled out of the open mouth. The front teeth were missing. There were five holes in his back in a tight pattern, from a .38 or bigger. Probably a .38 revolver. Baby Joe calculated the angle of the fall of the body and traced it back to the probable location of the shooter. One of the cushions from the sofa was on the floor, but otherwise, nothing else had been disturbed. No drawers opened, nothing obviously missing, nothing broken.

Being careful not to touch anything, Baby Joe whistled softly, twice, in case the frightened dog was hiding somewhere. Nothing. The doors to the patio were open, and he walked outside. The Vegas night air seemed a good deal fresher than when he had walked in. Something glittered on the floor, and he bent down to examine it. A whiskey glass. Expensive. Going into the kitchen to look again at Nigel, he noticed the mess in the microwave. Using a tea towel, he opened the door. The whole inside was encrusted with congealed blood, bits of flesh, feathers and bones, and sticking to the top was a large beak.

Baby Joe closed the door and stepped over Nigel, making sure he didn't step in the blood. He walked out of the apartment and closed the door behind him, carefully wiping the lock and the handle. As he walked down the two flights to the car, in his mind's eye he was running through what had probably happened. The perp had roughed the John Doe up some, probably wanting some answers. He must have gotten what he wanted, because dead guys don't tell. The perp had been on the couch, with a drink. The stiff had been in the kitchen, with his back to the room. For some reason the shooter had rolled off the couch—hence the cushion on the floor—and with a snub-nose revolver had put five shots into a two-inch circle, coming up from a roll. He had thrown his glass onto the patio and shattered it to destroy the prints, and left, taking the dog with him. Or else the dog had been somewhere else, because there were no paw prints in the blood. A pro! Baby Joe wasn't about to even try to figure out what the deal with the microwave was.

As he came through the door Asia was leaning against the hood of the car looking anxious, and Baby Joe's expression did nothing to allay her anxiety.

"What is it? What happened?" she asked.

"Get in, babe," Baby Joe said, gently. "We have to split. I'll tell you all about it in the car."

They were sitting in a dark corner of Jack's Irish pub, in the Palace Station. Baby Joe was on his third pint, and Asia on her second double Courvoisier. She was pale, and her mascara had run from crying. She had made no attempt to fix it. Her elegant hand, with its long fingers and beautifully manicured nails, shook as she set her drink back on the table, listening to Baby Joe and struggling to comprehend what had happened. A tough cookie from a hard upbringing, she had seen a lot of life in her twenty-three years, but nothing had prepared her for something like this. She was scared, and it showed.

"I'm fairly certain it was a professional job. Whoever did it was very good, and very careful. Nothing obvious had been touched or taken, so robbery was probably not the motive unless they were looking for something specific that we don't know about. There was only one glass, so it was probably only one guy involved. I believe he was looking for your friend Crispin, and I think your man Nigel was just unlucky. I think the guy smacked him around a bit, and we have to assume that Nigel told him what he wanted to know. Can you think of anybody who would want to hurt Crispin, or any reason why they'd want to?"

Asia shook her head. "Crispin is such a nice, gentle man. Why would anybody want to hurt him, and why did they have to kill poor Nigel?

Nigel didn't have a malicious bone in his body. He never hurt anybody. And what has happened to little Oberon?"

She buried her face in her hands and began to sob. Baby Joe let her alone for a minute, took a long pull from his pint, and looked around the room. It was starting to fill up, and the band was setting up. He turned back to Asia and gently touched her hair.

She looked at him and tried to smile. "I'm sorry. I know it's tough, but there are things that need to be done. Is there anything that can connect you to the place?"

"Well, I used to go around there all the time, but why would the police think that…"

"I wasn't thinking about the police," Baby Joe said.

"Then who?" she said, her eyes looking scared again.

"Never mind. We'll worry about that later. When is Crispin due back?"

"Not for four more days."

"Okay. We need to call him, now, and tell him to get the fuck out of there. Sorry, I mean, tell him to leave."

Asia smiled for the first time. "That's okay," she said, "I hear much worse than that every day."

Baby Joe nodded. "Would you prefer if I called?"

"Yes. If you don't mind."

"I don't mind at all. Will he believe me?"

"He will if I speak to him afterwards."

"Okay. We'll call now. Listen, Asia, I don't want to scare you, but it would be better if you didn't go home until I have had a chance to find out what this is all about. I suggest you come and camp out with me for a couple of days. It's not much, but you'll be comfortable. And safe."

Asia studied him. "Okay," she said, evenly, "if you think it's necessary."

"I don't really know what to think yet, Asia. But I undertook to protect you, and I will. Vegas is a much smaller place than people think it is. I'll need a couple of days to find out what's going on, and if you're connected in any way. If not, you go home. If anything comes up, we make a plan. Don't worry. I'll take care of you. I promise. I'm an old dog, but I've still got a few teeth left."

Asia smiled. "Thank you, Mr. Young. You're a good man."

"No, I'm not," he said with a grin, standing up. "Order me another pint, will you? I'm just going to phone Crispin."

"He'll be working. And you need the number."

"I'll page him."

# Chapter 9.

Baby Joe walked Asia out of the office. The manager had been waiting outside.

"Thanks, Pat," Baby Joe said. "I owe you one."

"Ah, fuck off, ya eejit," replied Pat.

Baby Joe nodded and escorted Asia back to the table.

"We finish our drinks, and then we go. Okay?" he said.

Asia nodded and they sat in silence. She did not seem inclined to speak, so Baby Joe didn't bother her. The band came out and started to play, and when Baby Joe asked Asia if she was ready to leave she shook her head and said she'd like to have one more drink.

"It feels cozy in here," she said. "Safe. Normal. Just people out having fun. As if all these other things never happened. As if nothing bad ever happened."

They had another drink each and stood to leave. Baby Joe let Asia walk in front. As they were halfway to the door the singer from the band wolf-whistled and said over the mike, "Sneakin' out like the thief in the night that yer are, are yer, Baby Joe?"

"Fuck off, you paddy twat," Baby Joe retorted, with a big grin. "I'm being a perfect gentleman, as always."

"Yer neither one, yer big thick pudden-headed Mick," said the singer, laughing. "This is for you and yer fair colleen, yer bollocks."

Baby Joe raised his hand in salute, and as he escorted Asia out of the door the band started into "The Girl from the County Down."


"This is the other side of Vegas. The shadow side. The demon that lives behind the lights. The side that people don't see and don't think exists anymore. They think it's Disneyland now, with fairy castles and magic carpet rides. All feathers and fun. But underneath that veneer, it's just as harsh and brutal as it ever was. Mr. Grim Reality wears a different hat now, and a more subtle disguise, but he still lives here, and if you stay here long enough you'll learn to see him in everything."

Baby Joe was talking quietly in his front room, lit only by the amber light creeping in from the streetlights outside and by candles in two ornate brass stands, one tall and one short. They were set on his coffee table, which he was leaning against as he sat on the floor, with Asia stretched out next to him on the sofa nursing a glass of bourbon. On the floor next to Asia's Italian shoes, a row of Guinness tins were lined up with military precision.

"I don't know if I want to stay here, now," she said, in a voice not much louder than a whisper. "I don't really like it anyway. It's just the money. I feel so alone here. Apart from Crispin, I don't really know anybody. I've got a couple of girls that I hang out with and have a laugh, sometimes, but nobody I could really call a friend."

"Vegas is that kind of place. It has a transient soul, if it has any soul at all."

Asia smiled in the half-light. "You're right," she said. "I've learned that much. I miss my family, and I miss the sea. I miss sitting on the levee under the moon, with my dog and no shoes, drinking a beer and listening to the sounds of the night. I came here because we had nothing, and I wanted to make things better for everyone, no matter what I had to do, but it sometimes seems that I had more back then when I had nothing than I do now, when I have all these things. It sounds funny, I know. It's hard to explain."

"No. I understand. It's the difference between being somewhere you're supposed to be and somewhere you're not. The absence of the subtleties and qualities that make the difference between living and existing. Requirements of the spirit unfulfilled. A feeling of the rightness of things, of waking up in the morning, and not wishing you were somewhere else. When there is some flaw in the fabric of our lives, when some color is missing from the palette that we use to paint our visions of contentment…no amount of material success will compensate for that."

"Whoa."

"Whoa, what?"

"It's the way you speak. It's not at all what I expected. I thought you'd be some kind of evil barbarian, but you're more like some sage or oracle."

"No, you were right the first time. It's just that you can't live as long as I have and not accidentally acquire a little wisdom."

"How old are you, Baby Joe?"

"I'm forty-four."

"My God! You could be my father…Oh, I'm sorry, I didn't mean…"

Baby Joe laughed. "That's all right. You're right. I could be your grandfather, actually."

She sat up and smiled at him. "Yeah, well, every little girl should have a granddaddy like you. Can I please have some more bourbon, granddad?"

Baby Joe poured her another shot, and as he was pouring she said, "Why are you here, Baby Joe? You obviously don't like it any more than I do."

"I stopped thinking like that a long time ago. The life I've lived, being anywhere is quite an achievement."

"No, I'm serious."

"Oh, I don't know. The wind just kind of blew me down here. I grew up in Boston. Ordinary Irish-American childhood. Old man was a cop. Tough guy, but a good father. Lyndon Johnson fucked me up. Lied about my age and joined the Marines. Thought it was the right thing to do. Went to the war. Came back. Joined the cops. Had a little situation, which meant I had to turn in my badge. Came out West and here I am, plugging away until I've got enough stashed for my boat. And then it's *sayonara*, baby."

"Where will you go?"

"Anywhere between the tropics of Capricorn and Cancer. Buy a little house on the beach, do a little fishing, watch the sunsets, get drunk, wait for the reaper, and spit in his fucking face when he comes. *Finis*!"

"That's a nice dream."

"It isn't a dream. It's a plan."

"I hope it happens."

"Me too. And now, we better call it a night. I want to be on the road early tomorrow. Can you handle Crispin on your own when he shows up, or would you rather I be here?"

"No. I'll be okay."

"Good." Baby Joe stood and turned on the light, and Asia covered her eyes against the glare. He went out of the room and came back with a towel and a denim shirt and handed them to her.

"Here, this is in case you get cold. The spare room is in there. There's an en suite bathroom, and the sheets are clean. If you want anything, just help yourself. I'll see you in the morning. Good night."

"Goodnight, Baby Joe. And thanks. I'm sorry I got you involved in this."

Baby Joe smiled at her. "I'm not," he said. "Now get some sleep."

After he had closed his door, Asia turned out the light and sat for a while in the darkness, finishing her drink. She held it cupped in her hands like soup, as if drawing some comfort from it. Then she, too, went through to her room and closed her door.

A soft footstep broke the spell of Baby Joe's fragile sleep and he was immediately awake, with his .45 Heckler and Koch pointed in the direction of the noise. In the faint ambient light, he saw Asia framed in the doorway and slipped the gun back under his pillow.

"Baby Joe?"

"Yes?"

"Baby Joe. I don't want to be alone. Can I come in?"

"Yes."

Without speaking further, she stepped into the room, softly closing the door behind her. She was wearing his denim shirt buttoned up at the front, and nothing else. He saw the sheen of her long legs as she slid in beside him. She wriggled up against him, and he put his arms around her and pushed his face into her soft, fragrant hair.

"That feels good," she said, quietly.

"Shh," he whispered into her ear.

Baby Joe tried to be still, but a part of him would not cooperate and was soon poking against Asia's perfect behind. He shuffled backwards and started to turn onto his back.

"Where are you going?" she whispered.

"I'm sorry, I can't help it."

Asia turned to face him. "It's all right. You can if you want to."

"Asia, of course I want to, but…"

"I want to. I want you to put it inside me."

Baby Joe kissed her, and her lips pushed back and her mouth opened, and a thrill went through him that was like a memory, something from another time and place. He slowly popped the buttons on whoever's shirt it was now and slid his hand onto her full breast. The nipple was proud, and very big. He pushed her gently onto her back.

"Baby Joe, I don't want you to wait. I'm ready. Put it in me now."

Baby Joe started to climb on top of her, and she put her hands against the hard muscles of his shoulders and looked up at him. He could see the faint gleam of her eyes, and her breath was the most wonderful thing that he had ever inhaled. He had his glans pressed gently against the lips of her vagina when she said, "Baby Joe."

He stopped. "What is it? Are you okay?"

"Yes, I'm fine. I feel wonderful," she whispered. "It's just, well…You know what I am?"

"Asia, what do *I* do for a living? I'm not a fucking librarian, am I?"

"But I'm a whore."

"No, you're not. Being a hooker is what you do, not what you are. I don't think you have the heart for it. But, even if you do, so what?"

"You don't mind?"

"Asia, shush," he whispered, kissing her and pushing slowly inside her.

They made love very slowly and for a long time, and Asia came three times, and it was real, and he could feel her tears in the darkness. He knew that she was crying not for him, but for herself, and for all the countless, nameless, faceless ones. He felt that he knew her, and recognized her, and he knew that he was too old and too far down the road for such foolishness. When they finally came together, as the first dove gray was in the east, he felt something leaving him that he knew he was never going to get back.

Later, when they had slept and were sitting up in bed drinking coffee in the golden light that streamed through the bedroom window, he smiled at her tenderly and said, "So, how much do I owe you?"

She smiled back and said, "Nothing. It's personal now. My services are gratis. How much do I owe you?"

"Nothing," he replied, setting down his coffee, and leaning towards her. "It's personal now. My services are gratis."

Asia smiled at him with her big amber eyes, put down her cup, and reached up to him.

Thumper Thyroid was feeling extremely pleased with himself when he walked into the Don's apartment. He had done the deed, come away clean, and spent an extremely entertaining evening in the company of a big bouncy blonde with massive jugs in Biddie's Roadhouse. He had had a steak the size of Texas for breakfast, and now he was walking in to see the Don, make his report, and receive his just rewards. Maybe the Don would be so pleased he would give him a permanent gig on the A Team, and no more hokey boxing matches and sweaty sock-smelling locker rooms. His pleasure grew when he saw the beatific smile on the face of the Don as he was ushered in by Stratosphere and Liberty.

"Ah. Mister Thyroid. What an absolute pleasure. Please, do have a seat."

Thumper eased himself into the chair in the center of the room, a smile spreading over his face like spilled honey.

"Now, Mr. Thyroid, in recognition of your efforts on our behalf in Lake Tahoe, your colleague has something for you."

Thumper grinned in anticipation of what he was going to get. What he got was a loop of piano wire, attached to two wooden pegs, slipped around his throat from behind and stretched tight. Thumper's hand automatically flew to his throat, and his fingers frantically tried to insinuate themselves under the wire, but it was already too tight. He could feel it biting into his flesh, drawing blood and cutting off his breath. He tried to stand, but Stratosphere quickly stepped around the chair and thumped him in the testicles. He sat down heavily, his face turning red and his tongue feeling twice its normal size. He stared, wide-eyed, at the impassive Don, and saw the light close in around him as his vision narrowed into a tunnel.

Just as he was about to black out, the wire was loosened. Thumper fell forward onto the carpet, gagging and gasping. Liberty and Stratosphere grabbed an arm each and hauled him back into the chair.

He put his hand to his throat, and it came away bloody. He tried to speak, but couldn't.

"I'm waiting for an explanation, Mr. Thyroid."

Thumper coughed and wheezed, and forced himself to say, "An explanation for what, boss? I did jus' like you tol' me."

"Well, then all I can say is Mr. Capricorn sings awfully well for a dead man."

"But boss, I drilled him right between the peepers. He had to be wasted."

"Oh, certainly you shot somebody."

A copy of the Revue Journal landed in Thumper's lap, with a picture of Morris Albright on the front page, looking like he was asleep in the snow.

"Not only did you shoot the wrong man, but you did it in such a manner as to attract the attention of the combined media of Nevada and California."

"But, boss, how do you know it's the wrong guy?"

"Because as you were driving back here, Crispin Capricorn was singing to a roomful of inebriated tourists."

"But how do you know?"

"Do you seriously imagine I would allow a lumbering, punch-drunk oaf such as yourself to go on an errand unsupervised?"

Thumper had nothing to say. Some ratfink fuckup had followed him and snitched.

"Would you mind telling me how you came to shoot the wrong person?"

"Jeez, boss. It was a fat guy, in the same color suit. I never figured for there to be two schlubs in the same gear."

"Thyroid, you bring new meaning to the word imbecile. Go and find Capricorn, and do what you were supposed to do. You have twenty-four hours. If, at the end of that period, he is still alive, you will not be. Do I make myself clear?"

"Yes, boss."

"Good, now get out. And do something about that neck!"

"Yes, boss." A cowed Thumper stood and shuffled towards the door. Stratosphere and Liberty followed him as far as the elevator.

"Hey, Thump. No hard feelins, huh?" said Liberty.

"Yeah. Sorry, Thump. You know how it is."

"Yeah, I know. No sweat, fellas. I'da done the same thing." Thumper Thyroid stepped into the elevator and pressed the button, waving to them as the doors began to close. His neck hurt, badly, and there was murder in his heart. Not like killing-somebody-for-money murder. Real murder. When you mean it. That fat fuck was gonna pay for this.

Back upstairs, the Don was talking. "Yes. It's a girl. I presume you have no problem with that. Yes, quite. I don't want to send Thumper because I fear the task is beyond him. Frankie is out of town. You'll have to stop by here and take one of the boys with you. They know what she looks like. One hour. Fine."

The Don clicked off his phone, and turned to Stratosphere. "Maxie is coming around to take care of that girl. I want it done today. This thing is getting too messy. Go with him, find her, do it, and come back. No fuss, and no mistakes. Got it?"

"Sure, Don Imbroglio."

"Good."

Crispin burst into tears as soon as Asia opened the door to Baby Joe's apartment. Great, huge, wracking sobs. He grabbed her in a bear hug, clinging to her so hard she could scarcely breathe. She guided him to a sofa, and he lay prostrate with the back of his hand on his forehead.

"Oh, Asia. I've had such an ordeal. You've no idea. No idea. I don't know where to begin."

Baby Joe came out of the bathroom and introduced himself. Crispin started to bluster, but Baby Joe cut him short. "Crispin, listen. I'm sorry for what's happened. We both are. But if I'm going to make sure it doesn't happen to you, you have got to get your shit wired. Can you think of anybody who would want you dead, for any reason?"

"N-no, nothing, nobody. I'm just a singer, for fuck's sake. Why would..." Crispin's voice was rising, building towards hysteria.

"Calm down. It's going to be okay. Now think. Do you owe anybody any money?"

"No, not a red cent."

"No gambling debts?"

"No."

"Can you think of anyone you might have upset, maybe insulted without knowing it?"

"No. When I insult someone, I like them to know about it."

Baby Joe grinned. "That's the spirit. Describe your movements over the days before you went to Tahoe. Everything that you did. Don't hide anything, or leave anything out. It's important that you tell me. Remember, I'm not judging."

Crispin began to unravel the threads of his life, gradually warming to the task, and getting a sparkle in his eye when he got to the party at Dorothy Deviche's (pronounced *ceviche*'s). Then he got to the part where he and Asia had gone to Monsoon's house and found the door busted in and a skeleton in the coffin.

Baby Joe said, "Whoa. Wait a minute. Run that by me again."

He listened intently as Crispin went through the story again, in fine detail—except for the part where he had shit in his pants, of course.

"That may be it. At least it's a place to start. Here's the deal. Asia, you and Crispin stay here. Don't answer the door or the phone. If I need you, I'll use your mobile. If anyone you don't know calls your cell phone, hang up immediately. If it's me I'll ring once, hang up, and ring again. I'm going to go by your place and check it out, then go on down to your man Monsoon's lair and see if I can come up with anything."

Baby Joe went into his bedroom and came out carrying a snub-nosed .38 Police Special and handed it to Crispin. Crispin shrieked and dropped it as if Baby Joe had handed him a hot turd.

"Guess not," Baby Joe said. "Honey, can you shoot?"

"Shit, yes. I'm from down home."

"This ain't squirrels, baby! Ever use one of these?"

Asia shook her head. Baby Joe carried it over to her and handed it to her.

"Hold it like this. If anybody tries to get in, don't hesitate. Shoot through the door. If someone gets in, aim for the middle, shoot, and keep shooting. This is just a precaution, you understand. Nobody knows you are here. So don't worry. I won't be very long."

Crispin raised his eyebrows and pursed his lips as Baby Joe kissed Asia on his way out the door.

Maxie "Slide" Grimmstein could walk under the belly of a rattlesnake with a top hat on. He was a complete and unmitigated lowlife of the first order, without a single redeeming feature, and was immensely proud of it. He had committed every criminal and deviant act described under the Federal Criminal Code, and a few that weren't, and was proud of that too. With his pointy, sallow face and unkempt, shaggy hair, he looked like a borzoi with lung cancer. He particularly enjoyed brutalizing women and was looking forward to this little escapade.

As he sat next to Stratosphere in the parked Mercedes, with his nasty little eyes glittering as they watched the girls working the street, he was becoming impatient. "How much longa 'fore the cunt shows?" he whined, in a voice that made mosquitos sound pleasant.

"Dunno. But I ain't sittin' here lissenin' to you pissin' an' moanin' all fucken day. I betta try sometin." A good-looking black girl was sashaying past, and Stratosphere leaned out of the window. "Hey, sweet cheeks, c'mere," he said.

Baby Joe left the Mustang in the next street, and walked down the road on the opposite side to Asia's house. Bingo. There was a big, black Mercedes parked three houses down, and he walked past it, catching a glimpse of the driver in the side mirror. It wasn't Uncle Al, the Kiddies' Pal, and he sure as hell wasn't selling vacuum cleaners. Baby Joe kept walking, following the curve of the street until he was out of sight. He turned down a side road and walked back in the direction he had come, watching the houses until he calculated he was in front of the one that backed onto Asia's place. The garage door was closed, and there was no car in the driveway. He went up to the side gate, whistled, and waited. No dog. Moving swiftly, he reached over and unlatched the fence, strode through to the back, grasped the branch of an overhanging apricot tree in Asia's yard, and hauled himself over the wall.

He squatted in the shadow of the tree, watching the windows and doors carefully for any shadow or any movement, then approached the French door at the back. He could hear the phone ringing. It rang for an unusually long time before stopping. Baby Joe knew from his previous visit that the house was not alarmed, and he took the door handles and pulled. He smiled. The door was locked, but the restraining bolts at the top and bottom were not fastened, and the two doors pulled apart. He would have to remember to speak to her about that. The phone began to ring again, and continued ringing, an insistent monotonous clanging. Baby Joe pulled his piece and moved swiftly through the rooms. Nothing.

The telephone finally stopped, and in the exaggerated silence Baby Joe heard a faint creak coming from upstairs. He started to walk up, silently, each foot placed with care, easing himself upwards on the balls of his feet. The doors at the head of the stairs were open, and Baby Joe stepped noiselessly across, set his back against the wall, and eased his head around the corner until he could see partially into the room. The doors to Asia's walk-in closet were open, and in the mirror on the inside of one of them he saw a thin figure stretched out on the bed. He had his trousers pulled down and was masturbating vigorously with a pair of Asia's silk panties over his face. Baby Joe could not restrain a grin. He stepped quickly into the room, put the cold steel barrel of the Smith & Wesson against the man's balls, and said, "Don't shoot!"

The man yelled in alarm and sat up, dropping the knickers. "For the love of Christ," he yelled, staring wild-eyed at the gun.

"Hey, Maxie," said Baby Joe. "Didn't come at an inconvenient time, did I?"

Maxie looked at Baby Joe's face for the first time, recognizing him. An embarrassed grin spread across his face. "Jeez, Baby Joe. I think I shit myself."

Maxie started to bring his legs off the bed. Baby Joe swung the gun in a lazy backhand, breaking Maxie's nose, and sending blood spraying from a deep cut across its bridge. Maxie squealed and fell back, holding his nose in disbelief.

"What are you doing here, Maxie?"

Maxie acted as if he hadn't heard the question. "My nose. You broke my fucken nose, ya cocksucka."

"Who sent you?"

Something in Baby Joe's voice should have told Maxie not to get smart, something that said getting smart with Baby Joe would be the worst thing in the world. But Maxie didn't listen.

"Fuck you. None of your fucken business. What the fuck are you doing here?"

Baby Joe clubbed him with the gun again, in the temple, hard this time. A deep, blue indentation on Maxie's head slowly filled with blood. He was out. The phone started again, relentless and unending. Baby Joe frisked Maxie. In his back pocket he found a straight razor and opened it, holding it against the light, watching it shine with latent malice. Maxie groaned, and Baby Joe slapped him twice and hauled him upright. The phone kept on ringing. Baby Joe pocketed the gun, grabbed Maxie by the balls, held the blade against them, and looked Maxie in the eye.

Maxie went to pieces. "Jeez, Baby Joe, for fuck's sake. The Don, the fucken Don. It's the girl, I dunno why, I swear. The fucken Don, man. You don't ask questions, you know that. You just do. It's just a job, man, it's just business. What the fuck am I s'pose to do? Nobody says no to the

Don. You know that. C'mon, Baby Joe, give me a break. Baby Joe, for fuck's sake."

Baby Joe lifted the razor, and held it in front of Maxie. Maxie seemed to shrink into the bed. The phone kept ringing.

"You were going to use this."

It wasn't a question. It was a statement. Now Maxie was listening. And what he was listening to was scaring him worse than the razor.

"You were going to cut her with this. You were going to hurt her, and watch her bleed, and then you were going to kill her."

"Baby Joe, I swear I…"

Baby Joe saw a picture in his mind's eye, a picture of Asia's beautiful face, cut and bleeding, and Maxie standing over her, leering, liking it.

Maxie made a small gulping noise, and his eyes went wide, and his hands flew to his throat as the razor separated his jugular, and separated Maxie Grimmstein from the seedy, squalid little existence that he had called life.

The phone was still ringing. Baby Joe dropped the razor, walked over to the bedside table, picked up the receiver, and listened.

"Hello, hello, who's there? Hello."

Asia.

"Hey, baby."

"Oh, Baby Joe. Thank God. Are you okay? My friend Rhonda called. She was crying. She said two guys pulled her, one great big guy and one small, ratty little guy with nasty eyes. They hurt her. They made her tell them where I lived. I was so worried. I thought something might have happened to you."

"I'm fine. Don't worry," he said, gently. "It's taken care of. Just sit tight. I'll be back as soon as I check out Monsoon's place. I'll bring you a few spare things. You're going to need them."

"Why?"

"Because you're not going to be able to come home for a while. I have to go. Bye."

"Bye."

Baby Joe found a small bag, stuffed it with an assortment of things, and left the way he had come in. As he drove out of Asia's street, the big guy was sitting in the Mercedes, picking his nose and smoking.

# Chapter 10.

The basketball dwarfs were standing on the corner as Baby Joe approached, trying very hard to radiate an aura of menace, and managing to look every bit as intimidating as garden gnomes in party hats. Baby Joe had made a swing by the place, then parked the car in a nearby 76 lot and walked back. Baby Kobe peeled himself off the wall as Baby Joe approached, and blocked his path. The others gathered round.

"'Sup, homes?"

"If you're looking for Snow White, I haven't seen her."

"Huh?"

A flicker of unease ran through the pack. This old dude wasn't playing the game.

"We the NV Street Posse," said Baby Kobe, trying to maintain face.

"Maybe I can get your autograph on the way back."

Baby Kobe looked confused. "Say wha'?"

"Listen, Rumpelstiltskin, I've got a really good idea. Why don't you get out of my way, before I kick the fuck out of you and steal your tootsie rolls."

One of the kids giggled, and a couple of them stepped back. Baby Kobe stood there, scared now, wanting to move but not daring to. The other kids were watching. If he backed down now, he would lose the gang. He spit. A big wet gob spattered next to Baby Joe's shoe. Baby Joe slapped him, grabbed him by the front of his Lakers shirt, and heaved him off the ground.

"Son," he said, "I don't know how old you are, but if you live to be a hundred you'll never know how lucky you are that that didn't hit me."

Kobe squirmed and let out a stream of invective.

Nearby was a yellow dumpster, daubed with graffiti, and Baby Joe heaved Baby Kobe into it. He landed with a loud, resounding clang. As Baby Joe walked away, he could he hear Baby Kobe's voice squealing from the metal depths of the dumpster.

"Get me out. Yo, mothafuckas, get me out!"

Baby Joe glanced back and the other kids were standing around the dumpster, laughing.

The door to Monsoon's house had been hastily repaired. Baby Joe had no trouble letting himself in, and entered to find that Monsoon had not made much of an effort to repair the damage that the Don's crew had done. The place stank, the unmistakable smell of poverty and neglect. Your average Depression-era hobo would have been embarrassed to stay there. Baby Joe went through to the garage, where Crispin had told him he would find the coffin. It was still there, on the floor, and there was some kind of scale next to it. Baby Joe pondered it for a few moments, but it didn't speak to him. Broken glass cracked under foot as he traversed the "living" room and went into the bedroom. If the lounge smelled bad, it was the Hanging Gardens of Babylon compared to the bedroom. A pair of skanky underpants lay in the doorway and Baby Joe briefly considered shooting them, just to be on the safe side.

His eyes were immediately drawn to the military equipment scattered on the floor next to the bed, and he bent down to retrieve the bayonet. As he did so, he saw—under the bed, lying in a decade's accumulation of dust—a set of medals. Baby Joe picked them up and sat back onto the bed, blowing the dust from them and rubbing them clean on his shirt. They were very impressive. Congressional Medal of Honor, Distinguished Service Cross, Silver Star, Purple Heart and oak leaves, Republic of Vietnam campaign medal, Vietnam service medal.

Baby Joe was suddenly angry. Some poor bastard had waded through that shit, fighting for his country in a war his country didn't want to fight, every waking day a living hell of booby traps and shrapnel and incoming, and mouth-drying asshole-tightening fear, getting royally fucked over by Charlie and the brass both, watching his friends die, watching surgeons sewing pieces of him back together. And the symbols of all this, the actual material manifestation of what it all meant, these small memorials to his comrades and his courage, had ended up underneath a piss-stained bed in some reeking shithole in a meaningless town in the fucking desert.

Baby Joe slipped the medals into his pocket. On the floor was an overturned military suitcase with the lining ripped out, and when Baby Joe picked it up to right it photographs cascaded out and landed at his feet in a black-and-white mosaic. He looked at the name, barely legible on the case. Philip Parker. Captain. He paused. The name rang a bell. Something rustled in the damp and darkened closet of his memory. A voice. He listened, but it would not come out into the light. He turned to the pictures. He gathered them up and sorted them out, carried them back into the living room, and sat at a table studying them in the light from the window, examining each one and then flipping it over to read the inscription of the back.

Suddenly he was right back there. He could almost smell it. The old familiar names, the equipment, the ancient looks on the faces of young men, little more than children — murderous, uncomprehending children, cops and robbers on an epic scale. Bang, you're dead. Except in this game you stayed dead, and if you lived you came back with a piece of you stolen away before you ever had the chance to understand what it was that you had. You came back with your mind altered and the course of your life altered, melted down in the forge of war and recast as something else, pummeled prematurely into a different kind of manhood, so that for the rest of your life you saw the world in different colors than the people who had not been there.

The same face appeared in a lot of the pictures: a tall, handsome black man with a broad, confident smile. You could see from the photographs that this one had not been afraid. This must be the man. Baby Joe took a full-face photo and studied it. Hawaiian shirt, flowers around his neck, a bottle of beer, and a smile to light the world. From the edge of the picture appeared some strands of long, wavy black hair and a slim, brown arm, its hand resting on the man's shoulder. He flipped the picture over. *Hanging ten in Honolulu, baby.*

Baby Joe turned the picture back over and gazed at it. Where are you now, bro? Did the cup pass? How did it turn out for you? Then, looking into the dark, laughing eyes from long ago, some veil of mist suddenly parted in Baby Joe's brain. He let the photo drop to his lap.

*Fuck me. I don't fucking believe it. Philip Parker.* He hadn't immediately recognized the face because it was an occurrence so completely unexpected that he just wasn't ready for it. Phil Parker. Christ! Baby Joe stared at the picture. The hairs on the back of his neck stood on end, as if someone long dead stood behind him, and he had the sensation that he was not alone.

And he wasn't, for in that instant some portal in his mind opened, and the carefully constructed dam that had kept those dreadful memories from flooding his brain burst, and the banshees came howling in. Baby Joe took up the photo again and stared at it, as if he was staring down a long tunnel. Because he knew now that Philip Parker's cup did not pass. And he knew why.

Subic Bay. He was on his way home, escorting some dickless desk-jockey General on a "fact-finding mission." The fact he had discovered was that if you stayed in your cabin and drank scotch all day, you could pretend that the war didn't really exist and that you were back in Washington, filling out forms and staring at your secretary's ass. General Bombast Bullshit! This fucking toy soldier had wanted to go to this bar, hang out with "the boys," as he called them, show them what a cool, unsuperior superior dude he was, maybe get some pictures to stick on his office wall back at the P. Only "the boys" had told him to fuck off back to his mammy and threatened to kick ten bells of shit out of him, and the general had skulked off back to the base to sulk and write a report about the lack of civility among the enlisted men. When he ordered Baby Joe to drive him, Baby Joe told him to fuck off as well. Where could they send him that was worse than where he had been?

So he stayed in the bar. Got talking about music to this seriously cool black dude. Airborne. Blew the fuck out of the harp and listened to Bo, and the Wolf, and Muddy. Said the heat and the water reminded him of Fort Benning, except back there it wasn't the zips you had to worry about, it was the white boys. The seriously cool black dude was Philip Parker.

The sound of a car pulling up snapped him out of his reverie. He pulled his gun and moved over to the wall next to the window, pulling an edge of the curtain aside and looking out. A taxi was pulled up at the curb, and an ancient, white-haired old man in some kind of yodeling outfit was climbing out of the back seat. The driver had gotten out, too, and was sitting on the hood of her cab, lighting up.

Baby Joe stashed the gun and moved over to the door, opening it when the old man knocked. Shock registered on the old man's face as he saw the carnage behind Baby Joe, quickly replaced by suspicion.

"Who are you? Vere is my grandson? I demand to speak vith him."

"Sir, I have no idea who your grandson is. Please, come inside. I'll explain." Baby Joe stepped aside to let the old man pass, and closed the door behind him.

"My gott. The stench, *ja*. Vat has happened here?"

"The house has been broken into."

"Who by?" said Bjørn Eggen, continuing to gaze around in bewilderment. "The Third Reich?"

"Did you say you were looking for your grandson?"

"*Ja, ja*. Sure. This is the address. He is a useless bastard, always asking for money, but he is all I haf left. I haf my son promised I vould take care of him, *ja*."

Baby Joe moved over to the table and picked up the picture of Philip Parker. He looked at the pale old man, and down at the grinning black face. It couldn't possibly be, but what the fuck?

"Sir, do you know this man?" he said, handing the old man the picture. The old man peered first at Baby Joe, and then at the picture. He looked at it for a long time, and as Baby Joe watched the old man's eyes began to mist over.

"*Ja*. Is my son. They haf killed him. From vere do you get this?"

It took a second before Baby Joe was able to speak. The suspicion crept back into the old man's eyes.

"I found it here, today, just now. I was in the war with your son. Philip Parker, right?"

"*Ja*. Captain Philip Parker. My son. The mother was very beautiful, *ja*. Very beautiful. From Alabama. I haf met her in Italy after vhen I vas fighting the Germans in the desert in the var. I used to take care of the dogs that found the mines."

Baby Joe extended his hand. "My name is Baby Joe Young. I'm a private investigator. Pleased to meet you, sir."

Baby Joe was surprised by the power of the old man's grip as he took the proffered hand, and said, "Bjørn Eggen Christiansson, at your service."

"Well, Mr. Christiansson, this is all something of a coincidence. I came here on behalf of my client and found the place deserted. I was just looking around when I found these photographs. Is your grandson expecting you?"

"*Ja, ja.* But vas yesterday. I am late one day. I vas in Alabama for to see the grave of me vife. Meet up vith some fonny kids. Get dronk, miss me damn flight. He wrote me this letter."

Bjørn Eggen took out the much-read letter and handed it to Baby Joe. Baby Joe scanned it, while the old man looked around him as if in a daze. Baby Joe looked at the clipping. He handed it back.

"Mr. Christiansson..."

"Call me Bjørn Eggen."

Baby Joe smiled. "Bjørn Eggen, I believe your grandson may have already left."

"No, my friend, this is not possible. He vould not go without me. I haf here the letter. I vil vait, *ja*. Sure he vil come back soon. Ve vil go together. Bring back my son, *ja*."

Baby Joe was at a loss as to what to say. The old man had had a long flight and a bad shock. Whatever other bad news he had coming, it could wait. "Well, Bjørn Eggen, perhaps you are right. I don't know what happened here, but maybe you should rest and we can find out about

Monsoon tomorrow. I will help you. This is not a good place to stay, right now. Have you someplace else to stay?"

"I hav an hotel, *ja*. The hotel Shimmer."

"The what now?"

"You know. Like ven the heat make the road move."

"Oh, the Mirage."

"*Ja, ja,* this is the name, *ja*. Mirage."

"Okay. This is my card. Call me when you get to your hotel."

"*Ja, ja,* sure," Bjørn Eggen said, not really listening. He had picked up the photographs and was looking at them, examining each one carefully.

"See you, then," said Baby Joe.

The old man waved absently, and wandered over to the chair with the pictures.

Baby Joe stepped out through the broken door. He stood for a second, looking down at the pavement, trying to interpret what he was feeling. A connection? Responsibility? Fuck, yes. How could you deny that? Indirectly, he was only standing here because of that old man inside. It was a coincidence so inconceivable as to defy credence, yet it was real. He looked up. The cabbie was still sitting on the hood of her cab, smoking a cigarette. She indicated the house with a nod of her head.

"What's the story there?" she said.

"Fucked if I know. Listen, did you get paid?"

"No."

Baby Joe looked at the meter through the window, took some money out of his pocket, and handed it to Maggie.

"What are you doing?" she asked.

"Fucked if I know," he replied, turning around and walking back towards the house.

*What the fuck* am *I doing?* he asked himself as he stood in the doorway, looking at the old man. Bjørn Eggen was bent over the photographs with his face in his hands, crying softly.

"Er, Bjørn Eggen, listen, er...perhaps you would be more comfortable staying with me, since your grandson is not here, and you don't know anybody."

The old man dried his eyes with the back of his veined hand and looked up at Baby Joe, studying his eyes. Something in the Baby Joe's demeanor told him he could trust him.

"Vell, I don't really like to stay in the hotels, *ja*. Okay, I make a deal vith you. If ve can stop for a beer on the vay home, I come vith you."

"Bjørn Eggen, you're a man after my own heart."


"Vat the hell is that?" Bjørn Eggen said, when they were sitting in a corner at the Whale and Baby Joe had sat down with a pint of lager and a Guinness.

"This is Guinness. Finest substance known to mankind."

"Looks like my vife's arse used to look like," said Bjørn Eggen, lifting his beer and causing Baby Joe to almost choke on his.

They talked about Phil Parker, and Monsoon, and Bjørn Eggen's life, and his dogs, and they talked about war, and Vietnam, and Phil Parker's Congressional Medal of Honor, and how the dice roll impartially for the wicked and the meritorious, and how Philip Parker had had his life taken from him in defense of his country. And, as they talked, Baby Joe came to the realization that the old man did not know the true circumstances of his son's death. He also came to the decision that Bjørn Eggen would not discover it from his own lips—for how would it benefit the old man, or serve his memories, to know that his son had died for nothing, in a place where he should never have been, in a war that was already over? Or to know of Baby Joe's part in it, even though it had not really been his fault.

While Philip Parker and Baby Joe were drinking in the Bay, the Cambodians seized the SS Mayaguez, which was on its way to Thailand. They took the crew to Koh Tang Island. Ford told Kissinger to ask the Chinese to tell the Cambodians to let the crew go. Kissinger told Bush Senior, who at that time was the US Liaison Officer in Beijing, to pass the word. The Chinese told George Senior to fuck off. Ford sent in the Marines. He sent the 1st Batallion 4th Marines, who were stationed in Subic Bay. Phil Parker and Baby Joe were Airborne, and so were the guys they were drinking with. For them, the shit was over. But when the Marines' transport pulled out, they were on it. It had seemed like a good idea at the time.

The Americans didn't know two things when they hit Koh Tang. They didn't know that the Cambodians had already released the crew of the Mayaguez, and they didn't know that the island was heavily defended—ironically, against the Vietnamese. When the shit stopped flying, eighteen Americans were dead. Phil Parker was one of them. Three guys got left behind. Their names are the last three names on the Vietnam Veterans Memorial. Phil Parker was killed by one of the very last shots fired in anger.

But that wasn't all. At the end of the fight, there were only two choppers left evacuating the Americans. The second to last to leave was an HH-53. Phil Parker was on it. He was home free. They were hovering four feet over the surf ready to pull out when this Airborne kid came running through the smoke out of the tree line. The call went out to wait.

The kid got to within ten feet of the chopper when a B40 grenade came in. It knocked him ass-over-tit into the surf. Without giving it a second thought Philip Parker jumped down, grabbed the kid, and heaved him into the door of the chopper. The chopper was heavy, and there was incoming, so Phil Parker waved them away. He ran back for cover and waited until the last chopper came in. They gave him the Congressional Medal of Honor for it. But he never got to use his free air travel, or get invited to a Presidential inaugural ball. Turns out the Airborne kid was cut to shit, and winded, but otherwise he was okay. The kid's name was Baby Joe Young.

And right now the kid was feeling confused, disoriented, and fucked-up in the head, just like all those years ago on the chopper. He was looking for the son of the man who had saved his ass, and gotten himself killed doing it, and drinking with his father. How did that work? What celestial haunting mechanism was clanking its chains here? Is there some karmic requirement that the present must be forfeit to the past? That debts from the past must be redeemed in the future? And if so, by what means or in what currency must the debt be paid? He was also feeling guilty as hell. Guilty about keeping the truth from the old man, and knowing he had no right to do so, even if it was the right thing to do. Or was he just telling himself that? How would the old man feel about sharing a drink with the man who had caused his son to sacrifice himself? And he felt guilty about his motive for asking him to stay, which in truth he was not entirely sure of himself. It was part sympathy, part instinct, part curiosity, and partly some uncanny and disturbing sense of the past reaching out to let him know that he could not escape it.

But it was also cynical pragmatism. He thought it might help him discover what the fuck was going on, and what Monsoon had that was so interesting to the Don. Asia and Crispin had obviously just stumbled into something...something big enough that the Don thought it necessary to get them out of the way. And what was the deal with the old man? He was obviously not aware that the clipping was a fake. Why had Monsoon gotten him involved? Why had the poor old bastard been dragged halfway around the world just so that life could give him another kick in the balls?

He knew that he should just walk. Every instinct and tenet of common sense told him so. He should just put the girl on a bus back to Baton Rouge, put the fudge packer on a plane to wherever, drop the old man at the Mirage, and walk away. Three people were dead already — one of them killed by him — and he knew it was only just beginning. He didn't give a rat's ass about that evil creep Maxie. That little shitbird had deserved it, and he had been doing the world a favor. But he knew how these things worked. One thing led to another and before you knew it, your ass was against the wall, and you had to either fight until it was over, or cut and run. He was going up against some bad boys, here. The worst. His boat was waiting for him at the edge of his dreams. And he was close...almost close enough to call it quits right now. Maybe now was the time. Do something smart for a change. What the fuck was he doing? For people he didn't even know. Sure, one of them he really liked, and she made him feel like he hadn't felt for twenty years. But she was a whore, a three-hundred-dollar-a-night trick twenty years his junior. You didn't need to be Stephen fucking Hawking to figure out how much time that one had left on the clock.

Baby Joe went to the bar for a last round. He looked back at the old man, sitting there in his leather shorts, with the sun from the high window lighting his hair Rembrandt-style. He was five thousand miles from home, worrying and hoping, with a picture of his dead son and a lie in his pocket. He thought about Crispin. Two hundred and fifty pounds of quivering jelly, almost as helpless as when he came screaming into the world covered in blood and shit. He thought about Asia. The taste of her breath, the smell of her hair, the weight of her breasts. That look in those exquisite tawny eyes. He thought about his promise to her.

And he knew he wasn't going anywhere until this thing was over. He was going to fight, because that was all there was to do. Because deep down in the dark recesses of his soul, where the dragon lived, he wanted to. Fuck the Don!

"Mr. Young, you are one stupid motherfucker," he sighed aloud as the drinks arrived.

"Excuse me?" said the barman.

Baby Joe shook his head. He went back to the table, set the drinks down, reached into his pocket, and sat.

"Bjørn Eggen. You should have these. I found them in the house, so they must have belonged to Phil." He placed the medals on the scarred and scratched wood, and they lay glinting silver and bronze in a beam of pale light.

The old man reached out slowly and took them up, and held them in his horny, wrinkled hand. His eyes misted over again as he looked up into Baby Joe's face. "*Ja,*" he said, very softly, "thank you. Thank you, my friend."

They finished their beer in silence, and as they drove down the freeway, back to Baby Joe's townhouse, Bjørn Eggen stared in silence out of the window. He saw the lights and the billboards, and the garish colors, and bizarre shapes of the hotels, and the monotonous, dun-colored desert, and the hazy, gray hills beyond. Then he saw the insides of his eyelids, and was asleep.

"What on earth is a safe house, Mr. Young?"

Crispin was tipsy, bordering on off-his-trolley. He had been drinking steadily since his arrival, hiding in the sweet, warm depths of a gin bottle, communing with the genie who lived there, the genie who could make everything all right, the genie who could make all the bad things go away. Poof! Like magic. He was using gin to suppress his pain and confusion and fear, and he had just about suppressed the fuck out of them by the time Baby Joe sat him and Asia down at the garden table to speak to them. Bjørn Eggen was lying in a deep, exhausted sleep in the spare room, dreaming of sunlit dogs running across the snow.

Baby Joe smiled indulgently. He was beginning to like Crispin despite himself. In fact, he was beginning to like a lot of people recently: Crispin, the old man, Asia. Rather more than like, in her case. What the fuck was wrong with him? Maybe there was something going around.

"A safe house is a place where you'll be safe, because nobody knows where it is."

"What a splendid idea," Crispin said, giggling, and taking another sip of gin. His fat face was florid, and his bouffant had collapsed down over his eyes, making him look like a jovial and overindulgent judge.

"Baby Joe, do we have to?"

"Some evil shit is going down, honey, and I don't want you anywhere near. These are hard words, but somebody wanted you dead. They'll keep trying until they succeed. You leave tonight. I'll rent you a car at the airport. You drive to LA and fly from there. You're sure there won't be any problem with Crispin staying?"

"It won't be a problem for us, but it is going to be a huge culture shock for Crispin. It might be more humane just to let the Don put him out of his misery."

"There's not much that can shock me, dearie, let me tell you," said Crispin, who had almost nodded off.

They both smiled.

"We'd better get him kitted out with more appropriate duds for down there, or they'll think Mardi Gras has started early," Baby Joe said.

Crispin fell asleep, slumped in his chair with his chins on his chest and his hair hanging down like a wilted sunflower. They were silent for a few minutes, knowing what had to be said, but neither one wanting to be the one to bring it up.

Finally Asia spoke. "Baby Joe? How long do we have to stay?"

Baby Joe took a deep breath. "Maybe you can never come back. I don't know yet. I don't understand what is going on, but it's bad. It isn't your fault, but you have walked into something, something to do with Bjørn Eggen's grandson. People are dead, and more will die. I'm going to make sure that one of them isn't you."

"But what are you going to do?"

"I'm not sure. I'm just going to play it by ear. But I can't do anything while I'm worrying about you."

"Are you worried about me?"

"You know I am. This wasn't part of the plan, and I didn't expect it, but it's happened now and I have to deal with it."

"What about us?"

"Asia. This is not the time. Okay? Let's just make sure there is a 'you,' and we can worry about 'us' later. I'm going to organize the wheels. You call the airline and sort out the tickets. I'll be back in a couple of hours."

Baby Joe stood up to leave, and Asia ran to him and threw her arms around him. "I want there to be an us. I feel so safe with you. So secure."

Baby Joe kissed her, and gently pried her arms from around his neck. "There's no such thing as security, baby," he said softly. "It's an illusion. This is a difficult situation. People get emotional under stress, and when they're scared. You said it yourself, I'm old enough to be your father."

"But I…"

Baby Joe put his finger to her lips. "Later," he said. "Things will be clearer with some distance between us. Now you know the drill?"

Asia pulled a face, and took a theatrical deep breath. "Don't answer the door, don't answer the phone, if anyone tries to break in, shoot them. Yeah, I know."

Baby Joe grinned, turned, and walked out of the door. Asia looked down at the slumped figure of Crispin, sighed, plunked herself down in her chair, and reached for the bottle.

Baby Joe drove to New York-New York, parked his car, walked through the lobby to reception, and took a cab to the airport. He rented a small, unobtrusive Japanese hatchback, drove it to the Crown and Anchor, got a pint, and sat down to ring around his contacts, finding out as much as he could about Monsoon Parker without divulging anything.

What he discovered left him more puzzled than before. Parker was nothing. Just a small fly buzzing around in the shit at the bottom of the food chain. No different than a thousand other small-time hustlers, feeding off the crumbs and scraps from the king's table. The kind of guy that people like the Don only noticed if they found them stuck to the bottom of their Italian loafers. This poor bastard must have done a state-of-the-art piece of fucking up to get himself in so deep with Don Ignacio Imbroglio. There was every chance that the reason he was not at home was because he was on a permanent vacation to Sleepville out in the sticks. The fucking River Styx. Which meant that, sooner or later, he was going to have to break it to the old man. His phone rang. It was Asia, with a corncob up her ass.

"Crispin has gone back to his apartment!"

"He what? The stupid bastard!"

"He's drunk. After you had gone, I laid down to relax and must have drifted off. When I woke up, he was gone. He left me a note saying that if he had to go and live in a swamp, he at least wanted to have some decent clothes. He said he would be back in an hour."

"Okay. I'll see what I can do. Sit tight. Usual rules." He hung up. That fat fucker! If Baby Joe had any sense, he would just leave him. *But Crispin knows the plan. He might spill. Shit.*

Finishing his drink, he dropped a twenty on the table and walked out to the hired car.

Thumper Thyroid knelt before the trussed-up and trembling Crispin Capricorn. Smiling, he held up a small black device with a bright red digital display that read 03:00. He waved it in front of Crispin's wide eyes and set it on the floor in front of him. Standing, he stepped over the reeking thing that had been Nigel and into the kitchen, with Oberon skipping at his heels. Thumper turned on the gas in the oven, propped the door open with a knife, and turned all four gas rings to full. He walked back over to Crispin and knelt again. He looked into Crispin's eyes, seeing the hugely dilated pupils, watching the sweat pouring down the pale, pudgy face. Oberon jumped up and licked Thumper's face. Thumper petted him, still looking into Crispin's eyes.

"Good boy," he said.

Thumper reached down to the little device and pressed a small green button on top of it. The digital display flicked to 02:59, and then 02:58.

Crispin screamed, "FOR CHRIST'S SAKE WHAT ARE YOU DOING? NO, NO, STOP IT, TURN IT OFF, TURN IT OFF!"

02:46, 02:45…

Thumper Thyroid smiled at Crispin and pinched him on the cheek. "Three minutes, fat boy," he said. "Enjoy."

He stood, made a clicking noise with his tongue, and walked out of the door with Oberon scampering happily behind him.

Crispin squealed. A high, thin, hysterical screech. "NO. WAIT. STOP. COME BACK. OBERON. OBERON, YOU TRAITOR. YOU JUDAS. YOU FUCKING FURRY LITTLE TURNCOAT. OBERON, COME BACK. NO. NO. PLEASE GOD NO. HELP. HEEEELP."

Thumper could hear the screaming as he trotted down the two flights of stairs and walked around the building to where the car was parked. As he climbed into the driver's seat, Oberon hopped in through the open back window and sat on the back seat. Thumper started the engine, turned on the stereo, and twiddled the dial until he found an oldies station. He heard Bob Dylan singing "Knockin' on Heaven's Door." Smiling at the appropriateness of the song, he carefully fastened his seat belt, put the car into reverse, and looked behind to make sure the way was clear.

He saw Oberon looking at him. Panting happily. Proudly displaying the small black device with the bright red numbers that he held between his teeth.

00:02, 00:01

Thumper Thyroid didn't even have time to complete the phrase "Oh, Fuck," before the exploding Semtex sent Oberon to that great big kennel in the sky, and Thyroid to wherever it is that inept boxers, murderers, and sometime-mob-enforcers go.

Baby Joe dispensed with a precautionary parking of the car, and, satisfying himself with a quick scan of the front of the building, drove around the back and into the parking lot. He saw the red Mercedes, and he saw the figure behind the wheel turned away, looking at something in the back. Before he had the chance to decide what to do, the sun rose for the second time that day. An immense orange flower grew in front of him, and a sudden violent wind rocked the little car on its chassis. All sound ceased, and the air seemed to be sucked out from his lungs, and then came a deafening WHUMP, and the devil breathed fire and brimstone on him. Baby Joe rolled out of the door just before the windows came out of the little hatchback in a tinkling silver shower.

Hertz was going to be thrilled. "Well, what happened was, I parked next to this Mercedes, and it exploded, see? Honest!" As he huddled against the tire, making himself as small as possible, a hard rain began to fall around him — glass and steel, copper and hot plastic. Something soft landed on his knee, something white and red and furry. It was a dog's ear.

Baby Joe stood up with his ears ringing and looked at the smoldering piece of twisted metal that had, only moments before, been a fine example of German precision engineering. Whoever and whatever had been inside it were toast. *Well, at least the Don's wage bill is getting smaller,* he thought, racing towards the fire escape as the first curious faces began to appear.

He didn't have to slap Crispin as many times as he thought he was going to, to get him to stop screaming. He killed the gas, severed the bonds with the knife that Thumper had used to prop open the oven door, and said, "Let's go, Crispin. You've been a very naughty boy."

As Baby Joe headed for the door, Crispin's plaintive voice pulled him up.

"Baby Joe," said Crispin, looking at the floor, "I need to change my underpants."

Baby Joe tried his best not to laugh, but it was like Canute trying to hold back the waves.

Crispin announced, "Well, I'm glad someone thinks it's fucking funny," and flounced into the bathroom, slamming the door behind him.

"Where are your car keys?" Baby Joe said through the door, still laughing.

"On the fucking table. Are you blind as well as ignorant?"

The sound of approaching sirens choked the laughter in Baby Joe's throat, and he banged on the door and told Crispin to stop looking at himself in the mirror and hurry up. As the flustered Crispin emerged from the bathroom, a volley of tomato ketchup caught him in the face and chest. His eyes went wide in shock and amazement.

"NOW WHAT THE FUCK? JUST LOOK AT THIS SHIRT. THIS SHIRT COST THREE HUNDRED FUCKING...!"

Baby Joe grabbed him and pushed him towards the door. Crispin shuffled up to the elevator and narrowed his eyes at Baby Joe when he said, "No. The stairs."

Out back there were already two squad cars, and two officers were pushing the crowd back while another one was looking at the torched Merc, and one was on his car radio. Baby Joe grabbed Crispin as he was about to go waltzing out.

"Where's your car?"

"In front."

"Good. C'mon."

He dragged Crispin down the short passage and into the crowd of people gathered in front of the door. "Make way, please! Let us through, this man is injured."

There were gasps and comments from the crowd as they parted, and Baby Joe pushed the Heinz-splattered Crispin in front of him to the car. A minute down the road they pulled over for an ambulance and a fire engine coming in the opposite direction, and two minutes later they hit the freeway.

"I don't suppose you have a tissue?" Crispin said hopefully.

Baby Joe shook his head.

"Oh, Baby Joe," Crispin said, with tears beginning to form in his eyes, "what is happening to me? Nigel is dead, Oberon is dead, people keep trying to kill me, my career is ruined, and I'm sitting in a hired car with a madman, covered in tomato ketchup. What did I do to deserve this? Why me?"

Baby Joe shook his head. "Fucked if I know, Crispin," he said, softly. "Fucked if I know."

## Chapter 11.

Frankie Merang always got nervous when he had to use the telephone. He didn't know why, but it was just one of those things, like some people stutter and some don't. It made his throat dry, and it confused him, so the right words were hard to find. On this occasion he was even more nervous than usual. So nervous, in fact, that a half a pint of bourbon had been required to relax him to the point where he felt confident of making sure he found the right words. On this occasion, choosing the wrong words would be like choosing the short straw. He was calling the Don.

"It's Frankie," he said, when Liberty answered.

"Yo, Frank. How's the dink pussy?"

"Like a shit-faced dwarf. Small and tight. Let me speak to the Don, will ya?" Frankie waited, listening to the faint hissing of the line.

"Mr. Merang. How are you enjoying your stay in the Orient?"

"Good, Don Imbroglio. I like it just fine."

"How gratifying. And how are our affairs?"

"Couldn't be better, Don Imbroglio. The slope has the stuff."

"Oh, he has? And?"

"The contact claims that what he has is all there is left. He wants ten mill for it. Cash."

"Ten million dollars. Hmmn. Somewhat less than the amount quoted by our friend Mr. Parker. Must be having a discount this week. Have you seen the merchandise?"

"Sure, boss."

"But didn't our associate, Mr. Parker, say that it would take time to bring in the goods from the jungle?"

"Yeah, but we fixed things up real fast, boss, and the stuff got here real quick."

"I see. And you have met the contact personally, of course."

"Sure thing, boss."

"And just who is our benefactor?"

"Some slant businessman, boss. I can't even pronounce the name. Our guy knows."

"Very well. I shall send out some associates to verify your findings, and make the purchase if all is satisfactory. I'll let you know when to expect them. By the way…how is our friend Belly Joe behaving himself?"

"Ah, well. You see, boss, Belly Joe screwed up."

"Indeed. In what fashion?"

"Well, see, boss, he went to this clip joint, see. Jeez, I tried ta stop him, but he wouldn't lissen. Anyways, he gets this bill for champagne for, like, five hundred bucks, and of course he don't want to pay it. The dinks start to come on heavy, so Belly Joe has to straighten a few of them out. Only, they call the cops, see, and Joe gets put in the wagon. They got him in the slammer, boss."

"How unfortunate. And what steps have you taken to remedy the situation?"

"Well, our guy is tryin' to fix it, boss. We think we can get him out for a coupla bucks, but it might take a few days."

"Hmn. And in the interim, are you able to handle things on your own?"

"Sure thing, boss. No sweat. I got it all sewn up."

"All right, then. Congratulations, Mr. Merang. Rest assured you will be rewarded commensurate with your endeavors. I shall be in touch."

The line went dead, and Frankie dropped the receiver and reached for his cigarettes. He blew a series of smoke rings and, poking his finger through them, reached for his bottle of bourbon.

"So, Donny baby," he said aloud, grinning at his reflection in the mirror in front of him, "yez ain't as smart as ya think ya are, are ya? Ya guinea fuck."


The Don had a theory. He called it his Matryoshka Doll Theory. It was how he liked to conduct his business. Like one of those Russian dolls, where each one opens up to reveal another smaller one inside. Painted dolls with inscrutable, relentlessly smiling faces, each one in turn concealing another secret self, none of them being what they seemed to be, until you reach the very last and very smallest, hidden away inside the layers of her sisters. The only one who was not a façade. The one who was the final truth.

The Don's schemes were like an elaborate jigsaw puzzle. Everyone who was involved had a piece, a partial image from which they could extrapolate whatever design their imagination would furnish, but only the Don had the box. Only he knew what the finished picture looked like. The Don also believed that no man should be required to support the burden of responsibility alone, particularly when the burden of responsibility involved large sums of the Don's money.

Therefore, each participant in his ventures was provided with not only an aide-de-camp, but also another pair of eyes and ears, just to ensure that he didn't inadvertently stray from the path. For reasons of practicality, the identity of the eyes and ears remained unknown to the participant, thus allowing the Don to indulge in some interesting games of I Spy to while away a tedious hour. And on really important errands the eyes and ears were themselves provided with someone to watch over them. This second observer's piece of the puzzle had a picture of the first pair of eyes and ears but not the original participant, in accordance with the Don's Russian Doll Theory.

Thus, the Don insulated himself by several degrees from the potential consequences of any unforeseen or unfortunate turns of event. Like the unfortunate turn of events that had resulted in the tragic demise of Thumper Thyroid, for example. Not to mention that distasteful piece of excrement Maxie Grimmstein. Not that either one was any great loss, but the point was there was untidiness here, unacceptable untidiness, by which the Don could not abide. Thyroid had presumably dispatched himself through the sheer carelessness and ineptitude which was his calling card, but that was by no means certain. Grimmstein had been a professional job, which meant that he had two problems. Neither of the people he had ordered to cease to exist had ceased to exist, which would have to be remedied. Furthermore, somebody was cutting up the help. Somebody dangerous. Steps would have to be taken, and quickly, before things got out of hand.

As a consequence of his belief in the fundamentally flawed character of human beings, the Don tried to ensure a secure and reassuring working environment for his employees. They could toil away happily, secure and reassured in the knowledge that if they even considered for one nanosecond pulling a fast one they were assured of being provided with a swift, certain, and excruciatingly painful demise. Don Imbroglio considered one of his greatest assets as an entrepreneur, and one of the key reasons for his success, to be his essential faith in human nature. His essential faith that people would try to slip him the Big Bamboo at each and every opportunity that presented itself. His essential faith that the people who worked for him were greedy, opportunistic, shortsighted, devious, untruthful, and basically lacking in those ideals of nobility, honor, and loyalty by which man distinguishes himself from the herd and rises above his base and brutish instincts and desires.

Take, for example, the case of Mr. Frankie Merang. Here was a man who had obviously failed to rise above his base and brutish instincts and desires. It is said that bats "see" sound, the way that we see light. In the same way, in his inability to see light, the Don had learned to take information from the sounds he heard with a musician-like skill. Subtleties and nuances of tone and timbre, alterations in pitch, slight hesitations, or changes in tempo were, for the Don, as obvious as a neon dildo. In short, the Don could detect bullshit at five thousand yards, in a thunderstorm, wearing a balaclava. It would take an extremely subtle weaver of tales to mislead Don Ignacio Imbroglio, and if Frankie Merang had sophistication of speech then Frankenstein's monster had good table manners.

Since Frankie and his simian companion were ensconced on the other side of the world, accompanied by a seriously suspect character of dubious origin, entrusted with the disposition of the Don's freshly laundered green, full precautionary measures had naturally been taken. Furthermore, in accordance with the essential neatness of the Don's thinking, he had sent his cleaning lady to tidy up the mess that would inevitably attend a venture of this nature. However, in light of Merang's cloddish and clumsy attempt at deception, additional steps would be required.

The Don wasn't sure exactly what half-baked plan Merang had cooked up, but it was sure to be something risibly transparent, and although he suspected that Merang would be too stupid to identify his tail and give him the slip he wasn't going to take the chance. And also, who else was involved? What despicable collusion was taking place between his minions in that far-off place? Independent arbitration was called for.

And then there was the small matter of the disappearance of the two missing parties, whose disappearance needed to be made a little more permanent, and also the issue of the improptu barber who had ventilated the late Mr. Grimmstein. All this would be best farmed out. The fewer people in his immediate organization who knew of his recent inconveniences, the better.

The Don reached for his phone, dialed, and said, "Ah, Mr. Harris. I wonder if you would be so kind as to pop round and see me. Yes. At your earliest convenience. Say, immediately, for example."

Watching the red taillights of Crispin's car receding down the road, Baby Joe came to an important decision. He decided to go and get shitfaced. He looked in on the old man, but he was still deep in the embrace of Elysium, so he made coffee and woke him up. He decided to level with him.

"You haf maybe something for to put in the coffee?" Bjørn Eggen said, looking odd and out of place in a pair of canvas pants and a thick woolly sweater.

"Sugar?"

"No. Fock the sugar," he said, with a devilish grin that made him look like some ancient mythical satyr. "I can say such vords now the ladies not any longer here, *ja*. Whiskey maybe."

Baby Joe smiled, walked through to the kitchen, and came back with a bottle of Jack Daniels. He poured a generous shot into the old man's coffee and poured a glass for himself. He paused for a second before he began.

"Listen, Bjørn Eggen, I have to talk to you. I think your grandson is in some kind of trouble. I don't know what, yet, but I know it involves some very bad people. People who want to hurt Asia and Crispin, which is why I had to send them away. I'm going to have to send you away for the same reason. These people might come here."

Bjørn Eggen nodded. "*Ja.* I am not yet the senile. My grandson's house did not do that to itself, *ja.*"

"I think the best thing for you to do is to check into your hotel room and hang about for a few days to see if I can come up with anything. If you go running off to Vietnam, you might be going on a wild goose chase."

"I haf chase many gooses in my time," the old man said with a gleam in his eye, and then, abruptly, "Is my grandson dead, Baby Joe?"

Baby Joe said nothing. He looked into his glass.

"Baby Joe, I am an old man, *ja.* I am not expecting much older to get. I do not know if even I vant to get much older. In a long life, such as mine haf been, is much pain. Is necessary. If you know something, you must tell me, *ja?*"

"Bjørn Eggen, if I knew I'd tell you. I only know what I've told you already. If you do as I suggest, I'll keep you posted and let you know as soon as I know myself."

The old man nodded and shuffled on his bowed old legs into the spare room to get his things. Bjørn Eggen reappeared wearing a parka.

"For fuck's sake, Bjørn Eggen, you're going to a hotel, not on a fucking caribou hunt."

"Maybe I do hunt. Old is not dead, *ja?*"

"Come on, you old fart, get in the car."

Baby Joe dropped Bjørn Eggen off in front of the hotel, saying, "Go well, old man. I'll call you tomorrow."

Bjørn Eggen took him by the hand and said, "I know you are a good man, *ja*. You know, the sapling cannot grow in the shade of the oak."

"What the fuck is that supposed to mean?"

"Think about it, my friend," said the old man, turning and humping his backpack into the lights and noise of the Mirage.

Baby Joe watched him go, shook his head, smiled, and headed for Tropicana and the Crown and Anchor.

Stratosphere and Liberty had been told what to expect from Baby Joe Young and had been warned not to take any chances. That's why, apropos of nothing, Stratosphere hit him on the back of the head with a leather sap in the parking lot behind the Crown and Anchor pub as Baby Joe was staggering towards his car, just about to break a fair cross-section of the rules in the Nevada Highway Code. Not hard enough to really do damage, just enough to drop him to his knees. And that is also why, when Baby Joe dropped to his knees, Liberty kicked him in the ribs—not hard enough to really tear anything, just hard enough to take the wind out of his sails.

"The Don is waiting," Liberty said, as Baby Joe rolled over and up onto his knees again.

"Don who? King? Tell him I'm retired. Can't make the weight," said Baby Joe, feeling his ribs, making sure nothing was cracked.

"Very funny, smart guy," Stratosphere said.

"Yeah, well, if you'd wanted snappy comebacks, you should have got Robert B. Parker down here."

"You talk pretty cute for a washed-up Mick wino laying on his ass in a parking lot," said Liberty, who, although he had never heard of Robert B. Parker, was fairly certain that Baby Joe was being pretty cute.

"You should listen to me when I'm sober. I think I smell KY jelly — whose turn is it to be on top tonight, ladies?"

Now, some fairly basic rules of the strong-arm business are: never underestimate your mark; if you are going to knock somebody down, make sure that you do so in a manner that precludes their getting up any time soon; and *never* lose your temper. Liberty and Stratosphere had been doing this kind of thing for a long time, and figured to have most of the angles covered. But, as they say, sometimes you get the bear, and sometimes the bear gets you!

Blame it on the steroids, but Liberty lost it and swung his boot at Baby Joe's face, hard. Baby Joe waited until he could smell the leather, then rolled his head, leaned in, and punched Liberty in the testicles. Stratosphere was already barreling in as Baby Joe rolled to his feet. Three heavy, killer punches came in quick succession. Baby Joe weaved between them, slammed his heel into Stratosphere's shin, and stabbed him in the eyes with two stiff fingers. The big man howled and put his hands to his face, and Baby Joe stepped behind him and propelled him by his own weight headfirst into the red brick wall of the pub. It was touch-and-go which one would give way, but the pub held out and Stratosphere fell to his knees and rolled over. Over and out! Liberty was back up and coming in, but cautiously now, watching, measuring. Respectful.

Baby Joe backed up slowly, until he felt the back of his legs against the fender of a parked Cherokee. He held up his hand, covered in blood from the other one's skull. "Oh, dear! Blood. Your girlfriend's tampon must have fallen out!"

Liberty charged, snorting like a bison and smelling not much different. Baby Joe ducked under his wild swing and turned, simultaneously snapping the antenna from the hood of the Jeep. As Liberty's momentum carried him into the vehicle Baby Joe stabbed him twice with the jagged edge of the broken metal, once in the back of the groin and once in the neck under the ear. He stepped back as Liberty turned around, the blood gushing from his neck looking black under the blue lights of the pub. He put his hand to his wound, looked at it, and looked at Baby Joe.

"The next one is in your fucking eye, big man."

Liberty held his hands out in front of him. "Okay," he said, "okay."

"Good boy. Now tell the Don that if he asks me nicely, I'll come and see him. And tell him that if either of you two refugees from the Guinness Book of Retards ever raises your hands to me again, he'll be needing two new pizza delivery boys. Understand, Shrek?"

Liberty nodded. Baby Joe backed off a safe distance and then sidled up to his car. He figured if either of the two goons had been packing heat, they would have used them—or at least pulled them—but he wasn't taking anything for granted.

Pulling off the 15 onto the 95, Baby Joe conceded to himself that when Handyman Harris had called earlier in the evening and summoned him, telling Handyman Harris that the only Don he knew was a fucking River and then hanging up had not been the shrewdest move he had ever made. But then again, Don Ignacio Imbroglio was seriously starting to get on his tits. Furthermore, the last time he had unthinkingly done as he was told he had been seventeen years old and had ended up, as a consequence, in two feet of stagnant water in a paddy field, covered in buffalo shit, with a half a key of Soviet-made shrapnel in his ass and tracers flying over his head like Tinkerbell with PMS.

As he peeled off onto the Summerlin Parkway he decided that he was sober enough to realize that he had probably made a bad mistake, but drunk enough to not give a fuck. That was a bad policy. When the Don's word was in the street, it was like the weather forecast to a sailor: you had better pay attention, or you could end up with more sea than you could handle. He decided he'd better camp out somewhere and think this through. The place he chose to camp out was his usual spot in the darkest corner of the Whale Lounge, where he told the waitress to keep 'em coming and settled down to ponder the situation.

As far as he was aware, until tonight the Don had not even known that he existed. All of a sudden he was being invited for a little tête-à-tête. If the Don had wanted him dead, he would be dog meat. It was that simple. So whatever the Don wanted required him to be alive in order to do it. So...what were the permutations here? He had been made for smoking Maxie? He didn't think so—it was too soon, and anyway he had been careful. The Don had eyes on Monsoon's place? Maybe. The Don had a soft spot for the miniature kid he had dumpstered and was upset? Probably not the case. The Don had put him together with Asia and Crispin? Possible, in the case of Asia, if the Don had eyes on her crib or was tracking her. If the Don had a crew on him they were very good, because he had been watching and had seen nothing unusual, nothing at all. And anyway, if the Don was onto him and knew who had been staying at his house, why hadn't he had a visit before now?

So what to do? Split now, and never come back? He had been through that already. Sooner or later—and probably sooner—the Don was going to send somebody else. He wasn't going to be thrilled about his goons being bloodied up, if nothing else. Bad for his reputation, having his muscle slapped about in public. The thing to do was to preempt the situation. He decided on a simple plan, always the best, which called for nothing more than taking a room in the hotel, listening to the band, drinking enough Guinness to be able to sleep, and confronting the Don in the morning.

He was on his third pint, while the band was halfway through a rousing version of "The Craic Was Ninety In The Isle Of Man," and he was just on the point of shouting "Yeeehoooo," when the manager tapped him on the shoulder and put his hand to his ear. He followed Deck into the office, asking with a jerk of his chin who it was. Deck shrugged.

Baby Joe took the receiver and said, "Young."

"Mr. Young. Don Imbroglio speaking. Enjoying the music, I trust?"

"Yeah, I'm all in favor of a good reel every now and then. How can I help you, Don Imbroglio?"

"I understand there was a little unpleasantness this evening. A slight misunderstanding, no?"

"Well, I think we came to an understanding, Don Imbroglio."

"Yes, quite. Actually, I'm rather impressed. Perhaps my people were just a tad overenthusiastic. But you know it was all entirely unnecessary. If you had accepted my original invitation, none of this would have happened."

"Well, Don Imbroglio, if you yourself had invited me, I would most certainly have come. But, you know, your man's telephone manner could stand a little work."

"Allow me to apologize on both counts, Mr. Young. We seem to have gotten off on the wrong foot. I would be most grateful if you could step round to my apartments tomorrow afternoon, say four o'clock. I have a proposition for you which I am sure you will find irresistible."

"Okay, Don Imbroglio, I'll be there."

Baby Joe hung up. A personal invitation, no less. Legit? Probably. Easier to send some better talent otherwise. At least the corny fucker hadn't said he was going to make him an offer he couldn't refuse. Now all he had to do was figure out what, exactly, the Don *did* want from him and, more importantly, who he had on his tail. He would watch as he left, although he was pretty sure that the dogs would be called off now. Unless he didn't show tomorrow, of course.

Baby Joe stood before the Don, and even though the Don could not see him something in the air—some perceptible tension in the web—made him realize that this was no ordinary fly. Don Imbroglio dispensed with his customary theatrics. The fingers clicked and the chair arrived.

"I am sure you would care for a drink, Mr. Young."

"Yes, Don Imbroglio, that would be nice."

Again the fingers, and Stratosphere arrived bearing a cold, perfectly poured pint of Guinness.

Baby Joe smiled. "You do your homework, I see, Don Imbroglio."

"I like to make my guests feel comfortable." The Don made an almost imperceptible motion with his head, and Liberty and Stratosphere vanished. "I feel a little privacy is in order for the proposition I am about to make."

"Yeah, well, thanks for the invitation."

"Ah, a regrettable incident…a misunderstanding, as you said. I understand you were in Vietnam, in the Special Forces, Mr. Young. I myself was involved in the conflict in Korea. Frightful business."

"Did you ask me here to swap war stories, Don Imbroglio, or are you going to get to the point?"

The Don was not used to being spoken to in such a manner, and red static flickered through his brain. He controlled it and continued in his smooth voice, "The reason I ask, Mr. Young, is because I would like you to go back there."

Baby Joe took a big swallow of his pint. Vietnam! He heard the sound of snapping fingers in his mind. His face remained completely impassive. The Don's acute ears could hear the gurgling of the fluid.

"Are you enjoying your stout, Mr. Young?"

"As ever, Don Imbroglio. As ever. What would you like me to do for you in Vietnam?"

"You were recommended to me by an associate whose opinion I value, as a man of integrity and ability, with the appropriate qualifications. As I learned from your unfortunate encounter with my employees, my associate was not mistaken in his opinion. Some of my colleagues have encountered some…difficulties, shall we say…whilst on business for me in the Orient. I have unfortunately begun to lose confidence in them. They were last seen in Ho Chi Minh City. I imagine they believe that the distance and the exotic location will allow them a certain independence of action that they would not enjoy here, but you understand a man in my position simply cannot allow that state of affairs to exist. I need you to locate these people."

"And then what? Contracts are not in my job description."

"No, no, Mr. Young, nothing like that. I merely want you to observe them and report their activities and movements back to me. 'Shadow them' is, I believe, the expression used in your profession. I am particularly interested in whom they might meet with. I have no doubt that the nature of their business on my behalf will lead them into negotiations with certain parties whose entrepreneurial enterprises might mirror my own. I would very much like to be put in direct contact with my Asian counterparts. I understand you speak the language?"

"I used to. A little. Enough to get by. So, what's the deal? I usually get two-fifty a day, plus."

"I'll pay you one thousand, plus expenses, and first class travel."

"When do I start?"

"You may consider yourself employed as of this moment, Mr. Young."

The fingers snapped. Liberty reappeared, and placed an envelope in front of Baby Joe.

"In there, Mr. Young, you will find your ticket, photographs and descriptions of the parties you are looking for, and a telephone number to use, which is not to be given to anyone else, you understand."

"Yeah."

"You will also find a generous cash advance, and a credit card with a five-thousand-dollar daily limit, which I must ask you to use for all your business-related expenses. I am very meticulous on the point of accountancy. It will also allow me to keep track of your progress, as it were. Are these terms to your liking, Mr. Young?"

"Deal," said Baby Joe, taking up the envelope and standing. Draining his glass, he set it softly on the table.

"I am sure you understand the need for absolute discretion, Mr. Young. Any information you may acquire is strictly for my ears only."

"Understood," Baby Joe said, and then, "You were very sure I would take the job, Don Imbroglio."

"Well, I generally get what I want, Mr. Young. And as you say, I do my homework. Your profession can have its ups and downs, can it not?"

Baby Joe nodded curtly. "Thanks, Don Imbroglio. You'll be hearing from me in a couple of days."

"I'm sure I will, Mr. Young, I'm sure I will. Bon voyage, as they say."

Liberty and Stratosphere followed him to the elevator door. They both wore dark glasses, and Liberty had a bandage tied around his throat and walked with a limp, which he was trying very hard to disguise, but couldn't. Baby Joe gave them a smile that was no smile at all.

"Nice shades," he said, as the doors closed.

They were strictly minor-league guys. Small fish hanging around the reef, picking up occasional scraps from the sharks that constituted the Don's A Team. If his looks were anything to go by, Poxy Purdy should have been as hard as they come. He had a face like a warthog drinking battery acid from a pisspot. But being ugly doesn't necessarily make you tough. His partner, Bender, knew that. He made Poxy look like Brad Pitt, but if he had ever tried shadowboxing, the shadow would have won. They were okay when it came to slapping hookers around or leaning on some poor stiff who was so terrified of the Don that he wouldn't defend himself, but when it came to the real nitty-gritty they were way out of their depth. Nevertheless, between the two of them they should have been able to handle an eighty-year-old man. The Don thought so, too, which is why he'd sent them to snatch Bjørn Eggen from his hotel. Well, even criminal masterminds make mistakes.

Bjørn Eggen had a way with animals, and with dogs in particular. To them, he radiated amicability in some canine spectrum that only they could see. From the sappiest show poodle to most vicious, psychotic pit bull, dogs loved him instantaneously. Cerberus himself would have loved Bjørn Eggen.

And Behemoth loved him. Behemoth was some kind of monolithic sheepdog from the Caucasus. Two hundred pounds of muscle and bone with Smilodon teeth at one end and a dick at the other, Behemoth belonged to the head gardener at the Mirage. When Bjørn Eggen would go to sit on a bench by the pool and drink beer while watching the children play, Behemoth would go with him. Which is why Behemoth was asleep under Bjørn Eggen's bench when Poxy Purdy and his partner Bender approached.

"You comin' with us, old man," Poxy said.

"Excuse me, vat haf you said?" replied Bjørn Eggen

"You deaf?" Bender said. "He said get up, you comin'with us."

"To vhere are ve going?"

"Just shut up and get up. You'll find out," Poxy said.

"*Ja,* okay, but I am old man. Please to help me stand up."

"Sure thing, Granddad," Bender sneered.

Bender reached down, grabbed Bjørn Eggen's shirtfront, and hauled him to his feet.

Bjørn Eggen reached down, grabbed Bender's nuts, and twisted them. Bender was surprised at how strong the old man's grip was.

Poxy stepped forward with his fist cocked, ready to punch the old man in the face. Then something distracted him. What distracted him was Behemoth removing three and a half pounds of his left buttock and swallowing it, together with his wallet.

People have certain expectations of old men. We expect them to be frail and forgetful, and to reminisce a lot. We don't generally expect them to head-butt us and break our noses—hence Bender's surprise. Behemoth was trying to decide between more buttock, or perhaps a nice slice of thigh, when Bjørn Eggen called him off and walked away without a backwards glance.

"Good boy," he was saying. "How about I buy you nice packet of beef jerky, *ja?*"

Bender looked over to where Poxy Purdy was lying, bleeding heavily, in an intermediate state somewhere between shock, agony, and disbelief.

"The Don ain't gonna like this," he said.

Baby Joe sat in his customary chair in the Whale Lounge, nursing his customary pint and staring at the ticket on the table before him. Vietnam.

There are many kinds of wounds and many kinds of scars. Some say the way of it is that the scars inside, the ones you can't see, are the worst. Scars of the mind, sucking puncture wounds of the soul that never close, damage that stays with you for as long as you breathe, damage so profound that a person becomes something else altogether. Baby Joe had come out of the maelstrom of the battle for Hue with his limbs and his sight and his faculties more or less intact, but something of his being had been left behind, something that wandered among the ghosts of his friends in the Forbidden City and floated down the Perfumed River with all the other wraiths on cool misty mornings.

Vietnam. Like most of the others he had tried to put it out of his mind, to not think about it, to push it out of his daily life. But it was like a swollen river. You can hold it at bay, but sooner or later it bursts its banks and the memories, like the water, come flooding in, washing away everything that you have made until nothing remains but the water.

He looked again at the pictures on the table in front of him. Monsoon Parker looked like he had been made up of spare parts—African skin and lips, Asian eyes and cheekbones, European nose, and hair from Discount Cheesy Greasy Wigs R Us. The other two guys were real beauties—the one looked like he shaved with a chainsaw, and the other had a face like an enema gone wrong.

Baby Joe was starting to wish he had read more Sherlock Holmes stories as a kid. What was the deal here, Lucille? It was like looking for images in a cloud…every time you looked you saw something else, something you hadn't seen before. Monsoon has got something, or knows about something the Don wants, something the Don thinks Asia and Crispin also know about, but they don't. The something is big enough for the Don to want to eliminate any inconveniences…like Asia and Crispin, for example. The something is in Vietnam. The Don sends Monsoon to Vietnam with Chainsaw and Enema as nursemaids. Monsoon does the ten-toe tango. The Don hires *him* to play watchdog. Why him? Because he knows the country? Or because the Don knows or suspects all or some of what has happened and is setting him up. But then, why the charade? Could it be a simple improbable coincidence? Was it dangerous to even think that way, to think that the Don would ever do anything except weave a web from razor wire and vipers' tongues? And even if the whole thing was coincidence—just the Olympians, bored out of their eternal skulls, having a little fun—he had to assume that the Don would make the connection between him and Asia, sooner or later, and therefore put him in the frame for Maxie Grimmstein. He had been careful, but he couldn't afford to assume that there was nothing he had overlooked. There was always something. And what was the story with the old man, and the fake newspaper cutting?

So much for what he didn't know. What he did know was that he was inextricably involved in something complicated, in the tight embrace of something that would not let him go. He knew that inevitably he would assume inconvenience status. He knew that he was back to his original choice. Go or blow! He knew he didn't want to spend the rest of his life in the shadow of the Don, and he knew that it would be more sensible to hire Hannibal Lecter as a babysitter than to underestimate him.

He knew that whatever was or was not between himself and Asia could not possibly endure very long. He knew it was a love affair—if that was the name for it—with the life expectancy of strawberry jelly in a kindergarten classroom, but he also knew that he wanted it. Whether it lasted ten days or ten years, it was his for now and he wanted it, and he wasn't going to let anybody take it away from him without a fight. He knew that the waters had suddenly become irremediably muddied, when a few short days ago all he'd had to worry about was where his next check was coming from. *That'll teach you not to answer your fucking phone,* he thought.

He stared into the bottom of his glass as if the answer would be written there, in some mysterious runic configuration of foam. All that was written there was that his glass was empty. He remedied that situation with a passing waitress, and continued his rumination. Asia was safe for the moment. The best thing was to go ahead as planned, see what developed, find out what it was all about, see if some way out presented itself, and just be good and ready for when the Don made his move. The move would probably not be until after he had hooked up with Mr. Monsoon Parker and his watchdogs and the Don had gotten what he wanted. And besides, as suicide missions go the pay on this one was pretty good.

But if it came down to it, if this thing grew into something so black and implacable that there was no way to get out from under it, then he was going to have to go after the Don. Even as he thought it he felt the rage, the stirring of the dragon, the absolute outrage that such people thought they could reach into your life and threaten to take away everything that you had and everything that you wanted. That they thought they were entitled to do that. Baby Joe didn't know for sure how much firepower he had left—if he still had enough to mock the boar in his lair, and walk away from it—but he knew that the creepy fucker would be shy a few soldiers by the time he found out.

After the little dance in the parking lot of the Crown and Anchor the Don would not be underestimating him, but there was one thing—and it might be a big thing. It might make all the difference. Not so much an ace up the sleeve but a whole deck of cards, a calculator, and a copy of fucking Hoyle. Something about the Don, about the way he moved his hands, about the way he held his head. If Baby Joe didn't know better, he'd swear the fucker was blind.

"They haf try to steal me, *ja*," Bjørn Eggen was saying, "but they focken pick wrong old man, sure. Wrong old man vith big focken dog. Focken stealers. Ve show dem. This Viking not so focken old, *ja*."

They were at the bar at the pool terrace of the Mirage. The house dick had called Baby Joe after talking to the old man. The two clowns had split before the cops and ambulance could arrive. Baby Joe had Bjørn Eggen explain everything that had happened. He didn't like it. Something was very wrong with the scenario. Poolside gardens at five-star hotels in broad daylight are not your average mugger's prime choice of venue. He looked at the old man—drinking his beer, watching the children, Behemoth lying at his feet.

"I'm sorry this happened to you," he said.

"For vhy?" replied Bjørn Eggen. "I not sorry. Best focken fon I haf in years. This one enjoy it too," he added, indicating the dog.

"Can you think of anything else, anything that they did, anything that they said, that might give me a clue?"

"Only maybe this guy Don."

"What?"

"I don't know. Some fella called Don. When I haf leave, the one with the broke nose say to the one with the bit arse that Don not going to like it."

*Shit*, thought Baby Joe, as the penny somewhat belatedly dropped. The Don had somehow made the connection between Bjørn Eggen and Monsoon and had tried to snatch him to use as insurance, to make sure that Monsoon played ball. He was almost relieved at the simplicity of the decision he had to make.

"Bjørn Eggen," he said, "Monsoon has already gone to Vietnam. I am going too. I think it will be best if you go home."

As he said it, he already knew what the old man's response would be.

"Fok that. If that no-good, useless grandson has gone der, den I go find him, *ja*? He is in trouble for sure. I vil try to help."

"Okay, then we go together. I know some more of what is going on now. I will explain everything to you on the plane."

For some reason, Baby Joe loved airport departure lounges. He always had. So, despite the circumstances, he found himself enjoying himself. He was enjoying the prospect of the flight, enjoying his drink, and enjoying immensely the fact that he had paid for Bjørn Eggen's ticket with the advance the Don had given him, using the Don's own bread to stick a spoke in his wheel. It felt like getting the first jab in, in what was sure to be a twelve-rounder.

Bjørn Eggen was on his third beer and locked in earnest conversation with a sweet little gray-haired lady next to him. You kept expecting her to whip out an apple pie from her knitting basket and start handing it round. Bjørn Eggen was busy explaining how you distinguish the lead dog in a team, and how important it was to have him at the front, and the old lady was looking at him as if she had waited her whole life to discover this piece of information.

Baby Joe was thinking about what the old bastard had said, about the oak tree. He figured it was something to do with Asia. He could try to figure it out later. In the meantime it would be behoove him to keep his mind on the job at hand. He could call her from the 'Nam, and make sure she was okay and that the locals had not used Crispin for gator bait. He heard their flight announced and nudged Bjørn Eggen, who had graduated on to the joys of ice fishing and how to stop your ass from sticking fast to the ice.

"Hey, Casanova, time to get your skinny, prehistoric butt on the plane."

"*Ja, ja.* I come vith now. This lady is Mrs. Mary Rose Muffin. She also is going to Vietnam. This is the coincidence, *ja.*"

Baby Joe smiled at the old lady, who beamed back. He had a mental image of her and Bjørn Eggen joining the mile-high club somewhere over the South China Sea. Well, it was a long flight. The old bastard might just have time to crank one up.

"We'd better go," Baby Joe said, as Bjørn Eggen offered Mrs. Mary Rose Muffin his arm and escorted her to the plane.

The 'Nam. He had never expected to go back, and the spirits were already calling to him. He expected to find it much-changed, but he knew that what was there now would only be laid over what was once there, and that underneath hotels and freeways and lights, shadow warriors still called out as they exchanged blood in streets and fields of ether and giant dream birds yet fell from the skies.

# Part 2. The 'Nam.

The Red River flows down from China, through northern Vietnam, and reaches confluence with the sea in the Gulf of Tonkin. Archaeological evidence suggests that humans settled its fertile banks almost half a million years ago. It further suggests that some of the earliest known human agricultural activity took place in its silted floodwaters, and that a distinctive culture has existed for twenty thousand years.

Vietnam is a country of spectacular natural beauty, of long sensual beaches, of verdant lush valleys, and majestic forested mountains. Of course, the lush valleys and majestic mountains are not quite as verdant and forested as they used to be, but then Agent Orange will do that.

If you include the western seaboard of the Zhanjiang peninsula across the Chinese border, start at a point near its tip across the strait from the island of Hainan, and follow a line along the coast of Vietnam, down through the Gulf of Tonkin, and around the South China Sea littoral past Ho Chi Minh City to the Mekong Delta, you will describe the approximate shape of an enormous letter S.

The S stands for the shit end of the stick, which is what the people who inhabit the region have been getting since the first Annamese prince lit a candle to his deity. The original inhabitants thought their country was a wonderful place to bring up the kids. Unfortunately for them, so did everybody else, and a whole succession of people started muscling in, including but not limited to the Hans, the Wus, the Jins, the Songs, the Suis, the Chams, and the Tangs. Not to mention the Mings, Mongols, and Manchus.

After a thousand years of feeding the Big Yellow Dragon to the North, the French bureaucrats moved in for a hundred years or so, which made all the previous occupations seem entertaining by comparison. At least the Mongols didn't bring Edith Piaf. During WWII there were some complications and the Japanese moved in for a while, but pretty soon the tricolore was gaily flapping in the oriental breeze once again.

After the Vietnamese had finally had enough of the French and persuaded them to leave at Dien Bien Phu and the frogs of Vietnam could breathe easily once again, the Domino Theory showed up and some gung-ho American politicians and top brass—who didn't actually have to go and fight, themselves, you understand—decided that a twenty-thousand-year-old civilization was in need of some real civilizing, Uncle-Sam style, and so introduced the locals to an interesting new cocktail of gasoline and palm oil, and made them listen to Beach Boys records.

After which, they got Communism and Oliver Stone. The poor little bastards just couldn't seem to catch a break. And it was about to get worse.

# Chapter 12.

Nobody knew for sure how old Woolloomooloo Wally was, especially Wally. But everybody who knew him knew that he could remember things from the before-times. The time of dreams, when things had been very different. They knew that he had the dreams, and that he knew what they meant, and that underneath his gray, grizzled curls and behind that wizened, puckered leather face, there resided profound and ancient knowledge, the wisdom of ages that heard things in the winds and saw things in the shapes of the flight of birds and took meaning from the light in the eyes of wild creatures.

They knew, too, that if you dropped him naked into the bush, a hundred miles from anywhere in any direction, and went back a year later, he would have built a village, started a herd, fathered a half a dozen kids, and painted every rock for miles around with elaborate and arcane symbols.

Wally was sitting on a junk at the mouth of the estuary of the Saigon River, surrounded by beer bottles, dogs, chickens, geese, pigs, and a multitude of dark-skinned, fuzzy-headed kids of varying ages. He wasn't really sure which were his kids, and which were his grandkids, and which ones had just wandered onto the boat. They all looked the same to him, and since he called them all son or daughter and valued them all equally, what was the difference? On the lower deck of the junk, five women in their late thirties and early forties were cooking, washing clothes, changing babies, sewing, and feeding pigs, respectively. Wally knew that one was his wife, and that the other four were her sisters, but he couldn't remember which was which. They all looked the same to him, but since he called them all Mrs. and valued them all equally, and impregnated them impartially and without preference, what was the difference?

Wally had been in three wars, and each time he had ended up fighting Asian people and, as is generally unavoidable in three wars, he had killed more than a few. But in the years between the wars, and in the intervening period since the last one, Wally had made it his duty to try to replace as many of the Asian people that he had killed as possible. Of course they weren't, strictly speaking, Asians, but they were close enough.

It was only nine o'clock in the morning, but the sun was already hot and reflecting back off the river in blinding volleys of light from the wakes of the small, motorized junks that constantly whizzed up and down. Wally's junk was moored at one end of a vast flotilla of similar vessels, all crowded with people and animals, and all with laundry waving in the breeze like the banners of some war-bent armada. Planks and rickety bamboo bridges connected the junks, and over these children raced, and people carried bundles and baskets, and some rode bicycles, and some even rode actual motor scooters, on which they zipped and zoomed over the precarious, narrow boards with nerveless and impressive skill. Over all lay an intricate and complex symphony of talking and yelling and singing, of shrill whistles, of obscure arguments that had continued unabated for decades according to some mysterious and inviolable set of rules, of bells and gongs and chimes, of the barking of dogs, the squeal of pigs, the honks and grunts and farts of a whole menagerie of creatures, bizarre and commonplace. As counterpoint was the competing blare and static of countless radios, all, by some unstated social contract or agreement, apparently tuned to different stations. And opposite, across the wide, slow-flowing muddy water, was the green line of the jungle, timeless and imponderable, like a vast, green army camped out at the very gates of the city.

Woolloomooloo Wally's skin was midnight black, so black as to make him appear almost a shadow on the deck of the boat where he squatted, finishing his breakfast beer; skin which, except for the folds over his belly, was still taut and glossy over his wiry frame. The toned muscles of a lifetime of physical toil still rolled beneath it. He wore a pair of ratty shorts that had been red at some point in their history, but which had faded over the years to an anemic pink, and an ancient T-shirt with an illegible logo and more holes than the Belfry. A green baseball cap, balanced atop the invincible mass of steel wool that he used for hair, completed his ensemble. As for footwear, no cobbler on earth could fashion a pair of shoes to fit those gnarled and scarred roots at the end of his ankles, the impenetrable, horny soles impervious to nail and thorn alike.

Wally had had a strange life, born at some undetermined time to the Ngadjonji people in the remote forests in the far north of what the Gumaring called Queensland, not far from where the Yarra had once fought with them at the place they called Butcher's Creek. Then, he had been Birring Barga. Birring had grown up living the way his people had lived since they wandered across the narrows before Australia was even a continent proper. He had hunted, and fished, and run with the animals, and learned their voices until they could speak to him of their lives, and he had listened to the stories of the dreamtime, and learned the songs of his people. He had learned to read the land, and to understand its meaning, and to respect and revere it, and to take from it what he needed and nothing more.

And one day, when he was little more than a boy by the standards of the West but already a man in the eyes of his tribe, and already a father, he had taken his woomera and his boomerang and spears, and gone walkabout. The moon became fat and then hungry again many times as he walked at right angles to the trajectory of the sun, stopping now and then to camp with people like himself, but whose languages he did not understand.

Eventually he had come to the place that the old ones had told him about, with houses made from flat trees, and machines that growled at him as they passed. Some Gumaring people had taken him, and made him sit in hot water, and given him a strange coat that was hot and stopped you from moving properly. They had given him the words of their tribe, which he remembered in case he ever had to speak to them, and they had given him a book, with little animals walking all over it, and they had made him understand that these animals, too, could speak to him. So he studied them until he understood, and the animals told him many wonderful stories of faraway places.

But the people kept making him listen to the same animals, who told him about a dead Gumaring with a hairy face who you were supposed to love without question, and about the way that you had to live, which was the only right and proper way. And in this right and proper way you had to sing boring songs all the time, and you weren't allowed to jump on any Sheilas.

So he climbed out of the window one night, and followed the river. At the end of it, he came to a place where all the people of the world all lived together in one big camp. Here buildings were made of square stones, and you could see the sea, and there was a huge bridge that you could use to climb into the sky and see the edge of the world. This was a cruel place, and he had been beaten and abused and spat upon, and so he wandered until he found the place where all the Yarra people lived together, and here he had learned about the white ones, and their machines, and about the pieces of colored paper that were so important to them that they even swapped them for food. And in time Birring Barga became Woolloomooloo Wally.

Wally did many things in those early years. He worked on the docks, and he had a job on the ferry to Manley, and one year he got work on a sheep station and all he had to do was ride around on a horse all day, mending the fences, and this was good because he was out in the bush, and when his work was finished he could go into the trees and do the old things. And the next year he went back, and they taught him to shear the sheep, and soon he could do it better than all but the very best of them. And he came back to Sydney with a lot of the colored paper that year, and he drank a lot of beer and jumped on a lot of Sheilas and went to a lot a races, where he always won because he understood the horses and knew which ones would win if the jockeys didn't interfere, until one day they chased him away. But life was still good anyway.

Then one day it said in the papers that a big war had started, and that Australia wanted all able-bodied men to join up and go overseas to fight the enemy. So Wally and some mates went, and they joined the army, where they made him wear a uniform and taught him to shoot a rifle, and they put him on a big ship, down in the hold where they stayed for days and days, pitching and rolling on the sea, and everybody being sick, except Wally, who just went to sleep. They were sent into a hot, steamy jungle, and small yellow people—like the Chinese merchants he had seen in Sydney, but much fiercer—shot at him, and so he killed a few of them.

One time he was sent with a group of white men as a scout. The white men were encircled, and they ran out of ammunition and became lost, and a lot of them died, and many more were wounded and sick. So Wally took off the stupid boots, which were heavy and noisy and no good to anyone, and he took off the sweaty, itchy uniform, and he painted his face in the old way with some white stuff that they used to clean the webbing, and he went out into the night, into the jungle, and he killed a lot of Japanese, and they never knew he was there. And then he went back to the white people and showed them the way to go back, and they followed him across a river at night, to where all the other white people were. And after, when they were back in Sydney, they gave him a lot of coins to wear on pieces of cloth, and his picture was in the paper, and smiling white people shook his hand, and nobody called him a boong, or told him to fuck off.

And after that, every time there was a war, some men in uniform would come and find Wally and ask him to go with them, to fight whoever it was that they were fighting, and Wally always went, because he liked the white people now and felt sorry for them and did not want them to get lost again.

The last war had been really bad. He had not felt the same way about it, because nobody was really sure why they were fighting, and so he had stopped fighting and opened a bar for the soldiers to drink in when they came in for R and R. He called it Wal's Outback. And when the war was lost, it did not feel like losing, and Wally was just glad that it was over. When the Americans left, he gave the bar to his Vietnamese Sheila and went home and decided that he wasn't going to fight in any more wars.

He opened a hotel in Queensland with his friend, and it was all right for a time, but he became tired of the despair and hopelessness that he saw in his people, who drank not as Wally did, because he loved the beer, but because they couldn't remember who they were and because they couldn't be Muramba anymore, and couldn't be Gumaring either. So he began to think of Vietnam, and of the mountain people they called the Montangards, in the hills, when it had been like being back in the old time, and of the good people that he had known, and how it was not like losing something but like finding something, and how easy it was to jump on the Sheilas. So when the time was right, he packed up and went back, and Wal's Outback was still there, although it was not a bar anymore. So he reopened it, and met Rodney.

Rodney could steal the wallet from your pocket and the sandwiches from your lunchbox with equal facility, and with a touch so subtle and gentle as to be barely felt. This was all the more remarkable for the fact that Rodney was only seven, and more remarkable still for the fact that Rodney was a four-ton elephant. Furthermore, Rodney was a she. Wally understood that Rodney was just naturally inquisitive and did not discourage her. Rodney and Wally made a decent living together. They did weddings and parties, and religious ceremonies, and sometimes they did shows for the tourists, and all the time Rodney's soft subtle trunk wandered, as she probed and poked and sniffed, slyly stuffing things into the little bag on her neck. When they got home, Wally would always find Rodney's sack filled with a cornucopia of goodies, some donated on purpose, and some unknowingly.

There would always be coins, and paper money, and fruit, and sweets. But there would be other things as well. Condoms, combs, mirrors, false teeth, lipsticks, cameras, wallets, handbags, tampons, purses, pens, chewing gum, pairs of knickers, lighters, keys, address books, personal organizers, CDs and cassettes, guns, photographs, one time even a frozen chicken, and once a small dog. The wallets and purses Wally always scrupulously returned, usually receiving a reward from the owner, but the rest of the artifacts he could not return because he had no way of knowing to whom they had formerly belonged, and so he considered them legitimate business revenue. He had a small stall on a street corner, attended day and night by one of his "Billy lids," where he sold the fruits of Rodney's gathering, sometimes even back to the original owner.

Wal's Outback was quite successful. The locals liked it, and Wally's kids hung around the hotels and the train station handing out flyers, and so they got a lot of tourists. Back in Australia he still had a half share in the hotel, and he knew that if he ever felt like going back, it would be there.

And so, in the sunset of his life, Wally was a happy man. His life was full and interesting. He loved his women and his kids, and his boat, and Rodney. He was still in vigorous health, with all his faculties. He had memories in abundance, enough to sustain him until it was time for the long dream, and he had enough money, and plenty of beer, and if he wanted to jump on a different Sheila every now and then, nobody minded. Life was still good.

Wally stood, scratched his balls, broke wind, shoved his empty bottle back into the crate, patted a passing kid on its head, said "Good on yer, son," waved to his Sheilas who all looked up from their tasks and gave him big smiles, trotted down the swaying gangplank, and headed down the crowded, dusty lane towards Wal's Outback.

Monsoon Parker's first evening back in the land of his birth had not been especially edifying. In fact, he had done nothing more than sit in his hotel room, smoking endless cigarettes and watching a cartoon on TV about some monkey with supernatural powers that kept switching between kung-fuing the shit out of bad guys, and turning itself into a handsome prince and trying to pork-sword the princess.

The reason that Monsoon was spending his first evening back in the land of his birth watching TV in his hotel room was that Frankie Merang, after giving him a gratuitous slap in the teeth, had handcuffed him to the bed while he and Belly Joe had gone out to pork-sword some princesses of their own. So Monsoon was laid there, under a creaking paraplegic ceiling fan that was having about as much effect on the climatic conditions as a fart in a hurricane, slowly dissolving into the pool of sweat that was rising around him, and fervently hoping that some new form of particularly virulent and incurable swamp clap was currently circulating among Ho Chi Minh City's ladies of the night.

The priapic monkey-prince was distracting Monsoon from keeping his mind on figuring out his next move, because Frankie had thoughtfully turned the TV up to full volume and placed the remote in the bathroom before moving the telephone out of reach, just in case Monsoon felt inclined to alert anyone to his distressing situation.

Monsoon had realized that it was going to be difficult to put the moves on Frankie and Belly and to give them the slip, but he had not anticipated just how difficult. They were keeping him tighter than a nun's snatch, and until tonight one of them had always been right next to him since they stepped off the plane. He had not been allowed to speak to anyone, learning this the hard way when he had attempted to speak in Vietnamese to the cab driver and Belly Joe had slugged him in the nuts. The only thing he could figure that was to his advantage, so far, was that they wouldn't be carrying any artillery. At least, not yet.

So, all he had to do was pick up a trail that had been going cold for forty years, find something that may or may not exist, con the Don into sending over a shit-load of money to pay for it, slip these cuffs, overpower two stone-cold killers who were both three times his size, steal the dough, and split. Piece of cake. One thing, though, was that they were going to have to cut him some slack with the Vietnamese lingo, or else how was he going to be able to even try to track down the hypothetically extant merchandise? That maybe could give him the opportunity to recruit some muscle of his own, and things might change. He had to figure Frankie for having thought of that, but what he couldn't see was how Frankie planned to prevent it.

He was just wrestling with this problem, and keeping one eye on the monkey-princess, who he had to admit had a pretty fair pair for a cartoon, when he heard a noise like a Kodiak bear's hoedown on the wooden stairs outside, and Frankie and Belly blundered into the room. Belly immediately came over and shoved his fingers under Monsoon's nose. They smelled like he had just wiped his ass with a dead mackerel.

"Ged a load of your sister's quim, zipperhead," he said, pleasantly.

Belly Joe went over to the wheezing fridge in the corner, took out a beer, and sat on the edge of the bed, guzzling it and smiling at Monsoon, while Frankie busied himself unwrapping a cloth-wrapped package that he had carried in with him.

Belly Joe was not named Belly Joe for his grace and agility on the parallel bars. Belly Joe was not even called Belly Joe because he was a fat, greasy, sweaty, malodorous bastard who had not been able to see his dick without standing on a mirror for twenty years. Belly Joe was known as Belly Joe because he claimed to have once dispatched a fellow inmate at Joliet by suffocating him in the showers beneath the prodigious folds of his stomach — a deed which, while greeted with considerable skepticism by the prison community, was considered sufficient in the telling to earn him the sobriquet. Belly Joe was indeed no slouch, though, when it came to shoveling away his grub, and it is reasonable to assume that, if Belly Joe had been present at the Sea of Galilee, then five fishes and a couple of loaves just wouldn't have cut it, and that unless Jesus had had a few Big Macs lying about that nobody knew about, a few ragheads would have gone hungry that day.

Knowing his friend's predilection for having his belly filled was probably part of the reason that, as Belly Joe turned to grin at him after a rafter-shaking fart, Frankie filled his belly with seven slugs from a Browning 9mm. Monsoon, manacled and helpless, looked on in horror as Belly Joe dropped like a poleaxed moose. Frankie stepped up and emptied the remainder of the clip into Belly Joe's forehead before whirling the automatic on his finger, Destry-style, and blowing the nonexistent smoke from the end of the silencer.

"This town wasn't big enough for the both of us," he said, grinning at Monsoon, who looked on with an expression that was a cocktail of equal parts terror and incomprehension, with a dash of curiosity, poured over the ice that filled his veins, severely shaken, not stirred.

"I've always wanted to say that," said Frankie, with a broad grin, flopping down on the bed next to Monsoon.

"Now, my little rinky-dink friend," he said, "let's you and I have a little discussion, shall we?"

Needless to say, Bjørn Eggen's first reaction when they stepped from the customs hall into the breathtaking heat and humidity was to look for the nearest cold beer.

"Before ve do anything, ve haf to…"

"I know," Baby Joe interrupted. "Find a beer."

"*Ja*, exactly."

Amid the cacophony of noise and the whirling kaleidoscope of color that assailed them, as they stood in the sunlit street and were immediately surrounded by a hundred importuning voices and hands, Baby Joe heard a different, familiar accent. He looked down to see a skinny, dark-skinned kid who appeared to have a scouring pad attached to the top of his head.

"Hey, mate. You want beer? Bloody cold, fair dinkum."

Bjørn Eggen heard only the word "beer," but immediately the kid had his undivided attention. "From vhere do we find the beer?"

The kid handed him a card. It read, *Wal's Outback. Karaoke Lounge and Bar. 'Tucker from down under.'*

Underneath was an address and a phone number.

"Where is this place, kid?" Baby Joe asked.

"Just around the corner, mate. Two minutes. It's me dad's place."

"Then lead on, young man, lead on," Baby Joe said, winking at Bjørn Eggen and setting off after the kid who was already skipping down the street.

They followed the boy through a sinuous maze of torturous streets, streets that looked like they had been designed by a snake on acid. Bjørn Eggen was fascinated, and watched the unfolding vista with great interest and a bemused smile on his face at finding himself on the exact opposite polarity of everything that was familiar to him: color instead of white, heat for cold, noise and clamor for serenity.

Baby Joe was feeling decidedly weird, as if he were following in the phosphorus trail of his own footsteps—when a young man with whom he shared a common name and destiny, a young man sanguine and unburdened, had stalked these same streets, or streets very much like them, a half a lifetime ago. The ghosts had gathered around him and were speaking to him a lot sooner than he had anticipated, as if they had been waiting for him for all these years.

Fifty yards in front of them, the kid stopped in front of some bamboo tables and chairs set out on the sidewalk, and into the actual road so that the traffic was obliged to navigate around them. He began to wave and skip up and down.

"Here, mate, in here," he yelled.

They passed under a painted sign upon which koalas and kangaroos were primitively rendered in garish colors, and the words "Wal's Outback" were spelled out in stick-like depictions of aboriginals striking elaborate poses, and entered the cool, dim bar.

A pretty girl in a red silk dress, with the same dark skin and wooly hair as the boy, smiled at them as they came in. "G'day, mates, howareya?" she said, extending a long elegant arm in welcome.

"Vat haf she said?" demanded Bjørn Eggen.

"She said hello."

"Vich language is this?"

"Australian."

"I haf think they are speaking English in Australia."

"They think so too," said Baby Joe, stepping up to the bar.

Like the furniture, the bar was constructed from bamboo and raffia, and behind it stood one of the ubiquitous, dark-skinned young people, this one a boy with his fuzzy curls stuffed into the confines of a felt hat with corks suspended from the brim on pieces of string.

"Nice hat, kid," said Baby Joe.

"No, it's not, it's bladdy stupid. Me dad makes me wear it."

"Is the girl at the door your sister?"

"Yeah."

"And the boy that brought us here is your brother, right?"

"Yeah, me kid brother."

"Are there any more?"

"Ah, yeah. Heaps."

"Your dad must be a busy man."

The youth grinned. "Too bladdy right, mate. What can I git ya?"

"Beers. Big and cold."

"No worries."

    The boy set two tall beers on the counter, so cold that that ice adhered to the outsides of the bottles. After three each the old man asked for the restroom, and was directed through a door and out into the bright sunshine behind the bar. Stepping into the relative gloom of the bamboo-roofed outhouse, he latched the door behind him and, kicking the commode, peered into it, making sure there were no inhabitants that might give him an unpleasant surprise, before dropping his shorts and sitting down. It was cool and peaceful in there, with the light falling in lines across his knees from the latticed door and the gentle buzzing of insects and the soporific effect of the cold beers.

Bjørn Eggen had already decided that he liked Vietnam and was enjoying himself immensely. He really liked Baby Joe, whom he thought he was a very good man, and he had enjoyed the flight over, having had a few drinks and talking with Mrs. Mary Rose Muffin. She was a very nice lady and had told him where she was staying, and he hoped he would get the opportunity to see her again once he had found his reprobate grandson.

Bjørn Eggen satisfactorily completed his enterprise and as he bent over to retrieve his shorts he became aware of a strange sound, like a leaking pipe or someone blowing their nose. He paused to listen, but the sound stopped. He was bending over again and had both hands on the waistband of his shorts when something warm and wet attached itself to his anus with a gentle sucking action. With a scream, and a dexterity that belied his years, Bjørn Eggen propelled himself bodily through the outhouse door, ripping it from its hinges and detaching whatever-it-was from his anus with an audible pop.

Baby Joe was already heading for the back door before Bjørn Eggen's yell had entirely cleared his larynx. He burst into the hot yard and saw the old man on his knees, covered in dust and straw, desperately trying to pull his shorts up over his wizened ass cheeks. He sprinted to Bjørn Eggen, helped him to his feet, and assisted him with his tangled leather braces. The old man was shaken and pale, but looked more angry than frightened.

"What happened, Bjørn Eggen?"

The old man pointed accusingly at the outhouse. "Focken arse bandit try to stab me arse in der."

The two of them peered into the outhouse, with its wrecked door, and saw nothing but the pale glow of the white commode in the shadows.

"How many beers have you had? There's nothing in there."

"Someone grab me arse in der for sure."

By now the courtyard was filling up with dark-skinned, wooly-haired kids of varying sizes and genders, and the eldest, the bartender, stepped forward.

"What's up, mate?" he said, looking concerned.

"My friend was assaulted while he was in the shithouse."

Laughter erupted among the kids.

"Vat so focken fonny?" said Bjørn Eggen, glowering at the children.

"Ah, no worries, mate. It's just Rodney," said the eldest, smiling.

"Who the fock is Rodney? Maybe I gif him the big punch in the nose, *ja*?"

"It's a big bladdy nose, mate," said the bartender. "Look."

He went to a gate in a fence immediately behind the outhouse, opened it, and whistled. Rodney came swaying into the yard, chewing a length of bamboo shoot and looking very pleased with herself. Bjørn Eggen looked appalled.

"Fock me. Focken elephant try to fock me in the arse with the focken nose, *ja*."

"If you'd have gotten that up your ass, you'd have known about it," Baby Joe said.

"*Ja*, for sure. Shame ve don't haf Crispin here, *ja*?"

The next beers were on the house, but Bjørn Eggen and Baby Joe could hardly drink them for laughing.

Monsoon was rubbing his wrists, staring at the destroyed features of what had, until recently, been Belly Joe. He had watched Frankie change the clip and shove the piece into the waistband of his pants, and then pour them both a shot of something that was supposed to be brandy, before un-cuffing him. Monsoon calculated his chances of taking Frankie as slightly less than the chances of the Clippers winning the championship any time before the sun expanded and burnt the earth to a cinder, and he was fairly certain that Frankie Merang had come to the same conclusion. This was all becoming very confusing, and while he was all in favor of Belly Joe catching a hot lead tattoo he knew it could very easily be his turn next. He decided to give Frankie his undivided attention.

"You probly curious to know why I dropped fat boy?"

Monsoon nodded.

"An' you probly curious to know why you still breathin'?"

Monsoon nodded again, a little more enthusiastically.

"Well. It's like this, see. I need ya. An' you need me. You gotta know that the Don was gonna have me bump ya, once you found the connection, or even if ya didn't. I know ya smart enough to have that figured, an' I know ya bin' busy tryin' ta figure how you was gonna give us the slip. Meantime, I bin doin' some figurin' of my own, an' it come out like this: Suppose we fix it so the Don thinks we made the deal. Now, he ain't gonna trust a putz like me with any kinda serious moolah. He's gonna send a coupla financial people, you know, bean counters. Supposin' I tell the Don I found a guy has the entire supply of the stuff that there is, and that he wants ten mill for it. Strictly cash. Ten mill is gonna sound like we cut a good deal, make the Don more likely to take the bait, and it's a nice handy number to split two ways. We get somma your slope pals on the team, and we set it up like they are the sellers. I got some samples from the Don, which we use to convince the pencil pushers that the deal is legit. Plus, and this is the kicker, I figure we need a coupla clowns to dress up like they's army personnel, an' we go through a little routine so's the money boys buy the scam. Then, when they produce the green, I waste 'em and we split the dough. You followin' me so far?"

"Yeah, Frankie. I'm with you, my man. That is a real cool plan. But how are we gonna fix it so the Don don't twig?"

"Okay. Good point. This is the most important part. The deal is, the Don didn't get to be the Don by bein' dumb. The only way this can work is if the Don thinks we are both dog meat. Otherwise they ain't never gonna be no escape. I know the Don put a tail on me. I jus' don't know yet who. That we gotta find out. When we do, we gotta make it look like we was double-crossed and iced by the slopes. And we gotta fix it so the tail sees us both go down. This guy will be one of the Don's most trusted people. He goes back, tells the Don what he seen, the Don swallows it, and you an' me are away clean an' on the next plane to Graviesville. Capisce?"

"Yeah. I'm impressed. That's smart, Frankie-boy. Real smart."

"Thanks. Now, I figure we spend a few days goin' around like we looking for the stuff. Only we ain't. We looking to flush out the tail, and set up the phony sell. The more runnin' around we do, the more chance I have to pick him up. In the meantime, I keep the Don sweet, an' figure some story to explain how come the late, lamented fat fuck ain't with us no more, an' you get a crew together to help us pull the con. An' we both keep 'em open. Wide open, baby. Right?"

"Right."

"Okay. Now you know it's in your own interest to go through with this. You speak the lingo, and now lardass ain't in a position to help, you can probably ditch me. But how far you goin' to get, and what you goin' to get out of it? 'Cos, without me, there's no do-re-mi, correct? Plus, you gotta figure the other character, who we don't know who it is yet, an' who is on our asses twenny-four-seven. I can't make the set-up without you, so you know I won't be dealin' you no seconds. The only way for us to come out of this alive and in the green is if we play it straight with each other. The fact that you ain't dead, an' he is, an' I done it in front of ya, has to tell ya that I'm on the level. So, what say we shake on it, pal?"

Monsoon was smiling as his hand disappeared into Frankie's huge ham. He was smiling because he knew he had just rolled a big seven. So, all along Frankie had been planning a carbon copy of the scam he had been planning—minus a few essential details, of course. He knew he had a few days' grace to figure things out. The tub of lard with the glazed eyes lying on the carpet had just halved his odds. He knew he couldn't outmuscle big Frankie, but he was damn sure he could outsmart him. He was damn sure Foghorn Leghorn could outsmart him. What he needed now was a place to start, and the place to start was with Woolloomooloo Wally.

# Chapter 13.

It was a contest of wills, and Handyman Harris was losing. He was doing a little research on behalf of the Don, research that involved pumping hookers for information. And one he was pumping at the moment was writhing about underneath him like a con in the chair, trying to get the job over with, while Handyman was trying to slow the proceedings down and get his money's worth. In the end he had to settle for one minute and thirty-eight seconds, and the smell of burning rubber. Handyman liked them proud, which was just as well because this one had trouble sitting upright as Handyman rolled off. As she finally made it, with a small romantic grunt, rivulets of sweat ran down her sides and formed little creases in the folds of her belly.

"Gee, that was great, hon," she said, idly evicting an errant piece of wet lint from the hole that contained her belly button. As she bent over to retrieve her capacious knickers, a wet used condom smacked into the cheek of her considerable ass.

"Hey," she yelled, "playtime's over, asshole."

"No it ain't, Miss Piggy. It's only just begun. Now sit the fuck down."

The girl studied Handyman with a professional eye. He didn't look like rough-stuff material and, anyway, wasn't built for it. Pushing fifty, small-framed and skinny, he didn't get that baggy paunch and those pipe-stem arms and spindle legs in Gold's Gym. She decided she could take him without having to resort to either the .22 or the straight razor she kept in her purse, and walked over to give him an instructional slap in the teeth with her pendulous melon breasts wobbling on her chest. She pulled up sharp as Handyman swiftly grabbed his coat and reached into the inside pocket. As the girl started to take a backward step, reaching for her purse, Handyman pulled out...an envelope.

This was getting intriguing. The girl decided to play it coy and produced the approximation of a seductive look from her limited repertoire.

"Now, that ain't no way to talk to a lady."

"You're lucky I didn't holler sooey. If you want what's in here, you betta lissen."

"I'm all ears, baby."

"No you're not. You're all ass. I need some info. You tell it right, the grand that is in here is yours."

In light of his continued personal remarks concerning her gravitationally-challenged condition, the girl was reconsidering her decision not to slap Handyman silly, but the magic word, "grand," restrained her.

"Lemme see."

Handyman zipped open the envelope, pulled out ten crisp centuries, and flipped through them like he was flipping through the pages of a book. The girl held out her fat, sweaty palm.

"Uh-uh. First the word, then the deed. W'as your name?"

"Ethel."

"Sure. And I'm Winston Churchill. How long you been around here?"

"Ten, twelve years."

"So you know the score."

"Honey, I know the score, the line, the players, their jockstrap sizes, their wives' phone numbers, and the schools their kids go to. What you wanna know?"

"You come across a tall redhead working the same beat? Good body, nice face, long, wavy, auburn hair, yea long?"

"Yeah. I seen her. I seen every piece a meat that ever got slapped on the counter round here."

"You ever talk to her?"

"Yeah. Couple a times. Nice kid. Not really cut out for the business. Too soft."

"Know her name?"

"Yeah. Anna, Aysha, somethin' like that. From some place south. French name."

"Orleans?"

"Maybe. I ain't seen her around lately."

"Lemme ax you something else. You know a fat faggot by the name of Crispin Capricorn?"

"Sure. Everybody knows him. He's a scream. An' a gentleman," she added, giving Handyman a pointed look.

"Seen him around?"

"No. Now you mention it, I ain't."

"Well, lissen, Ethyl Nitrate, this ain't much for a grand. You gonna have to do betta. Can you think of anything that she said, or mighta did, that might give you a clue to where she is?"

Ethel was thinking hard. In fact, she was doing a thousand dollars' worth of thinking. With a grand she could afford to keep her legs closed for a couple of days. That Anna was a nice kid, but whatever it was that this creep wanted her for was none of her business, and she knew better than to ask. Suddenly, trawling through the gutter of her mind, she hit pay dirt.

"Wait, I got sumthin'. I remember this one time, a few of us was hanging out. It was a cold night, and the johns was thin on the ground. We went for coffee and got to talking, and this Anna tells us how she sends a money order home to her mom, every week. I remember 'cause nobody said anything, but that was when we all knew she wouldn't last long in the business."

"Hey. That might be something. You done good, Ethel. Here."

Handyman tossed the notes onto the bed, and Ethel snatched them up. She was so busy counting them that she wasn't really listening when Handyman said, "Oh. An' here's a little sumthin' else for ya."

"Huh?" Ethel said, looking up just in time to receive a caustic blast of mace in her florid, porcine face.

"Squeal, piggy," Handyman said, as he lifted the money from the bed.

Pulling away from the curb, Handyman was feeling relieved. Working for the Don was a double-edged sword. It gave him protection in the city, and he could go about his enterprises unmolested by either side of the law, but the sword of Damocles was always hanging over him like an Italian switchblade shiv dangling on a piece of spaghetti. It was like cheap fireworks. You never knew when something was going to blow up in your face. Like, he had put the Don onto that Mick gumshoe Baby Joe Young. The Don had wanted someone to go to Vietnam, and he knew the Paddy had seen combat there. But he knew Young liked the sauce, and if he fucked up, then Handyman himself fucked up by association.

But at least, after assuring the Don that he could get it done, he had taken care of the job at hand. The Don had pointed out to him that pulling in and leaning on half the hookers in Vegas would be a time-consuming and labor-intensive affair and would be bound to attract attention. He had also said how he felt sure that Handyman, with his knowledge of the streets, so to speak, would be able to save him all that trouble, and how grateful he would be if Handyman would just do him this little favor. Well, my greasy wop friend, Handyman Harris delivers, yet again.

A phone call told him the locations of all the post offices in the immediate vicinity of where the girl lived, and he had scored on the second attempt. The guy in the post office had been most helpful. Let's hear it for the good ol' US Mail customer service. Handyman had been sympathetic. He knew how hard postal work was, and he knew how nobody appreciated postal workers, and he knew that they worked long hours for doodle-squat and had to put up with lip from every jackoff in the country with the price of a fucking stamp in his jeans. In fact, he had been so understanding of the post guy's situation that they had exchanged pieces of paper. One had a picture of a president on it and the other, the one Handyman Harris had safe in his pocket, had Mrs. Evangeline Birdshadow, 1527 Neanderthal Drive, Baton Rouge, LA, printed on it, in a neat, efficient hand.

"So vat ve do now about the grandson?"

Baby Joe and Bjørn Eggen were onto their seventh beer apiece, and neither one felt inclined to move. It had been a long, wearying flight, and, after the traumatic events of the few days prior to their departure from the States, Baby Joe was in need of a little R and R, and Bjørn Eggen never took much persuading when there was beer involved.

"Well, Bjørn Eggen, today is just about wasted. It's already nearly four o'clock, and we still have to find a different place to stay. I need to check into the Rex, but I'm not going to stay there."

"Why for so?"

"It has bad memories. The war."

"Ah, *ja*. This I understand."

The real reason he didn't want to be in the hotel the Don had booked him into was the old man. In the hotel the Don would have eyes on him, and the eyes would clock the old man for sure. Of course the Don might have put someone on their asses at the airport, or even on the plane, but unless he had employed a local, a tail round here would stick out like King Kong at a scout jamboree. He was still dreading having to give the old man the hard word about his grandson, if the news was bad, and he didn't want to worry him any more than was necessary. He had thought that if the old bastard drank enough he would want to sleep, and he would be able to go and have a scout around, but it wasn't working. The old goat was punching his weight and not showing any sign of fading in the later rounds.

"Anyway," Baby Joe continued, "the first step will be to recruit somebody local to be our mouthpiece. Then we check all the hotels and the most popular bars. Check out any back room gaming joints. Check the airport and the train station, ask around among the cab drivers. Then we can approach the government. Find the people who deal with the repatriation of remains, and see if your grandson has contacted them.

But we'll start tomorrow. One more day isn't going to make any difference, and we're both tired. I like this joint. Maybe we can eat here."

"*Ja.* Good idea. Maybe I eat dat focken Rodney, *ja?*"

Baby Joe slapped the old man on the back and went to get a menu from the waitress. The place was filling up slowly — a few backpackers, a couple of tourists, and a lot of locals. Baby Joe noticed the karaoke machine in the corner, which was, thankfully, not turned on.

"Hi. Can I have a menu, please?" he asked the girl in the red silk dress.

"Sure." She smiled, handing him one. Baby Joe smiled back. She was exotic and very pretty.

"What time does the karaoke start?"

"Ah, later on, mate, after dark. You want to sing?"

"No. I want to eat without some tone-deaf bastard murdering country and western songs in my ear."

The girl laughed. "No worries. You've got a few hours yet."

"Good. Listen. Do you know a decent hotel, within walking distance from here?"

"Yeah. For sure. Me dad's got a boarding house next door. It's cheap and very clean. Air-conditioned and everything."

"Have you got any rooms?"

"I dunno. But me dad will be back in a bit. He's been out since this morning, so he won't be long. You want me to send him over when he gets here?"

"Yes. Thanks very much."

The girl winked at him. "No worries, mate," she said.

As soon as he walked out onto the roof, the hairs went up on the back of Baby Joe's neck. They called it the Rooftop Garden now, and tourists were drinking the kind of technicolor cocktails that only people on vacation drink. Looking out over the city you could see neon and streetlights, and not mortar fire and tracers.

They could call it anything they wanted. They could call it the Garden of Fucking Eden if they wanted, but it didn't change anything. Baby Joe looked into the mirror behind the bar, and a seventeen-year-old boy gazed back at him. A boy who didn't know that you could die. A cocky manchild drinking hard liquor that they wouldn't have served him back home. Too young to drink in America, but old enough to get killed for it.

He looked around. The only uniforms now were the ones the waiters were wearing. He closed his eyes, and the ghosts of kings and pretenders past instantly invaded his brain, sweeping through the valleys of his mind and overrunning the perimeter of his consciousness. He saw the journalists and photographers. The real ones, the Tim Page guys, the ones who lived the life and walked the walk, with the shit still on their shoes; and the others, the ones who talked the talk, and walked around with eight cameras strung around their necks, and their fatigues still new and their press creds in their hats, calling themselves war correspondents. And he saw the brass and the ribbons, revved up on bourbon and bullshit, the mighty gods of war safe in their towers, behind their impregnable egos, talking too loud about kill ratios and quotas and attrition, while in the hills all around boys were dying and Charlie lurked in the treeline and stalked through the shadows, and drew close. And waited.

He opened his eyes. A group of tourists were laughing in a corner. The tigers were paper tigers now, and the dragon was asleep. He ordered a triple Laphroaig 40-year-old single malt, and a Kirin beer chaser. He viewed the bar tab with satisfaction.

*That's put a pretty decent hole in the slimy bastard's card,* he thought, as the rich peat sent his tasebuds into orgasm. He eased down onto his stool, but then caught himself. He didn't want to get too comfortable, even though he would have liked to stay. He had told the old man he would be back in a half hour, in time for dinner, but he wasn't going to commit the sin of rushing the scotch.

While he was savoring his drink and fighting to keep his mind out of the past and fixed on the immediate future, he spoke to the bartender. "Hey, man. See that table full of tourists over there?"

"Yes, sir."

"Good man. Send them over a Singapore Sling apiece, and put their dinner bill on my room tab."

"They are many, sir, it will be…" The barman hesitated.

"It will be what?"

"Excuse me, sir, but it will be very expensive."

Baby Joe grinned, a big shit-eating grin. "Right on," he said.

After Baby Joe finished his drink, he took the stairs down to the lobby and walked over to the concierge.

"How may I help you, sir?"

"Could you reserve me a first-class ticket to Cambodia for tomorrow evening, please? Open return. And then I would like a limo."

*That'll keep the meatball motherfucker guessing for a while,* he thought, as he handed his card to the concierge.

The meal was delicious. Bjørn Eggen had fish in coconut sauce, and Baby Joe had a curry, which contained pieces of meat that he hoped hadn't been recently chasing the postman. He tried some red sauce from a bowl in the center of the table.

"Jesus wept. We used to drop this stuff on the Viet Cong, during the war, and now they're feeding it to us."

"Vas bad var, *ja?*"

Baby Joe nodded. "There aren't any good ones," he said quietly.

"*Ja,* my friend, this I know. But we survive, *ja?*"

Bjørn Eggen raised his bottle, and Baby Joe did likewise. He looked at Bjørn Eggen's lined, weather-beaten countenance and tried to imagine him as a young man in uniform, tried to imagine the expression on his face as young men around him were wrenched from their lives, as he waded through noise and blood and dismemberment, to imagine him with a weapon, firing at the enemy with no light in his eyes. Somehow, he wasn't able to do it.

A shadow fell across the table and Baby Joe looked up to see a thin figure, wearing some kind of outsize Russian hat silhouetted against the overhead light.

"G'day, mates," a cheery voice said. "Reckon you two blokes need a place to kip. No worries. Got jus' the place."

As Baby Joe shaded his eyes, the dark figure sat down. The grinning features appeared timeless, with deep-set eyes sparkling in a face like ancient parchment, and a wild and wooly thatch, like Don King with a bad hair day.

"Woolloomooloo Wal's the name," he said, extending a gnarled talon. "This is me place. You blokes ready for more grog?"

"Baby Joe Young," Baby Joe said, taking the proffered hand. "Pleased to meet you. This is my good friend Bjørn Eggen."

"Nice to haf the pleasure," said Bjørn Eggen, taking Wal's aged and midnight-black hand in his own pale and veined talon.

Baby Joe watched the two old men smiling at each other and was reminded of a line from Kipling. "But there is no east and there is no west, when two strong men meet face to face, though they be from the ends of the earth," he said.

"Vat the fock you sayin now?"

"It's a poem."

"Fock the poem. Vat about the beer? *Ja?*"

Baby Joe smiled ruefully and shook his head. "Wal, can we buy you one?"

"Nah, mate," Wal grinned, "you get the next one."

Wally held up three fingers, and a girl—different from the other one, but obviously her sister—brought over three cold brews.

"So you blokes 'ere on 'oliday, or business, or what?"

Baby Joe was about to make a non-committal reply when Bjørn Eggen whipped out his increasingly frayed letter and the newspaper clipping. Baby Joe said nothing. He hadn't had the heart to tell the old man that the clipping was a fake, made up in some downtown casino souvenir shop.

Wally was taking a swallow of his beer as he reached out and took the papers. There followed a sound like the breaching of a porpoise, and Baby Joe and Bjørn Eggen were drenched in a fine, cold beer spray.

"Strewth. I don't fucken believe it."

Wally reached over to where Bjørn Eggen was wiping his face with a napkin, grabbed his hand, and began to shake it vigorously.

"Ah, mate. You dunno what this means to me. Good on yer, cobber, fucken good on yer." Wally snatched the napkin from the startled Bjørn Eggen and wiped his eyes with it.

"Vat means vat now?"

"Your son. Phil. 'E was me mate."

"You haf know Philip?"

"Is a croc's arse green? Course I fucken did. Me mate, 'e was."

"This is very queer, *ja*? Baby Joe, also, he know him."

"Ah, yeah?"

"Yeah. Not very well, but I remember him. We were on a mission together. I recognized him from a picture I saw in Bjørn Eggen's grandson's apartment."

"*Ja*, is so. I haf it here." Bjørn Eggen produced the photograph and handed it to Wally. Wally's wrinkles softened into an unfathomable faraway expression. He turned from the picture to Baby Joe.

"You were 'ere too, eh?"

"Yeah. Two tours."

"Fuck me old boots. This calls for a serious pissup. Let's go in back. I'll get you blokes a towel. Sorry, eh?"

The three walked through the bar and down a narrow corridor and into a small office, which was a masterpiece of disorder. Wally cleared them some drinking room and gave orders that they were not to be disturbed. A bottle of whisky was produced, dispatched, and replaced, and the beers kept showing up like second cousins at a will reading.

While the faint, discordant sounds of the now-commenced karaoke drifted in from the bar, they talked of friends, and fortune, and fights on foreign fields, of loss, of red pain and black terror.

They spoke of childhood, and children, and innocence sacrificed. They spoke of love and futility and, when Wally told of how he had not been there when Captain Parker had died, and how, if he had been, it would not have happened, tears were shed. Baby Joe knew at that moment that the truth must not be withheld for any reason, because these men were entitled to know, and his own honor would be forever forfeit if he did not speak. As Bjørn Eggen and Wally listened in silence he recounted with difficulty, as he fought back the tears, exactly how Phil Parker had lost his life.

The silence continued when he had finished speaking, as if a spell had been woven, a truth so sacred come into their midst that it must not be profaned by mere words, for there are things that are known and understood by men that are beyond words. Nor would any words suffice to account for the inexplicable, astounding, mournful, and beautiful weaving of the stories of their days that had brought them to that moment in that place. They, each man, separately and in unison, felt the presence of Philip Parker in the room.

When Bjørn Eggen struggled to his feet Baby Joe stood to meet him and as Bjørn Eggen embraced him Baby Joe lost his fight with the tears, and the ghost of a handsome black man smiled down upon them.

"You is focken brave man. I am knowing how hard vere these vords," Bjørn Eggen said. "Philip give his life for focken gud man. You is me focken son now, *ja*?"

"Thank you," said Baby Joe, "Thank you."

Wally was having his own struggle, and his eyelids were about to give out under the strain.

"Strewth. Will you two bludgers knock it in the fucken 'ead?" he said. "You'll 'ev me fucken bealin in a minute, ya barstads. Are we drinkin grog 'ere or what?"

And as the whiskey went down, they pulled from their memories the songs of their fathers, and more tears were shed. And later, as they spoke of their women, and their dogs, Wally went out into the yard and fetched Rodney. She stood outside the office, rumbling deep in her ribs and drinking beer through the window, lifting the bottles in her trunk and pouring them down her throat, and Bjørn Eggen kissed her and forgave her for grabbing his ass. And as the three staggered out into the morning light and headed for Wally's junk, half-blind and happy, with their arms around each other's shoulders, they were strangers no more.

Frankie and Monsoon were having a sociable breakfast together—a breakfast consisting of a bottle of vicious swamp whiskey and a packet of Russian cigarettes whose tobacco kept spilling out of the tube. Just for good form's sake, Monsoon had a cup of coffee, which had obviously been dredged instead of filtered. Monsoon had just finished explaining how he had set up the people who were needed to play soldier, when two clean-cut young men in their late twenties approached the table.

"Ciao, fellas," one of them said, with a big smile.

Frankie looked at Monsoon. "You betta not tell me that these two pansies are it."

The young man's smile evaporated.

Monsoon stood up. "He don't mean it, guys. He's just joshin', ain't ya, Frankie? Sit down, boys. What can I get you?"

The two men sat down, pulling their chairs as far away as possible from Frankie, and ordered Campari and sodas.

"So, guys," Monsoon said, pleasantly, "you want to run through it again, so's Frankie can hear?"

The two men both started to speak at once, stopped, looked at each other; both started to speak at once again, stopped again, and giggled.

"For fuck's sake," Frankie growled.

They stopped giggling. One nodded to the other, who said, "Okay. We make sure the uniforms fit. If not, we take care of it this afternoon. The office is ready, and I've got the keys. We meet you there at ten tomorrow. I'm the captain, he's the lieutenant. When you arrive with the other men, we give you all the documents to sign, and the flag, and explain all the travel and customs arrangements. Then I make a speech and say how wonderful it is, and how proud you should be and how grateful your country is, etc."

"Okay, boys, good. I'll give you the rest of the cash tomorrow."

"Oh, goody. We really need it. We heard about this most wonderful cultural site that we simply must go and see, and we want…"

"Who gives a fuck what you want, miss," interrupted Frankie. "Just don't screw up, or else the only sight you are going to see is the sight of a fuckin' slope doctor askin' ya where it hurts."

"Yes, well. Erm …we'd best be getting along. Nice meeting you, Mr., er…"

"Mr. fuckin' Ed."

Smiling feebly, the two men waved and walked away.

"Shit, Frankie, you didn't have to scare 'em to death."

"How the fuck is anyone goin' to buy those two faggots as the fuckin' military, Monsoon? We need Sergeant Rock, an' you get the fuckin' Village People."

"They'll do good, Frankie. They're actors, over here on vacation."

"They betta do good, or you fuckin' won't."

Crispin looked and felt ridiculous. He had been compelled to stuff himself into some outrageous country bumpkin dungarees that made him look like a gigantic blue salami, and to confine his luscious curls under a hat that resembled an inverted douche bag. Furthermore he was hot, humiliated, sweaty, and uncomfortable, and the entire insect population of Louisiana was lining up to bite him on the ass. He had a rash in an unmentionable place, an upset stomach, his feet had swollen up, and he hadn't had a shower since he got here, having being forced instead to endure the demeaning ordeal of squishing himself into a zinc tub that had obviously been designed by a dwarf, while Asia's giggling sisters poured frigid water over him from a plastic bucket, and heaven-knows-what horrific waterborne organisms insinuated themselves into his orifices.

He was sitting on the levee with Asia, which she apparently found enchanting, with the grass scratching his bug-bitten ankles, trying to block out the incessant and insane buzzing of insects and the racket from the tinny and out-of-tune piano that some inept hayseed was pounding on in the bar across the street. Even the fat full moon, which he usually found so romantic, and which here, in the hot humid night, appeared to be twice its usual size, seemed to be leering down at him, mocking him with a greasy yellow grin. And now the silly bitch proposed to make him get into a tiny boat, manned by a disreputable crew of gibbering inbreeds, and sail around in a fetid swamp populated by God-knows-what bloodsucking creatures, in order to "hunt gators." The only alligator skins Crispin was remotely interested in had "Bally" and "Size 9" printed on the soles, and he would rather stick bamboo shoots under his fingernails than brave the wilderness in an obviously unseaworthy vessel full of foul-smelling rabble. But the alternative was to remain behind on his own, which was unthinkable. Who knew what perverted and homicidal brigands lurked in the darkness?

Crispin decided the only reasonable solution was a solution of gin and vermouth, and proceeded to anesthetize himself with a pint of the blue paraffin that was served as gin in the honky tonk across the street. When Asia informed the clientele that Crispin was a performer they importuned him to play a few songs, but he declined on the basis that his Zydeco repertoire was somewhat limited. However, when one unhinged-looking individual—who appeared to have some form of deceased quadruped hanging from his belt—helpfully suggested that he didn't have to play if he didn't want to, but he didn't have to spend the next six months walking round in a truss if he didn't want to either, Crispin obliged them with a rendition of some Dr. John songs, which went a long way towards raising his standing in the community. Drinks were on the house from then on. By the time a smoking, clattering pickup truck—which looked as if it had served as a troop transport in the War of 1812—clanked to a halt outside the bar, Crispin's trepidation about the forthcoming excursion into the depths of the moonlit bayou had entirely dissipated.

The front seat of the truck was occupied by the driver—who appeared to be all of twelve and who had, for reasons fathomable only to himself, elected to smear his face with half a pint of used motor oil—and a fat woman sucking on an unlit cigar and squeezing a big stone jug between her thighs like a giant ceramic dildo. She smiled when she saw Asia, revealing a set of gums devoid of anything that could be said to resemble a tooth, unless you counted the one discolored corn-stripper protruding from her lower jaw, just about in line with the large hairy mole on her chin.

"Hey, dollface," the woman screeched, "how the hell y'all bin? Get yo' narrow ass in here, child."

"Hi, Irene. Hey, Nate. This is my friend from Vegas, Crispin."

Nate rearranged the oil smears on his face, which was presumably intended as some form of greeting, while Irene proffered the jug. "Yanta get yo' gums round this boy?"

Back in his natural habitat, Crispin would have called in the exterminators to have the jug sprayed before even looking at it. Now he was so far gone into despair and confusion, so far removed from anything that he recognized as his life, that he reached out robotically for the jug, hefted it, and sucked back. The experience was similar to what he imagined an unanaesthetized tonsillectomy followed by a jalapeño gargle would feel like.

As he was trying to recover his breath, Nate addressed him. "Moon be damn near straight up. Might be y'all wanna haul it over the tailgate, boy, so's we kin get the ball to rollin.'"

"What language is this?" Crispin wheezed, peering at Asia's watery image through tear-filled eyes.

"Nate wants you to sit in the back. Hey, boys, how y'all's doin' back there?"

Grunts and mutterings greeted Asia's remark, emanating from the huddled figures perched in darkness in the back of the flatbed. Crispin handed the jug back to Irene, who nestled it back into the folds of her crotch and assisted Asia into the cab. Crispin walked around to the back and waited for the tailgate to be lowered, standing there in some confusion when that event did not occur. His dilemma was solved when two pairs of immensely strong hands grabbed him by the straps of his dungarees and hauled him in, depositing him in an undignified heap on the bare steel floor with his nose about three inches away from the wrinkled anus of the large bloodhound who was sound asleep in the back. Three silent, unshaven men dressed in cutoff jeans and T-shirts and sporting more firepower than a SWAT team, regarded him with some curiosity. Crispin could see the light from the bar glinting on the blades of hunting knifes and on the barrels of shotguns and rifles.

Asia banged on the roof and shouted out of the open window, "This here's my buddy Crispin, boys."

"What time's the revolution start, fellas?" Crispin said, struggling into a sitting position, but his feeble attempt at camaraderie was drowned out by the grating of gears and his companions disappeared in a cloud of white smoke.

They drove into the hot night, with fireflies winking in the undergrowth and the river appearing and disappearing as flashes of silver between the moss-festooned branches of the trees. Fortified by the jug circulating among his anonymous confederates Crispin stoically endured the bouncing and banging of the truck, which threatened to undo twenty grand's worth of cosmetic dentistry as they rattled over rutted backcountry roads, until they pulled up next to a broad expanse of still water, glowing pale under a majestic moon hanging in the cloudless night.

As soon as the rattletrap truck creaked to a halt, and before the sound of the engine had echoed into silence over the flat water, the three men had leapt over the side and were heading towards a low jetty extending out over the lagoon. The dog raised its concertina jowls, peered at Crispin with a bloodshot eye, cocked its leg, pissed on him, and bounded over the tailgate.

Crispin regarded the spreading stain on his leg and uttered a deep, heartfelt sigh. "Oh well," he said to himself, "at least it can't possibly get any worse."

Asia's smile rose like the morning sun over the side of the truck. "Hey, Crispin. Guess what?" she said, repressing a giggle. "Irene thinks you're really cute."

"Oh, for fuck's sake," Crispin said, burying his face in his hands.

An hour later, Asia was still teasing him as they sat on a blanket by the edge of the water, listening to the symphony of frogs, the whine of mosquitos, and the regular slaps of Crispin's beefy palms as he tried to prevent himself from being exsanguinated. They had the jug between them and had managed to unburden it of a fair proportion of its contents since the men had disappeared into the darkness in two small skiffs.

"I really don't see how we are going to capture any crocodiles sitting here," sniffed Crispin, who was beginning to experience difficulty distinguishing the fireflies from the stars.

"They ain't crocodiles, they's gators. An' we only come to watch the truck."

This wasn't strictly true, as they had originally been invited on the expedition until Nate had calculated that his skiff was not up to the task of containing both Crispin and Irene. And since it was suspected that Crispin could neither navigate, bale, shoot, skin a gator, nor suck off the other members of the hunting party if things got slow, Irene got the nod. Crispin would have been outraged had he known. Of course he couldn't bale, navigate, shoot, or skin gators, but…!

"I wish you wouldn't talk like that, either. You sound like you're on the Grand Ole Opry."

"I can't help it. When I get among the folks down home it just happens. Anyway, stop trying to change the subject."

"What subject?"

"Irene."

"My dear, Irene is not a subject, she's an object. Not only is she a woman, which in itself is inexcusable, but she has a mouth like a malfunctioning garbage disposal, a face like a perforated hemorrhoid, and, if she has a g-spot at all, it would have to be on her fucking face.

Furthermore, she smells like rancid sheep dip and has the cognitive power of an aardvark."

"So you're not interested, then?"

"Asia. Let me tell you something. In the course of my illustrious career I have had only one encounter with a person of the female persuasion, which was, needless to say, an unmitigated and embarrassing fiasco. If I were to ever attempt a repeat performance, which would have to be at gunpoint, I assure you it would not be with..."

Crispin's next words were drowned out by the sound of a loud explosion coming from the trees behind them. Crispin felt a pull on his arm as if someone was tugging at his sleeve, and jumped as something splashed into the water in front of him. Two more explosions followed, and whatever had pulled at his sleeve now ran hot fingers through his hair. Confusion was replaced by fear and amazement as he realized what was happening.

"Those redneck assholes are shooting at us!" he said.

Asia was not there. She was already slamming the door of the truck closed behind her, and Crispin began to squeal in terror as the smoke from the starting motor washed over him and the wheels began to roll. Earth spattered his face as Asia spun the truck round in a tight circle, so that it was between him and the source of the gunfire. Three more shots rang out, dinging into the driver's side door as she screamed at him to get in. In a total panic, Crispin wobbled to his feet, slipped, fell headlong, struggled up again, and clambered into the cabin, panting like a hot dog.

As Asia gunned the engine the windshield came out with a bright, metallic glitter, and one of the headlights popped. Feeling the wind in her face, she pressed the pedal to the floor and was headed for the gap in the trees that marked the beginning of the track when she felt the sudden heaviness in the steering that told her one of the front tires had been hit. Struggling to control the leaden vehicle on the soft earth, she saw a flash of white in the remaining headlight, and realized that a car had been parked sideways across the track. Asia aimed for the car's front fender and plowed forward. Crispin's door was still swinging open, and it slammed shut as the heavy truck crumpled the car's front panels and propelled it from the road. Crispin—who was in shock and carefully brushing pieces of glass from his lap as if the cause were nothing more serious than a spilled drink—was thrown backwards onto Asia, preventing her from steering. She was yelling at him to move when another set of headlights directly in front suddenly burst to life, blinding her. She instinctively swerved, saw an oncoming tree, tried to swerve again, heard a deafening noise, and was briefly aware of a flying sensation before the bright lights around her were extinguished.

When she came to, someone was playing with her tits. She tried to sit up, but heavy hands restrained her. Looking up she saw a pair of hairy balls and a hand stroking a semi-erect penis and felt her jeans being tugged over her feet. She screamed and began to struggle, but someone kicked her in the stomach, knocking the wind from her. She lay still, trying to catch her breath. Crispin was slumped in the door of the truck with blood dripping from a gash over his forehead.

"May as well have some fun with this before it gets cold," someone said.

Asia felt a hand trying to invade her, and pressed her thighs together. She heard laughter.

"Oh. She's worried she ain't gonna get paid. You gonna pay, ain't ya, Joey?"

"Sure. I'm gonna give her a pounda flesh."

More laughter. The one who had been playing with himself had managed to attain a serviceable erection and he knelt between Asia's thighs, trying to force them open with his knees. She could smell the booze on his breath and see his leering, pockmarked face. Two hands were still reaching over her shoulders and roughly massaging her breasts, and the one kneeling over her slapped these hands away and then slapped her hard across the face, twice. Backhand and forehand.

When she opened her eyes, his expression had changed from lascivious to surprised. He had his hands on his shirtfront as if he had suddenly discovered that he had spilled something on his tie. The man looked inquiringly at Asia, as if expecting her to explain the red flower that had mysteriously appeared and begun to grow across his chest. Asia felt herself released and she brought her knees up and kicked the man viciously in the nose with both feet, sending him toppling backwards.

Just then an impromptu fireworks display began, and a bright cannonade erupted from the nearby tree line, painting the night white and orange. Asia rolled over in the cool grass into the lee of a tree trunk as men began to run and fall around her with odd, jerky movements, illuminated intermittently by the strobe lights of the gunshots.

The banging and flashes abruptly stopped and the blackness and silence rushed in to take their place. Asia lay still, the after-glare of the gunfire descending like blue flares across her pupils, straining her ears to pick up the shuffling and scraping noises she could hear. She heard the unmistakable sound of shell cases being dumped out of a cylinder, and then a woman's voice.

"Asia. Asia, hon. Y'all okay?"

"Irene. Yeah, I'm all right. I'm over here."

A torch beam found her, and she tried to cover her nakedness with her hands. The beam remained steady.

"Kill that flashlight, you asshole," she heard Irene say.

The light blinked out and Irene came waddling over, carrying a blanket in one hand and a smoking .45 in the other. Nate followed accompanied by the bloodhound, who immediately tried to shove his snout into Asia's beaver.

Nate booted him up the ass. "Yodel, cut that out fo ah whupp yo ass, y'hear?"

If Yodel heard, he didn't say anything. The three other men gathered around, also holding smoking weapons. Irene handed her the blanket. It smelled like a bear's outhouse.

"Here," said Irene, "cover them jugs with this for these un's here get to droolin'. It's okay. Yodel don't need it for a while anyway. Y'all hurt?"

"No. Couple of bumps and bruises, but I'm okay. What about Crispin?"

"Oh, he's fine. Bit of a knot on the haid, but he'll live."

"Thank God. I think I went through the windscreen. Lucky the glass was already out. And lucky you all came back. They were going to…"

"We know," said Nate. "We saw. An' t'weren't no luck, neither."

"What do you mean?"

"I mean, we picked them fellas up just after we left town. Rolled behind us with no lights. Figured they's the law, or else after the truck maybe. We dint wanna say nuthin case y'all wuz frit. Anyways, we lef' the boats in yonder grove and doubled back. Soon as we seen the gunfire we let 'er rip. Dropped all them fellas."

"I don't know what to say. I don't know how to thank you."

"Thanks, shit," said one of the men. "Hell, girl, that was more fun'n a turkey shoot."

"Jus' like the good ol' days back in the 'Nam, when y'all could shoot anyone y'ant to, an' wouldn't nobody say nuthin to ya," said another.

"Hell, yes," said the third. "Anyways, we dint see no gators nohow. Who the hell are these assholes, anyway?"

"I don't know who they are. But I know who sent them. And I know he'll send more. We'll have to go away."

"Shit, if all them sumbitches'r dumb as these here, they can send all they want."

"Yeah. Me'n the boys'll take care a y'all, missy."

"No. Thanks anyway. But we'll have to leave. What about the police? What shall we do?"

"Sheriff don't like to come this far out lessen he's fishin'. 'Sides, paperwork'd seriously piss him off. We just push them vehicles into the swamp and let the gators take care a this carrion here."

"Where y'all thinking 'bout goin?" Irene asked.

"I don't know. I really don't. But I've got a friend. Baby Joe. He's in Vietnam now. I'll call him and tell him what happened. He will know what to do. He always knows what to do."

Asia and Irene attended to the stricken Crispin while Nate and the others patched up the truck and changed the tire. By flashlight they carefully collected all the weapons and the spent shell cases. Two of the men went to fetch the boats while the others stripped the three bodies, and an hour later the corpses were gator bait, slowly settling into the sediment at the bottom of the river. The men drove the two cars to a remote section of the swamp and pushed them into the water, waiting until the last of the bubbles had disappeared before painstakingly erasing any tire marks and walking back to where Nate, Irene, Asia, Crispin, and Yodel waited by the pickup. As they set off they heard a splashing, away in the distance, and Yodel leapt over the side of the slow-moving truck and went baying off into the bayou. Nate retrieved him with a long, piercing whistle and gave him another boot up the ass to help him back into the truck. By midnight, they were all sitting back in the bar on the levee.

Asia took Crispin off to a side table and sat him down. He had not spoken since the incident and looked pale and sad and tired, and utterly defeated.

"Crispin, we have to leave. First thing in the morning. We can't stay. I have no idea how they found us, but they did. And if they can find us here, then where can we go that's safe? I have to call Baby Joe. He's the only one I trust and the only one who will know what to do. Okay?"

Crispin nodded, and Asia started to get up to rejoin the others. Crispin laid his fat hand on her arm. Quietly he said, "Asia?"

"Yes?"

"Wherever Baby Joe tells you to go, promise me that I can go, too."

Asia turned back and put her arms around Crispin's bowed shoulders. She kissed him on his fat cheek.

"Of course," she said.

## Chapter 14.

Monsoon Parker was badly shocked. He was badly shocked for three reasons. One reason was that whoever had done the wiring in the shithouse at Wal's Outback had not done a very good job and, when Monsoon had flicked the light switch while standing in a pool of misaimed urine, he had gotten quite a jolt. The second reason was that when the light eventually flickered into existence, it revealed not row upon row of shiny silver packets, but a whitewashed wall. The third reason was that as he had stepped, cursing, into the sunlight, he had seen his grandfather wobbling out of the door.

The first item on the agenda, once he had reached his gentleman's agreement with Frankie Merang and had been allowed a little fighting room, had been to discover if his perhaps-delusionary hopes concerning the existence of the king's ransom's worth of mind-altering chemical substance in Wally's outhouse were substantiated. Electric shocks, plaster, and grandfathers did not come under the category of delusionary hope. However, as shocked as he was Monsoon had had the presence of mind to duck down out of view—although given Bjørn Eggen's condition it is doubtful that he would have noticed Monsoon if Monsoon had been riding a fluorescent orange Mardi Gras float with an ostrich on his head and a pineapple up his ass.

Monsoon recognized Wally, although he looked much older than his photo. Actually, he looked much older than the Declaration of Independence. The other guy seemed vaguely familiar, but he couldn't place him. Monsoon decided that he was now officially seriously confused.

Monsoon had arrived via an ancient Peugeot taxi, its circa-1950 engine busily contributing to the miasma of toxic lung soup that served the locals as air. He had decided to be incognito until after he checked out the outhouse, so he was wearing a pair of unobtrusively obtrusive Bootsy Collins shades and a Rasta wig, which was threatening to implode his skull at any moment in the outrageous heat and humidity. A rivulet of sweat, resembling a small but significant tributary of the Amazon, was roiling down the back of his neck, soaking his shirt and shorts both. A pair of airport-bought leather Jesus boots completed his ensemble.

Pulling up outside Wal's Outback he had bidden the driver wait, slipped gratefully into the cool interior, and ordered a beer and back. The beer had been scintillatingly cold and, despite his anxiety to get to the head, he had savored it. He had gobbled the whisky, ordered the same again, asked about the outhouse, and strode breathlessly towards the back.

What he was seeing conformed—allowing for a little modification here and there—to the images in the somewhat-soggy photos in his top pocket, and a rising tide of hope flushed him into the bathroom, only for harsh reality to abruptly terminate its flow with AC/DC and plaster. After recovering somewhat from the shock he was confronted by a wall daubed with standard-issue barroom bathroom graffiti, unremarkable except for one especially well-executed drawing of an improbable sexual position accompanied by the legend of what Mo the Schmo could do to himself.

As Monsoon stared at the wall and its messages, meaningless and infinitely significant at the same time, attempting to deal with the volcanic surge of disappointment and despair that was welling up from his intestines and threatening to make him nauseous, he saw a glimmer of hope. Literally. The plasterwork had obviously been done by the same guy that did the wiring. A section at the top left corner was unevenly covered, and the faintest glimmer showed between the cracks. Monsoon spat on his finger and rubbed at the crack. It didn't tell him much either way.

Earlier, he had made a few calls and had tracked down a sister of his mother's. He had given her some bullshit about his roots and his birthright and his father and his mother's grave, and she had swallowed it and was sending some cousin to pick him up that evening. He would return like the prodigal bum, and ingratiate himself back into the bosom of his family in case he needed to pull a Houdini. Later, he would recruit some muscle from his family and come back and open the wall. He went back to the bar, downed his drinks, and had one foot in the stark, glaring street when he saw The Three Lushketeers come bobbing and weaving out of a back room.

"What the fuck?" was the question that came immediately to mind. Other questions followed hot on its heels. What was the old man doing here, how had he gotten away from the Don, how had he found Wal's Outback, did it mean the money was here, what was the connection between the old man and Woolloomooloo Wally, did they know each other, what else did the old man know about, what had he told Wally about him, what was he going to do now? Etc., etc.

In the absence of a better idea he was on the point of shouting his grandfather's name, when a venerable oriental proverb leapt into his mind. When the way is not clear, do nothing. He skulked back over to the waiting cab and told the driver to keep Baby Joe, Bjørn Eggen, and Wally in sight, trailing them until he saw them stagger precariously up the swaying gangplank of an old junk. Across the street was a small café. Monsoon cut the cab driver loose and sidled into its dim interior for a drink and a think. He decided to stake out the boat for a while and see what developed.

He pondered the permutations, complications, and consequences of the sudden and unexpected appearance of his grandfather. He searched for his conscience, but decided he must have left it on the plane. Nobody had ever really given a fuck about him, so why should he care about some old duffer that he barely knew? He took a seat by a small, flyspecked window, ordered a bottle of what professed to be vodka but turned out to be crank oil, and eyeballed the boat. Taking a drag from his cigarette, he studied the junk through the smoke.

It had more animals on it than Noah's Ark, and looked to be around the same vintage, and how many kids did that old bastard have? There was this fucking tribe of them, swarming all over the boat like pirates with afros. He watched as they all gathered at the foot of the gangplank with their wild hair waving in the breeze, looking like a field of giant black dandelions, with one of the older ones addressing them and pointing. Then, as if a sudden big wind had dispersed them, they all scattered and went racing off in every direction.

Monsoon leaned forward to sip his crank oil, and then sat back into the shadows. As the crank oil, which he was beginning to get a taste for, slowly went down, he formulated his plan, rather more practical than scintillating in this case. He would buttonhole Wally on his own and give him the spiel. He would tell him that he had a big surprise planned for his grandfather, and decoy everybody away from Wal's Outback. Then, with the help of his cousin, he would open the outhouse wall and take it from there.

Wally had appeared at the top of the gangplank with his grandfather and that other guy. Again Monsoon searched the backrooms of his memory for something to hang onto him, a name or an incident, but it would not come. The guy looked dangerous, though, kind of compact and contained, like a cocked hammer. As Monsoon watched the three men shook hands, and the guy helped his grandfather down the swaying plank. They waved back up at Wally and flagged a cab. As they climbed in the guy looked directly at the window that Monsoon was looking out of, and Monsoon shuffled further back, deeper into the gloom. As the cab pulled away he watched Wally scratch his belly, pat one of the dogs on the head, and disappear back into the boat.

Waiting until the taxi was gone, Monsoon chugged the crank oil, took a drag from his cigarette, and flicked it, still burning, into the street. As he stepped onto the gangplank, some kid picked up the cigarette and walked away, smoking it.

The Don was seriously, seriously pissed off, and Stratosphere and Liberty knew it. The reason that Stratosphere and Liberty knew that the Don was seriously, seriously pissed off was because the Don was saying, "*Gli idioti. Che ho fatto per meritare questo. Sono circondato dall'imbecilles. Catso. Vaffanculo stronzo!*" and waving his arms about like an Italian.

And the only time the normally imperturbable Don waved his arms about like an Italian and said, "*Gli idioti. Che ho fatto per meritare questo. Sono circondato dall'imbecilles. Catso. Vaffanculo stronzo!*" was when he was seriously, seriously pissed off.

The man sitting opposite Don Imbroglio was terrified in direct proportion to the Don's pissed-offedness. And not only was the man terrified, he was wounded. He had a patch over one eye, a bandage around his throat, one arm in a cast, and a dressing on the left side of his head where his ear had formerly been attached. Oh, and a fat lip.

Except for this latter, the wounds he displayed were a result of being caught up, two days earlier, in a gunfight with a crew of psychotic, moonshine-soaked rednecks in an alligator-infested swamp. The fat lip was a result of Stratosphere punching him in the mouth, two minutes earlier.

The Don strode from the room onto his balcony, and when he returned he had stopped waving his arms about like an Italian and had resumed his customary, reasonable, dulcet English tone, which caused the man to become even more terrified than previously.

"So, what you would have me believe is that I sent four well-armed men to dispense with an overweight, middle-aged, homosexual lounge singer and a novice prostitute, and not only are three of these men dead, but I am missing two expensive vehicles, and the overweight, middle-aged, homosexual lounge singer and the novice prostitute are not only still alive, but have disappeared, after I went through a great deal of trouble and expense to find them in the first place."

"I'm sorry, Don Imbroglio."

"I imagine you are. Explain to me again how you think that might have happened."

"Well. Me an' the boys went down there, just like you said. We made the marks, and then laid low till nighttime. We see them goin' off in some truck, so we follow and they head out into the sticks, which we figure will be a good place to take care of 'em. Then it looks like things are working out real good, cuz the people that they're with leave them two alone, saving us the trouble of offing the others. Anyway, Joey gets a little anxious, and lets fly too soon. They hop into their wheels, and try to make a break for it, but we put a few rounds into the truck, and the broad runs it into a tree, so we got them, see? Then just as we're just about to do the deed, these hicks start blazing away from the trees. They nail everybody except me, although they wing me pretty good in a coupla spots. I'm down but not out, so I crawl away into the water, and hide under some trees. While I'm sitting tight there, is when I hear the broad say sumthin about this guy Baby Joe, and him knowin' what to do, and something about Vietnam. Anyway, soon as they pull out I walk back the nearest town, boost a set of wheels, and get back here as soon as I can, to tell you."

"I see. And what conclusions do you draw from all this?"

"I figure it was a setup, Don Imbroglio. The way these guys collected the cases, and stripped our guys, I figure them to know what they're doin', whereas they wouldn't if they was just a bunch a hicks."

The Don considered what had been said in silence. The man could feel the days of his life being weighed in the balance. Sweat ran down his face and when the Don spoke he could barely hear the words for the pounding of his heart.

"How long to you expect to be incapacitated?"

"Inca-what?"

The Don sighed. "How long before you will be well enough to be of some use?"

"Oh, I'm ready now, Don Imbroglio. This ain't nothing. I can…"

"That won't be necessary. Go home, and stay by your telephone." The Don dismissed the man with an abrupt flick of the wrist, and Liberty wrenched him from his seat and propelled him towards the door.

"Bring the other two incompetents."

Stratosphere manhandled Poxy Purdy and Bender into the room and compelled them into a kneeling position by main force.

"Do you know," asked the Don, "how much they charge to clean carpets these days?"

Poxy managed a whimper but Bender, who was apparently suffering from an attack of St. Vitus Dance, contented himself with quivering uncontrollably.

"Quite obviously you do not. But if you did, you would realize that it is only the exorbitant cost of stain removal that prevents me from having my associates here splatter the sheep offal that serves you for brains all over the room. Let me ask you an easier question. How is it that, between the two of you, you were not able to overpower and subdue an ancient man with one foot in the grave?"

"There wuz a dog, Don Imbroglio, a really big dog. It bit me in the—"

"The nature of your wounds are of no concern to me whatsoever. My only regret is that it was not your puerile head that was removed. What became of your conqueror?"

"I don't know anyone by that name, Don Imbroglio."

The Don sighed again, deeply this time. "What happened to the old man?"

"Er, well, we dunno, Don Imbroglio. After I got my heinie stitched, we went back to the Mirage, but the old geezer checked out."

The Don decided that he did not owe humanity the favor of removing these two halfwits from the gene pool and motioned for their removal. He pondered that he had, in his rage, almost extinguished more inconsequential lives, but it was a question of simple economy. He was getting short-staffed. This drug nonsense was getting entirely out of hand. It had seemed such a simple and risk-free affair, and now it was not only infringing upon his other activities, and threatening to undermine his credibility, but it was seriously depleting his workforce. And it wasn't like he could just put an ad in the Revue Journal: "Wanted. Stone-faced assassins. Unsociable hours. Previous homicides an advantage."

Radical measures were required. He was going to have to recruit from outside, which he was loath to do. And now there was apparently a further complication. He had quickly sensed that Mr. Young was not the beer-soaked Irish donkey that he appeared, but this latest development was unexpected and not a little suspicious. Our boy from Boston had coolly accepted a commission, while simultaneously and knowingly assisting the quarry. That would explain the efficient demise of the late-and-not-lamented Maxie Grimmstein. *What game are you playing, Mr. Young? Well, whatever it is, you are about to get a suspension. A very long suspension.* The ringing of the phone interrupted the Don's thoughts.

"It's overseas, boss. Vietnam."

"Mr. Merang, I presume?"

"No, boss, some foreign guy. One of them."

Curious, Don Imbroglio held out his hand for the receiver.

Baby Joe had felt better. A school of salmon were spawning in the pit of his stomach, and the bears that were chasing them were trying to burrow in through the back of his head. Somebody important must have died, because every time one of the kids ran past on the deck overhead a twenty-one-gun salute went off in the roof of his skull. Bjørn Eggen, on the other hand, looked and felt ridiculously good, as if he had spent the previous day and night drinking milk and honey instead of rotgut whisky and piss-barrel beer. Furthermore, he was being distressingly cheerful as they sat, cross-legged, on the large raffia mat on which they had lain throughout the night in an alcohol-induced coma, attracting the attention of every mosquito, midge, gadfly, and cockroach between there and the Cambodian border. One of the kids had bounced into the cabin and deposited in front of them a large bowl of coffee and two elongate brown objects, oozing grease, which looked like the fried scrapings from the bottom of Rodney's paddock. A bite confirmed Baby Joe's suspicions and he tossed it through the adjacent porthole, half expecting it to come flying back in.

"I vould haf eaten that. Is not good to vaste food, *ja*."

"Oh, I agree. Wasting fricasseed elephant turds is a different matter."

The mat that served as a doorway to the tiny cabin flapped open, and Wally's woolly noggin poked through. He wore his habitual piratical grin, and if he was feeling even the slightest effect of the previous day's excesses there was nothing in either his appearance or manner to betray it.

"G'day, mates. Sleep all right? Bangin didn't keep you awake I 'ope," he added, with a salacious wink.

"*Ja, ja.* I haf very gud the sleep. Dream about me son."

"What about you, cobber? Jeez, you look rough. Eyes like piss holes in the snow, mate."

"You should see them from my side. How much did we fucking drink?"

Wally pushed through the matting and sat next to them. "Heaps, mate. Fucken plenty. Hair of the dog's what yer need."

"I think you might be right."

"Vat dog is this? I very much like to see the dog."

"No, Bjørn Eggen, it's just an expression."

"I see, *ja*," Bjørn Eggen said, not seeing at all.

"Come on, then. 'Ands off cocks and on socks. Let's go up top and I'll get somethin to fix you blokes up."

They followed Wally up onto the already-hot deck. The sun stood at about eleven o'clock, and Baby Joe calculated that they had slept for about four hours, if that. Wally appeared with a case of Foster's lager. Tossing one to each man in turn he cracked his own with a loud hiss and stuck it to his mouth, where it appeared to adhere to his lips by force of suction. He swallowed loudly, his pronounced Adam's apple bobbing in stark relief, as if some small creature scurried beneath the skin.

He finished his beer, opened another, and said, "Good on yer, mates. Crack a bladdy tube. She'll be right."

Baby Joe regarded his tin with suspicion, wondering if his churning stomach could accommodate it. He watched Bjørn Eggen, who entertained no such reservations, empty his tinny and reach for another.

Baby Joe took the plunge, sucked down a deep draught, and instantaneously felt better.

"I bin thinkin 'bout what you blokes were telling me yesterday. I reckon I'll round up a few of me Billy lids, and send 'em out on a recce, so to speak. Don't reckon it'll take too long to bring this grandson fella to heel. What do ya reckon?"

"That would be a great help, Wally. Thanks."

"Ah, no worries. I'd go meself only I got a show to put on with Rodney in an hour. What about if we meet up at the bar, say six, for a couple of sundowners."

"Last time was the sun-uppers, *ja?*"

"Too right, mate," Wally said, clinking tins with Bjørn Eggen.

A fuzzy head popped up at the top of the stairs leading down into the bowels of the junk. "Hey, dad, there's a Sheila on the phone wants to speak to Baby Joe," the boy said, before disappearing back down the hatch.

Baby Joe jumped up and followed the kid. It could only be Asia. After speaking to Wally he had called her and told her where he would be staying, in case she had tried to call the hotel where they were originally booked and been worried not to find them. He had been trying to keep her out of his mind and, given how emotive his return to the 'Nam had been, had expected it to be easier.

Putting the still-warm receiver to his ear, he could tell she was upset before she even spoke, as if her fear was somehow transmitting itself down the line.

"Asia?"

"Oh, Baby Joe."

Her voice broke down, and Baby Joe murmured to her, soothing her, giving her time to gather herself. He listened to the quiet sobbing.

"Asia, are you hurt?" he said, finally.

"No, no, I'm all right. I'm just so very frightened. They tried to kill us."

"Who did?" he asked, already knowing, and already feeling the long black veil descending behind his eyes.

"I don't know, some men. We were out in the bayou. They followed us. There was a big fight. The people I was with killed them."

"How many?"

"Three."

Why the fuck would the Don send three men to blow away a young girl and a singer? He should have thought it through better. He should have known it wasn't far enough away. It had been stupid to think the Don wouldn't find them. What had he been thinking?

"What about Crispin?"

"He's all right, but he's badly shaken up. He hardly speaks. He got a nasty cut over his eye that we had to stitch, and they shot two holes in his pompadour."

Baby Joe laughed. He couldn't help it.

"It's not funny."

"I know. Forgive me. I'm sorry. Where are you now?"

"I'm at a bar, close to where my mother lives. I'm worried about her too, now, and my family. I want to leave. It's not safe here, it's not safe anywhere."

Asia broke down again, and Baby Joe let her cry. Listening to her weeping, he made himself a promise. He promised himself he was going to cut that pompous little greaseball fucker's heart out and piss into the hole.

"Asia, stop crying. What do you want to do?"

"I want to be where you are. I want to come there."

Baby Joe's serious-error-of-judgment alarm went off, and rang long and hard. This was not right. Everything about it was wrong. There was no provision in his plans for this scenario. He was too close already, and he knew it. This was when you made mistakes. If you got involved, you couldn't see clearly. Sooner or later you would make a bad call, a professional decision on an emotional basis, and that would be it. Walking a fucking tightrope, on ice skates. There was absolutely no way he could do what he needed to do, either for her or for himself, if he had her to worry about. It was a distraction he didn't need. How could he watch his ass, if he were continually watching hers?

He pushed the mouthpiece closer to his lips and said, "Okay."

"I knew that's what you would say. Crispin wants to come, too."

*Oh, well, bring the dog then, bring your mother, bring a couple of friends, bring Larry, Curly, and Moe, bring Uncle Tom and his fucking cabin.*

"All right," he said.

"Are you sure? You don't sound it."

"How do I sound?"

"You sound angry."

He had tried to keep it out of his voice. He was angry, but not with her. With himself. It was a bonehead play, and there was no way to see it other than as it was.

"I'm not angry," he lied, "I'm just concerned. Tell me exactly what happened, right from the beginning. Give me as much information as you can remember."

Baby Joe concentrated as she spoke, watching the changing images in his mind like an action replay, assuming the different roles, asking himself questions and answering them. When she had finished, he said, "Is there anything else that you can remember? Some detail that you left out that you didn't think was important, but that might be?"

"No. That's everything I remember. It happened so fast. And I was scared."

"I know, baby. I know. So there were no survivors, and no witnesses other than your friends?"

"No."

"You're sure."

"I'm sure."

"Okay. Listen to me. Leave there now. Tonight. Don't worry about your family. The Don will send somebody to find out what happened, but will figure on you being smart enough to have left. Send your mother and sisters to stay with friends for a few days, just in case. Make all your arrangements, and call me at this number. If I'm not here, leave a message with whoever answers the phone. They all speak English. I'll be at the airport to meet you. Put the phone down now, and do as I told you."

"Baby Joe…"

"Yes?"

"Baby Joe, I…"

"Asia, tell me when you get here, okay? Don't worry, it will be all right. Now get going. I'll see you soon."

"Okay. Bye."

Baby Joe walked slowly back up to the deck, to where Bjørn Eggen and Wally were laughing. His face was bleak. He was thinking about Asia lying naked with those men's hands on her. He was thinking about Don Ignacio Imbroglio. They looked up as Baby Joe's shadow fell across them.

"All right, Blue?" Wally said.

"Yeah."

"Vas Asia, *ja*?" Bjørn Eggen wanted to know.

"Yeah. She's coming out."

"Here. Something has happen?"

"Yeah."

"I tell you, my friend."

"I know."

"You got trouble, mate?"

"It's all right."

"No, it ain't. It may as well be painted on yer kisser in big fucken letters. I seen too much agro not to know it when I see it starin me in the bladdy mush."

"You're right, Wally. But I don't want to get you involved."

"Listen, mate. This old barstad 'ere was Phil Parker's dad. I owe it to Phil's memory to lend an 'and, if I can. If you don't wanna tell me, it's all right. If you wanna tell me it's none a me fucken business, fair dinkum, that's all right, too. But let me tell ya somethin'. When you put yer 'and in Woollomooloo Wally's 'and, that means yer 'is mate. An' if yer 'is mate, your trouble is 'is trouble. Okay?"

Baby Joe smiled. "Okay, Wally. Thanks."

"No worries. Now let me go an' sort these little barstads out. What are you two blokes gonna do?"

"We'll go and have a scout round ourselves. We'll be back at the bar about six."

Wally nodded, tossed his can into the boat, and let out an unearthly cackling sound. Fuzzy heads immediately began to materialize from every corner.

Wally grinned. "Me fucken kookaburra impression," he said.

With the sun almost directly overhead, Bjørn Eggen and Baby Joe walked down an alley divided into equal sections of light and darkness by the ruler edge of black shadow that ran along its center. A gaggle of silent children followed a few paces behind them, stopping when they stopped and proceeding when they moved on. Baby Joe was following the directions on a map, a mental map etched so dimly on the fabric of his brain that he struggled to recall its true contours.

"I know it's around here somewhere," Baby Joe said.

He paused, looking around him, half in sun and half in shadow, bisected by the sun line into some kind of harlequin, a dweller between night and day. One of the older children detached himself from the group and approached, smiling shyly.

"America," he said.

Baby Joe smiled and nodded. "America."

"Me Hung."

"Congratulations."

"Me can very good the America."

"Good man."

"You lose you fren."

"What did you say, son?"

"You look you fren. Crazy man." The boy drew circles around his temple with his finger and crossed his eyes.

"Yeah. You know where he lives?"

"Sure. You wrong street. You follow."

Hung walked towards the open end of the alley with Bjørn Eggen and Baby Joe behind, followed at a few paces by the silent posse of solemn children. Just before the intersection with the street another passage intersected with the alley, a passage so narrow that Baby Joe could easily touch both sides with his outstretched hands.

Hung stopped at the foot of a bamboo ladder that was propped against an opened second-story window and pointed up. "You fren here."

"Sure?"

"Sure."

Watched by his silent audience, Baby Joe climbed the frail ladder until his face was level with the window. He could hear wind chimes and guitars.

"Hazy?" he shouted. "Hazy Doyle?"

"Hey, baby."

Baby Joe looked down at Bjørn Eggen and Hung and gave them the thumbs up. "Bjørn Eggen, this ladder is not too steady. Can you make it?"

Bjørn Eggen gave him an impatient look and waved him on.

Baby Joe climbed through the window, and it was like climbing through a time portal into another world. He stepped into a chamber decorated with moons and stars and rainbows, reverse swastikas, astrological signs and runic symbols, crudely painted nudes in various acts of copulation, all rendered in psychedelic colors, underneath a painted parachute canopy which was suspended from the ceiling, forming a kind of Bedouin tent. On one wall was daubed a huge peace sign, and next to it a faded life-size poster of Jimi Hendrix and painted slogans adorned the adjacent walls, applied at random in various hands. Make Love Not War. Keep On Truckin'. Here Come the Judge. Burn Baby Burn. An old stereo was set on a low table, surrounded by actual albums scattered on the floor around it and stacked up in uneven piles. *The White Album, Electric Ladyland, Ogden's Nut Gone Flake, Abraxus, Joe's Garage, Mad Dogs and Englishmen, Goats Head Soup…*

Baby Joe recognized the voice of Janis singing "Ball and Chain." In one corner, a huge brass Buddha glowed in the light from the myriad-colored candles that surrounded it. In front of it, leaning back against it, sat the person Baby Joe had sought out.

Hazy Doyle was busy rolling an enormous joint, carefully crumbling the leaves and spreading them evenly on the paper, and he did not look up from his task when Baby Joe climbed in through his window.

"Hey, man. All right. Park it, baby."

Baby Joe simply smiled and sat down. Hazy continued with his rolling, concentrating, intently peering through his round wire-rimmed glasses. Nor was he distracted when Bjørn Eggen maneuvered somewhat stiffly over the windowsill and into the room.

"Hazy, this is my friend Bjørn Eggen."

Hazy paused, and looked over the top of his spectacles at the surprised Bjørn Eggen. He was wearing a green silk sarong, and over his bare and narrow chest a scarlet Sergeant Pepper-looking military dress tunic with braid and silver buttons, at least two sizes too small, so that his thin arms with their protruding veins stuck out up to the elbows. A headband with pictures of the Road Runner and Wile E. Coyote contained his long gray tresses, and something shone above it, as if he wore some kind of metallic skullcap, like a Hassidic robot. Hazy smiled at the old man and made the peace sign, but did not speak.

Bjørn Eggen did not know what to say and sat in the window, bemused, looking from Hazy to Baby Joe and back to Hazy.

"So how have you been, man?"

Hazy lit his joint, and disappeared behind a billowing smoke screen. His hand appeared from the midst of the smoke, proffering the joint to Baby Joe, who declined.

"Oh, you know, man. Shinin' it on and kickin' back. Keepin' the faith, man, makin' sure the flame stays lit."

Although almost a quarter of a century had elapsed since they had seen each other, Hazy addressed Baby Joe matter-of-factly, as if he had just been out for cigarettes, as if strangers and shades from the past climbing unannounced through his window were an event so commonplace as to not require acknowledgment or comment, as if he lived with such apparitions as a permanent part of his consciousness, so that people coming thus was no surprise, because they were never gone.

"That's good, man. You feel okay? You need anything?"

"All you need is love, man."

Baby Joe regarded his friend. It was like addressing a hologram. As if he could wave his hand right through the image that appeared to be Hazy without disturbing it. Reaching out and touching Hazy on the shoulder, Baby Joe removed an envelope from his inside pocket and placed it by Hazy's foot. "Here you go, bro. We have to go. I'll stop by later."

Hazy looked at the package, and then at Baby Joe. He smiled, looking into Baby Joe's eyes, but Baby Joe knew he was seeing something else. "Okay. Later, man."

At the bottom of the ladder, the children maintained their silent vigil. Baby Joe handed Hung a twenty-dollar bill. "Don't forget your buddies," he said.

Hung stood to attention and saluted. "Me no forget. Thank you, America."

The kids formed into a circle with the twenty-dollar bill at its center, regarding it with reverence as Baby Joe and Bjørn Eggen headed for the street at the end of the alley.

"Who the fock is that?" said Bjørn Eggen, wishing to be polite but unable to contain his curiosity further.

"He's a guy from the war. He lost it. After he got fucked up they shipped him home, but he couldn't handle the States anymore. He went to Thailand and later, when things changed, he came back here. A few of us send money, to the mission here. To keep him going. He was like our company talisman. A lot of people started dying after he got hit."

Bjørn Eggen said nothing, and they walked in silence to the junction and flagged a cab.

# MACHINE GUN JELLY

"He saved my life," Baby Joe said, opening the door for Bjørn Eggen.

In the absence of the kids, the junk was strangely quiet. Somewhere below a woman was keening a sad song in a high, quavering voice, and from the bow Monsoon heard a rhythmic whacking noise as he clambered up the gangplank. Ducking under a clothesline he saw on the deck below him a row of drying fish glittering in the sun, and next to them a woman who appeared to have an inverted lampshade on her head, repeatedly raising something gelatinous and slimy and smacking it onto the sun-baked wood. He was about to call out to her when he was distracted by a commotion in the shadows between the stacked rows of chicken cages in the stern of the boat. He became aware of a sudden pungent odor, a new ingredient added to the rich olfactory broth emanating from the boat, and an improbably large ginger cat with one ear missing ghosted across the beam in front of him. Something huge flapped into the periphery of his vision, causing him to duck, and he looked up to see a fat goose settling into the complicated tracery of the rigging.

He heard a peculiar snuffling sound and, simultaneously, something resembling a cross between an animated grass skirt and a Rastafarian bear emerged from behind a bale of cloth and began to advance towards him. Monsoon had to assume it was a dog, or possibly a small, ill-kempt buffalo, and stepped back in alarm, at which point he tripped over the large, black and white sow that was standing behind him rooting for insects in the seams between the planks, hitting his head on the deck with a loud crack and momentarily stunning himself. Only his Rasta wig saved him from completely concussing himself. He was immediately brought back to full consciousness by a wet rasping sensation on his face and a forceful intrusion into his groin, as if he were being molested by something large and unpleasant that was trying to decide whether to eat him or fuck him. The creature-presumed-to-be-a-dog had bounded over and was licking his face, wafting him with breath like a skunk's jockstrap, while the sow rooted happily in his trouser pocket. Grabbing the pig's ear in one hand, and a clump of the dog's matted fur in the other, he thrust both animals away and struggled to a sitting position, which was the moment the goose in the rigging chose to void the runny and pungent contents of its bowels down the front of his Hawaiian shirt. The creature-presumed-to-be-a-dog turned its attention to the fallen Rasta wig, which it began to favor sexually with considerable enthusiasm.

Just then an object sailed over his shoulder and smacked the pig on the rump, sending it galloping down the deck, squealing. Monsoon heard soft steps and a stern voice sent the dog retreating back behind the bale.

"See ye'v met me mates."

Monsoon looked up into a face like a laughing walnut.

"Mr. Woolloomooloo, I guess," Monsoon said, trying unsuccessfully to muster some dignity.

"Ya guess right, mate," said Wally, holding out his hand and hauling Monsoon to his feet. "An' who might you be?"

"I'm Monsoon Parker. Captain Parker's son." He took the proffered hand.

"Strewth, the prodigal fucken grandson!" Wally exclaimed, dropping Monsoon back onto the deck.


The five faces, averted and unseen under the traffic cone hats, were smiling, and shrill giggles tinkled in the hot air. Monsoon struggled to keep the folds of his skimpy towel together, while Wally's wife and her four sisters, whichever was which, simultaneously laundered his soiled clothes and attended to the throbbing swelling on the back of his head.

Wally squatted on the deck in front of him nursing a beer, saying, "No worries, mate. They've seen bigger shrimps than that on me barbie."

Wally continued to regard the discomfited Monsoon. "Strewth. 'Ere I 'ave alf me bladdy tribe scourin the city for yer, an' yer stroll right onta me fucken boat."

"Yeah. Coincidence, huh?"

"Too right, mate. Wait till Bjørn Eggen gets back."

"Who?"

"Your bladdy granddad, yer dill. 'E'll be as 'appy as a dipshit in a dirt box. 'Ow in the name of Ned Kelly's mare's galloping minge did ya end up 'ere?"

Monsoon was presented with a quandary. He did not know how much Bjørn Eggen had revealed. His decided to do what he did best and lie through his teeth, and so contrived his features into a perfect expression of pathos and sincerity. He considered a slight quiver of the lips, but decided not to go overboard even though it was one of his best effects.

"Mr. Woolloomooloo," he said, with just the faintest trace of a quaver in his voice, "this has been a very emotional time for me. Things have not been going very well for me just lately, to say the least. I got to the point where I didn't know what to do. I was fucked. I had nowhere to turn, and nobody to turn to. Then, I got the news about my father. As you know, I never had the chance to know him, but at least it gave me some direction, some purpose. As I was going through his old case, trying to find out anything I could, I found this."

Monsoon reached down to where the contents of his pockets were piled on the deck next to him, produced the letter from Captain Parker, and handed it to Wally. He watched as the other man read, his lips moving ever so slightly. Then the man gave him a weird, painful-looking smile.

"Scuse me a sec, son," he said, and rose lightly and walked away.

Monsoon Parker mentally heard the sound of fishing line whizzing off a reel. *Hook, line, and fucking sinker,* he thought.

After a few moments, the old man came back, carrying a bottle. "Sorry, mate," he said, "but it ain't true."

"What's not true?" Monsoon said, too quickly, suddenly not so sure of himself.

"It's not true that time 'eals all wounds, mate. Some wounds never 'eal. Yer old man was me best mate. A top bladdy bloke in every respect, and I still miss 'im. Yer done right comin 'ere, son. Shit, yer even look like one o' me tribe. Get yer chops round this." Wally handed Monsoon the bottle. It had no label. Monsoon could not personally attest to the flavor of wombat piss, but he was fairly convinced that it must be similar to what the bottle contained.

Wally began to talk to Monsoon at length, of his father and of the way it had been. It was clear from Wally's intonation that Monsoon was not expected to contribute to the conversation in any way other than to listen. The shadows grew long, and Wally's reminiscences grew longer. Monsoon recognized that he was at a key point in the game and concealed his boredom behind his best display of rapt interest, while simultaneously figuring how quickly he could get away from this senile buffoon and get the fuck off this pestilent, pox-ridden ark full of diseased animals before his grandfather showed up again.

"'E was a top bloke, yer old man, a top bladdy bloke," Wally was saying, for the fiftieth time. "'Ow d'ya say ya managed to dig 'im up again?"

"Oh, you know, man. DNA. Seems some rebuilding was taking place in Hue, and some American bones were found. The military was called in to investigate. I got a letter from the Pentagon."

"Is that right?"

"Yeah. Anyway, lissen, Wally, I'm sorry, but I gotta split. People to see. You know. When's the old man back?"

"We're meetin at the bar at six. 'Ere's me card with the address. You want me to send someone to pick yer up?"

"Er, no. I'd like to surprise him. What's the best restaurant?"

"Yer mean the poshest, or the one with the best tucker?"

"The best tucker," said Monsoon, wondering if a tucker was some kind of a burger.

"Ah, yeah, well, apart from me own, a course, that'd be the Perfume River Prawn Palace. Fucken delicious yabbies."

"Great. Well, do you think maybe we could all go there tonight? On me, of course. Say about ten. I could just walk in and surprise him."

"Ah, yeah, dinkum idea."

"Good, then. Oh, lissen, before I split. Do you know anything about Machine Gun Jelly?"

"Yeah, I 'ear it's real good on shrimp. What the fuck are ya talkin' about?"

"Never mind, it was just a thought. Well, gotta go." Monsoon retrieved his still-damp clothes and slipped into them as discreetly as he could.

Wally stood upright. "Don'cha wanna finish yer beer before yer go?"

"No thanks. I'm in kind of a rush. I'll have one with you tonight."

"Fair enough. See yer, mate."

"Yeah, see ya."

Wally watched Monsoon as he walked down the jetty and climbed into a taxi. Something was wrong. Some flaw in the weave, a bum note somewhere. Wally didn't like him. Wally was a skilled reader of people, able to interpret the aura each carried and to quickly find the essence of a person and establish a rapport. But with this man something was missing, and it disturbed him. He was the son of his old friend, the grandson of his new friend, and Wally would have liked to have been his friend too, but there was something that just wasn't there. And something else. He was lying through his fucking teeth.

Wally leaned on the boat rail, watching Monsoon's cab pull out into the traffic. Machine Gun fucken Jelly. There was something queer in the woodpile here, and no mistake. And it must have been a hell of an explosion that killed Captain Philip Parker, if they found his bones in Hue. Phil Parker had been killed in Cambodia.

# Chapter 15.

Ten o'clock became eleven, then midnight, and the clock continued its relentless progression, but of Monsoon Parker there was neither hide nor hair to be seen. The old man had lapsed into silence, and his dinner lay cold and untouched before him.

At one o'clock, he said, "I do not think so my grandson vill be to coming this night. I am a little tired-feeling from yesterday. Maybe I vill to sleeping be going, *ja*."

Wally summoned one of his kids and instructed him to take Bjørn Eggen home to his room. The old man smiled a sad smile as he bade them goodnight.

"Poor old bastard," Baby Joe uttered, watching the suddenly frail-looking old man shuffling from the room.

"Something's up, mate," Wally said, when he had gone. "I dint wanna say nothin in front a Bjørn Eggen, but that grandson's a bladdy lying mongrel."

"How do you figure that out?"

"Well, first off, when I tells 'im 'is granddad's 'ere, 'e don't seem surprised. Like 'e already knew. Then, when I asked 'im about 'is dad, 'e tells me some 'orseshit about Phil bein found outside Hue. Which is fucken strange, seein as 'ow 'e was killed in Cambodia. Then 'e asks me about Machine Gun Jelly."

"About what?"

"Machine Gun Jelly. Only an 'andful of people would 'ave 'eard of it. I was attached to a Lurp unit, as a scout, and we come in from a walk in the bush an' sucked back a few tubes. Anyway, these blokes decide to break into this compound to piss the army off. They come out with this shitload of something they called Machine Gun Jelly. Nobody knows what the fuck it is. Turns out to be some kinda drug. I never 'ad no use for the stuff meself, though I 'ear it was pretty fucken 'ot shit. Anyway, these Lurp blokes go back a coupla days later, to try an' get more, and the whole fucken compound's been torched by an air strike. The Lurps was off on a mission, so they left the stuff with me. Only, they never came back, see. I gave one to me mate Phil, knowin 'e was partial to the old Bob 'Ope. The bricks were covered in 'eavy duty silver foil, and an 'andy size, so I used the rest of 'em for building me shithouse. Never thought about it again till now, when all of a sudden Phil's son shows up askin' about it."

"This is starting to make sense."

"You could have bladdy fooled me, mate."

Baby Joe considered for a second, and came to a decision. "Okay, listen, Wal, I think it's time you knew the full story."

Baby Joe carefully explained everything that had happened: Asia, Crispin, the Don, Monsoon, the dead people, the whole shooting match. When he had finished Wally went quiet, staring into space with a solemn expression that made him look even more ancient than he was. Baby Joe studied his face: an old god, fixed in contemplation of the foolishness of man.

"I should've said something sooner. The truth is, I'm not really sure what I'm doing. The old man doesn't know everything, and I'm trying to keep him from knowing the worst of it, but it's going to come out. There won't be any way to avoid it."

"No worries, mate. Yer doin the right thing. Good on yer," Wally said, looking at him.

It was Baby Joe's turn to look away. He stared down into his glass.

"I'm struggling to get my brain around it, Wally," he said. "Phil, Bjørn Eggen, that shithouse, Monsoon, the connection, the coincidence. It's just too fucking weird for words. I feel fucking haunted, there is no other way to describe it. Haunted and fucking responsible."

"For what, Blue?"

"I'm just thinking that if, back then, I hadn't been so gung-ho to go, if I would have said 'fuck that shit, I ain't going,' then maybe Phil Parker wouldn't have gone either."

"Now yer talkin out yer fucken arse, ya bludger. It was a fucken war, mate. You can try an' analyse it till the fucken cows come 'ome, but it don't make no difference. Some people come 'ome, and some don't. That's all it is, mate."

Baby Joe smiled at him. "Yeah, Wal. You're right. I know."

"Too right. That was then and this is fucken now. So wadda we gonna do about this can o' fucken worms? 'Ow can I 'elp?"

"Wally, you can help best by forgetting the whole thing. I told you I don't want you to get involved. Bjørn Eggen and I will move on tomorrow."

"My arse ya will, yer barstad. I don't want to 'ear any more o' that shit. Now 'ow can I 'elp?"

Baby Joe shrugged. "All right, then. You can start by getting the beers in. Then, I need to find out more about this Machine Gun Jelly. I have a friend here I can see who might know something. Then I need you to keep an eye on Bjørn Eggen for a day or so. And I'm going to need somewhere to put Asia and Crispin. Somewhere out of the way."

"No worries, mate. Leave it to Wally."

"Wal. You know this might get nasty."

"Then you'll need yer Uncle Wal to watch yer arse, won't yer, yer fucken nong?" said Wally, grinning and waving to his son behind the bar.

It may have looked like dinner to the other people seated around the table, but to Monsoon it looked like the aftermath of a particularly nasty freeway pileup involving multiple dismemberments and at least one thorough cranial debridgement. Platters of unidentifiable animal parts, impaled fish, and various species of amputated birds' feet, together with suspicious soupçons full of seething liquids, were spread among bowls of steaming rice and little packets of pastry, glazed in garish colors. Closest to him was a pig's head, which kept staring at him, possibly in an attempt to elicit sympathy for its condition. Unfortunately for the pig's head, Monsoon's reserves of sympathy were entirely reserved for himself.

He had cramps in his feet from sitting under the long, low table, and some ancient fucker kept wafting smoke about and banging on a big gong every time somebody said anything. Despite having unwittingly disregarded or infringed upon every known rule of Vietnamese etiquette Monsoon was doing his level best to be polite and sociable, but he was just about sociable'd out and his face was aching from the constant grinning.

He had quickly realized that his Vietnamese wasn't so much rusty as congealed, with the result that the conversation was making about as much sense to him as a Polish dyslexic. There were representatives of at least four generations around the table, to whom he was presumably related in some fashion, including the venerable old lady at the far end who was so far gone that her food had to be spooned between her gums and her jaw manually worked up and down by the youth sitting next to her.

The only one he actually recognized was his mother's sister, who was sitting next to him being relentlessly polite. He got the impression that for all their hospitality, he was making them feel uncomfortable. He thought about his old man's letter. Maybe he had been right.

He turned to his auntie and asked her in fractured Vietnamese if she could remember any English.

"Sure," she replied brightly. "I like speak English. We long time no see you? Why you no come see family?"

"America's a long way away."

His auntie considered this while studying his face, and he had the weird and discomforting sensation of looking at his mother.

"No so far," she said. "You go see mother?"

"You mean the grave? No. I don't know how to find it."

"Must go. Very important. You come me, tomorrow. I show you. Pay respect. She wait long time."

Thinking that he didn't have time for this superstitious bullshit, Monsoon reluctantly agreed to meet his aunt. Then he said, "I need to do some business while I'm here. Do you know somebody who can help me?"

"What kind business?" His aunt said, looking at him in a way that told him she knew exactly what kind of business.

"I just need some help with some local stuff."

"Sure. No problem. You cousin. I send tomorrow after you go see mother."

"Is he a good man?"

"You no worry. Very good man. Very clever. Whatever you want, he can do. Now no more business. Now eat."

Monsoon's aunt reached over and handed him a dish of suicide pie.

Take a picture of this. A Shau Valley. Operation Texas Star. The worst both-barrels, full-tilt boogie, shitstorm of terrifying insanity you can possibly imagine. Two determined, committed, well-equipped modern armies with their tail feathers up, going head to head for an ultimately meaningless piece of jungle real estate in some abandoned corner of Southeast Asia. Fifty mills, claymores, napalm, M14s, mortars, shells landing according to Chaos Theory turned mean, random geographic grid patterns turning healthy young men into soup. Phantoms zipping overhead like enraged hornets on steroids. Fire and heat, the stench of burning flesh, impenetrable smoke, abject and bowel-moving petrifaction, adrenaline-rush madness, shotgun, grenade, switchblade, hunting knife, stick and stone, eyeball-to-eyeball visceral death struggle.

Baby Joe Young, seventeen years old, lied about his age to hustle himself into the uniform in which he now lies bleeding from a multitude of shrapnel wounds, some of which still sear and smoke in his flesh. The light, otherworldly and eerie, rotors chugging and churning overhead in seeming slow motion, shadows flitting at the periphery of his vision. Baby Joe in pain, and maybe dying.

And then, through the mist of smoke and hot breath and fine blood spray a man walks, upright and calm, making no attempt to protect himself or even acknowledging the carnage around him. A strange light glows around him, an aura, like a translucent shield that no bullet or malicious intent can pierce. He walks towards Baby Joe at a dreaming pace, lifts him to his feet, drapes him across his shoulder, and carries him unhindered, unchallenged, and unharmed, through Armageddon and down the hill to the medevac.

He is Jack "Hazy" Doyle, so mesmerically and invincibly stoned out of his stack on acid, marijuana, reds, greens, blues, and purple bombers, that he is not actually aware of the battle that is in progress around him, other than as a psychedelic backdrop to the Spanish guitar music that plays in his head. He floats on his unassailable island of tranquility — serene, majestic, and wise,the Prince of Peace wandering through his enchanted kingdom of light and color in his shimmering cloak of hummingbird feathers and python scales. For Hazy it is midnight at the oasis on Cloud Nine, somewhere over the rainbow, and as he lifts the stricken and frightened Baby Joe to his shoulder, tenderly wiping the blood from his ruined lip, he smiles beatifically and says, "Far out, man."

Monsoon sat in the back room of the Pearl River Cabaret sucking on a noxious black stogie while having his own noxious blackish stogie sucked on by a seventeen-year-old Cambodian hostess. At least, she said she was seventeen. The fact that her teeth were on the bench next to his glass of industrial ether masquerading as vodka gave Monsoon cause to doubt the veracity of her calculations. Not that he gave a galloping fuck. He was too busy enjoying the experience to be concerned, thinking pleasantly that the girl could probably suck the lips off a bull moose.

Monsoon was killing time, waiting for the local muscle that his auntie had promised to organize for him. The meet was set for noon and he had a half-hour to spare, so he thought he might as well get his wick trimmed in the meantime. He closed his eyes so as not to let the bundle of jellied chicken feet that was suspended from a coat hanger in front of his face distract him from the erotic image of a foursome with Destiny's Child that he was trying to conjure up to coincide with his ejaculation.

He was approaching the vinegar strokes when someone tapped him on the shoulder. He opened his eyes to see some kind of bonsai Sasquatch staring intently at him with yellow eyes.

"Eyeyoucussin," it said.

"Say what now?" said Monsoon, as Destiny's Child abruptly left the stage.

"Eyeyoucussin," it repeated.

Monsoon tapped the Cambodian hostess on the top of her head, which was still moving rhythmically up and down. She stopped.

"Listen, Tokyo Rose, ask this yeti what it wants, and then tell it to fuck off back to Nepal."

The hostess addressed the newcomer politely, and then nodded sagely. "He say he you cousin. He name Ung. He say mama-san send him help you."

"Oh, yeah, well, tell him he's early, and that he can help me by getting the fuck out of my face till I finish shootin' my load in yours, baby."

"No me finish," she said. "This one interrupt big time. No can work like this. It unprofessional." She stood up abruptly, grabbed her teeth, and flounced out, leaving Monsoon scrabbling with his fly as he stared at her round retreating rear, mentally reminding himself never to pay up front again.

The Sasquatch stood, impassively staring. Monsoon examined him. He stood about four feet tall and was approximately as wide. Dense hair covered his body and, beginning from just above where his eyebrows would have been, thick, oily coils dangled almost to his waist. His tresses appeared to have pieces of bone woven into them. His arms and legs were knotted like hawsers, and he had the biggest hands that Monsoon had ever seen. Monsoon didn't know whether to offer it a drink or throw it a bone.

"Man," he said, "you is one unsightly-lookin' motherfucker. How the fuck can you be my cousin?"

"Eyeyoucussin," it said.

"For fuck's sake," said Monsoon, downing his vodka. Gesturing at the Sasquatch to follow him, he strode out of the back room into the noisy bar. The Sasquatch followed with surprising grace.

*Looks like, on this side of the family, my family tree is a real fucking tree,* thought Monsoon as the clamor of the streets engulfed them.

The guns have been silenced on that killing floor for almost forty years, but Hazy Doyle remembers it as if it were yesterday. He remembers that day, and many days like it. It's just the present that old Hazy has a problem with. He has been fixed in place and time, like a photographer's image on celluloid, locked into a permanent sixties groove, an endlessly repeating loop of reruns and recorded highlights that flickers to a stop in '69 and starts all over again from the beginning. A part of Hazy will forever remain on some foreign field...the part being the two-ounce lump of his brain which was scalloped out of his head by a rebounding piece of shrapnel and deposited neatly on top of a pile of fresh buffalo shit in a the bottom of a mud-filled paddy in the Mekong Delta.

Having survived, Hazy was a classic case about whom people always say, "He was lucky."

If he had been lucky, he wouldn't have been smacked in the back of the crust by a flying splinter of hot steel. If he had been lucky, he would have been in the back row of some fleapit in Charleston, SC, with his index finger embedded in the pudenda of the local homecoming queen and her tongue thrust halfway down the back of his throat instead of in some mosquito-infested swamp in Vietnam with a sizable portion of a full-strength NVA battalion seemingly intent upon obliterating him.

Hazy was fortunate in two ways, however. One was that he got hit right at the beginning of the assault, before the medevac crews were overwhelmed by the sheer volume of casualties, and was very quickly under the care of the skilled and courageous surgeons who saved his life. The other was that a couple of ounces of gray matter were neither here nor there to Hazy Doyle. His neurons and synapses being already so irremediably fried by constant exposure to every hallucinogenic and mind-altering substance known to mankind, he didn't really miss the bit that was missing. Then, as now, Hazy was a walking pharmacological experiment.

Hazy had a steel plate in his head, which, rather than being the inconvenience it might at first glance appear, was actually a blessing in disguise. Hazy loved his steel plate. His steel plate absorbed the solar rays, which he used to power the intergalactic journeys he made every day on his psychedelic surfboard. Furthermore, it allowed him to receive interplanetary messages that gave him directions from one solar system to another, so he never had to worry about getting lost. Better still, he could tune in to some really groovy alien radio stations. Hazy knew that not only was there life on Mars, but there were some seriously funky bands as well, and that sometimes, Jimi sat in.

When Baby Joe pushed aside the beaded curtain that served as Hazy's front door, and stepped into the diaphanous swirling cloud of incense and marijuana smoke, Hazy spoke to him as if no time had elapsed since their last meeting, as if he had just gone out for smokes again. Peering myopically through the round, wire-framed lenses of his shades, he said, "Hey, man. What kept you?"

Baby Joe had brought a crate of beer. "I went to buy beer," he said, handing one to Hazy.

"Outta sight, baby. Shit, man, what happened to your hair, man? The Man come down on you, or what?"

Baby Joe regarded Hazy fondly. He sat cross-legged in the folds of something that looked like Jackson Pollock's shower curtain. His gray hair hung almost to his waist, restrained by a bandana of purple silk. Looking down, Baby Joe could see the gleam of the partially exposed plate. The operation had saved Hazy's life, but subsequent scalp grafts had not taken well. Baby Joe sat studying him, wondering what scenes played out in this ruined mind as Hazy set his beer down, untouched, and began to roll a joint.

"You need to chill out, man. You look wore down." He smiled into the ether as he spoke, without taking his eyes from his task, sounding like Keith Richards with laryngitis.

"Ain't that the truth?"

Hazy looked up, an expression of mild confusion on his face, as if he wanted something but he couldn't remember what it was. He held up a finger as if he were about to disclose something important, then, reaching behind him, pulled out a frayed black beret, an authentic relic of the French occupation. Moving slowly and methodically, he placed the beret over the exposed piece of plate.

"Got to block the transmissions, man," he said, pointing heavenwards. "The only way to do it. I can't hear nothing otherwise. So, what say?"

"I said, how have you been, Hazy? Are you okay? Do you need anything?"

"Love is all you need, man," Hazy said, smiling. Behind him, candlelight reflecting from the polished brass Buddha glowed around his head like a halo.

*You are a saint,* Baby Joe thought. *A harmless, gentle man who was put into the grinding machine, into a place where he didn't belong, where nobody belonged, and who never came back.* Hazy Doyle never really survived the war at all.

Baby Joe drank down a beer and opened another. "I'd still be on that hill if it wasn't for you," he said.

Hazy had turned his attention back to the joint, which was assuming such proportions that it wasn't clear whether he was going to smoke it or play it, and he looked up again when Baby Joe spoke. "We all still on the hill, baby. You dig?"

Baby Joe nodded. He understood that he should not talk about it.

"Hazy, you know what Machine Gun Jelly is?"

Hazy lit his joint, filled his lungs, and held the smoke for a long time, all the while looking at Baby Joe as if he was looking through him to something that waited in the light behind the beaded curtain. Baby Joe wasn't sure if Hazy had understood what he had said, or even heard it.

Hazy released a voluminous cloud of sweet smoke and held out the joint to Baby Joe. "Sure, man. I'm hip to that shit. Bad karma, baby. Heavy traffic. The heaviest. A stone killer. That motherfucker kills people, man."

"Lots of drugs kill people, Jack."

"No, man. Dig what I'm putting down. You got to get your mind round it, bro. You don't chase this dragon. It chases you. Ain't nobody can ride this horse. It ain't a white swan, it's a crow. A black raven. This shit don't blow your mind, bro. It blow your soul."

"What do you mean?"

"Boom. Five thousand light years from home." Hazy reached out and took the spliff from Baby Joe, filling his lungs again as he shuffled closer. Another swirling cloud filled the space between them, dissected by a vertical ray of light coming through a hole in the ceiling.

"Jack. I'm not following you at all here, man. What are you talking about?"

"Okay, man. But be ready. What I'm going to lay on you is the weirdest of the weird, bro. This is the fucking Twilight Zone, man. The Outer fucking Limits. This was top-secret, for-your-eyes-only classified city, baby. Only the top, top brass, some Pentagon pen pushers, and a few screwheads were hip to what was going down. Machine Gun Jelly was supposed to end the war, man. It was a fucking weapon! It goes all the way back to WWII and something the Krauts were getting together."

"What, like the V2s?"

"No, man. Nothing like that. This was way more uncool. Fucking Dr. Mengele stuff, man. The final fucking solution. You know that after that war, the big one, the Pentagon was worried about the Reds getting their nuclear shit together, and there was this, like, race, man, to see who could get hold of the most Kraut eggheads. Well, one of these guys has this formula, see, a chemical formula that he lays on the military. It gets him into the States, but his idea is just too radical to lay on the people, and it gets eighty-sixed. About the time of the Tet, when old Walter is saying the party's over and the commies are all watching to see what will happen, somebody digs out this old Kraut's formula and starts fucking with it, and all of a sudden the end is in sight. The most devastating new weapon since the Enola Gay torched old Tojo."

"And what was it?"

"Machine Gun Jelly? It's a like cipher or something. MGJ is the acronym for the actual formula of the chemical compound that, like, only three cats in the whole world can pronounce. It's a drug, a, like, hallucinogenic aphrodisiac speed trip. The most mind-blowing trip since Neil Armstrong. The plan was to mass-produce it, and lay it on the gooks, man, drop it all over their positions, and into the villes. Even the big H, man, Hanoi. Get old Ho Chi high."

"What the fuck is a hallucinogenic aphrodisiac supposed to do?"

"It's beautiful, man. It messes with your mind and your manhood. LSD at warp speed, and Spanish Fly to the power of a thousand squared. Men become obsessed with their dicks, possessed by the demon reamer from Hades, oblivious to everything except the electric rainbow inside their heads, and the irresistible desire the fling themselves upon the nearest animate object—man, woman, or beast—and shag it senseless."

"And then what? Charlie becomes so ecstatic that they stop fighting? They are too busy fucking each other to fuck with us?"

"No, man. That's only part of it. The seriously freaky part is this. Machine Gun Jelly insinuates its way into the testes, and infiltrates the seminal fluid. The motherfucker seeps into your balls, man, you dig?"

"So it's chemical castration?"

Shaking his head, Hazy took another deep toke from his reefer and stared at Baby Joe.

For a second Baby Joe thought he had lost him, but his voice followed the smoke into the room, softer even than before. "You could say that, man. Machine Gun Jelly is audio sensitive. It responds to a specific frequency, or rather a specific combination of frequencies."

"And does what?"

"It fucking explodes, man!"

"It what?"

"It explodes. It blows your fucking balls into the outfield. It's a chemical Bouncing fucking Betty, man."

Baby Joe stared at Hazy, who stared back from out of his cloud, sitting under his beret with a sad smile. It was such an unbelievably outlandish story that, coming from anyone else, Baby Joe would have dismissed it as the imaginings of a drug-addled mind. But something in Hazy's eyes, in his ingenuous expression, something in his matter-of-fact delivery, something in what Baby Joe knew about the man who had once been Jack Doyle, told him that it was true, or at least that Hazy believed it to be true.

"Jesus H. fucking Christ. That is un-fucking-believable. What about the frequency? What about the delivery system?"

"This is the truly wonderful part, man. You have to dig the irony in this. The detonation signal obviously has to be something unique, something that won't trigger this shit by accident, right. So, you know at the end of 'A Day in the Life' on *Sergeant Pepper* there's thirty seconds of white noise, inaudible to humans, a kind of sonic practical joke, yeah? Well, that's it."

"You have got to be shitting me, man."

"No, man. That was the plan. Wait till every gook in the 'Nam is hopped up to the eyeballs on MGJ, and half of them are getting it on with their mama-sans down in the paddies. When every hut and tunnel in the 'Nam is crammed full of incendiary slope nuts. And then send in the cavalry, man. Air Cav in squadrons of Hueys, specially equipped with state-of-the-art hi-fis and massive multi-megawatt speakers, flying all over the country, blasting out Sergeant Pepper, and it's 'Goodbye Yellow Dick's Load.'"

Baby Joe sat back, shaking his head, and reached for another beer as Hazy temporarily disappeared behind his smoke screen. He listened to the sound of Hazy exhaling.

"So, what went wrong?" he said.

"Dig this, bro. One night, some Lurps came in from the shit and were in town on furlough. They got FUBAR. The compound had a heavy-duty MP guard, and the Lurps decided to fuck with them by breaking in. These mothers had their shit wired so tight, man, they were in and out without anybody knowing, except this one guy loses his chevron patch. They found the MGJ and, not knowing what it was, decided to boost some. As soon as the brass found out the next morning that some of the shit had been scaled, by *Americans*, they had to eighty-six the operation. Imagine every head between San Diego and Venice fucking Beach surfing round with no nuts. Hanging ten, with none hanging. Only a little had been made at the time, so they shut down production, and ordered a controlled detonation. But before that could happen, some dipshit second lieutenant, just arrived from the boonies, called in an air strike and fucked up the coordinates. He greased the compound, man, and all the techs that worked there, which was all very convenient for the brass."

"So Machine Gun Jelly was history."

"Yeah, man. Except for what the Lurps took. Nobody knows what happened to that."

"How do you know all this? I was here, and I've never heard of it."

"Well, you know, man. We moved in kinda different circles. This story was going round among the heads. You know, just one of those bullshit stories like the incurable pox, or the Vietnamese girls with broken glass up their pussies. Then, after I got hit, and I was in the intensive care in Saigon, they moved a guy in next to me who had been seriously torched, on account that the burns unit was full. This poor bastard was higher than fucking Telstar on morphine, baby. One night he starts talking to me, like, babbling in the darkness, and he tells me this whole thing. He was one of the techs that bought it from Lieutenant Dipshit. Next morning he was gone, and I heard later that he didn't make it. I also heard later that Lieutenant Dipshit got fragged. Draw your own conclusions, man."

They sat together in companionable silence listening to Hazy's sounds, drinking beer and smoking, Baby Joe trying to get his brain around what he had been told and Hazy slowly fading back into the ether after his moment of lucidity. When Baby Joe left, an hour or so later, after kissing Hazy on the forehead and telling him he would be back to see him, Hazy wasn't really paying attention. He had removed his beret and was busy rolling another joint and listening to the directions to the Shores of Orion.

Monsoon knelt down and frantically scrabbled at the quarter-century's accumulation of dust, spiderwebs, and bat shit that covered the wall of the outhouse at Wal's Outback. Behind him lurked his cryptozoological cousin, holding a twenty-pound hammer as if it were a lollipop.

"Think you can break this wall?" Monsoon asked, realizing the stupidity of his question even before the Sasquatch pulverized a significant section of plasterwork with a seemingly effortless flick of the wrist. From where the plaster had fallen away came a faint gleam where the hammer blow had scraped the grime off some kind of foil-covered package.

"Take the walls down. See what's inside, take it out."

Sasquatch moved bricks like a child destroying a jigsaw puzzle and began to lift out oblong packages. Monsoon snatched one up and rubbed it frantically with his shirttail.

Despite the steaming humidity, and the passing of the years, the letters were clearly visible. His ears were ringing. They were ringing with the same kind of strident clanking that silver dollars make spilling into the well of a slot machine. His almond eyes were round for the first and only time in his life, stretching like ardent moons to encompass the immensity of the wealth lying before him. He was hyperventilating like a scuba student with a constricted O-ring. His hand touched the cool silver. He felt an electric tingle run up fingers.

"Got a knife?" he managed to say, through a larynx constricted by dreams of excess and revenge, excess against the years of struggle, of nickel-and-dime sleepless worry-sick poverty, revenge against bitter years of disdain and humiliation. Sasquatch produced a malevolently glinting sickle-bladed knife and handed it to Monsoon, blade first, looking at him as if he would rather be sticking it into Monsoon's liver.

With as much care as he could summon, Monsoon made an incision in the corner of the uppermost brick, and carved the merest sliver from the corner of the claylike substance within. He held it to his nostrils and inhaled deeply.

He closed his eyes and indulged himself in the sweet, sweet glow of success and relief. At last. At long, long last. This was it, baby. This was the gentle kiss of Venus, Aphrodite's sensual caress, the golden shower of Danaë, and Cleopatra's great, gaping, glistening, Greek minge, all rolled into one.

He stood up. Sasquatch reached around and snatched the knife from his grasp.

"Yes?" said the Sasquatch, in a passing semblance of human speech. "You find what you look? Is it?"

"Damn straight!" replied Monsoon, as if from somewhere far away.

Suddenly, Monsoon felt as if he could not breathe and needed to sit down. The reason he felt as if he could not breathe was because of the slender silken cord that was wrapped around his throat like a rock python with cramp. The reason he needed to sit down was because the Sasquatch had kung fu'd him in the kneecap and traumatized his patella and, in a continuation of the same movement, kicked him in the groin.

Pain is only a vague description of what he felt. Nauseating, unbearable, box-jellyfish, fires-of-purgatory, Prometheus's-eagle-eating-your-liver agony would be more like it. The rock python recovered slightly from its cramp attack. Monsoon lay panting like a dog eating a habañero, and only the lack of volume in his windpipe prevented him doing a Tarzan-with-piles impression.

Something glinted at the corner of his eye and a tiny pricking added to the symphony of soreness that his body was conducting, and then he heard swelling violins and a smiling, buxom angel kissed him tenderly on the lips, and the last thing he saw, as his eyes rolled into the back of his head like a great white shark at suppertime, was the Valkyries coming to carry him off to Valhalla.

Mrs. Mary Rose Muffin was just hanging up the telephone as the doorbell rang. She liked to call home, every day, and make sure that everything was fine and dandy and just the way it ought to be. Now she glanced at herself in the mirror on her way to open the door. She looked very nice, even if she thought so herself. Her pretty blue frock was just the right length, and her blue-rinsed hair was curled and tidy, and her sensible shoes were neatly polished.

She had decided against the gloves, since it was just so stifling hot over here, but she had kept the hat with its white brim and nice satin band, fastened into place with a long antique hatpin with a real pearl at the end. Satisfied, she opened the door and smiled a big welcome to Bjørn Eggen, who was looking very smart in his pale gray suit and holding a dozen roses.

"Oh, my," she said, "just look at these beautiful flowers. And you look so handsome and distinguished. Come in. Come and help me pin one of these lovely roses on my dress."

Bjørn Eggen stepped over the threshold and did as he had been bidden, fumbling with the pin with his veined, old hands.

"There, now," Mary Rose Muffin said, admiring herself in the mirror. "Now, how would you like a little drink before we go?"

"*Ja.* Very much I would like that. Beer if you haf."

"I'm sure we do. And if not, I shall ring down." She fumbled in the mini bar and came out with a bottle of imported beer and a miniature of gin. "Would you? My old hands are not strong enough, I am afraid."

When Bjørn Eggen had prised open the bottles and poured Mary Rose's gin into a glass with tonic and ice, she patted the bed next to where she was sitting and said, "Now, come and sit next to me and tell me all about what you have been doing since we saw each other last."

Bjørn Eggen was happy to see her. He liked her and she was cheerful company. After leaving the others the night before he had lain for a long time in the darkness, thinking. A strange melancholy had come over him, a sadness and longing he could not shake, as if he were coming to the end of something. He had wanted to go home, where things were simple. It wasn't just the disappointment that his grandson had not shown up to see him. Knowing that something was going on he had half-expected it, and he didn't really know the boy anyway.

It was what it signified. Maybe the story about his son being found was not true, either. Maybe that was it. Maybe he secretly knew that he had come all this way for nothing, and that he wasn't going to take his boy home. Maybe he had known it all along. Maybe he was just a foolish old man messing about on the other side of the world on some wild goose chase. And maybe somewhere in all that was the fear that he would die in some foreign place before he could get back where he belonged. Before he could get home.

He had finally drifted off to sleep, and in the morning he had felt much better. Baby Joe had had somewhere to go, and Wally had been busy, so he had a couple of beers by himself and talked to Wally's kids, and decided that since he was here, and couldn't go home until the situation was sorted out, he was going to enjoy himself. So he had found the piece of paper on which Mary Rose Muffin had carefully written her number in a neat hand with looping letters, called her, and asked her to dinner. And she had said, yes, she'd love to.

And now here he was, telling her about Wally, and the coincidence, and about Monsoon, and about his adventure with Rodney—although he censored that story a little bit—and Mary Rose Muffin laughed until tears ran, and she had to wipe her eyes with a handkerchief. And then she said she would have to go and redo her makeup, and Bjørn Eggen took his beer onto the balcony and looked down at the bright and chaotic city until she reemerged.

"Come along, Bjørn Eggen," she said, "it's time we should be going. I asked that nice, young man at the reception desk, and he told me the very best restaurant to go to, and he made us a reservation and ordered us a taxi, and I'm so looking forward to our evening together."

"*Ja,* me too. I also look forward." Bjørn Eggen offered Mary Rose Muffin his arm and she took it, and he escorted her out of the room and down the long corridor, past brightly colored panels, to the elevator.

"You know who lose you war?"

Unless he had a wager on the outcome the result of a war was of no interest whatsoever to Monsoon, but he feigned interest for diplomatic purposes. "Er, the fucking politicians, right?"

"Wrong. Fucking Beach Boys lose you war."

Monsoon had more or less come to his senses and was without actual pain, although he could feel it pacing at the periphery of his consciousness, waiting for the opium to wear off like a predator waiting for its prey to grow weak from loss of blood. He was tied to a chair under the obligatory sinister naked bulb in a damp stone cellar. To either side stood two standard-issue evil henchmen, their bare, oiled, muscular torsos girdled by fully laden bandoliers, staring unblinkingly at him with implacable hostility. The Sasquatch squatted beside a dais, upon which stood a seriously heavy, ancient teak chair.

On the chair sat Generalissimo Long Suc, and the cellar lay beneath the Long Suc Extravaganza of Exotica.

"Fucking Beach Boys lose you war, American," the generalissimo repeated.

Even for someone as disinterested in military strategy as Monsoon, and under his current circumstances, this was an intriguing theory, which deserved attention.

Long Suc had, since his retirement from the military, become a purveyor of items not generally available. And he purveyed them to people of discerning and discriminating tastes, people with unique appetites, people unperturbed by such intangible and inconvenient concepts as extinction, deforestation, pollution, exploitation, et cetera. So General Long Suc's shelves were stocked with such trinkets and delicacies as ivory, rhino horns, whale meat, tiger's dicks, and a few dozen drug-addicted Cambodian teenagers of both genders.

Also on display were such practical items as land mines, rocket launchers, automatic weapons, Agent Orange, and a few canisters of Chinese nerve gas. Being a shopkeeper, the General saw it as his entrepreneurial responsibility to make sure the merchandise his customers wanted was always available at a competitive price. So if a couple of herds of elephants got wiped out in Thailand by an off-duty game warden entertaining himself in his spare time, it was all done in the name of commerce. And if the odd whale got harpooned in the lungs as part of ongoing scientific research, it was just the free market economy at work. And if a few kids happened to end up hopping round on one leg, or with no legs at all, the General didn't see how he could be held responsible for the use his customers made of the goods he sold them.

Long Suc was inordinately proud of the name of his shop, which he had plagiarized from the title of a hardcore porno mag he had once read in Sweden while part of a peace delegation, and he enjoyed entertaining his clients—such as the young man in front of him—with stories of his war experiences, as part of his marketing strategy.

"What the fuck have the Beach Boys got to do with the war?" Monsoon asked, somewhat understandably.

"Okay. I show you. American start bomb Hanoi. Okay? Very bad. Many kill. No food. No medicine. Everybody start think this too hard. Better we quit. We have big meeting try decide. All top people. Then one guy he say, 'If surrender, American make us listen Beach Boys all time.' So we decide keep fighting. And we win."

"That's an interesting theory, General," said Monsoon, not really knowing what else to say.

It was either the grinning old Mongol-looking fucker's idea of a joke, or he was not playing with a full deck. Sitting there laughing at his own story the General looked like Genghis Khan enjoying a rare lighter moment, taking a break from conquering the known world. He had dark, almost black, almond eyes, peering from between high cheekbones. The skull was shaven, save for a long braid extending from the back of his head and down over his shoulder into his lap, and an incredibly long, wispy, white Fu Manchu mustache completed the picture. Monsoon was half expecting a maniacal cackle.

"I agree," said the General. "Now we make deal."

"Oh, good, yeah, okay, great," said Monsoon, with genuine enthusiasm.

Long Suc indicated with a slight movement of his hand a neatly stacked pile of briquettes, about a foot long by six inches wide by an inch deep. There were stencil marks on each package, very badly faded, but just legible:

*Government Property. Top Secret. MGJ. Strictly Authorized Personnel Only.*

There was also a little motif, just visible, of a yellow skull and crossbones, like the small flag of an optimistic pirate.

"Deal we make as follows. You tell me what is merchandise, what it do, what you plan do with it, how much it worth, and I don't cut both you Achilles tendon and drop you off in gay leper colony."

Monsoon weighed his options. They didn't weigh very much. He decided to come clean. "Okay, okay, I'll tell you everything."

Long Suc assumed his best inscrutable oriental expression and nodded almost imperceptibly.

Monsoon laid out the whole story in all its labyrinthine complexity, ending on a note of legitimate indignation with the part about how his own auntie had set him up with the Sasquatch, who had obviously turned him over to the General.

Long Suc spread his features into a jovial grin, which didn't do much for his oriental inscrutability. "You auntie good business woman. And you plan very good. This number one plan I think we use."

"Well, thanks, No Suc. Don't mind if I call you No Suc, do you? First, though, I have to tell you, these are some seriously evil motherfuckers we dealin' with. I'm talking about the mob."

"Ah, gangsta. Al Capone. Dadadadadadadada." Long Suc fired an imaginary Tommy gun, spraying hot lead at the G-men. Then he smiled gently at Monsoon, the way you would smile at a child who had just made an inaccurate statement. He made an expansive gesture with his skinny arm. "You forget you history. Chinaman, Frenchman, American, Al Capone-man. All same. No problem. Ho Chi Minh City no same Chicago."

"So you're ready to rock and roll?"

Long Suc nodded sagely, although not really sure what dancing had to do with it.

"So where do I come in?"

"You DNA."

"Say again?"

"You DNA. Same same you father. You about same age you father when he die, no? We bury you one year, two year, no problem. Asia people patient. Know how wait."

"But wait," Monsoon said, his voice rising in panic, "what about my auntie?"

The General smiled benignly. "Oh, she be okay. Get new microwave. No problem."

Before he could start to beg and plead in the required manner, Monsoon felt a pinprick, and a rainbow-colored ferryman came to take him across the river to the land of Nod. The general made a sharp movement with his head, and the two henchmen cut Monsoon loose and began to drag him to the far recesses of the cellar. Long Suc rose laboriously from the chair and, aided by the Sasquatch, shuffled slowly up to his office, where he sat in red silk-upholstered luxury. He sent the Sasquatch to fetch tea and reached for the phone.

To find out the number of one Don Ignacio Imbroglio of Las Vegas, Nevada, USA.

# Chapter 16.

Rodney was a really good judge of character, and she liked Asia immediately. For one thing Asia smelled really nice, and she didn't object to a gentle bit of sniffing and probing from the old trunkaroonee. Furthermore, giving her a bun right off the bat was a great way of earning Rodney's immediate and undying affection, and that is exactly what Asia had done. In fact, Rodney liked Asia so much that she wanted to stand as close to her as possible whenever she was near, a fact that resulted in not a few people getting unceremoniously shunted aside.

Crispin, for example. Crispin was not enamored of Rodney. The fat bristly beast smelled atrocious, had no manners whatsoever the way it kept rudely shoving him, and it got way too much attention for a dumb animal. In truth, there was probably a bit of professional jealousy mixed in with Crispin's antipathy, since Rodney enjoyed celebrity status and Crispin's career was in something of a slump, to say the least. However, Crispin's spirits had risen considerably since arriving in Vietnam. It was really pretty, and exotic, and colorful, and the shopping opportunities were mouthwatering, and nobody had tried to shoot him or explode him for almost a full week. And anything was an improvement over that nasty, smelly, sweltering, bug-ridden swamp and all those gauche peasants that infested it.

They sat in the Thao Cam Vien botanical gardens, sitting under a large candy-striped parasol at the foot of a towering red and gilt pagoda eating delicious glacés and watching Wally and Rodney run through their repertoire for a busload of tourists on the lawn in front of them. Beyond was a tranquil lake with willows hanging into it and elaborately plumed birds like overgrown ducks sailing serenely by. It was early morning and the temperature was warm but not oppressive, and if Crispin closed his eyes he could almost imagine himself on a bench in a park back home on some sunny summer's morning.

Crispin was wearing baggy yellow Bermuda shorts and a billowing magenta short-sleeved silk shirt, and the gentle breeze flowing around his appendages was very soothing. Next to him Asia was chatting to the nice old lady that Bjørn Eggen had brought with him. When they had first arrived, and Baby Joe had met them and taken them to Wally's bar and then to the boat, Crispin had imagined, for one horrendous moment, that they were going to be required to stay on that floating barnyard. Much to his relief they had been driven over a bridge on the Saigon River and down quiet tree-lined streets to a charming little colonial bungalow set in lovely gardens with a lawn that ran down to the river, where there was a jetty with a little sampan tied to it. Crispin had been given his own room, which had a big bamboo fan in the ceiling and a veranda that opened onto the garden, and an old, old lady in black pajamas with a beehive on her head had smiled a toothless smile and given him clean towels. If he tried very hard he could imagine that he was on vacation and that all those horrible things had not really happened to him at all.

Peals of laughter drifted over to them from the lawn, and he looked over to see Rodney flourishing an oversized straw hat with flowers all around it and placing it on her dome head.

Asia giggled and tapped him on the thigh. "Oh, look at Rodney. Isn't she adorable?"

"Isn't she adorable?" Crispin mimicked. "If you like overgrown, show-off pigs with vacuum cleaners instead of faces, then yes."

"I think he's sweet," said Mary Rose Muffin.

"I am liking him too, now, *ja*. Only he is not he, he is lady elephant."

"Really?"

"*Ja*, sure. Only one trunk this elephant."

Mary Rose giggled and slapped Bjørn Eggen on the shoulder. "You naughty old man," she said.

Applause signaled the end of the show and Rodney came swaying over, with Wally gliding beside her with a fluidity that belied his years, appearing to barely touch the ground. Rodney lifted her trunk and began to nuzzle Asia's cheek, simultaneously treading on Crispin's foot.

"Ow! You fat oaf," he said, retreating down the bench and regarding his discolored loafer with dismay.

"'Owareya," said Wally brightly. "You blokes enjoy the show?"

"It was very nice, Wally, thank you."

"*Ja*, vas gud, *ja*?"

"Rippa. Well, Baby Joe said 'e'll be tied up this afternoon, so I thought you might like to take the boat out for a spin on the river. I'll send one o' me Billy lids to steer yer round."

"*Ja, ja*. I like very much. Mary Rose?"

"Oh, yes, I love boats."

"I'll need a hat," said Crispin.

"No worries, Crispy. I'll get you one. Come on, then."

Asia stood and straightened her skirt, and Bjørn Eggen offered his hand to Mary Rose. Crispin lifted his ice cream cone to his mouth and closed his eyes in anticipation of the cold, delicious raspberry taste. He opened them in surprise when his lips encountered dry pastry, and stared in puzzlement at his empty cone. He looked round to where Rodney stood, softly swaying, with her trunk in her mouth, gazing at him with her enormous brown eye. Crispin narrowed his eyes.

"You fucking fat sow," he hissed. "Ooh, just you wait. I'll fix you, snake snout."

As they set off in procession across the grass, with Wally leading, Bjørn Eggen holding hands with Mary Rose, Rodney plodding as close to Asia as she could get without actually pushing her over, and Crispin sulking behind them, a nondescript man—a European in a khaki suit who had been sitting, unnoticed, three benches away—rolled up his newspaper, flicked his cigarette at a passing duck, and sauntered after them.

Although the Don's pleasures were, of necessity, mostly in the mind, he did not begrudge himself a little enjoyment. As one of his favorite Gilbert and Sullivan pieces pointed out, being a despicable villain did not necessarily preclude the ability to have a little harmless fun. Having just hung up the phone, and being alone, the Don permitted himself a little un-Don-like giggle.

One of the things that the Don always found highly amusing was when somebody thought they were smarter than he was. Not morons like Frankie Merang, you understand—that was merely the equivalent of a puppy hiding one's slippers—but people capable of formulating some kind of a plan, counter to the Don's own, and seriously expecting to get away with it. That was the really funny part, when people actually thought they could put one over on him. Take the Irishman, for example. Following some torturous, unfathomable Celtic logic, that misguided

Mick gumshoe had not only seen fit to spirit away the grandfather of Monsoon Parker, but now, as a little bird had just finished telling him, had the girl and the portly singing sodomite under his wing.

Quite how, and for what reason, this circumstance had arisen, the Don was not sure, but it seemed to the Don a delicious effrontery that the Paddy should not only deliberately interfere with his plans, but actually do so while being in his employ, thereby causing him to pay for his own inconvenience. No doubt the Gael was enjoying gales of laughter at his own cleverness. *Well, Mr. Young, he who laughs last, laughs loudest, as they say, so enjoy your little schemes while you may.*

Monsoon was in the shit, again. In this case it was about six feet deep, with the consistency of goulash, and artfully decorated with a smattering of dead rat, tastefully set off by a sprinkling of used sanitary towels. Furthermore, it was rising, and Monsoon was failing dismally in his desperate attempts to keep his head above the surface, due to the fact that ship's chains and padlocks are not very efficient flotation devices.

Long Suc had concluded that the best way to add a little authenticity to the skeleton scenario would be to lower Monsoon into the sewer that ran beneath his emporium and leave him there until nature took its course. Monsoon had, like most of us, heard the survival stories from people who had had near-death experiences, stories about one's entire life passing before one's eyes, but all that was passing before his eyes was a procession of rancid turds. It was when one brushed against his actual lips that his wild-eyed, hysterical panic turned into wild-eyed, demented laughter. His brain disassembled completely by terror, Monsoon began to cackle like a pack of stoned hyenas watching Saturday Night Live.

A voice inside his head said, "What so funny?"

"This," he struggled to answer, gasping through the stench of the effluent that was now flushing past his nose, "this, dying like this, after a life full of shit, now I have to drown in it, hahahahahaha…"

"You lucky."

This struck Monsoon as even funnier. He wanted to tell the voice in his head to fuck off, to stop being so fucking stupid, to ask it how the fuck drowning in a fucking Vietnamese shit drain could possibly be considered lucky, but was unable to speak because of the large, semi-solid hunk of unpleasantness which was now lodged in his mouth.

"You lucky. America big boss say he want you alive."

Monsoon just had time to realize that the voice inside his head was actually a voice beside his head before he passed out.

Frankie Merang was really enjoying his sandwich. The reason being that it was the kind of sandwich which required him to lie on a soapy, inflatable rubber mattress with two petite, naked, and very slippery Vietnamese girls sliding all over him. On a tray next to him was a half-empty bottle of whiskey, and on a big-screen TV in the corner young girls were performing improbable acts with a variety of household objects.

"A taste of what's to come, Frankie my boy," he was thinking to himself, as one of the girls expertly slipped a condom over him using her lips. After the girl had perfunctorily performed her act of fellatio Frankie waved dismissively, watching her leave through a cloud of cigar smoke, and grabbed the ass of a passing waitress. It was firm and rubbery. "I might just have to get me some more in a little while," he thought, miming the drinking of a beer. The waitress, who looked about twelve, smiled and nodded. Frankie grinned like a happy stegosaurus.

It had always secretly annoyed him that people thought he was slow just because he was big, but now he was beginning to understand that it was actually an advantage. The more people that dismissed him as dumb, the better. Like El Greaso the Don, back there. That little wop dipshit was sending Francis A. Merang a present, a great big fat bag of used green, special delivery. The Don had called him that morning.

He smirked again as he recalled the Don's faggot limey voice. "Our congratulations, Mr. Merang. You have done extremely well. You can expect my financiers tomorrow. And since your partner has fallen by the wayside, as it were, you can expect his share of the proceeds as well."

*I got ya share of the proceeds right here, ya Spick prick,* thought Frankie, grabbing his crotch with one hand and reaching out to grab a passing ass with the other.

"Buddha teach us know our self. Me, I know myself very good. I know very good I no good. Good for you I no good, because if I no no good, you still be in smelly place, very dead."

Monsoon was doing his best to follow Long Suc's philosophical dissertation from the far corner of the room where he had been placed, surrounded by incense, due to the fact that several brutal scrubbings had failed to entirely remove the stench of the sewer from his skin.

"If I no no good, I no double-cross you and call Don, and Don no tell me better me no kill you, so you see, it good for you I no good. See?"

Monsoon managed a vacant nod, which was about all his motor neuron system could muster at the moment.

"I see you no see," continued Long Suc. "Confucian think very hard for American too small brain. No worry. No important. We friends again. You go now my office, call America Big Boss. Tomorrow we make deal. Everyone happy. Okay. You cousin go with you, make sure you okay. Have nice day."

Frankie and Monsoon were on the veranda of their hotel, drinking whiskey and having their shoes shined. A small Vietnamese boy, with the tools of his trade in a cardboard box, knelt at Frankie's feet, zipping his cloth over the toe of his boot.

"Mistah," he said, "you feet too big. You pay extra."

"Lissen, ya little dink bastard, you'll get that boot up ya yellow ass if you don't shut up. An' watch the fuckin' socks."

The boy grinned and continued polishing furiously.

Monsoon had somewhat recovered from his ordeal, although despite several more showers a faint miasma of effluent still bloomed in a delicate cloud around him. Frankie and he had spent the morning attempting to deceive each other, and discussing the deceptions they were planning to perpetrate on everybody else. Frankie had, in truth, been a little more honest than Monsoon, insofar as his conversations with the Don had actually taken place as described, and the money was actually on its way. It was not Frankie's fault that he did not know that the money was on its way not because of his deception of the Don, but because of the Don's conversation with Long Suc. Frankie's only real dishonesty was in not revealing to Monsoon that he had figured out who the tail was that the Don had put on them, and that after the deal had gone down he was planning to blow Monsoon's brains out.

Monsoon's fabrications had been a good deal more complex. He had altered the details of his conversation with Long Suc, studiously avoiding any mention of near-death-by-toxic-shit drowning experiences, or the fact that the Machine Gun Jelly actually existed, or the fact that Long Suc and the Don were now dealing directly with each other.

As for his own very recent conversation with the Don—in which the Don had indicated that they were now all just as cozy as can be, and that they would go ahead with the original plan save for one minor detail—he had deemed it prudent to withhold from Frankie the details of the minor detail, because *he* was the minor detail.

The conversation had gone along the lines of, "Our congratulations, Mr. Parker. You have done extremely well. You can expect my financiers tomorrow. And since Mr. Merang has fallen by the wayside, as it were, you can expect his share of the proceeds as well. However, given the rather egregious nature of his transgressions, I wonder if you could prevail upon your friend Mr. Long Suc to make certain arrangements for me."

Monsoon felt certain that Frankie would not especially care for the arrangements, especially the part about the Sasquatch waiting for him in the hotel room with his evil sickle-blade knife at the ready.

Frankie turned to Monsoon. "So, we all set?"

"As ready as we gonna be. You nervous?"

"Na. Whatever's gonna happen is gonna happen. Ya get nervous, ya screw up. You okay? Ya ain't goin' to pieces on me now, are ya?"

"No sweat, Frankie, I'm good to go. But what about the tail?"

"Don't worry, I'm on it. Wait here while I go upstairs and get my piece."

Monsoon smiled to himself as he reached for his smokes on the table and, as he did so, saw a boy of about ten with wild, wavy hair, looking closely at him.

"What the fuck ya looking at, kid?"

"Dunno, ya prawn," replied the kid, "I never seen one before."

Monsoon made as if to stand, and the boy scampered off.

The remarkable thing about Horatio Herbert was that there was absolutely nothing remarkable about him whatsoever. Horatio was everyman. Average height, average weight, unremarkable features, nondescript hair, conventional dresser. The kind of man who went unnoticed in a crowd. In fact, Horatio could go unnoticed in your bathroom while you were trying to take a shit.

Horatio's bland appearance was complemented by his even blander personality. He had no extreme likes or dislikes, no strong political views, no preferred food, no favorite color. The relative merits of cats and dogs were of no consequence to him, the outcome of a football game an irrelevance, and music a distracting noise. He had no wife, no children, no friends, and no sexual preferences. He drank in moderation, smoked sparingly, and did not indulge in the weed. He was not unduly concerned with financial matters and lived a modest lifestyle, well within his means, in an average house, in an average neighborhood. Meticulous in his personal habits, punctual, reliable, and diligent in his professional life, Horatio Herbert was a strong contender for the most uninteresting person in America.

Oh, except for one small thing. He really enjoyed killing people.

Baby Joe was beginning to see the light. He had needed to get away on his own for a while, to think things through, and had rented a sampan that had drifted him down to the little bar where he now sat, overlooking the colorful noisy chaos of a floating market. Slimy stone steps led down to the murky water, and his boatman squatted at the foot of them smoking a brown cheroot and holding the rope between his toes. Baby Joe had a tall, cold one in front of him. It wasn't Guinness, but it would do. It would have to.

He had met Asia from the plane and spent the night with her, and his skin remembered her touch and the feel and the smell of her body was still with him. He had hoped that when she arrived it would have felt different for one of them, or both of them, but it hadn't. It had been better—or worse, depending on how you looked at it. One of those deals where people say things like, I feel I've always known you, or, I feel so comfortable and natural with you, although I barely know you, or, I feel like I've always imagined I would feel.

It was romantic bullshit, but unfortunately it was true romantic bullshit. The way he felt inside her, the way she kissed him, the way she tasted, the way her hair felt against his face, the small sound of her voice in the darkness…this was exactly the way he had always imagined it would be if it was real, and right, and meant anything at all.

And now he found himself wishing for things. Wishing he was twenty years younger, wishing the circumstances were different. For fuck's sake! The next thing, he'd be tossing coins into the fucking river or crossing his fingers or clicking his fucking heels together. You don't see too many fucking pagodas in Kansas. Fucking wishes. I wish my dick was bigger, I wish I had fucked my school teacher, I wish I spoke fucking Mongolian, I wish my dog would have had better eyesight, then the fucker wouldn't have gotten run over. I wish I could erase the memory of flames over this city and bloated bodies floating down this river. I wish I hadn't pissed thirty years away without knowing or understanding, not for one minute, what any of it was about.

Well, there was only one thing to do about Asia. Surrender. Fucking capitulate. Let it roll, and be ready for when the tide burst. Enjoy it while it lasted, and live with it when the fucking roses died. If you can't stand a bit of pain in this life, you're on the wrong fucking planet. And you have to be alive to be in pain. Which led to the next problem: the problem of making sure they both lived long enough for their blossoming romance to come to its sad and inevitable conclusion and become a tear-stained note under an empty whiskey glass on an empty, perfume-smelling dresser.

At least that side of things was becoming a clearer, if no less complicated, equation. Evil gangster plus opportunist shakedown artist plus incendiary drug minus two mobsters and two innocent bystanders plus one ill-advised love affair in the midst of a potentially life-threatening situation, multiplied by a shitload of dollars, equals an all-singing, all-dancing, state-of-the-art fuckup of biblical proportions.

So what was the score now? From the fragments that he had to hand, the mosaic looked something like this: After the Captain cashes in, the MGJ somehow comes into Monsoon's hands. What a fucking family heirloom that turned out to be! Monsoon starts passing it around town, which attracts the vultures. Crispin is just looking to get high, but somehow gets connected, which also puts Asia in the shit. Somebody, either the Don or Monsoon, figures there's more of the stuff, hence this jolly little excursion. If what Hazy says is true, there is no more Machine Gun Jelly, and if there was it would be dangerous beyond any reasonable definition of the word.

Is the Don aware of either of those facts? What happens if he finds out? What is the Don's next move? Has he made the connection with Asia yet? If he is convinced that there is no Machine Gun Jelly, hence nothing to protect, and does that mean the heat is off?

*There is only one way to find out. Call him! Fuck this cat-and-mouse shit.* Wondering, waiting, watching. What if this, what about that? Enough. Time to mock the boar in his lair.

Frankie Merang's nose had been an embarrassment to him all his life. It had subjected him to much verbal abuse from his peers, with wisecracks such as "Frankie's hooter is so big, it generates its own weather system," and "Frankie's beezer is so immense, small dogs attempt to stand under it in the rain." The thing about it was, though, that for all its size and deformity, it actually worked very well. Frankie could always smell a rat...or in this case, a Sasquatch.

As he opened the door to his room, his beak immediately informed him of a presence, and he knew that either the cleaning lady had not changed her underwear for about fourteen years or that some diseased animal was in his room. He stopped abruptly, which is what allowed him to avoid the wicked curved blade that came slashing upwards towards where his throat would have been if he had not done so.

At this point, Frankie could have stepped back and slammed the door, but it was not in his nature to do so. Furthermore his gun was inside the room, hidden in the cistern. Instead, he grabbed the fist that held the knife and forward-rolled into the room, twisting the wrist completely around. He was surprised when instead of the sound of a cracking wrist he heard the sound of a cracking fist against his skull.

Whoever it was had rolled with him and delivered a blow of astounding force to the side of his head. Ironically, it was the very force of the blow that saved him, for despite his enormous bulk the punch actually knocked him end over end and out of reach of the vicious blade that came swooping down again. He rolled to his feet and saw some kind of incensed chimpanzee attempting to wrest the knife from the carpet where the force of the strike had driven it. Frankie stamped on the blade and snapped it, and brought his other foot up flush under the Sasquatch's chin with all the weight of his massive thigh behind it. The kick would have certainly stunned, and perhaps even killed, most men, but the Sasquatch merely shook its head and advanced, weaving in a mesmeric sway.

Frankie Merang had been in a great many confrontations during the course of his coarse and brutal career, but nothing had prepared him for the strength and speed of the blows that began to rain on him, and he began to fear for his life. The fear came to his rescue, leading to the desperation that caused him to grab the long, greasy tresses that hung down the Sasquatch's back, and dive over its head and out of the third floor window. The sound of the shattering glass mingled with an unmistakable crack, and Frankie found himself dangling ten feet above the street, clinging to the hair that was attached to the now-lifeless head that was wedged up against the windowsill.

As he clung to the braids, turning in a slow circle, he saw Monsoon sprinting towards the nearest taxi.

The Don's ears were burning. He had just fielded his third consecutive long-distance phone call, which had occupied the best part of an hour and caused his cigar to go out, and he was about to summon Liberty when the phone rang again. Oh well, such is the price and cost of success. He picked up the hot receiver, and waited for the other party to speak.

"Don Imbroglio?"

"Mr. Baby Joe Young. How nice of you to think of us. We were beginning to become concerned about your welfare. Those foreign climes can be so unpredictable, can they not? How's the hangover?"

"What are you talking about?"

"The Irish propensity for strong drink is well known, but I doubt that even you can consume twenty-six Singapore Slings without repercussions. Cambodia was a nice touch, too."

"I know what's going on."

"Well, I'm certainly glad somebody does. Would you care to enlighten me?"

"I know about the drug. Machine Gun Jelly. You can forget it. It was all destroyed by the army during the war."

"Oh, really? How disappointing. I assume you have this information from a reliable source."

"From the horse's mouth, Don Imbroglio."

"I see. And what of my associates?"

"That's up to you, now. I just want to know if you're prepared to call your dogs off."

"My dogs?"

"Come on, Don Imbroglio. Playtime's over. You know exactly what I'm fucking talking about. There's no percentage in this anymore. Just let it go. We'll call it quits."

"Mr. Young. Whatever you are making reference to appears to have eluded me. Perhaps you could clarify matters."

"All right. If you don't already know, you are bound to find out sooner or later. The singer and the girl had nothing to do with any of this. They were just in the wrong place at the wrong time. Bad luck. You lost a few of your people. You were doing what you thought you had to, and so was everybody else. But there is no point anymore. Just leave it."

"Well, since you choose to be so frank, Mr. Young, I am indeed aware of your role with regard to the missing parties. Not very ethical of you when you were under contract to me."

"Yeah, well. Call it a conflict of interests."

"You can call it whatever you so desire, Mr. Young, but the fact remains that you not only interfered in my affairs, but you also attempted to mislead me."

"Yes, Don Imbroglio, I did. I had my reasons. I'll refund you your advance. Just leave it alone."

"You seem extremely concerned about the welfare of our little refugees, Mr. Young. It wouldn't be something more than just professional interest, would it?"

"Don Imbroglio. I know you're a reasonable man. I know you value economy of effort. There is absolutely no point in you pursuing this now."

"Well, that is not quite true. I still have my reputation to consider. You know how important that is to a man in my position."

"Well, Don Imbroglio, I'll leave it to you to decide just how important that is."

"Are you threatening me, Mr. Young?"

"Let's just say I'm appealing to your sound business sense."

"You are very sure of yourself, Mr. Young. I admire that. You realize, of course, that I shall have to verify the nonexistence of the merchandise myself, before I come to any decision."

"That's fair."

"All right, Mr. Young. Let us leave it like that for the nonce. Goodnight, Mr. Young; give my regards to your friends, and don't forget to return your advance."

The Don hung up. He summoned Liberty to light his cigar and pour him a drink, dismissed him, and sat sipping brandy under a swirling cloud of smoke and listening to the faint beeping of horns far below. Presently he reached for his phone again. The voice that answered spoke for five minutes before the Don said anything.

"Good," he said, finally, "very good. Now, tomorrow afternoon, call Mr. Flowers. Verify that the merchandise exists. Once that is ascertained, then I want you to clean up this mess. Yes, all of them. Oh, and I want you to give Mr. Young the deluxe service. Oh, yes. Very slowly. Take all the time you need."

The Don hung up and went to his cigar. He inhaled deeply and smiled. He did appreciate a good Havana.

Monsoon had changed cabs three times and had driven halfway around the city before he figured it was safe enough to stop for a drink. He chose a bar directly across the street from the police station, and after surveying the other customers to assure himself that none among them had, at present anyway, any reason to want to kill him, sat down outside to ponder the latest complication.

When his drink came he grunted and reached out to take it from the waiter without looking up, which was unwise because the fist holding the drink turned out to belong to a very seriously pissed off Frankie Merang, who had just spotted Monsoon after having negotiated his release from the police station with a number of small, green, oblong pieces of paper. Frankie had an impressively swollen lip, a burgeoning and colorful black eye, and a plaster across his broken nose.

"Ya fucken slimy little piece of zipperhead shit. Ya set me up," said Frankie, by way of greeting, before lifting Monsoon bodily out of his chair and head butting him.

While this was taking place a taxi pulled up, and a compact, middle-aged man climbed out. The taxi waited. As he stepped forward to put the boot in, Frankie noticed the compact, middle-aged man standing very still, watching him.

"What the fuck are you looking at?" said Frankie.

Baby Joe ignored him and spoke to Monsoon, where he lay on the ground holding his bleeding nose. "Your grandfather wants to see you."

"I said, what the fuck are you looking at?" Frankie repeated, leaning forward.

Baby Joe continued to ignore him. "You'd better come with me now, Monsoon."

Frankie reached out and grabbed Baby Joe's shirtfront. "Lissen, shithead, I..."

Frankie never finished his sentence. Baby Joe straight-fingered him in the eyes with his left hand while grabbing the hand that held his shirt in an underhand grip with his right. Rotating his elbow sharply, Baby Joe heard the wrist crack. Frankie bellowed and stumbled backwards, upsetting the table. He began clawing at his eyes with one hand, and fumbling at his waistband with the other.

A heavy stone ashtray stood by the table on a bamboo stand, and Baby Joe lifted it and swung it backhand in a lazy arc. It cracked against Frankie's temple and he dropped where he stood, like a brain-shot bison.

Baby Joe looked at Monsoon, who was trying to decide whether to run for it or not. The bleakness in Baby Joes's eyes made up his mind for him, and he walked towards the taxi.

Frankie Merang was half drunk, sweating, and in a great deal of pain, and the scotch wasn't killing it. His left eye was bloodshot, his vision blurry, and his wrist throbbed mercilessly. There was a huge knot at his left temple. But if the scotch wasn't dulling the pain, the anger was helping, and at least it wasn't his gun hand.

It was all goin' to shit. The guys were showin' up tonight, an' here he was, all banged up, an' no fuckin' Monsoon. That fucker had been fast for an old guy. It had surprised him. Well, he wasn't going to get another chance. He was goin' down to that shitbox boat, or maybeez that sleaze-pit bar, where he figured Monsoon to be. Anybody that got in his way was dog meat. In fact, anybody that didn't get in his way was dog meat. Then, once he got ahold of Monsoon, everythin' would be sweet again. He knew what that ratfuck little zipperhead bastard was up to. They get to the meet with this character Long Suc, carrying the green, and all of a sudden it's Vietnam Part Two. Yeah well, it wasn't goin' to work like that. There was gonna be a little traffic accident on the way, see. An' the only survivors were gonna be Big Francis Merang and ten million dollars. This clown the Don had on his ass would see the bonfire, an' assume that Frankie was toast. Some fuckin' tail. If the Don had sent a wildebeest in a fuckin' tuxedo it would have been harder to spot.

Frankie took another heavy slug of whiskey, then rang the bell captain and asked him to send a couple of girls up. He was goin' to show these fuckers that you don't fuck about with Frankie Merang. He was gonna give these two slopettes the high, hard one, take care of this joker who suckerpunched him, and then take care of business.

It was a face Jordan Young reserved for those occasions when he was so angry that words would not suffice, and looking into it Monsoon Parker was afraid. The Incredible Hulk would have been, if not exactly afraid, at least a little concerned. It was a face that contained no recognizable element of humanity or compassion. It was winter in Stalingrad, midnight in Birmingham, shit-out-of-luck in the Mojave, the dark side of the moon, and stormy fucking Monday all rolled into one.

Monsoon was desperately trying to decipher the thoughts that were taking place behind those bleak and lusterless eyes. He would not have found them comforting. Baby Joe was thinking that if Philip Parker had survived to guide his son, then maybe Monsoon Parker would not have turned out to be such a contemptible shit bag, and that therefore he himself was in part and indirectly responsible for some of what had occurred. He was also considering how he would feel about sending the son of the man to whom he owed his life to eternity, and what Philip Parker would have made of all this. He was wondering which way the scales tip when love and sacrifice and regret in the one cup are balanced against guilt and justice and necessity in the other. He was thinking that moral implications are the domain of the living, and that the dead don't give a shit one way or the other. And he was concluding that this treacherous little ratfuck had it coming whichever way you looked at it.

Looking into those colder-than-penguin-shit eyes, any ideas that Monsoon may have entertained of attempting to lie, con, prevaricate, hedge, play for time, or just plain bullshit, evaporated like the mist on the glen.

"This is the bit where people usually say, 'You've got two choices,'" Baby Joe was explaining. "Except you don't. You've got one. Tell me what the fuck is going on, and why. The other one, you don't even want to contemplate."

They were on the end of the jetty at the bottom of the garden where Asia and Crispin were staying. In lieu of a belt, Monsoon was wearing about twenty pounds of reef-knotted anchor chain, the other end of which was attached to a piece of iron protruding from the anvil-sized lump of concrete to which the sampan was normally attached. The concrete was balanced precariously on the very lip of the jetty and Baby Joe's booted foot rested lightly against it, rocking it gently back and forth. Feeling an entirely understandable sense of déjà vu, Monsoon was wondering what he had to do to pass a day without finding himself chained to eternity.

Wally and Bjørn Eggen were standing slightly off to the left, behind Baby Joe, and Monsoon looked anxiously into their eyes, searching for a glimmer of empathy or sympathy and finding none. Bjørn Eggen's eyes were as cold and hard as the ice upon which he was accustomed to fish, and Wally's as distant as his ancestral home.

"Lissen. Wait. I..."

"Before you start, I want to explain something to you. Because of you, at least seven people are dead. Oh, and a dog. Two of them were innocent people, minding their own businesses. Just trying to get through, you know. Just trying to squeeze whatever drops of happiness they could from all this, however they could. Because of you, people that I care about have been inconvenienced, frightened, wounded, dispossessed, humiliated, threatened, and assaulted. Your own grandfather has traveled halfway across the world to end up in the middle this shit, because he imagines that you are all he has left in the world, and through you, something of his son lives on. Because of you my life, and the lives of other people, will never again be what they were. Because of you more people are going to die, and I may very well be one of them. So. Speak. And choose your words very carefully. Don't give me the slightest reason to drop you deep into the slime at the bottom of this river, because you have absolutely no idea how much I want to."

For emphasis, Baby Joe tilted the concrete.

Monsoon let it all hang out. The accumulation of fear and anxiety he had built up while tripping precariously from one near-catastrophe to the next finally burst the bubble, and his words came out in a babbling stream without cohesion and without the slightest attempt at deviousness. The truth, the whole truth, and nothing but the truth. When he finally ran out of steam, a silence descended as the others looked from one to the other.

"How much money are you talking about?" Baby Joe asked, flatly.

Monsoon hesitated. Baby Joe looked at him and eased his foot forward. The concrete block teetered on the brink of the jetty.

"Ten mill, man, ten big ones. Ten million fuckin' dollars, in cold blood."

Baby Joe stared at Monsoon for a long moment. The foot rocked. Monsoon held his breath, his eyes fixed on the toe of Baby Joe's boot. Baby Joe lifted his foot, and the concrete thudded back onto the jetty.

"Mr. Parker. You just got yourself some new partners," he said.

# Chapter 17.

Across from Wal's Outback was a ritzy little poon parlor called The Wild Wild East, replete with buxom little Vietnamese girls wearing cowboy hats and rhinestone gun belts with dildos in the holsters and very little else. Outside was a dejected-looking stuffed horse, minus its ears and deprived of the majority of its hair by some form of mange, which the girls would take turns mounting at night after the neon came on, firing cap pistols in the air and importuning passersby. Behind the horse tables were set on the pavement, and skulking at one of these sat Frankie Merang, glaring at the group sitting outside Wal's from between the horse's moth-eaten withers.

In terms of being bombed, Frankie was on a scale somewhere between Dresden and Hiroshima, but that had not prevented him from consuming three double whiskies as he spied upon the comings and goings across the road. He had seen the little dink come out of the back, together with the old dude, and sit with the guy that had cold-cocked him with the ashtray, and the old dinge. The broad and the lardass had gone through in back someplace. Somewhere among the short-circuiting neurons of Frankie's alcohol-flooded brain, an old-fashioned flashbulb went off. He suddenly remembered where he had seen that guy before. Back in Vegas, at the fights. *Well, ya seen ya last slugfest, pal.*

Like an old steam train building up momentum, a plan slowly hissed and chugged into Frankie's addled mind. The guy was drinkin' beer like it was goin' out of fashion. Sooner or later, he's gotta take a leak. Nine to five the john is out back. It would have to be, in a fleapit like that. So. Ol' Frankie would slide around the back, nice n' easy, an' find out where the head was, an' wait. An' when the sucker came out, Frankie would ventilate him while the dumb fuck still had his pecker in his hand. Frankie produced his very best evil leer and grabbed a passing girl by the cheek of her ass.

"Hey, baby," he said, flourishing a ten-dollar bill, "show me the back way outta this joint."


When it came to dealing seconds or switching dice, Monsoon was pretty good with his hands. When it came to using them for anything practical, he wasn't worth shit. Which is why the temporary shithouse that Wally had compelled him to build—under threat of severe genital rearrangement—didn't have a straight line in it, and didn't look like it could withstand a decent fart...which was a definite liability, given the clientele.

Inside, Crispin was trying to perform the almost-impossible feat of taking a crap while preventing his cheeks from touching the seat and holding his Bermudas off the dirt floor with one hand, at the same time. To his credit he was doing a pretty fair job until something large and heavy crashed into the frail structure. Unbalanced, he plopped backwards onto the commode, dropping his shorts, and grabbing at the chain in an effort to steady himself, giving himself an unexpected partial colonic irrigation in the process. His reaction was predictable.

"ASIA! GET THAT EXCREBLE FUCKING BEAST AWAY FROM ME."

A reasonable request, under the circumstances. The only problem was, it was nothing to do with Rodney. Rodney was in seventh heaven.

She was in the cool shade of her stall, with Asia's sweet perfume filling her trunk, being fed ripe mangos and having her ear scratched. She was gazing longingly at Asia while she rumbled her pachyderm love song.

It was Frankie Merang who, stalking the yard on unsteady pins, had stumbled into the outhouse, spiking his bruised head on a sticking-out nail and contriving to drop his gun.

"Shit," he said.

"What did you say?" Crispin asked, desperately looking around for something to dry himself on.

"I didn't say anything," Asia replied. "What are you shouting about?"

Frankie steadied himself against the fence and, after picking up the Browning and wiping it on his trousers, peered unsteadily in the direction of Asia's voice. The broad! Somewhere on the other side of this fence. Might as well have a little fun with the bitch while he was waiting.

Asia had shrugged and gone back to scratching Rodney's ear when the gate suddenly burst open and she turned in alarm to see the enormous figure of Frankie Merang framed in the doorway, supporting himself with one hand and waving a big cannon in the other.

"Don't fuckin' scream, bitch. C'mere."

Crispin's muffled voice came from inside the outhouse. "Asia. I can't hear a word you are saying."

Asia didn't move. She was watching the swaying barrel of the gun.

"I said, fuckin' c'mere," Frankie repeated.

Rodney made a deep growling noise and began to sway her head backwards and forwards.

345

Frankie looked at her as if he had just noticed her. "Wha' the fuck's tha'? Fuckin' elephant. I'm gonna shoot the fucker."

Frankie raised the Browning and pointed it over the top of Asia's head, aiming the unsteady barrel in the direction of Rodney's eye.

"NO!" Asia screamed, rushing forward. She charged Frankie with her nails clawed like talons, raking towards his face. Frankie let go of the doorpost and punched her in the stomach, dropping her. As he raised his boot to kick her in the face he was frozen by an earsplitting squeal and raised his eyes just in time to see what appeared to be an irate mountain bearing down on him. He focused on a bright red eye as a huge bristly forehead smacked into him, lifting him off the ground and slamming him into the outhouse, which collapsed like a house of cards. Frankie landed hard on the packed earth, dropping the gun. If you ever want to sober up in a hurry getting battered to death by an enraged elephant will do it, and Frankie's mind was stark, daylight clear as he desperately scrabbled towards the Browning. His fingers were inches from the butt when he felt a steel vise close around his ankle and felt himself being whirled aloft.

Rodney began to play with the 260-pound Frankie as if he were a rag doll, slapping him from side to side, jerking him up and smacking him into the dirt, squealing at an unbelievable volume as she did so. Her squeals were echoed by Asia's piercing screams from where she sat in the dirt in the corner of the paddock, by Frankie's agonized bellows, and by the muffled shrieks of Crispin from where he lay trapped under the wreckage of the collapsed outhouse.

In the corner opposite Asia was a prodigious pile of fresh elephant dung that Rodney had carefully deposited an hour before, and she now flipped Frankie towards it, sending him cartwheeling end-over-end through the air, flailing like an inept oversized gymnast. As Frankie landed face down in the manure with a distinct plop Baby Joe came crashing into the yard, with Wally close on his heels and Bjørn Eggen bringing up the rear. Baby Joe snatched up the Browning and grabbed

Asia by the arm, pulling her aside as Rodney charged past to where Frankie was making a feeble attempt to rise. Spinning with surprising agility and grace, Rodney sat down, planting her enormous butt squarely on Frankie Merang's head. Then, flapping her ears and raising her trunk vertically, she let out a peal so loud that the others had to cover their ears against the blast.

There followed a moment of stunned silence, a cameo in which nobody moved, everyone staring in amazement at Rodney, who sat proudly gazing at Asia. A low groan broke the spell, and Wally and Bjørn Eggen lifted the crumpled tin roof of the outhouse to find a splattered and soiled Crispin looking as if he were about to cry, which he was. He had his shorts around his ankles, a bamboo splinter piercing his squashed pompadour, and the toilet seat slung over his shoulder like some bizarre accessory.

Disconsolate, he hung his head and began to weep, saying in a high feeble voice, "I can't stand any more of this. Really, I can't."

As they tried to console him, while trying equally hard not to burst out laughing, Rodney stood and lumbered over to Asia and began to nuzzle her face with her trunk.

Asia stroked the animal's forehead. "Good girl," she said softly.

Rodney rumbled. Baby Joe went over and rolled Frankie over. The shape of his face was neatly imprinted in the dung. Frankie's besmeared eyes were opened wide in horror, and his open mouth and nostrils were packed with fibrous, vaguely green elephant shit. He was stone dead.

Asia was having a hard time calming Crispin down, especially as Wally and Bjørn Eggen were pissing themselves laughing. He had been hosed down and was sitting on a bar stool, wrapped in towels, nursing a half a pint of gin.

"I can't tolerate much more of this. I shall go quite mad. I'm not used to it. This is pure insanity. I'm a musician, a singer, an *artiste*, a fucking *star*. My boyfriend is murdered, I nearly get blown up, my fucking turncoat dog is killed, I'm chased from my home, my career, my fans, I have people shooting at me in some festering swamp while some leering, toothless hag is drooling all over me, and I end up in fucking never-never land, where I can't even take a decent dump in peace without some fucking circus refugee flattening the shithouse. My nerves are shot to pieces, I can't sleep worth a shit, and my hands are shaking so much I can't even wank myself into oblivion."

When he said wank, Wally and Bjørn Eggen, who had been struggling heroically to restrain their laughter, exploded once again, rocking back and forth on their stools with tears streaming down their faces.

"WILL YOU TWO FUCKING GERIATRICS KINDLY ATTEMPT TO ACT YOUR AGE?"

"Yes, c'mon boys," Asia added, "you can see that he's upset."

At that moment Baby Joe came in, carrying the things he had dug from Frankie's pockets, and the gun. "What's going on?"

"Crispin vants to haf a vank but it is not possible," Bjørn Eggen said.

Wally, who was just taking a mouthful of beer, sprayed it across the room and collapsed. Asia tried to give Bjørn Eggen a dirty look, but had to bite her lip and turn her head away.

Baby Joe had something that he wanted to say, but he could see that it wasn't a very good time. Grabbing a beer, he turned and walked back out into the yard.

"Aah, what?" Asia said, with her eyes still closed. She had just enjoyed the most wonderful meal of delectable spicy dishes done with coconut milk, coriander, lime, and ginger, with exotic names like *cha gio*, *bun ho*, and *cuon diep*, washed down with a couple of bottles of chilled French wine, and she now lay on the deck in the sun, dozing as the boat rocked gently up and down.

Bjørn Eggen, Asia, and Crispin had gone to meet Mary Rose Muffin for lunch on a floating restaurant that gave them a tour of the harbor while they ate. Baby Joe had been against their coming and had wanted them to lay low but they had all prevailed upon him, arguing that he was being over-cautious now that Merang was dead, and against his better judgment he had relented, and Asia was glad that he had because they were having such a marvelous day.

Crispin laid next to her, wearing a garish kimono that he had bought to console himself after his ordeal, a pair of massive Elton John sunglasses, and a huge floppy straw hat to protect his delicate complexion from the sun. At the back of the junk, Bjørn Eggen and Mary Rose dozed on a large hammock under the shade of a canopy. They were under sail, and as the skipper idled across the bay the only sounds were the wind and the lapping of water against the hull and the soft clinking sounds of the chef clearing up the galley below. A loud splash went unheeded, but when Asia heard someone say "Aah," she spoke to Crispin.

"Hmn?" mumbled Crispin, who was almost asleep. The rocking of the boat was soporific, and the breeze divine, and the meal had just been to die for, especially after that fucking roadkill that he had been forced endure in the bayou.

"You said 'aah.'"

"You're dreaming, sweetie. I didn't say anything."

"Well, somebody did."

"That would have been the captain," an unrecognizable voice said.

Crispin opened his eyes and saw a figure standing over him, featureless because of the glare of the sun immediately behind it. Crispin shaded his eyes.

"Yes," the voice continued, "that would have been the captain saying 'Aah' as I pushed him overboard."

Asia sat up, her feeling of wellbeing instantly dissipated and replaced by a tautness in the pit of her stomach. She saw the figure standing over them, extending an object towards them. It was a gun. With a silencer.

"Don't speak. Stand up and move to the back of the boat," the man said.

Crispin was already whimpering, and as Asia stood she could see the black-clad figure of the captain, flapping in the green water in their wake. The man herded them to the back, to where Bjørn Eggen still lay on the hammock, fast asleep. Mary Rose Muffin was awake and standing over him. The man shoved Crispin hard in the back, and he stumbled into the hammock, waking Bjørn Eggen.

"Vhat the fock?" he muttered, rubbing his eyes.

"Shut up and get up," the man said.

The old man struggled to his feet, his mind foggy, still not fully comprehending what was happening. Instinctively, he reached out to put a protective arm around Mary Rose. She avoided his hand and moved away, opting instead to stand next to the man. Expressions flitted across the old man's face in quick succession. Surprise, confusion, hurt, and finally resignation.

"Sorry," Mary Rose said, "nothing personal."

"You fucking bitch!" Asia hissed, spitting at her.

The man slapped her across the face, hard. Crispin flinched, as if he himself had been slapped, and he looked from one face to another, bewildered, still not getting it.

"What's going on?" he muttered.

"Can it, fat boy," the man said, and then, "Mary Rose, I presume."

"You presume correctly, and you must be Horatio, if I am not mistaken."

"You are not mistaken, madam, the very same."

"Yes, I thought it must be you when I saw you at the park," Mary Rose said, removing the pin from her hat and shaking her hair loose.

"You got good peepers for an old dame," Horatio said.

Mary Rose gave him a sharp glance. "One question, Horatio. Unless your surname is Nelson, how do you propose to get us back to port now that you have seen fit to throw the captain overboard?"

"No sweat. I got the other coolie trussed up down below. Now, if we're through with the chitchat, what say we do what we came here to do? Who wants to be first?"

"How haf you come on the boat?" Bjørn Eggen said, his expression changing again to one of resolve. Crispin was crying, and Asia had her arm around his shoulder. She was glaring at Mary Rose with absolute malice.

"Fuckin' Spock beamed me aboard, what do you think, you old fart? Okay, you're first."

Mary Rose looked at Bjørn Eggen with sadness in her eyes.

"Where do you want it, pops?" Horatio said, leveling the gun at Bjørn Eggen's heart.

"No," Mary Rose said, quietly, as she carefully placed her hat on the seat next to her.

"No, what?"

"He's not first."

"Oh, no?" Horatio said. "Then who is?"

"You are," said Mary Rose, stepping forward and driving her hatpin up to the hilt into his eye.

Horatio stood for a second, a look of blank incomprehension of his face. His ruined eye began to drip down his cheek like a broken egg, and a trickle of blood appeared. He dropped the gun, the light went out of his remaining eye, and he crumpled to the deck with a dull thud.

Nobody spoke until Mary Rose said, "Oh, dear. It looks like I'm out of a job."

Take a grab bag, stuff it full of conflicting emotions, give it a shake, tip it out, and you will have an approximation of the confused feelings that were running through the group assembled belowdecks on Wally's junk.

Mary Rose was crying, dabbing her eyes with a lilac handkerchief, and Bjørn Eggen sat next to her, holding her hand, looking at her with different eyes. Crispin sat by himself, mumbling incoherently and looking stunned, as if he had been bludgeoned over the back of the head with a blunt object. Monsoon was smoking and biting his nails, glancing at the hatch every few seconds as if he feared what might be coming down it. Asia was looking at Mary Rose, vacillating between disgust, gratitude, and forgiveness. Wally was passing out beers from a crate in the center of the cabin and Baby Joe was leaning against the bulkhead and drinking from a bottle of scotch, looking from one face to another, considering the connections between them, the coincidences that had brought them here, and the fragile bonds that bound them all together.

There was brittleness in the room, a palpable tension, almost audible, like a violin string stretched to its breaking point.

"I'm so sorry, everybody," Mary Rose, was saying. "It was supposed to be just a job. I never meant to get involved. I'm just a silly, sentimental old lady. At first I was just supposed to watch and report back to the Don, keep an eye on everybody. But then it kept changing, and I was getting different instructions every day, and all the time I was getting closer to you all, and especially to Bjørn Eggen, until I didn't know what I would do when the time came. And even when I had made my mind up, I had to go through with the arrangement to protect everybody. I had to make it look real, and to be sure that that creature Horatio was the right person, and then put him off his guard. I couldn't say anything, in case somebody panicked and gave the game away. I'm so sorry."

She bent her head again, and Bjørn Eggen stroked her hand.

"Do not cry. Ve understand. You haf anyway do the right thing, *ja*. Only Crispin haf shit himself again, I think."

Wally sprayed beer again and, of course, just happened to be standing next to Crispin when he did it, and it was as if the fine beer mist washed the tension from the room. Everybody cracked up except for Crispin, who just stared at his ruined new shirt and said, "I fucking give up."

The laughter swept away the last fragments of unease, and the room dissolved into small talk, the beers went down, the bottle was passed, traumatic events became anecdotes, and for an hour it seemed as if it were nothing more than just a pleasant social gathering of friends, and not of fugitives, as if no evil shadow stretched across half a world to threaten them.

Asia's conflict resolved itself, her anger dissipated, and she went to sit next to Mary Rose and took her other hand. Mary Rose stopped crying. Monsoon went to sit by his grandfather, who proceeded to bend his ear and to tell him what a useless waste of space he was, how he was nothing like his father, and, if not for the promise that Bjørn Eggen Christiansson had made to his own son, he would not cross the road to piss on Monsoon if he was on fire, et cetera. Crispin was coaxed out of his shell and began to elaborate on the adventure of Rodney and the latrine, and Wally dispensed beer, wisdom, and shit-eating grins all around.

Baby Joe let them enjoy it, leaving it for as long as he could, letting the poison drain out of it and the fear melt away. He watched Asia, laughing with Mary Rose, the beer making her voluble and theatrical, seeing how her body moved beneath her clothes. She glanced at him and smiled, and her hand went up to touch her hair. Twice now he had almost lost her, and would have if not for the intervention of others. There would be no third time.

When he felt the moment was right he clinked two bottles together, and into the suddenly quiet room said, "Okay. Time to get serious. Mary Rose, do you know of anyone else that the Don has sent out here?"

"No, Baby Joe. Apart from myself and the one from the boat, I don't know of anyone."

"Okay. Monsoon, what about you?"

"No, man. I come out here with Frankie, an' another guy called Belly Joe. Frankie took care of the Belly, and the elephant took care of Frankie."

"So as far as we know, the only two guys the Don has out here at the moment—who are still breathing, anyway—are the two money guys. What's your take on that, Mary Rose?"

"Well, we never get the full story, dear. All we ended up with was a shopping list. And I'm afraid you were on it and our friend here."

"Fuck," Monsoon opined, grabbing the whiskey bottle and glugging noisily.

"I see. Well, the most important thing is to get everybody safe. That's where Wally comes in. Wal?"

"Yeah, right. We're all goin on a little cruise. I'm about ready to 'ead 'ome anyway. It's time. I got a mate who's the skipper on a freighter, runs between 'ere and Fremantle. Brings me all me Aussie grog so's I don't 'ave to swaller the local piss. Anyway, I fixed us up berths, an' we sail tomorrow night. It ain't exactly the QE2, but it's comfortable and there'll be plenty of good tucker and loads a cold tubes."

"Where the hell is Fremantle?" Crispin wanted to know.

"Australia, ya bladdy ignorant petrol pooftah," grinned Wally. "We'll 'ead up north, I reckon. I've got 'alf a share in an 'otel up there, and that's where me people are from. It's fucken bush up there, mate, nothing but roos, crocs, dingo shit, and fucken billabongs. Sherlock fucken 'Olmes'd never find ya."

"Everybody okay with that?"

Nobody spoke.

"Mary Rose?" said Baby Joe.

"Well, I might as well. It wouldn't be very wise for me to go back to the USA, and I really don't have anywhere else to go. Besides, a sea trip will be fun."

"Bjørn Eggen, what do you want to do? Go home?"

"No, fock dat. For sure, I go vith you," said Bjørn Eggen. "Vil be great adventure."

"Asia?" said Baby Joe.

"You know I'm with you," she said with a soft smile, then added, "Crispin, you're in this too."

Crispin was pouting because even though he wasn't quite sure what a "bladdy ignorant petrol pooftah" was, he was sure that it wasn't something nice.

"Oh, sure," he said, "a long sea voyage on an unseaworthy vessel in the company of geriatric assassins, alcoholics, and jungle bunnies. How delightful."

"Well, if you prefer, you can always go back to Vegas and get shot."

"No, thank you very much. I'm coming with you. Where else have I got to go?"

"What about me?" Monsoon said. "I won't have no place to go neither."

"Bjørn Eggen?"

"This little bastard is not deserving to come with, *ja*, after all the trouble he make, but I think ve must not leave him."

"Anybody else object?"

Again there was silence. Crispin looked as if he might be about to say something but did not.

"Okay, then, you're in. But you have to earn your keep."

"What do you mean?"

"I mean this: According to what you say, a lot of money is on its way here. A lot of the Don's money. I say we make it our money. We have all had our lives irretrievably altered because of what that man has done. I say he owes us. Monsoon is at the root of all this. He owes us, too. It's payback time, ladies and gentlemen. Time to take the money and run, as they say."

"But what about the Don?" Crispin blurted out. "He'll find us again. He'll never stop looking for us. Never ever."

"Yes, he will," said Baby Joe quietly.

"How do you know?" said Crispin, half-hoping, half-despairing.

"Leave it to me," Baby Joe said.

The way he said it made Crispin believe him.

The light had faded from the western sky as Asia and Baby Joe stood together on the bow of the junk, watching the endless and unintelligible semaphore of reflected, flickering lights glistening on the water. The wood of the deck was cool in the afterglow of the recently descended sun, although the night was yet hot. An uncountable host of crickets added their stridency to the general din surrounding the junk. A slight breeze had risen from the east, cooling their faces. Bjørn Eggen and Mary Rose were asleep, and Wally had gone ashore to make some arrangements.

Even though Baby Joe knew that the plan would not work without Monsoon, and even though he knew that Monsoon was aware of the score and realized his best and perhaps only chance of coming out of this thing anything like okay was to play it straight...he didn't like it. Monsoon was a joker when you needed a jack, any way you looked at it.

Apart from the Monsoon Factor, it looked okay in theory. Monsoon would meet the money people at the airport. Later, he would take them to Long Suc to see the MGJ. Wally's mob of kids would be watching every step of the way. Then, theoretically, the actual exchange would take place later, at which point he would relieve the Don's men of the burden of their responsibility, with Wally acting as unseen backup. The others would be waiting aboard the tramp steamer. Once they had the money, they would hightail it to the ship and set sail immediately for Australia. Simplicity itself!

What could possibly go wrong? If you discounted double crosses, triple crosses, accidents, mishaps, coincidences, the fickle finger of fate, the winds of change, the icy finger of destiny, divine intervention, blind luck, shooting stars, the prophesies of Nostradamus, and the potential, sudden, unexpected appearance of the Harlem Globetrotters.

"I'm scared," said Asia. "Are you sure this will work?"

"I've never been sure about anything in my entire life," Baby Joe said. "And I'm certainly not about to start now."

"This is no time to be funny," she said. "Tell me."

"Okay. I'm sorry. You're right. Asia, this is the only way. Whatever happens, he won't let go."

"What are you saying?" Asia said.

"I'm saying this. As Crispin said, after we do this, the Don is going to come after us with everything he has. Here, somewhere else, wherever we go, it won't make any difference. It will be relentless, unending pursuit. We'll never be safe again. There's only one way that it can really be over."

"Which is what?"

"The Don."

"What do you mean? What are you going to do?"

"I'm going to kill him."

"You what? They'll kill you if you try."

"They'll kill me if I don't. I'm tired now. Enough. I didn't ask for this. The only way to end it is to walk right up to the heart of it and kill it. The Don is just a man. I'm through hiding. It's not my way. This fucker has threatened me and people that I care about, and it's like with a rabid dog. You can't give it a fucking biscuit. You have to shoot it."

"Oh, please." Asia grabbed him and clung to him. "Oh, please don't. Please don't do this."

Baby Joe pushed her away, gently but firmly, and held her at arm's length, looking at her. "I have to. For you. For me. For us. I'll be all right. I'll do what is necessary to stop this, and then I'll come and find you."

"Will you?"

"You believe me?"

"I believe you."

# Chapter 18.

Put an image in your mind of a typical male banker. Early middle age, conservative suit, conventional tie, briefcase, laptop, glasses probably, something discreet, possibly with a silver half-frame, expensive platinum-tipped fountain pen. Put this image in your mind, and then forget it.

Booby Flowers looked nothing like that. For one thing, Booby was only twenty-three. For another he wore Blues Brothers shades, sported a ponytail, chewed gum, and favored jeans, sneakers, and T-shirts with corporate logos that he got for free at all the conventions he attended. In lieu of a laptop he had an MP3 player almost permanently attached to his ears, which he used for listening to esoteric classical works by composers that nobody else had ever heard of. He also had more degrees than a protractor, had declined membership of Mensa due to a paraphrased version of the old Groucho Marx gag—insofar as he didn't want to be a member of any intellectual elite who were not intellectually elite enough to recognize his unsuitability as a member—and had been laundering, expediting, and transferring funds for shady individuals from Buenos Aires to Toronto since he was seventeen years old.

For a description of his partner, Giuseppe Scungulo, refer to the original concept. Giuseppe was a bit long in the tooth, but what he lacked in street cred he made up for in experience, sound judgment, and the fact that he was Don Ignacio Imbroglio's cousin. Approaching similar financial views from opposing ends of the philosophical scale, Booby and Giuseppe worked well together and the talents of each complemented the abilities of the other. If it hadn't been for the fact that they hated each other's guts, it would have been a really cool partnership.

Being used to the vagaries of their chosen profession, neither man was unduly surprised when the expected people were not at the airport to meet them as they stepped into the arrivals hall. Nor were they surprised when, having stopped in the bar for a little something to take the cabin pressure dryness out of their throats, a perspiring and breathless person bearing a certain resemblance to Tiger Woods approached them and asked them if they were from Las Vegas.

"*Vaffanculo*," Giuseppe explained.

"What?" said Monsoon. "I said, are you from Vegas?"

"What did he say?" Booby said, without removing his earphones.

"He wanna know if we're from Vegas?"

"What? I can't hear you."

"Well, turna the fucking radio off."

The piece that Booby was listening to was coming to a particularly important passage, so he held up one finger until the stanza came to an end, then removing his earphones said, "What did you say?"

"I say you a fucking ignorant *stronzo*, an' wanna these days I gonna kicka your ass."

"I see. And who is this person?"

"Are you from Vegas, pal? I don't think your buddy speaks American too well."

"He's an Italian peasant. He should be selling ice cream, actually."

"So, where ya from?"

"My mother's pussy. And you?"

"Look, pal. I asked you a simple question. Are you from Las Vegas, and are you on business for the Don, because if you are, I'm supposed to meet you."

"I thought you'd be taller."

"What?"

"Never mind. Yes, quite. I'm Booby Flowers."

"Booby?"

"Short for Beauregarde. Old-fashioned family. This is my associate, Giuseppe Scungulo."

Monsoon nodded, noting that old Giusseppe looked less than thrilled to see him.

"Monsoon Parker," he said.

"Monsoon?"

"Short for rainy season. You bring the dough?"

"Don't be ridiculous, Mr. Rainy Season, one does not bring such amounts, one withdraws them. Do you have the merchandise?"

As he said the word "withdraws," drawing out the letter A, he made an effete stretching motion with his hand. Monsoon wasn't much of a fighter, but he'd lay eight-to-one he could take this fairy and made a mental note to give him a slap in the chops if the chance presented itself.

"I got the meet set for this afternoon. You get to view the stuff."

"Very good. Once that has happened, you get to see the money."

"All righty, then. There is a place called Wal's Outback. Everybody knows it. I'll meet you there at three, and we go. Okay?"

"Wal's Outback. Sounds exotic. Super. At three, then."

Booby gave a supercilious little wave as Monsoon was leaving. Monsoon left a supercilious little gobbet of spittle on the pavement.

"*Cazzo.*" Giuseppe said, as Booby was about to re-attach his earphones.

"What?"

"I say *cazzo*. That cocksucka. I am noa to trust 'im. Ain'ta straighta."

Booby shrugged. "Oh, what a tangled web we weave."

"What the fuck you talkin about now, *frocio*?"

"Nothing. It's of no consequence. After this evening, it won't matter."

Booby plugged in his earpieces, turned the volume on his player up to full, closed his eyes, and began to conduct an imaginary string quartet.

"*Vaffanculo catso*," said Giuseppe.

In the cab on the way to their hotel Booby's enjoyment of an especially complex piece was disturbed by a cheeky kid who was riding next to them on a scooter, peeking through the window. He interrupted his listening experience momentarily to give him the finger. The rider, who dropped back, was wearing an oversized crash helmet. Otherwise

Booby might have noticed that it was a girl, and that she had hair like an electrocuted Yorkshire terrier.

As Asia cried out Baby Joe put his hand over her mouth, holding her tight around the waist with his other arm as she writhed and convulsed under him, waiting for her to be still. When she was calm again he looked into her face, into her dilated pupils, huge and shining in the half-light coming though the opening in the canvas that surrounded them, and began to move again, very slowly. He kissed her and felt her tongue insinuating itself between his lips and his teeth, and inhaled deeply, sucking her sweet breath into his lungs. They lay together like that for a long time, barely moving, caressing each other gently, listening to each other's heartbeats, feeling the rising tide, which, gathering, grew until it filled them both, and there was nothing else in the world but their coming together and flowing together, like the confluence of two streams.

And afterwards they lay in stillness, listening to the muffled noises from outside, the clucking and cooing of birds as the sun dispersed the mist, seeing the subtle changes of light on the inside of the canvas over their heads. They lay in a makeshift bivouac at the very stern of the junk, barricaded from the rest of the boat by stacks of birdcages, with ducks and geese and chickens bearing witness to their intimacy. When Baby Joe sat up his head made an indentation in the fabric above him and he had to lean back against the material, feeling the sweat cool on his body in the rising breeze. Asia lay on her back, her disheveled hair arrayed around her head in wild curls, tracing the outlines of the scars on his body with her finger.

"You're full of holes," she said.

"So are you."

"You should know."

Baby Joe brushed a strand of damp hair from her forehead.

"Do you have to go?" she said.

"If we want the money, yeah."

"Can't I come with you?"

"No. It's liable to get hairy. Anyway it's best if you stay here with Crispin. He's just about at his breaking point."

"I don't like it when you go away."

"Nobody likes it. That's just the way it has to be sometimes."

"Why can't *we* just go away? Wally said there is a place where no one can find us."

"We've been through this. Maybe Wally's right. But I couldn't live like that. Hiding. Waiting. Watching every stranger. Never knowing it's over, even after years. I've got to make it over."

"But couldn't we be happy, in a small place, where nobody knows us? Who we are, or what we were?"

"Maybe."

"We're happy now, aren't we?"

"Yes, Asia. We're happy now. And now is all there is. I wanted to let it go, but I can't. I'm so much older than you, and…"

"But…"

"Let me finish. I'm older than you and can see the end of things. But I realized that it is foolish to not pursue something that you want, just because you can foretell the end of it. Because you know it can't last. What does? So I've decided to take it one day at a time, and enjoy it while it's here, and remember it without bitterness when it's not."

"You're going to make me cry."

"No, I'm not. There have been tears enough. Come on, get dressed. I've got to go."

"You're not leaving before the ship sails?"

"No, of course not. I'll stay and see you safely away. I'll be back when it's done." Baby Joe dressed quickly, kissed Asia's hair as she struggled with her underwear in the confines of the cramped tent, and slid out into the gathering heat.

Baby Joe and Monsoon were out back of Wal's Outback, waiting for Booby Flowers and Giuseppe Scungulo. The appointed hour had come and gone, and there was as yet so sign of the expected pair. Monsoon had a severe case of the jitters; he'd had second thoughts, and third thoughts, and was now well on the way to fourth thoughts.

"So what do we do now?"

"We wait."

"For what?"

"To see what happens."

"What is going to happen?"

"What am I, a fucking prophet?"

"So how long do we wait?"

"Until something happens."

"When will that be?"

"Monsoon, for fuck's sake, man."

"Well, it's all right for you. You do this all the time. I don't know how you do it. I'm bored shitless."

"Oh, I'm sorry. I forgot to bring the portable TV. How silly of me."

Monsoon sat quietly for all of eight seconds and then said, "But what…"

"Listen. I don't know any better than you. The meet was supposed to be at three, right? Then you and the two guys go see the General?"

"Yeah, but maybe they ain't comin'."

"Well, maybe they are."

"But what if they don't?"

"Who the fuck knows? Let's just wait and see."

"And then what?"

"Just wing it. Have you spoken to Long Suc?"

"No. With everythin' that was happenin' I never had the chance to go. Not since Frankie bought the farm. I tried phonin', but I couldn't get ahold of him."

"Did you call their hotel? See if there was a message?"

"Yeah."

"And?"

"No."

"What do you think that means?" Baby Joe said.

"Fucked if I know."

"So as far as you know, the deal is on."

"Are you fucking deaf? I don't know."

"Without Frankie's sample, you are the only one that can positively ID this shit, right?"

"As far as I know, yeah."

"And the Don wants you on the team because of the coffin scam, correct?"

"Could be."

"Which is why he told Long Suc to let you out of the shit pit?"

"That's the only reason I can think of."

"So Long Suc can't do the deal without you?"

"Yeah, I mean, no. I mean, maybe not, I guess."

"And the bankers won't produce the cash until they're convinced that the merchandise is legit, which is what you set up with the General, no?"

"Yeah."

"So how come they ain't here?"

"Well, you're the dick. You figure out what's goin' on."

Baby Joe consulted his watch. It was close to four-thirty. "They ain't coming. So we go."

"Go where?"

"Wonderland to see Alice, dipshit. Long Suc's, where do you fucking think?"

While Baby Joe and Monsoon had been fruitlessly waiting for Booby Flowers and Giuseppe Scungulo, at Wal's Outback, Booby Flowers and Giuseppe Scungulo were fruitfully conducting business with Long Suc in the antechamber of his business emporium. The conversation was going smoothly, or at least as smoothly as a conversation involving a retired Viet Cong warlord and a monosyllabic old-school Sicilian gangster — neither of whose commands of English could be said to be impeccable — and a smart-assed college grad bean counter who insisted upon conducting the proceedings with his earphones in, could go.

As a nod to his American friends, Long Suc had added a Yankees baseball cap to his ensemble, worn with his long braid protruding through the adjustor in the back, which had the effect of making him appear as every bit as trustworthy as a rat with a gold tooth. And, in a touching gesture of concern for his business partner's sense of security, he had added to his complement of oily, bare-chested, bandolier-wearing, expressionless evil henchmen, bringing the number to five. As the Americans entered the doors were closed and two henchmen immediately took up positions behind them, denying them exit. Long Suc smiled and half-raised his right hand, which for him was an effusive gesture of affection.

"Ah. Welcome, friends. Very pleased you come see me. You bring money?"

Giuseppe stepped forward to the accompaniment of the harsh click of an automatic weapon being cocked. He stopped.

The general smiled. "Please, my friend. You lift arm. Like this."

The general raised his hands above his head and Giuseppe did likewise, as if they were playing a sinister version of Simon Says.

"Please. You also."

Booby joined in the game, wrinkling his nose as the evil henchman who frisked him breathed the obligatory foul breath into his face.

The frisking concluded, Long Suc said, "Thank you. Is necessary, you understand. Please. You bring money."

Booby grinned at the general. He was loving it. It was some kind of whacko late night TV show. Raiders of the Lost fucking Ark. He couldn't believe this kind of shit still went on. Groovy.

"Er, well, actually, Mr. Suc, we are under instructions to see the merchandise before we produce the money. Is necessary, you understand."

There are those who might consider imitating the accent of homicidal Asian warlords, especially in front of their men, to be a trifle unwise. Long Suc smiled pleasantly at Booby. He was smiling pleasantly at the mental image of the insolent little *du ma* suffering the death of a thousand cuts.

He snapped his fingers, and an engine burst into life. A cloud of smoke accompanied by the stench of diesel filled the room as a forklift trundled in through an archway, balancing a pallet on which were neatly stacked a perfect pyramid of briquettes of Machine Gun Jelly. Each one had been thoughtfully numbered by Long Suc in big red letters. The driver killed the engine. He was diminutive, very young, wore black pajamas, and although a henchman was obviously not qualified for evil status. In fact, he seemed quite pleasant.

"You count. Okay. All there."

Giuseppe had just about had enough of this B-movie-looking slope clown, and even though the pieces were patently all there, he made a point by sauntering over and methodically counting them.

"*Tutti bene*," he said, after taking his time.

"Good then. Now you go bring money, yes? But I forget manners. You want drink?"

"Sure, why not. Giuseppe, our host is offering us a libation."

"*Quello che hai detto*?"

"Do you want a drink?"

"Bourbon, straight."

"He would like…"

"Okay. I hear. You same?"

"Could I have beer?"

The general made a subtle gesture, and the pleasant henchman scuttled down from the forklift and disappeared through a door at the back.

"Now, about money."

"Ah," began Booby. The general held up a hand.

"How come you all time speak? How come you friend no say anything?"

"*Vaffanculo*, slant," Giuseppe said.

"Ah, okay," said the general, turning back to Booby. "Okay. About money."

"We'll go and get it now. We can be back in a couple of hours."

"Very good. But no come back here. Different place. Much better, safer. Also have very good karma. Bring good fortune."

"Where?"

The general smiled, and said proudly, "Temple of the Dawn of the Living Buddha. You bring money, we bring drugs, have nice dinner, all friends."

"Whata kinda fortune cookie bullshit isa this?"

The general turned his gaze to rest upon Giuseppe. He was imagining the death of ten million rabid leeches.

"Okay, General, fine, we'll be there," Booby said, hastily, before Giuseppe could make any more helpful comments, and then he quickly added, "General, there is another matter to be discussed."

"What you need?"

"Monsoon Parker."

As unfortunate coincidences go, think Titanic and iceberg, for Monsoon chose this precise moment to step through the door with a beatific grin on his face.

"Ah. Mistah Parker. We been expecting you."

Long Suc turned expectantly to Booby, who felt a little embarrassed speaking in front of Monsoon as he said, "The Don would like to know if you could kill him for us."

Monsoon had one hand on the door before the karate chop felled him.

Long Suc snapped his fingers in order to demonstrate of what little consequence the demise of Monsoon Parker would be. "Easy. But you friend Don say he no want me kill this man. I very confuse."

"That's right," affirmed Monsoon, in woozy voice, from where he lay on the floor.

"Yes, well, what the Don actually meant was, don't kill him until after we saw the merchandise."

"Ah. Very clear now. Okay."

It was as unexpected and surprising as it was beautiful, like a green bud in autumn, or a ragged wedge of geese flying north for the winter. Mary Rose Muffin had been marking time, waiting for the curtain to close on the part-tragedy, part-black comedy that had been her life. Waiting for the death scene, which she had been expecting for years, the mistake or miscalculation, the betrayal or bad luck that would herald the beating of black wings coming to take her troubled soul.

When she reflected upon her years, which she did with increasing frequency now, in the evening of her life, her descent into darkness seemed, with the benefit of hindsight, almost inevitable, as if her life had chosen her and not she it. As if she never had a choice. What constantly amazed her about it all was that she was not essentially a wicked person, but was—and had always been—a kind and compassionate woman. It was just that she had been the sort of kind and compassionate woman who had a tendency to shoot people. Or stab them, or poison them, or push them out of windows.

The first time had been almost an accident, back in the days when she was just a young girl from Baltimore, struggling for a living in sleazy New York burlesque, battling to feed the infant son who had gotten her kicked out of college and booted out of the family home. Her parents had been professional people, staunch Catholics, and pillars of the academic community, and one of their daughters being knocked up by some sweaty jock in the back of the family Plymouth was just not done. If they had known it had actually been several sweaty jocks, it would have been even worse. Back in those days Mary Rose had been quite a looker and a girl of healthy appetites.

The clientele at the joints where she worked were your typical scum-sucking, douchebag dirty-raincoat types, and one night one of them—who was a lowlife even by scum-sucking, douchebag standards—had accosted her on a rainy, neon-lit street as she was vainly trying to get a taxi to stop. He had pushed her over, and ripped open her blouse, and was kneeling over her, holding her by the throat with one hand and attempting to masturbate onto her tits with the other, when she had clattered him over the head with a dustbin lid. Then she had grabbed his dick and twisted it really hard. Apparently the guy was into severe dick twisting, because he promptly spunked all over the front of her skirt. She having just paid three bits that she could ill afford having it cleaned, this seriously pissed her off and she wielded the bin lid in both hands, Sir Lancelot style, and smacked him good, right in the kisser. He staggered off the curb and into the path of a passing beer truck, and went off to sing the low-life lullaby to the angels.

She had gotten off with a self-defense rap after the beer truck jockey testified in her favor in return for a quick tour of his cab, and the thing that she remembered most about the incident was standing over the broken stiff in the rain wishing he was still alive so that she could kill him again.

At that time, most off your mob hitmen were your standard five-o'clock-shadow, broad-shoulder, pin-stripe-suit, gat-bulging-under-the-lapel types, so there was a definite gap in the market for a sexy ruthless femme fatale, and Mary Rose had cashed in on it. In the early years she had had a kind of morality even in an immoral profession and had adopted a strictly scum-sucking, douchebag-only policy, refusing to whack anyone she didn't think deserved it. But the years, and exposure to the hard face of things, and personal tragedy, had coarsened her to the point where she no longer made the distinction, although pregnant women and children remained a big no-no.

She had eventually lost the kid to scarlet fever and later another one, in childbirth, and wars, alcohol abuse, and automobiles had taken four husbands, and after that she had given up on romance as a bad job. She had eventually hooked up with the Don, and followed him on his rise to the top, and the years had zipped by until she had found herself old and alone and wondering where it had all gone. And, as is the way of things, she had begun to worry about issues of her own mortality, and atonement, and to question the waste of a life, and a road that had started on a rainy night in the Big Apple, or maybe even before that, in the back seat of a Plymouth with a gang of sweaty and fervent boys.

And now, out of nowhere, the sun had risen in the west and a white-haired old man with bandy legs and a silly accent had awakened something in her that she had thought had been as dead as her children. Something that she did not understand, other than to know that it was something warm, and that she wanted to be near it, and to stand in its light for what remained of her days. And that maybe, even this late in the day, if she could put something back, however small, it might in some way count in the balance for what she had taken out, when the final measure was taken.

They were sitting in camp chairs, holding hands under a green-striped parasol, she with a gin and tonic and he with his inevitable beer. It was as if they sat not on the grimy, cluttered, and noisy deck of Wally's junk, looking at a muddy river, but on the deck of an elegant liner in a turquoise bay overlooking the palms and beaches of some Caribbean paradise.

Mary Rose put her drink on the packing crate she was using as a table, and a pig immediately tried to steal the lemon from it. She gave him a resounding slap on the snout and then, feeling guilty, took up the slice and tossed it to him. He caught it with a dexterity that would have brought appreciative applause from any seal and then sat staring at her, waiting for an encore. She giggled.

Bjørn Eggen returned from the frontier of slumber, and opened his eyes. "Vat for is funny?"

"This pig is harassing me."

"You vant I should kick him in his arse?"

"No. The poor thing has already had a slap on the nose."

"The pig is best in the frying pan, *ja*, or the pork pie I am also very much liking?"

"Shush, he'll hear you."

The pig wasn't taking any chances and lumbered off to the other end of the boat.

"See, now you've scared him away."

"Good. He was bad smelling, *ja*?"

Mary Rose laughed, and then stopped abruptly. "Bjørn Eggen?"

"This is me."

"Tell me it hasn't changed."

"Vat haf not changed?"

"This. You knowing what I do. What I used to do. What I have done."

Bjørn Eggen sat up, removed the dark glasses he was wearing, and looked at her. "You haf save me."

"It doesn't bother you, all those people I killed."

"I also haf the people killed. Many people, *ja*. Many."

"But that was different. It was in a war. Everybody kills in a war. I killed people in cold blood. Murdered them."

Bjørn Eggen shrugged. "Dead is dead, *ja*. I am not to be the judge."

"Did you think I was going to let you be killed?"

"For a moment, *ja*."

"What did you feel?"

"A bit sad, *ja*. Surprised. But not so surprised as this other one haf been, *ja*?" Bjørn Eggen chuckled, and reached for his beer.

"Were you afraid?"

"No. I haf no longer the fear. At my time, the death is a small matter, *ja*. I haf loose many things and only vait. But now, is a little different I think, *ja*?"

"How?"

Bjørn Eggen reached over and took her hand.

"Now I meet you, I think I haf reason for to try to hang on a bit longer."

Mary Rose reached up and put her fingers into his snowy hair. She said, "Thank you."

"For vat haf you me to thank?"

"For saving me."

"I think you haf me saved, *ja*"

"Then we saved each other."

"*Ja*. I think so ve did. I think so ve did."

Bjørn Eggen swallowed an improbable amount of beer, sat back, replaced his shades, and closed his eyes. Within moments he was snoring softly. Mary Rose adjusted the parasol to head off the sunbeam that was advancing across the deck towards his face. She looked down at him, and smiled.

# Chapter 19

Throughout history, people's lives have been saved by a bewildering and astounding variety of circumstances, contrivances, and personalities. Ninety-pound women lifting automobiles off their children; people saved from a fall by their suspenders; pilots plummeting thousands of feet, sans parachute, and landing in deep snow; emergency tracheal surgery performed with a bamboo stem or the barrel of a ballpoint pen; mountaineers rescued by big, furry, brandy-serving dogs; drowning people saved by dolphins; clairvoyants not taking doomed flights because of dreams; canaries in coal mines; cannibalism at sea; the sudden mutation of a virus; the random non-selection of a salmonella-contaminated dish; the inexplicable remission of a tumor; the inhalation of tainted breath from the lips of complete strangers; airbags, seatbelts, tourniquets, vaccines, antibiotics, electric shocks to the chest cavity, and so on and so forth, ad infinitum. Take any circumstance, and the odds of its being unique in the incomprehensible fandango of human experience are extremely slim. But, in all probability, Monsoon Parker was the first person to ever have had their life saved by a Polaroid camera.

Long Suc studied Monsoon, who was now viewing the world through a narrowing tunnel due to the pressure of the evil henchman's steely fingers on his throat. He indicated that the choking should stop long enough for Monsoon to be dragged forward, closer to him. The general's eyes were not what they had once been, and since he felt it was only ethical to honor the terms of the contract himself he did not wish to lose face in front of the Americans by missing with the giant .357 Magnum Colt Python hog leg that he now withdrew from his waistband.

As Monsoon lay, gasping and gagging on the floor, unable to voice even the feeblest of protests, one of the evil henchmen grabbed his hair and jerked his head back, so that his unfocused eyes were pointing approximately in the direction of the general. Long Suc cocked the hammer of his piece and, leaning forward, placed the barrel against Monsoon's forehead. His eyes swiveled inward, seemingly independent of one another, and aligned themselves with the cold blue metal.

It's amazing what the contemplation of a .357-caliber mercury-filled hydroshock bullet exploding into your brain cavity will do for your powers of recuperation and, given that time appeared to be at a premium, Monsoon decided upon a policy of begging, pleading, protesting, bargaining, and abusive invective, all combined.

"NowaitpleasedontI'lldoanythingI'llpayyoucan'tdothiswhyI'minnocentIdidn'tdo ithelpfuckyouyoustinkingslanteyedfaggottcocksuckerohGodnopleasedontshootmercy."

Because Long Suc did not actually understand a word Monsoon said, and because he actually didn't give a frog's watertight fanny anyway, he ignored him, and instead addressed Booby. "Okay. You see. You tell boss. Okay?"

The general was about to squeeze the finger that would relieved Monsoon Parker of the burden of existence, when Booby said, "No, wait. Hang on a minute."

The general was suddenly embarrassed by his lack of manners. He uncocked the weapon and extended it to Booby. "Oh. So sorry. Excuse me. You want do you self."

"No, General, thanks, I'm sure you understand, but our employer would like to have some kind of proof."

"Like head in basket?"

"No. Shit, no. That's not my bag, man."

"Ah, you want bag for head. No problem. I give."

"No, man. I need a photo. I want to get my camera from the car."

"Ah. Photo for boss see. Very good idea. Okay. I wait."

Escorted by two evil henchmen Booby headed for the door, while Long Suc instructed the pleasant henchman—who had just arrived with the drinks—to go and fetch him a mirror. After all, even cold-blooded, murdering, son-of-a-bitch Asiatic warlords want to look their best for the camera.

Baby Joe had chosen a spot outside Long Suc's where he would be concealed by the shadow of a magnificent banyan tree, which marched its multiple trunks in a stately procession all down the length of one side of the street.

There had occurred a period of unhelpful bickering, during which they had decided that the best thing to do would be for Monsoon to brazen it out, and to go in and find out what the fuck was going on. Or rather, Baby Joe had decided that the best thing to do would be for Monsoon to brazen it out, and to go in and find out what the fuck was going on. Monsoon had decided that the best thing to do was for Baby Joe to go and fuck himself, and for him to go back to the boat. Baby Joe then revised his thinking, and had decided that the best thing to do would be that if Monsoon wouldn't brazen it out, and go in and find out what the fuck was going on, he was going to shoot him.

After weighing up the relative merits of brazening it out and getting shot, Monsoon had decided in favor of the brazening.

Once this decision had been arrived at Monsoon had—uttering a fervent prayer, spiced with a decent helping of foul and abusive language—reluctantly crossed the road and pushed open the doors of Long Suc's Extravaganza of Exotica.

Ironically, it now appeared that the decision between brazening it out or getting shot had been pointless, as he was about to get shot anyway. Under the circumstances he decided the best thing to do would be to assume a ghastly pallor, vomit in terror, tremble uncontrollably, hug his knees, and rock back and forth, blubbering incoherently.

Baby Joe, meanwhile, was standing behind the bole of the banyan tree, hefting the Browning he had inherited from Frankie Merang. Cleaned of its coating of dust and elephant shit it contained one full clip, as Frankie had helpfully refrained from shooting anybody since he reloaded after emptying it into Belly Joe. When he saw the door open and the kid with the ponytail emerge, flanked by two tough-looking gooks, Baby Joe took a step backwards, deeper into the concealment of the tree's tangled and overhanging limbs.

Watching, Baby Joe weighed his options. There was no way of knowing what was going on inside, but he could speculate. Having more or less compelled Monsoon to enter, did he feel any sense of responsibility for his wellbeing? Not really, given it was all that little shit's fault in the first place. Infinitely more important than Monsoon's state of wellbeing was the money. If the dough was already inside, then it was too late. Perhaps the cash was in the car, but he seriously doubted it.

So what was he going to do? Sit under a tree all night, scratching his ass, or vent some of the frustration and anger that had been building inside him to furnace intensity—anger that he was storing inside, holding, waiting for the moment when he would need its energy.

Ponytail was rooting about in the back of a black Toyota Celica that was parked outside, with the one guard behind him and the other watching the door. They looked like two Dobermans, taut and alert, and Baby Joe knew all too well the folly of giving them anything less than the full respect they deserved. And how many more inside? How many more to come swarming out like angry hornets if he disturbed the nest? There was only one way to find out.

He stepped into the street, looked at the two men, and spat on the floor. The two men exchanged glances, and the one guarding the door began to walk across the street, with the other's eyes following him. Baby Joe ran diagonally away, doubled back, and trotted up to the Toyota. The first henchman started back, not running but walking quickly, and the second stepped forward.

Baby Joe, smiling, said, "Good evening."

The man hesitated, unsure, leaning forward slightly, one hand reaching behind his back. Baby Joe engaged his eyes and, still smiling, whipped his hand up, caught hold of the bandolier, and pulled the man forward and down, crashing his head into the doorsill of the Toyota. The man's knees buckled and Baby Joe pushed past him, knocking him over. As he attempted to rise, Baby Joe brought his boot down onto the back of his head, driving it into the pavement. There was a noise like a coconut being struck with a machete, and the man lay still.

Baby Joe looked up to see the other guard advancing upon him, swiftly but unhurried and relaxed. This would be a lot different. This one was ready. He glanced over to where Booby stood frozen in the headlights like a startled doe, his comic book characters having suddenly jumped off the page, forgotten the script, and turned scary. Baby Joe had the gun drawn, not wanting to shoot but ready if the man showed the slightest sign of reaching. He had to be sure the man was coming for him and not making for the door. He suddenly sprinted away from the car. It worked, and the man changed direction and dashed forward to cut him off, a boxer cutting down the ring. Baby Joe grabbed the petrified Booby, spun him in between himself and his pursuer, cracked him over the back of the head with the butt of the gun, and pushed him down.

The man stepped easily over the fallen Booby, stopped, and stared steadily at Baby Joe and at the gun pointed at his heart.

"You no shoot. Others come." He smiled and started to walk away.

"Stop," commanded Baby Joe, feeling foolish saying it.

"You no shoot," the man repeated over his shoulder, still walking away.

Fuck it. The nerveless little bastard was right. He looked at the retreating figure, at the tight muscles rolling under the oily skin of the shoulders, at the loose, balanced walk. Shit. Baby Joe didn't fear size or strength, or skill, but at his age he feared speed. The guy was a lot smaller than he, but less than half his age. As he stepped forward, he hoped that meant he only knew half as much. He knew he was going to have to take some incoming to get close enough and prepared himself.

The man whirled, and three fast and accurate blows thudded into Baby Joe's head and stomach. Rolling and tensing, Baby Joe took as much of the sting out of them as he could, but they still sent bells ringing. He pulled up, as if hurt, and let the gun fall from his fingers. Before it had hit the ground, the man was already bending down to retrieve it. As the fingers closed round the piece, Baby Joe's boot crunched down, splintering them.

Amazingly the man did not cry out, but stepped back and up and into a defensive posture. A foot came whirling up, which Baby Joe just managed to avoid by rolling against the Toyota, letting it support his weight. A second kick came zipping up and, hoping it wasn't locked, Baby Joe grabbed the door handle and wrenched it open. The glass popped and tinkled to the pavement as the man's foot drove through the window. This time he did cry out as Baby Joe slammed the door with his shoulder, breaking the leg. His pain was brief as Baby Joe stepped around and elbowed him hard three times — once in the temple, and twice at the base of the neck — each time cannoning his head off the doorframe. The man went limp.

Leaving him dangling from his trapped leg, Baby Joe took up the gun and walked back across the road into the shelter of the tree and waited a couple of minutes to see if the fight had disturbed the hornet's nest or not. As he waited Booby groaned and rose to his knees, rubbing the back of his head. Keeping a sharp eye on the door, Baby Joe strode quickly up to Booby, grabbed him by the collar, hauled him to his feet, and pulled him back over to the tree. Booby did not resist. Suddenly it was not cool anymore, and his detached irony had detached itself.

Once safely concealed by the branches, Baby Joe stuck the muzzle of Frankie's Browning against Booby's temple.

"You must have seen lots of movies," Baby Joe said, pleasantly.

By way of answer Booby cranked his eyes wide open to maximum, and his eyeballs rotated slowly in opposite directions like a pinball machine with a serious tilt. Baby Joe debated whether slapping him hard in the kisser would bring him to his senses or make him worse. He decided to experiment. The sound, like a haddock hitting a stone slab, could be heard across the street. Booby focused.

"I said, I'll bet a young guy like you goes to lots of movies," repeated Baby Joe.

"Sure," Booby managed.

"Well, this ain't one of them. The cavalry ain't coming, and the good guys don't win in the end. I'm going to ask you some questions. If I get the right answers, you get to go home and jerk off to Pet Shop Boys records. If I don't, you get to be part of someone's chicken chow mein. Now all I need are simple, yes-and-no answers. Are you following me so far?"

"Yes."

"Good boy. Is my friend still alive?"

"Yes."

"Is the other guy that was with you inside?"

"Yes."

"Is the money inside?"

"No."

"Can they get to it without you?"

"No."

"How many other guys inside, not including your buddy?"

"Five, maybe six."

"Well done. Now, repeat after me. 'A man has got me. A very bad man, with a big gun. The other two are down. Let Monsoon go, or my brains will be chop suey.'"

"A man has got me. A very bad man, with a big gun. The other two are down. Let Monsoon go, or my brains will be chop suey."

"Very good. Now we are going back over the street, and you are going to repeat what you just said through the doorway, as loud as you can."

Baby Joe stood with his back to the wall, holding the gun tight against Booby's head, as Booby did as instructed. There was momentary silence, followed by the sound of stealthy footsteps.

Inside, Long Suc was very annoyed. He was looking his absolute best, and now it looked as if he wasn't going to get his photo taken after all. He shouted, "What you say?"

Baby Joe tapped Booby on the head with the barrel of the Browning, and he dutifully repeated his words.

"So what?" said Long Suc.

"Tell him, 'So you don't get the money, asshole,'" whispered Baby Joe.

"So you don't get the money, asshole."

After a moment's reflection, Long Suc conceded the point. "Okay. Me let nigger go."

"Tell him," whispered Baby Joe, "that anyone who comes out of that door and don't look like Tiger Woods gets blown away, and so do you."

Booby repeated the word verbatim.

A brief period of tension ensued before Monsoon came hurtling out of the door and landed face-first on the pavement. Baby Joe shoved Booby inside, fired three shots in quick succession into the ceiling just behind the door, hauled Monsoon to his feet, and dragged him across the road, through the twisting trunks of the banyan tree and into the darkness beyond. After a few feet he came to a steep incline leading down to a rivulet. He pushed Monsoon down the hill, and turned and lay prostrate with the gun pointed towards the door. All that happened was a muscular figure appeared briefly in the doorway, glanced up and down the street, and closed the door.

Inside, Long Suc gazed at the zombiefied Booby, tenderly straightened his collar, and then slapped him very hard in the teeth. "That for calling me asshole."

Back at Wal's Outback, a man known to his few friends as Hmong Hmong whistled tunelessly as he labored to reconstruct the outhouse. From what he had been told, first somebody had vandalized it and stolen all the bricks and then, after a temporary affair had been knocked up, an elephant had apparently trampled it into splinters.

Hmong Hmong had heard many stories in his life, but he knew from his teachings that all was truth and illusion at the same time, so what difference did it make what had happened to the building? It was true that there was a large elephant in an enclosure next to where he was working, but his teachings told him that it was unfair and unwise to put blame upon an innocent animal, whose spirit was pure, and in truth he had no interest in what had happened to the building. What did interest him was that he was getting very well paid to rebuild it, and was getting free food and free drink, and with the money he would be able to buy a new bicycle and have a little left over for some jiggy jiggy at the weekend.

As he reached a leathery hand down to grab another brick, he noticed a strange substance on the ground and picked it up. It was a small, malleable lump with the texture of putty, but a very dark gray-brown color, much like the elephant. He raised it to his nose and sniffed, but it had no recognizable odor. He licked it, but it had no discernible taste. He was about to discard it when he noticed that his tongue was tingling with a most pleasant sensation. He gave it a bigger lick. The tingling grew stronger and even more pleasant. He decided to bite off a little piece.

The world suddenly looked brighter and clearer, and the sky appeared radiant, and the singing of the birds became enchanting and magical. He swallowed the whole piece. The sky turned into an atomic rainbow, and the singing of the birds became symphonic, and a huge bulge appeared in the front of his cotton pants. His tongue felt ten times its normal size, and flicked in and out of his mouth like a cobra's tongue, moving with a will of its own.

He looked at the elephant. It had turned bright pink, and its eyelashes were three feet long, and its trunk was a sinuous, sensuous, provocative delight, and its eye was as big as the harvest moon and gazed at him with tender longing. His eyes fell upon the elephant's vagina. It was swollen, bright gorgeous purple, and glistening and gaping and then, joy of joys, it was singing, singing to him alone.

Hmong Hmong dropped the brick he was still holding and, grabbing a plank of the elephant's enclosure, tore it from its fittings, creating a gap large enough to squeeze through. He was sobbing with ecstasy and love as he thrust himself into the hole.

The secret of the survival of species is adaptability. Baby Joe Young knew this, as he also knew that the secret of the success of a game plan is its fluidity, its ability to change when confronted with an unexpected move by an opponent. He knew all the mantras. Expect the unexpected; if something can go wrong, it will; blah blah blah, ad infinitum, and so on and so forth, et cetera et cetera.

So the trick here was to subtract the known from the unknown, add the possibilities, subtract the impossibilities, multiply by the intangibles, and come out with ten million dollars and a deck chair on Bondi Beach with a cold lager in hand, watching the surfers fall on their asses.

The known was that Monsoon had overheard Long Suc set up the exchange at the Temple of the Dawn of the Living Buddha, and that Wally knew where it was and what it was. It was, apparently, a legitimate place of Buddhist worship, but with a decidedly secular addition. In the back was a dining room where all manner of dodgy deals went down under the watchful eye of the Living Buddha, who represented the deity, served the tea, kept an eagle eye open for the fuzz, and slipped surreptitious messages between the conspirators in return for a discreet donation.

The unknown was how many people Long Suc had on his team, and what kind of hardware were they packing. Given the circumstances, and in the light of recent events, Baby Joe was fairly certain that the Don had not given the help the night off to attend their croquet match.

As a pre-game analysis, the team matchup didn't look too promising. The home team had — apart from home field advantage — an unknown number of fit, well-trained, fearless martial artists led by a cunning, unscrupulous former general who had survived and won two wars and seen more action than Errol Flynn's codpiece.

The away team consisted of himself, who was in fact a shadow of his former self, two old warriors who were sterling individuals but forty years past their prime, a homicidal lady pensioner with a heart of gold, a woman who was hell on wheels in the sack but probably not any great shakes in a shootout, a small-time shyster who was as much use as a chocolate condom, and a 250-pound puffball who couldn't take Winnie-the-Pooh.

All things considered, a full-frontal assault was probably doomed to failure. He couldn't even count on the element of surprise. Obviously, subterfuge and subtlety were the order of the day. Plus tea — the root of downfall of the British Empire — and the fact that, according to the tourist brochure published by the Temple of the Dawn of the Living Buddha, the Living Buddha bore a remarkable resemblance to Crispin Capricorn.

# Chapter 20.

In the private dining room of the Temple of the Dawn of the Living Buddha Long Suc, Booby, and Giuseppe sat around a long, black-lacquered Japanese table, which was a legitimate antique from the Edo period. They were seated on low chairs, which Booby thought were groovy and Giuseppe thought were fucking uncomfortable.

The room was painted, floor to ceiling, entirely in gold leaf. The furniture was likewise gold, as were the carpets, curtains, cutlery, plates, goblets, decanters, candelabras, and mirrors. Lined against each of the longest walls was a row of huge, identical, bronze Buddhas, sitting in smiling judgment upon the proceedings like a jury of benign uncles. At one end of the room was a low dais, on which sat two even bigger Buddhas. Enormous, imponderable, obese, golden, and laughing — laughing open-mouthed at the delicious folly of it all.

In between, in front of a golden filigree screen, on a golden throne, an obese bald-headed man, wearing only a loincloth and painted head to foot in gold paint, sat cross-legged, with a seemingly perpetual benevolent smile attached to his shiny cheeks. In a semicircle around them, seated cross-legged on the bare wooden floor, were thirteen men who would not have looked out of place at Kublai Khan's stately pleasure dome, except for the incongruity of the AK-47 that each had on his lap. Another incongruity, which did not quite fit the décor but which was at least color-coordinated, was the yellow Hyundai forklift parked in the corner next to the back door.

Long Suc was being a genial host, his geniality generated by the suitcase that lay on the table between them.

"This one of most beautiful and sacred room in all Asia," he said, smiling like a Burger King trainee on his first day in the job. "Much history, many famous people. Open case and show me money."

Booby and Giuseppe both leaned forward and fiddled with the combination locks, each having the code to only one end, although Booby had long ago figured out Giuseppe's code on account of the fact that he silently mouthed the numbers as he turned the dial. As the lid slapped against the table, Long Suc's lips almost met on the top of his head. He removed a wad and hefted it, as if he could tell from the actual weight that it was all there.

"You are welcome to count it," said Booby, somewhat unnecessarily.

Long Suc gave a small, disparaging wave. "No my fren, me no need count. He count."

Long Suc snapped his fingers, and two of his crew hefted the case and took it over to the forklift where one of their colleagues had a counting machine. A soft whirring noise began to purr into the room.

"And the, er, merchandise?" Booby asked.

"Merchandise already here, there, see?" Long Suc pointed to the dais.

Booby's eyes followed his finger, but he didn't see. He looked at Long Suc and shrugged.

"Buddha," he said, "very clever. Have to be Asian be so smart. You take Buddha back USA, no problem."

Giuseppe had had enough. "*Ma che cazzo dice*. Whata kinda Mickey-Mouse bullshit you-a talkin', for fucksa sake. Is oldest trick in fucking book, hide drugs insida statue. Yousa thinka US customs borna yesterday? *Che cretino.*"

Long Suc smiled pleasantly, thinking of the death of the twelve gay pandas. "No, no, no, my fren. You no understand. Buddha *is* drug. We melt, put in mold, paint gold, very clever, no? We put in crate, send straightaway USA. Okay, now we drink tea, celebrate."

"Fuckina tea, fuck that shit," said Giuseppe, tea apparently not being to his taste. "Whiskey."

Booby concurred.

"Okay, no problem," said Long Suc, thinking of the death of the barbed wire underpants.

He motioned to Living Buddha, who rose ponderously and shuffled out of a door behind the dais. After an uncomfortable silence of about ten minutes he returned, carrying a gold-lacquered tray with sixteen large gilded cups on it, fourteen of which contained tea, and two containing an approximation of whiskey. Pointedly serving the foreigners last, the Living Buddha wobbled through the company, smiling relentlessly and dealing out the drinks.

Crispin was feeling better than he had for days. He had never thought of gold as being a particularly becoming color for him, but after admiring himself in the full-length mirror of the Temple of the Dawn of the Living Buddha's luxuriously appointed restrooms, he had to admit that he looked pretty wonderful. Not that it was surprising, given what he had been through these past few weeks, but he might even have dropped a couple of pounds, and there was the faintest inkling of a cheekbone rising under the gold-painted skin of his pudgy cheek. With his pompadour firmly squashed under a close-fitting gold swimming cap, and the rich sheen of the gold paint on his limbs, and the oriental slant of his eyes where they had been cleverly taped at the corners, and his gilt eyeliner, and his tight-fitting stretch spandex bicycle shorts under his golden loincloth, and his heavy Cupid's bow lips all golden and inviting, he could almost fancy himself.

At first he had flatly refused to even consider what Baby Joe had suggested. But then Asia had spoken to him of how the others were relying on him, and how without him there could be no money, and he had started to reconsider. When Mary Rose had told him how stunning he would look, and how he was the only one who had the talent to pull it off, the old trooper had started to come out in him. When Baby Joe had called him a whining, sissy sack of shit who had been nothing but trouble from the beginning and that if he didn't do it Baby Joe was going to kick the shit out of him in front of God and all the world, it had just about tipped the balance.

When he first stepped out onto the dais he had been petrified, certain that he would be discovered immediately. His anxiety was quickly dispelled and replaced by relative calm as it was soon apparent that no one had noticed the switch. The relative calm was gradually replaced by irritation that no one was paying any attention to him. The Living Buddha's perpetual smile was on the point of becoming a perpetual pout when Long Suc motioned him to go and fetch the drinks.

The real Living Buddha was, meanwhile, struggling with his worldview, his inherent belief in the all-wise beneficence of the universe, and the fifteen yards of duct tape that bound his wrists and ankles.

Living Buddhas have certain expectations. For example, when they are approached by angelic, but dark-looking, teenaged girls bearing garlands and they bow their shaven heads to receive the same—all the while smiling serenely—they expect to be adored, embraced, and perhaps kissed.

They do not expect to be sapped to their knees, rabbit punched, and knee-dropped into unconsciousness. The object of Buddhism being heightened consciousness, not unconsciousness, they furthermore expect to awake to light and enlightenment, not bound and naked in complete darkness with an ominous scratching taking place somewhere in the surrounding obscurity.

Wally, Baby Joe, and Monsoon had staked out the Temple of the Dawn of the Living Buddha, with all entrances covered. Two of Wally's older kids, a girl and a boy, were acting as runners, delivering acerbic messages between the three.

"Listen. How many guys did the general have with him?"

"That I could see, a fucking football team."

"American or English?"

"You mean soccer?"

"I mean how fucken many?"

"Ten, twelve, maybe more."

"Armed?"

"Is a baboon's ass red? Fucken heavy artillery, man."

"Showtime!"

"What?"

"Look."

There was the case. A Black Toyota rolled to a halt and Booby and Giuseppe climbed out. Giuseppe had an embossed leather case attached to his left wrist by handcuffs for security's sake. Obviously, machetes were not real big in the old country.

"Maybe it's the money," said Monsoon.

"Maybe it's the Don's laundry," suggested Baby Joe.

Maybe it was filled with pornographic videos or kitchen appliances. Maybe the general was a closet model railway aficionado, and it was a train set. Maybe it wasn't. Maybe it was filled with the Don's money. A very large amount of the Don's money. Enough of the Don's money to repay him for the shitstorm that the Don had sent to rain on him, and to put a serious burn on Don Ignacio fucking Imbroglio.

He watched as Giuseppe and Booby proceeded up the long, tree-lined gravel walkway, and under a golden arch into the gilded pagoda that formed the vestibule of the Temple of the Dawn of the Living Buddha.

"Those ratfuck sons of bitches," Monsoon pointed out.

Baby Joe looked over to where Wally's son was standing behind a blind streetlight, and gave him the prearranged signal. The boy grinned an exact replica of his father's grin, and raced off.

Crispin was so far into character Lee Strasberg would have been proud of him. He was doubly concentrating. Concentrating on being the Living Buddha, and concentrating on the instructions he had been given. Serve the general first. Use your left hand, and spin the cup three times counterclockwise before offering it. Do not speak. Do not look into anybody's eyes. Maintain the smile. If spoken to, put the fingers of your right hand to your forehead and bow slightly. Don't fart. Serve the foreigners last, and quickly. They are the only ones who will look at you.

Leave as soon as possible. As soon as it has taken effect hit the gong three times — twice, then pause, then once more.

His performance was flawless, except that at the end he couldn't resist giving the cute one with the ponytail a little coy wink. He retired to the dais and assumed position as the general stood, followed by the henchmen. Booby caught on and stood as well, nudging Giuseppe, who gave him the evil eye and creaked to his feet.

"Very good do business with America man," said the general. "Also no hard feeling for war. Betta luck next time. To my fren, the Don."

For the sake of good manners he repeated the toast in Vietnamese, smiling at his guests: "I hope these two pederasts contract incurable wasting disease and die in writhing agony while on second last page of very long novel."

One of the most remarkable features of industrial rhino tranquilizer is the speed with which it becomes effective. No sooner had the assembled company knocked back their drinks than they keeled over in unison, like the soldiers outside Fort Knox in Goldfinger. The choreographed collapse was so fast and hard that Crispin thought he might have overdone it a bit with the syringe. He was unable to restrain himself from performing an impromptu victory Charleston twostep, before rushing across the room and enthusiastically banging the gong. Within seconds Wally, Baby Joe, and Monsoon slid into the room and began gathering the weapons from the unconscious men.

Monsoon's none-too-subtle sidle towards the case was halted by Baby Joe's voice. "Leave the fucking case alone and get the weapons, dickhead."

Wally began tossing the guns out of the window, under which were waiting his two children. Monsoon reached under the general's tunic and pulled the .44 from the shoulder holster under his arm, and then drew back his foot to give the general a gratuitous kick in the testicles, to give him something to think about when he woke up.

As he did so the general, who was already awake, gave him a gratuitous kick in the testicles. Monsoon's agonized scream and the general's shouted order coincided with the sound of thirteen henchmen jumping to their feet. They stood at the ready, waiting for the general to give the signal. The room became a tableau, each participant held in place by the force of the tension that invested the moment.

"You think you more smart than me, America?" the general barked. "You think I no tell revered and divine Living Buddha from fat number-ten perfume pansy? You think we fall for old industrial-rhino-tranquilizer-in-tea ploy? You ignorant. You born ignorant, you live ignorant, and now you die ignorant. And, one more thing…"

Nobody ever found out what the "one more thing" was. In view of the fact that thirteen only-partially-disarmed deadly assassins were about to launch themselves at him, it seemed to Baby Joe an opportune moment to hurl the smoke grenade he had retrieved from one of them. He followed this with simultaneous fire from two AK-47s, one in each hand, set on automatic.

That's when everything switched to slow motion, and it turned into the Chinese New Year. The Year of the Scapegoat. Lights began to flash as if he had just stepped out of a limo at a Hollywood premier, then a hundred jackhammers started up at once, Beelzebub lit a sulfur cigar and began blowing smoke down the passage, and someone started giving him a marble chip tattoo. He found himself rolling slowly forward like a scuba diver turning turtle, and in front of him someone was making popcorn and throwing firecrackers. The room went suddenly dark as a henchman decided to shoot all the lights out of the ceiling, and then—tired by all the activity—lay down on the stone floor and went to sleep. Forever.

## MACHINE GUN JELLY

The world fast-forwarded to real time, and Baby Joe rolled to his knees. A thick pall of red smoke hung in the air and a swarm of incensed fireflies zipped through it in all directions. A man fell at his feet, his mouth open to make some final comment about the injustice of it all, but the words died in his throat. Along with him.

A growing pool of blood spread along the smooth stone, insinuating its way into the cracks between the golden tiles. The dead man had two grenades attached to his vest. Baby Joe took one in each hand, pulled the pins with his teeth, threw one baseball-style in the general direction of the general and rolled the other across the floor. Two terrific explosions followed in quick succession, amplified by the closed room. Bizarrely, the gong resonated above the din, with a syncopated rhythm as if Buddy Rich were playing it. Something seared into Baby Joe's arm, and he glanced at the small smoking holes in his sleeve. He saw shadows moving towards him through the smoke, and looked around frantically for another weapon.

A rhythmic percussive banging came from beside his ear. One two three, one two three. Like a waltz. The last waltz. The shadows fell over.

Wally kneeled beside him, grinning in the smoke like a deranged medusa. "Are ya gonna sit on yer bladdy arse all night, yer nong, or are ya comin to the dance?"

Wally had dived out of the window as soon as the smoke grenade had left Baby Joe's hand, his first thought being for his children. He had had to give them stiff clout apiece to get them to run to safety. He had sat under the window with three AK-47s and emptied them over the sill in a spray pattern. He had then taken a .45 in each hand and rolled away to the next window and, standing back from the light, began to fire rhythmically at the shadows moving in the clearing smoke. One two three, one two three.

The firing had stopped, and there was an exaggerated silence after the twin explosions of the grenades. Wally handed Baby Joe a gun, and they crept behind a massive bronze Buddha and waited as the smoke slowly drifted out of the shattered windows.

Monsoon Parker felt strangely calm, almost euphoric, as if this latest in a series of seriously terrifying, life-threatening situations were just one seriously life-threatening situation too much for his brain to handle. His terror receptors shorted out, his brain switched from reality TV to MTV, and, as the bullets hissed past his ears and snatched at his actual clothes, he walked calmly through the maelstrom singing "Dreadlock Holiday" to himself.

As he strolled towards the forklift he did not break step or rhythm, even when a piece of the shattered gong smoked across his scalp and took out a three-inch strip of hair and his left earlobe. He even found time to say a pleasant "Hi" to an evil henchman, who was frantically struggling with a jammed weapon and was much too busy dying to respond to Monsoon's greeting. Monsoon climbed into the forklift and started the motor, carefully looking behind him as he began to slowly reverse, exactly as if he had been pulling out of a lot in the local mall. The horrifying scream that came from under the forklift did not affect him one way or the other, and the bullets clattering off the bodywork and forks went unheeded.

He motored leisurely across the room to where the Machine Gun Jelly Buddha sat, smiling implacably. He was not hindered by the smoke and continued unfazed, as if he could see right through it, sliding the forks underneath the Buddha and hoisting it to waist height. He remained oblivious to the death and destruction raging all around him, even when the concussion from an exploding grenade ruptured his right eardrum.

When Long Suc materialized from the turmoil and smoke, snarling like a rabid hyena, and aimed a vicious swipe at his head with an enormous scimitar, he simply swayed his head enough to avoid the blade, and nonchalantly swung the steering wheel so that the vast MGJ Buddha bludgeoned Long Suc to the floor and under the wheels.

Monsoon carefully chose a spot in the outside wall, midway between two of the avuncular Buddhas, and gunned the engine. He was still singing as the forklift splintered the wooden wall, crashed out into the night, dropped miraculously down a six-foot embankment, and rolled away across the manicured lawns, through the immaculate flower beds, out onto the road, and headed downhill towards the docks.

It goes without saying, or ought to, that the Living Buddha's golden makeup was completely organic—in this case made of a base of beeswax—and a little-appreciated fact about golden beeswax body makeup is that when hot, especially when compounded with sweat, it becomes very slippery. This fact can come in unexpectedly handy when Living Buddhas happen to find themselves restrained by duct tape in complete darkness.

The Living Buddha was able to writhe free of his bonds and struggle to his feet just in time to hear what appeared to be a reenactment of Gettysburg start up above his head. The heady smell of incense gave him a clue as to where he might be and he shuffled forward, stubbed his toe on something hard, made a very un-Zen-like statement, and lumbered into the wall where he groped for and eventually located the light switch. He found himself in the inner sanctum, a small room behind the main hall where the Living Buddhas could relax from relaxing, and where people seeking enlightenment could find out exactly how deep the Buddha's wisdom was, and be initiated into one or two yoga positions that were not featured in the average meditation session.

Against the wall there was a gold-painted wooden chaise longue, replete with gold cloth-covered cushions, and a golden, lacquered Japanese table was set at right angles on the gilded tile floor. Next to it was a rather moth-eaten gold rug. The obligatory Buddha, this time solid brass, sat next to the table on a small platform on which oversized incense sticks smoked gently. Unfortunately for the Living Buddha the only door led into the main room, from where the noise was now truly alarming.

Some serious transcendental meditation was called for and he was about assume the position on the rug when the door burst open and a nightmare apparition hurtled itself breathlessly into the room, collided with him, and knocked him flat on his face. With an effort he struggled to his knees and then to his feet and turned to see Crispin staring at him, wide-eyed and panting, fanning himself desperately with his pudgy hands.

The Living Buddha had lived a life of study, and had applied himself religiously to his studies, but his studies were not of a temporal nature, and did not include languages. He was therefore compelled to draw upon the only two English words he knew.

"Fuck you," he said.

Crispin stopped panting and fanning himself with his pudgy fingers. "I beg your pardon."

"Fuck you."

Straws and camels' backs came to Crispin's mind. Something clicked in his brain. He heard it. Audible, like a switch. From hot to cold. He began to speak, slowly and softly at first, and then gradually building up steam.

"All right, that's it. Enough is enough. Listen, you fat cunt. In recent weeks, I have been beaten, threatened, shot at, kidnapped, humiliated, terrified, dispossessed, and upstaged by a fucking elephant. I have been dragged halfway around the world from one festering shithole to another. I have lost my house, my career, my lover, and my dog. Furthermore, I have literally shit myself. And I've had it. I am not taking any more shit from anybody. Especially, and I mean fucking especially, from a grotesque, ridiculous, circus-looking ponce like you. And you know what the difference between you and me is? I mean, apart from brains, looks, talent, intelligence, and charisma? The difference is, I make this shit look good, you fat turd!"

"Fuck you," said the Living Buddha, making up for what he lacked in vocabulary with succinctness. After all, he hadn't exactly had the best day of his career, either.

Crispin clenched his pudgy fists, lowered his head, and propelled himself at the Living Buddha. The Living Buddha decided it was time for a temporary abandonment of pacifism and did likewise. The two charged headlong at each other like two golden sumo wrestlers. The Living Buddha's education did not include languages, but it did include the rudimentaries of the martial arts, which meant that as Crispin charged, head down, bellowing like a bull walrus with its nuts caught in an ice floe, the Living Buddha was able to nimbly sidestep him and karate chop him on the back of the neck. Crispin's stunned momentum carried him forward onto the golden Japanese lacquered table. This Japanese lacquered table had not been constructed with weight support as a major concern, either, and, as Crispin landed square upon it, all four legs surrendered to gravity simultaneously, with the customary sickening crack of breaking bone. Amid all the pain and rage and confusion, Crispin suddenly became aware of an acute sense of déjà vu. *Oh, here we fucking go again,* he thought. *All I need now is a fucking dog to bite me.*

At which point the Living Buddha's Lhasa Apso came charging out from where it had been sleeping under the chaise longue and sank its teeth to the hilt in Crispin's beefy calf.

The silence was eerie, in some ways more frightening than the noise of the battle. In the drifting and dissipating smoke, Baby Joe and Wally had risen to their feet. They were the only ones that were able to. Baby

Joe felt the incipient sting of a dozen flesh wounds as the adrenaline wore off. Wally was bleeding in several places, but if it bothered him he didn't mention it. Even for two such experienced warriors, the scene facing them was as amazing as it was improbable and unlikely.

All the henchmen were gone, lying around the room in those grotesque, contorted attitudes that only death can give to the human body. All the walls, the floor, the ceiling, and the furniture were perforated with hundreds of bullet and shrapnel holes. Of the gong, only a jagged circle remained.

But not one single Buddha in the whole room had so much as a scratch. No fewer than five hundred rounds of ammunition, plus two live grenades and a smoke grenade at close quarters, and not one Buddha had even been grazed. They sat, smiling and laughing at the survivors, enjoying the immense absurdity of what they had just witnessed.

Giuseppe Scungulo had died without knowing what had hit him. The Italian's body lay in an enormous pool of blood, and fifteen feet away, upside-down and looking extremely surprised at the turn of events, was his severed head. Booby Flowers was still alive. He had suffered some superficial wounds but had slept peacefully through the whole thing. The Americans had been drugged for real.

Long Suc had reasoned that he could use events to keep the MGJ and the money and blame Baby Joe. He had reasoned wrongly. At the back of the room General Long Suc was on his hands and knees, shuffling through broken glass towards the door, dragging the suitcase, and leaving a bloody trail behind him on the polished stone. The blood came from his ankles. His feet were still attached to bottom of the forklift.

The silence was broken by the sound of sirens, and Baby Joe moved over to the gaping hole in the wall. He could see a line of flashing lights winding up the hill from the sea. He could also see the silhouette of Monsoon's head as he gunned the forklift through the gardens.

The Lhasa Apso was savagely chewing Crispin's leg, and frustrating his cumbersome attempts to get to his feet and defend himself as the Living Buddha advanced upon him with a twenty-pound copper Buddha raised above his head and a very unspiritual expression of his face. The Living Buddha wasn't sure how many levels of consciousness he would have to drop down for beating this fat arse-bandit to death, with a statue of Buddha no less, but at this point he didn't give a fuck. Nirvana would have to wait. He was going to pound this fucker's head into meatloaf. And eat it.

Unfortunately for the Living Buddha a lifetime of meditation, pacifism, and vegetarianism do not accustom one, even one with murder in his heart, to the sight of blood. As the Living Buddha was preparing to bring the copper Buddha crashing down on Crispin's helpless skull, he caught sight of the blood gushing from the blue-rimmed puncture wound in Crispin's fat calf, and fainted clean away.

As he went down he released his grip on the Buddha, which plummeted forward and down, landing clean on the back of the Lhasa Apso's head, cutting it off in mid-chew and sending it to join Oberon in the big kennel in the sky.

# Chapter 21.

Baby Joe had known that the smart move would have been to put the muzzle of the general's .45 against the unconscious head of Booby Flowers and drop the hammer, but it just wasn't in him to do it, and as he drove away in the opposite direction to the sound of the police sirens that were now very close he was reflecting upon the fact that he might live to regret it.

Sometime later, on the other side of the world, Don Ignacio Imbroglio was reflecting upon how he was going to make Baby Joe Young regret being alive. When he had received the call from Booby, his English manner and mannerisms had dissolved in a stream of Sicilian invective that would have made a Borgia blush, and his incandescent rage had sent Liberty and Stratosphere scurrying into the furthest recesses of the apartment. The Don, in his anger, was like a volcano. He didn't go off very often, but when he did everybody knew about it and nobody ever forgot it.

But Don Imbroglio, despite his Latin origins, was essentially a man of calculation rather than passion, and once the fire in his brain had subsided to a smolder he set about picking through the ashes to assess the situation in a rational manner. To borrow a phrase from his army days, this venture was FUBAR and becoming more FUBAR'd by the day. This fiasco was turning into his own private meltdown, and the casualty list was fast becoming as big as Chernobyl. Any organization such as his is based on respect—read "fear." Fear of pain and death. Fear of the all-seeing eyes, the ears that miss nothing, the hydra that can never be destroyed no matter how many heads are lopped off, the tentacles that reach into people's lives, that root them out no matter where they go, the shadowy nemesis from which there is no escape. At the minute, the Don's mob was more like blind and deaf Siamese twins who couldn't root out a fucking turnip.

This could get really serious. Already there were whispers. Rumors. Too many people had disappeared. Cracks were appearing, the mystique beginning to wear thin. Soon there would be insurrection, disobedience, disrespect. Warnings ignored, debts not paid, desertions and defections, small resistance gradually becoming bolder and more flagrant until you had outright rebellion. Until there was no longer any respect, and then you had nothing but a blind and helpless old man, sitting in an ivory tower, waiting for someone to end it.

Sooner or later, the story of what was really happening would come out, and when the word hit the streets that a hooker, a fat fruit, an Irish rummy, and a small time schwarz bunko steerer had taken down two of his best people, taken him for ten mill, and probably instigated an international incident with some Golden Triangle gook warlord, it would be *arrivederci*-fucking-Roma. He had to resolve this, and fast, and in such a spectacularly, unforgettably brutal fashion that the status quo would be restored and reaffirmed. PFQ.

But what to do? He had already lost more people than he could spare, and he could not afford to take anybody out of his local operation, especially at a time like this when a show of strength was needed. Admittedly, most of those he had lost had been strictly minor league, but Mary Rose and Horatio had been on the all-star team. This Mick must really be something, to pick those two out of the lineup. What kind of a sick mind would suspect a sweet little old lady like Mary Rose? Not to mention slicing up Grimmstein like a pizza and feeding knuckle sandwiches to his two so-called bodyguards. And then there was that *paisano* creepo ex-cousin, Scungulo. It was going to be really entertaining explaining that one to his aunt. Maybe he should just hand the Mick over to her. But no, even he wasn't that cruel. There was only one solution.

One of the Don's remarkable mental facilities had been a phenomenal, almost photographic, memory, but it was failing him with increasing regularity lately, and for phone numbers that he didn't use very often he had adopted the ingenious device of having them embossed in braille on a brass plaque attached to the underside of his desk. He now reached down and read the number he needed, a number he hadn't had to use for over eight years.

It's strange how sometimes that which appears the ugliest by day can be the most beautiful at night: like a steel works, or Las Vegas, or a skid row hooker. Crispin was thinking along these lines as he leaned against the railing at the stern of the MV Wollongong, watching the lights from the docks shimmering on the water and the little toy-looking boats cutting back and forth across the bay.

With the cool breeze carrying the faint scent of spices from the estuary it was almost romantic, and Crispin's mind's eye was filled with warm and reassuring images. In particular, the warm and reassuring image of the ten million dollars that was sitting in the cabin below. The ten million dollars which they had appropriated as compensation from the Don, damages for loss of life, property, reputation, and dignity, and expenses for travel costs and replacement of possessions. Also, in his case, two dog-chewed legs — even though the first one hadn't been the Don's fault, strictly speaking — and several changes of underwear.

He almost required another one when the ship's horn sounded with rib-vibrating intensity right next to his ear, signaling two hours to sailing and summoning the Wollongong's inebriate and no doubt pox-ridden bilge rat crew from every seedy gin mill and knocking shop along the waterfront. When his heart stopped pounding he strolled around the deck to the bow, and stared out beyond the flashing red and green lights to the faint white swirls on the dark water beyond. A sickle moon balanced on the eastern rim, and pale seabirds ghosted past on silent wings. In less than two hours a new life would begin, past buoys and the green headland and out onto the vast churning Pacific. To a new continent, and to who-knew-what?

Crispin thought about Nigel, and Oberon, and his apartment. About the life he had known for so long that was gone forever. The salty sea breeze blew the tears like tiny rivers across his fat cheeks. He thought about the bomb, and the shooting in the swamp, and that horrible scary man on the boat, and the throbbing pain in his lacerated leg.

He sniffed and wiped away his tears. *You have to be alive to be in pain*, he thought, heading for the stairs and the lights of the bridge above them.

Baby Joe climbed through the window and into the flickering light from the hundreds of candles that Hazy Doyle had burning, candles of every conceivable size, shape, and color, like the cave of some maniacal Catholic hermit. The turntable spun around, the arm clicking, the record's label spinning hypnotically, and Hazy sat in the lotus position staring at it, too far away, too deep in interstellar space to notice that the music had stopped. Baby Joe lifted the arm and dropped it into the groove, and Hendrix's voodoo guitar writhed into the smoky air, summoning Hazy back from the Sea of Tranquility.

He looked at Baby Joe over the top of his round spectacles without the slightest trace of surprise or curiosity, as if Baby Joe were as permanent a fixture as the fat Buddha who glowed happily in the corner. Hazy smiled and made the peace sign. "Man, they got a band out there that's a motherfucker."

"So how's Elvis?"

"No, man. Elvis is on Venus, you know that."

Baby Joe shook his head and opened one of the beers that he'd brought with him. He offered one to Hazy, who took it and stared at it as if it were some mystical artifact from a lost civilization. Baby Joe took it back from him, opened it, and handed it back.

"Far out, baby. You know, a big wind is comin', man. A cosmic wind. I hear the bells."

"And then what happens?"

"The fuckin new millennium, man. They gonna show us. No more color, no more hatred, no more hunger, no more religion. No more fucked-up brass sendin' lambs to the slaughter. Just fat happy babies, laughin' in the sunshine, man."

Baby Joe smiled. "Listen, Hazy. What are you going to do?"

"Shit, bro. Shine it on and kick back, man."

Baby Joe leaned forward and gently removed Hazy's glasses. His black dilated pupils were in actual orbit, rotating around his eyes very slowly and ever so slightly out of sync. He was already on his way out to Venus, to dig Elvis. Baby Joe kissed him on the forehead and replaced the dark glasses.

He took the package he was carrying and unwrapped it. Inside was fifty thousand dollars. He moved over to the Buddha and hefted it. Hollow. Peeling off a bunch of hundreds, he stashed the rest under the Buddha and set it back down. The Buddha smiled at him. Picking up the inner sleeve of a record from the chaotic pile around the player, he scribbled a note.

*Look under Buddha. Stay frosty bro. Baby Joe.*

He propped the note against the player, set the bundle of bills next to it, and sat finishing his beer, staring into the colored smoke and into the mist of older days, seeing lost, remembered figures appear and disappear into its slow liquid swirl.

As he walked away from the foot of the ladder, the diminishing strains of "Little Wing" followed him down the unlit street.

Among his peers, Captain Joe Brew was known as "Penguin" Brew, the reason being that it was maintained, in some uncharitable quarters, that he had once fucked one while three sheets to the wind on an Antarctic expedition with the Australian navy. Joe Brew swore blind, to this day, that it had been a nun.

Penguin Brew was of average height. Average height for a Lilliputian schoolboy, that is. This dimension being almost matched by his girth, he was practically circular in profile. Add to this a nose that made W. C. Fields look like Matt Damon, a full red beard that appeared to have been acquired secondhand from a down-on-its-luck muskox, a state of permanent inebriation stretching back to 1974, and a vocabulary that included every expletive—Anglo-Saxon and otherwise—utilized throughout the English-speaking world, and you have a reasonable description of the man and his mind.

Baby Joe being ashore, and Mary Rose catching a few Zs below in order to feel fresh for the sailing, Penguin was entertaining Asia, Wally, and Bjørn Eggen on the bridge of the Wollongong when Crispin chugged up the stairs.

As he stepped onto the bridge a heavy object hit him in the stomach and a beer can rolled away across the deck.

"Ya meant ta catch it, ya fucken dingbat," Penguin explained.

"I don't drink beer, actually. Isn't there any gin?"

"Gin. Fucken mutiny. I'll 'ave no fucken gin drunk on my fucken bridge."

"Asia is drinking gin."

"That's different, mate. She's a good-looking Sheila. You're a just fat shit-stabber with a dead fucken jumbuck on 'is 'ead."

"Listen, you unsightly dwarf, I didn't come on this rust-bucket boat to be insulted by a talking doormat."

"So where d'ya usually go? An' she ain't a boat. She's a bladdy ship, ya drongo, and in the old days, you'd'a bin in the bilges, getting the golden fucken rivet, mate. An' I'll tell ya sumthin else for nuthin, London to a fucken brick you're talkin into the big white telephone before we clear the fucken harbor."

"This is outrageous. How to you expect to get us to Australia in your condition? Anyway, you are so stunted I don't see how you are able to see over that wheel-thing."

"It's a fucken helm, ratbag, an' if there's any more insubordination you're swimmen, mate, if the Norgies don't fucken harpoon ya by mistake."

Penguin tilted his head back and bellowed. Asia was trying to sympathize with Crispin and bite her lips off at the same time, and Wally and Bjørn Eggen were holding on to each other and hooting like a pair of ancient gibbons.

Crispin stuck his nose in the air and turned to leave.

"Ah, come back 'ere, ya silly fucken gallah. I was only pullin yer plonker. Sheila, break out the gin rations fer me shipmate."

Placated, Crispin took the proffered gin and sat next to Asia, and an hour passed in tales of storms and ice and wild places, and Penguin sounded the horn again, and they heard singing as the last of the crew came rollicking up the gangplank. Behind them came Baby Joe.

He stepped into the wheelhouse and deftly caught the can that was flung in his direction.

"Just in time, mate," Wally said. "This fucken pirate is just about to 'aul away."

"I just came to say goodbye."

Wally walked over and shook Baby Joe's hand. "Good on yer, mate. Watch yer arse. We'll see ya down under, eh? You 'ave the address and all that shit?"

"Yeah, thanks, Wal. See you, hey."

Crispin stood and approached. "Baby Joe, you know I…"

Baby Joe patted him on his shoulder, and shook his hand. "I know. Don't go getting sentimental on me now."

Crispin smiled a sad smile and sat back down.

Baby Joe walked over to Bjørn Eggen. "See you, you old fart."

The old man grabbed Baby Joe's hand, and wrung it. "You watch what you focken do, *ja*. I haf the beer ready for vhen you are coming under down."

"That's fucken 'down under,' ya antiquated old dingbat," Penguin informed him, and then told Baby Joe, "See ya in Oz, mate, maybe, if we don't fucken sink."

"Yeah, see you, man, and leave those fucking birds alone."

"It was a fucken nun, ya dill. 'Ow many times do I 'ave ter tell ya?"

Baby Joe moved towards the door, and Asia stood up to follow him.

Bjørn Eggen stopped them. "Baby Joe, vhat are you thinking about the idiot grandson?"

"I don't know what to tell you. The last I saw of him, he was heading downhill fast on a forklift. He could be anywhere. If he turns up before I leave for the States, I'll send a message to the ship. Tell Mary Rose goodbye for me, will you?"

"That won't be necessary," Mary Rose said, coming up the stairs. "You didn't think I was going to let you escape without a kiss, did you?"

She reached up and hugged him. "Now you be careful. It is a very dangerous thing that you are going to try. Many before you have failed. Remember everything I told you. It will help."

"I will. See you in Australia," he said, waving as he left the wheelhouse, with Asia holding his hand.

"Yeah. See yer when the moon comes over the shithouse door," Wally called after him.

Asia walked with him to the bottom of the gangway. He pulled her close and held her for a long moment, feeling her breathing, trying to absorb as much of what was her as he could. She resisted as he pushed her away and held her at arm's length. The light from the ship shone on her copper hair and on the tears that were beginning to form in her eyes.

"I wish you would change your mind," she said.

"I can't."

"But now we have all that money, we can…"

"We can't. The money doesn't make any difference. You know what has to be done."

"But what if you don't come back?"

"Listen, Asia, I don't know what will happen, and I'd be lying if I said I did, but if I don't go, there can't be any us. This thing will hang over us, and I will always be thinking about it, and always worrying, and, if something were to happen to you because of what I didn't do, then... you know."

"I know," she said softly. "I wish there were something I could do to help."

"There is. You can kiss me, and then you can turn around and walk up that gangplank."

"The ship is not sailing for half an hour."

"I know. But you're just making it harder for me to leave you. If we have to part, let's just get it over with."

Asia nodded and reached up to kiss him.

Baby Joe suddenly felt tired and old. He wanted it to last forever. He wanted to feel her sweet lips on his for a lifetime. He wanted to take her back up the gangway and make love to her as the ship rolled across the waves on the way to a new day, in a new place. He wanted to be warm, like the child who lies in bed listening to the footsteps passing in the rain outside.

Instead, he turned and walked away into the darkness at the end of the dock. Asia watched him go, watched the lonely figure getting smaller and smaller until it disappeared into the night beyond the lights. When she got back to the top of the gangway, with the tears streaming down her face, Mary Rose was waiting to take her in her arms.

It was a typical waterfront bar and the dregs who had washed up there, left behind by time and tide, looked at him as he walked in. But no one bothered him. He did not look at anyone, nor meet anyone's stare, but he had that kind of light about him and they steered clear. The stumblebums and panhandlers and hard cases left him alone; the ladies stayed away. He stood at the bar and pointed to a whiskey bottle. The barman brought him a glass, without meeting his eyes.

"Beer," he said. He took a bill from his pocket and, without looking at it, placed it next to the glass of whiskey.

While he waited for his beer he stared at his reflection in the grimy, smeared mirror behind the bar. It stared back at him, as if at a stranger. Beyond his reflection, smoke played in the color and the light and he heard whispers in the ambient noise and knew they whispered about him. When the beer came he took it up, and the whiskey, and carried them outside to a bamboo table set unevenly on dirty cobbles.

Looking down into the dock he saw hawsers being cast off and watched the Wollongong slide from her moorings, and he saw the turbulence in the water and heard the distant roar of the tugboat engines as they hauled her bow seaward. He saw the lights on the ship diminish as she turned beam on to him and headed out of port, and he watched the fading stern lights and the dimming glow from the bridge until they were far out to sea. The mournful echoing of the horn carried back to him over the water. He sucked back the whiskey and looked around at the darkness and knew that out there, under those moving specks of light, were his woman, his friends, and the reason that he was sitting here alone.

What he didn't know was that, concealed in the hold, sweating in the humid heat and just about deafened in his one good ear by the vibrations, was Monsoon Parker, sitting on top of a golden Buddha molded from extremely unusual material.

What do you do with a drunken sailor? In Monsoon's case, you get him even more drunk, slip him some *dinero* to help you get holed up on the ship with all your bags, chattel, and stolen property, and then you send him to get you a bottle of something. Under the circumstances, it should be fucking champagne! This story had more twists than Chubby fucking Checker, and deserved to be celebrated in style. All that glitters isn't gold! Absolutely co-fucking-rrect. Sometimes it's worth much more than that.

He hadn't really known what he was doing. He had been so completely stupefied that his head had been devoid of any structured thought, empty of everything except the vague notion that he should escape, and that somehow the Buddha would protect him. And how, brother? And how! It was not until the night air got to him, after all the guns and sirens were far behind, that he noticed that the Buddha had something sticking in its head. That didn't seem right, so he pulled it out. It was a fragment of the gong…just like the gong that went off in his head when he saw the congealed substance sticking to the fragment. He still couldn't quite believe the astounding improbability of what had just happened.

And now, he was going to make it. Anyone who could drive a bullet-hole-filled forklift—with two chopped-off feet stuck to the chassis, loaded with illegal contraband stolen from a fucking Attila the Hun impersonator—away from a murder scene, right through the center of Ho Chi Minh City and into the docks without being arrested, robbed, shot, lost, or involved in at least a five-car pileup, was definitely going to make it. He was still struggling to get his brain around it. It was totally, mind-blowingly, no-fucking-way-you've-got-to-be-shitting-me impossible, and yet here he was. One minute he expected to be fish food, and the next he's in the navy and in the motherfucking gravy, man.

And nobody to stop him. One by one, the threats had been removed. Belly Joe, gone. Frankie Merang, history. Sasquatch, in the big Yukon in the clouds; the third man, gone to meet Orson Welles; Long Suc, footloose; Mary Rose, the murdering granny, converted; that lunatic pisshead Paddy on his way back stateside to get himself wasted. An amusing ditty came unbidden into his head. Ten little psychopaths sitting on a wall, ten little psychopaths sitting on a wall, and if one little psychopath should accidentally fall, there will be nine…

Okay, so he could be a little more comfortable, but you had to be breathing in order to be sweating your balls off inside a giant vibrator with a rivet up your ass and in need of a change of underwear. And as soon as he figured they were far enough out to sea so they couldn't turn back, he'd show himself. What were they going to do, throw him overboard? The way his luck was running they'd probably give him a stateroom, feed him a T-bone and a case of cognac, and airlift him in a couple of hookers to play with on the trip. And in the meantime, he'd just entertain himself by calculating the street value of the little stash that he just happened to have inherited.

He jumped when the sailor came weaving around the bulkhead door with a bottle of gin. He hadn't heard him on account of his bum eardrum. Well, what the fuck. When he got to Australia he'd get it fixed by the top man, who'd have a receptionist with massive tits who could really go for a guy that looked like Tiger Woods and had ten million dollars in his back pocket. The sailor plunked himself down next to Monsoon, took a swig from a bottle, and handed it to him.

"I got this, mate. Gin. S'all I could get."

"It'll fucking do. Cheers, pal. What you say your name was again?"

"Norm."

"Well, Normy baby, I hate fucking gin. It stinks. So here's looking at ya."

Monsoon was still flying at altitude from the adrenaline and from the overwhelming fact of not being severely dead, and as he poured the gin down his throat it was the best thing he had ever tasted, and as the recollections of the night's events assaulted his fevered brain he was gripped by the need to recount his adventures to someone. He began to babble at the befuddled Norm, who stared at him with blank, uncomprehending eyes, his head weaving slightly from side to side.

Even in the retelling of a tale as fabulous as the one he had just featured in, the simple unembellished truth would not suffice for Monsoon, so the version that the besotted Norm heard differed slightly from factual events, particularly with reference to the ingenuity and heroism of Monsoon Parker.

"Ain't that a hell of a fuckin story?" he said, finally.

Norm didn't answer, and Monsoon looked round to see him stretched out on the deck with his eyes tight shut, his tongue lolling out, and a pool of glistening drool gathering next to his slack jaw and baggy, unshaven cheek.

"Some fuckin audience you turned out to be," Monsoon said, raising the gin to his lips.

## Part 3. Down Under.

A long, long time ago, when TV evangelists and game show hosts were just a distant, horrible future nightmare, all the continents of the world were joined together in a big lump, floating around on the molten magma at the earth's core. Eventually some bits snapped off and floated away to become places like France, and China, and Russia, and Birmingham, Alabama. Some of these bits kept bumping into each other and changing shape and splitting up again, but the bit at the bottom sailed off into the great southern sea and stayed there.

Left to develop all on its own some extremely improbable creatures evolved, like animals with built-in handbags that bounce up and down, and mammals with beaks, and lizards with umbrellas round their necks that run on two feet, and men that wear funny clothes and throw little red balls at three sticks stuck into the ground and think it's fun.

For a long time there were no people in this place, but then about forty thousand years ago, deciding they needed a bit more room, some dark-skinned people wandered in. When they got there they found as much room as anyone could possibly need, and they spread out over the whole continent in small groups, living off, and in harmony with, the land, and for millennia all was tranquil and as it should be.

Then, a few hundred years ago on the other side of the world, some people on a small island invented the steam engine, the puddling process, and the spinning jenny, and decided to go around the world annoying everybody. The way they annoyed people was usually by killing them and taking away their land and making them sing songs about fat Germans and old ladies and dead carpenters.

While they were sailing around the world, looking for new people to annoy, they found this continent, but nobody really knew what to do with it. Then someone had this brilliant idea. Why don't we use it as a place to keep all the bad people who have committed horrible crimes? Crimes like being hungry, or not having any money, or wanting to have their own country back, like the Irish. So they gathered up all these people and put them in boats with soldiers, and sent them to the other side of the world to build a new country.

And as has been repeatedly demonstrated throughout history, when building a new country it is always a good idea to begin by killing as many of the people that are already there as possible, especially when you have muskets and pistols and sabers and horses, and they have sharpened sticks.

In the fullness of time this new country, which they called Australia, became a great nation with fine, independent people. But they never forgot the heritage of their country, which was born in strife and blood, injustice and misery.

And it wasn't over yet.

## Chapter 22.

The smell of eucalyptus was powerful in the cool dawn air. At the far horizon, a huge domed rock began its chameleon display with a becoming shade of phallic purple. In the high branches of a tree a kookaburra berated the morning, and a couple of branches below a koala yawned and scratched its balls. Beneath, in the leaf litter, a wallaby stirred and took a few tentative hops, the low sun glistening russet on its dew-damp fur.

In the shade of the tree the skeleton of an old, abandoned Holden Kingswood stood with its tireless wheel rims sunk deeply into the red earth. Stretched from its roof, which in some forgotten past had been red, a faded canvas was suspended from two poles, forming a rudimentary bivouac, the whole resembling the construct of some inept refugee. Under its sheltering folds the car seats had been placed to make a rude bunk, upon which a long slender figure with black, bushy hair and skin so dark it appeared to absorb the light lay sleeping upon his back, his chest rising and falling as he softly snored.

The trampled bare earth around him was littered with crushed beer tins and empty wine bottles. In the propped-open trunk, where an old torn mattress was stuffed, a fat wombat opened its eyes, clambered onto the ground, shat out a prodigious turd, clambered back into the trunk, and was immediately fast asleep again. From a low branch above, an outraged cockatoo summoned Australia to wakefulness with its shrill squawking. Flaring its bright yellow crest it began to strut along the branch, posing and preening, tilting its head to peer at the world below through its wild eye. The kookaburra's manic yodel answered the cockatoo, and a low-circling flight of parakeets joined in.

A general shrieking and trilling ensued, ravaging the peace of morning until another more subtle sound entered the mix: a soft whirring noise. The cockatoo pivoted its head in alarm the instant before the swirling blade of a boomerang ferried it into oblivion in a spectacular cloud of feathers. The return to the former silence was instantaneous.

Wombat Jimmy deftly caught his returning boomerang and wiped the blood and feathers from its edge against his bare buttock.

"Bladdy screeching drongo," he muttered.

Wombat Jimmy had been rudely awakened from a particularly vivid and pleasant dream involving a proud-breasted half-caste girl from Parramatta, a case of Castlemaine XXXX, and a didgeridoo, and was not impressed, especially as he had been dragged into wakefulness before he had reached the vinegar strokes.

Jimmy strolled to the front of the car, idly scratching his narrow asscheeks with the blade of his boomerang, and lifted the hood. Wombat Jimmy loved his car. It was older than he was. In lieu of a motor was an ingeniously rigged, battery-operated fridge. Reaching into it, he grabbed an ice-cold tube of XXXX and cracked it with a loud hiss. In the trunk the wombat's eyes sprang instantly wide open and it leapt from its mattress and galloped round to where Jimmy leaned against the hood, pouring the amber nectar down his throat. Jimmy eyed the beast, who stared up at him intently with its beady eyes.

"Ah, g'day, Walkabout," he said. "'Owareya."

By way of reply, Walkabout farted loudly.

"I see. 'Ere ya go then."

Jimmy grabbed another beer, cracked it, and poured the frothing brew into an upturned hubcap at his feet. Walkabout planted his front paws in the beer and began slurping noisily.

"Good on yer, mate," Jimmy said, raising his own tinny.

As he tilted back his head to drink he saw the high droning speck of a small plane circling overhead in the faultless blue sky. Crushing the can in his hand, he tossed it over his shoulder onto the enormous pile of its predecessors, retrieved his spears and woomera from where they were propped against the bole of the eucalyptus, and, taking his boomerang in his free hand, headed into the bush.

"See yer, Walkabout," he said over his shoulder. "I'm off to see about me mornin' tucker."

Walkabout farted.


Stavros "Big Bazouki" Papastopalotovus was having a hard time. He was having a hard time keeping up with the demand for beer caused by the celebration attending the sudden and unexpected arrival of Woolloomoloo Wally, an occasion of such momentous consequence to the community of Blue Billabong, Queensland, that it had brought out every sheila, bloke, dingbat, ocker, and drongo for miles around. And keeping them topped up with amber nectar at the correct temperature of just above freezing was like trying to barbecue ice.

He was having a hard time making himself heard above the noise in the packed room, over which the overhead fans were churning impotently in a humid funk of sweat and smoke. He was also having a hard time keeping his eyes off Asia's tits and on the register, which was apt to end up shy a few shekels if he didn't watch it like a pit bull watching a pork chop. And all this while trying to conduct an investigation into the mysterious disappearance of Captain Cook, Captain Cook being the stuffed koala that had adorned the lintel of the Big Blue Billabong Hotel for as long as anyone could remember, and whose loss was widely predicted to portend impending disaster, rather like what is supposed to happen if the ravens ever leave the Tower of London.

Wally was obviously ecstatic to be back home, and would have been even more ecstatic if he had actually had any idea of where he was, having been more or less legless since they had arrived in Cairns. He was currently staring with rapt attention at the Coke machine in the corner, in the belief that he was watching a rugby match on TV.

Crispin was feeling better than he had since the whole dreadful episode had begun. Beginning with the glorious and enchanting arrival into Sydney harbor, the five-star hotel, the shopping, the sightseeing tour, the Blue Mountains, the day at Bondi, he had found everything just wonderful, and not at all what he had expected. Then there had been the first-class flights, the dinners, the days in Cairns, the trip on the cable car to the rainforest at Kuranda. And now here he was in this charming little country hotel surrounded by all these rustics who were really very nice, even though most of them were drunk and didn't have shirts on and you couldn't understand a word they were saying. Bit like Louisiana, really. And these dark fellows, well. They were just so, you know, svelte and mysterious. Crispin had decided to get into the swing of things, so he had bought himself a hat with corks hanging from it, and a vest, and was sitting drinking beer just like the others, just one of the fellows. He had considered spilling something down the front of his vest for the sake of authenticity, but decided against it.

Baby Joe's ghost had followed Asia to Australia, and it slept with her, and ate with her, and walked with her everywhere she went, and the longer that went by without her hearing from him the stronger its presence became, so she had decided to build a house of beer cans to hide in, and had so far finished the dining room and the kitchen and had made a good start on the garage. Seated in one corner an ancient, burly man with an eye patch and no front teeth grimaced and grinned as he kicked the shit out of a wheezy accordion. Asia swayed and weaved in front of him, doing the too-many tango.

Bjørn Eggen was sitting happily on the sunny front porch, having an earnest conversation with an Australian stock dog — a blue heeler — and the dog was making a great deal more sense than most of the other people at the gathering. Mary Rose, having seen which way the wind was blowing, had sensibly retreated to the cabin that had been given to them and was sitting in the shade of a eucalyptus, reading and drinking tea. Monsoon, who had arrived to join them only that morning, having stayed behind in Sydney to make some "arrangements," was *hors de combat*, having been punched in the eye by a Greg Norman fan, and was lying in his room with an ice pack on his face.

His sudden appearance on the ship had naturally been a great surprise to them all, and Penguin Brew had had to be dissuaded from administering some suitably nautical stowaway punishment like keelhauling, and had had to satisfy himself with a relentless barrage of abuse that lasted the entire journey. Monsoon's explanation that he had been so traumatized by his harrowing experience and skin-of-the-teeth escape that he had been too afraid to come out of hiding until he was sure that they were well away elicited suitable sympathy from the ladies, and he was once more restored to the cautious good graces of the company. It had been generally agreed, however, that it would be a wise course of action to refrain from mentioning the case full of the Don's liberated moolah to that particular young man.

The journey thereafter had progressed uneventfully and pleasantly. Neptune had smiled upon them, and the sea had remained balmy and tranquil under blue Capricorn skies. They had passed the time reclining on deck, and playing cards, and reading, and one day Bjørn Eggen captured a yellowfin tuna from the stern. They gathered in the evenings and dined and drank, and while Wally and Bjørn Eggen and Penguin regaled each other with tales of derring-do, Asia and Mary Rose and

Crispin spoke of gentler things, and Monsoon went below to hang out with Norm and the crew.

And thus the days passed, until one evening just after sunset they steamed around the heads and saw the Opera House, and the harbor bridge, and the towering lights of Sydney. They all went ashore together that night and enjoyed a splendid dinner, and while they were thus occupied a crate went ashore under the supervision of Norm and was delivered to an address in the Five Docks.

They all took rooms in the InterContinental — all except for Monsoon, who had accepted Norm's kind offer of hospitality — and they breakfasted overlooking the park the following morning and later went back to the ship to collect their belongings.

And it was later that day, when Monsoon stopped by to speak to his grandfather, that he saw a large black suitcase sticking out from a closet.

They spent a couple of days in Sydney, and Wally took them around to all his old haunts, and they went back down to the docks to say goodbye to Penguin Brew and watch the Wollongong set sail, heading back to Ho Chi Minh City; and the following day, when they took the plane up to Cairns, Monsoon did not go with them.

In any other era, they would have been pirates. They looked like pirates, thought like pirates, fought like pirates, and between them had more plastic limbs than a Macy's window. In recent years, at least one of them had been involved in every armed conflict, major and minor, in every poverty-stricken third-world shithole from Angola to Afghanistan.

They had all been through the gates at Fort de Nogent at Fontenay-sous-Bois, outside Paris, all knew what Legio Patria Nostra meant, and all got religiously fuck-faced every thirtieth of April in remembrance of Capitaine Danjou. They had all left the tricolor behind, with French passports and new names, and they were no longer the people they had been before, and the people they had been before were no longer them, or anybody else for that matter. They had reunited in Zurich, formed the Association Sans Sympathie, and earned their living resolving little difficulties for people who could afford them and who were not especially particular or squeamish about how their little difficulties were resolved, as long as it was discreet.

A.S.S. was a democratic organization and each member's voice had equal weight, and no project was undertaken unless all were in agreement. They sat now around a large cherrywood table in their headquarters, which was part office, part clubhouse, and part cathouse, and discussed the telephone call that they had just received. They had a strict policy about drinking and business—they never contemplated any business unless they were suitably well oiled—and to this end, they all had their tipple of preference in front of them.

Magnoon Piastre, a one-eyed Greek Egyptian from some stench-ridden chicken shack on the outskirts of Alexandria, sat with a bottle of ouzo in front of him. Curtains Calhoun, the product of a failed abortion in a cold water Dublin workhouse, favored John Powers whiskey. Gaspart Descourt—the result of a vigorous ten-minute union between a Belgian lieutenant and a teenage Congolese virgin during a brief respite in an artillery barrage outside Katanga—drank Courvoisier. Dugong Heartache, an overweight child of the prairie—the only son of a born-again Baptist who had drowned his mother, in the name of Jesus, during an overenthusiastic rebirthing ceremony in the Ohio River—was a Wild Turkey man. The final member, who was of course drinking vodka, was Vladimir Pizda, conceived during the sacking of Berlin by an inebriated Cossack cavalry major who had missed his aim while attempting to bugger a fat Bavarian seamstress.

Dugong Heartache had taken the call, and he addressed his comrades.

"Yeah. Fucking Vietnam, I said."

"I sink zis war is over, no. You lose already?" said Gaspart Descourt.

"So did you, you French fuck. Diem Bien Phu, remember? At least we didn't fucking surrender like a bunch of pussies."

"I am not fucking *français*, monsieur. I am 'alf Belgian, and 'alf Congolese, as you well know, and I'll thank you to remembair it."

"When you ladies have finished bickering, perhaps Dugong would care to elaborate on the nature of the call," Curtains Calhoun said.

"I've never fucked a Vietnamese," Magnoon Piastre added, helpfully.

Displaying the stoicism of his forefathers, Vladimir Pizda declined to comment.

"Ah don' know if we want to fight with ze Vietnamese. Zey are ze tough cookies, non?"

"We don't have to fight them, you frog-eating dipshit. If you'll shut the fuck up long enough, I'll explain. This is a guy we did some business for a couple of times before. Last time was a few years back. You remember, that boat at LA. The creepy English-sounding Italian fucker in Vegas, yeah? Well, it seems someone has absconded with some of his dough and also some merchandise belonging to his business partner. This is a simple search, destroy, and recover job. The only wrinkle is that whoever did the deed amputated the partner's fucking feet in the process, so we might be facing some incoming. This wop wouldn't have called if it was going to be easy. For one, I'm in. Anything is better than sitting round here looking at you ugly motherfuckers. What do you say?"

"How were the feet amputated?" Vladimir asked.

"With a fucking sushi knife. How the fuck should I know? What difference does it make? Yea or nay?"

"Da."

"Okay, good. Magnoon?"

"I've never fucked a Vietnamese before."

"So you're in. Now we're getting somewhere. Gaspart?"

"Fucking *oui*. *Pourquoi pas*?"

"Curtains?"

"You might need to draw on my experience."

"All right, gentlemen, it's a done deal. We go. Raise your glasses, and leave us toast Operation Xanadu."

"For fuck's sake, you corny twat," said Curtains.

"Got any better ideas?"

"Yeah."

"Such as?"

"Such as Operation fucking Ho Chi Minge."

Coarse laughter pierced the room, and as the five men clinked their glasses together their arms were reflected in the high French polish of the cherrywood table.

"*Sláinte!*"

"*Sherefe!*"

"*Na zdorovie!*"

"*Salut!*"

"Up yours."

The draft from the air conditioner felt strange and cold blowing onto the back of Baby Joes's newly shaven head and he rubbed his hand over his skull, feeling the weird smoothness of his skin as if he were touching somebody else. He was drinking in unfamiliar surroundings, wearing unfamiliar clothes, and feeling disoriented and out of place, as if he had accidentally stepped into someone else's life.

He was parked in a joint called Trez Chez, and the ritzy décor, the muzak, the chintzy furniture, the garrulous, exhibitionist patrons who may as well have had "look at me, look at me" tattooed on their foreheads all amounted to a place that he wouldn't normally have been seen dead in. But then, the reason he was in there was because he didn't want to be seen dead anywhere else, either. In fact he didn't want to be seen dead, period. His leather trousers creaked as he reached for his drink, and he looked around self-consciously from behind his shades as if the whole room could hear it. He felt like an actor at a screen test and knew that he was blowing the part and that he would have to do better, to learn to be comfortable and at ease, to learn to accommodate his new identity for as long as he needed to.

His apartment had, of course, been trashed. He had expected it, and would have been surprised to find anything other than the wreckage he had encountered when he went around. It had been a professional job. A message. Nothing had been taken, but everything of any value had been destroyed or defaced beyond repair. Not that there had been anything that had been really worth anything to him, either materially or as sentimental value, but the fact of its happening was another coal on the fire of his anger.

He had flown into LAX, rented a set of wheels, and checked into a cheap hotel where the noise of the couple arguing and making up in the next room had been drowned out by the almost constant roar of jet engines overhead. Sitting by the window in a bar he had watched people playing pool and dancing to country and western songs on the jukebox, and he had watched the people standing at a bus stop outside waiting in the darkness for the light and warmth to come. It came and went, and one old lady stayed where she was, sitting on the bench with two plastic bags. Baby Joe walked the block back to the hotel and lay awake for a long time, staring at the slow fan and watching the lights from the passing cars traverse the walls.

In the morning he shaved his head, bought new clothes, and drove back to Vegas. He took a room at the Budget Suites on Lake Mead and holed up in it all day. As night fell he ventured out to eat, staying away from places he knew and was known, avoiding anywhere where he might be recognized. He bought a bottle of whiskey and drove to the apartment at three in the morning, driving past it in both directions twice before parking the car a street away and walking back. He entered the place in darkness, stepping over broken glass and splintered wood into the bedroom.

The mattress had been razored and the stuffing pulled out, but he turned it over and lay down on it and it was good enough. He lay there for a couple of hours, drinking from the bottle and staring at the darkened ceiling, listening to the small noises that accentuated the silence. Somewhere a dog barked, and later a motorbike roared past heading for the freeway.

He stood again and walked over to the wall that separated the bedroom from the kitchen, and punched it. A thin piece of paper-covered plywood gave way, and Baby Joe reached inside and pulled a Glock 9mm and a spare clip from the cavity. He checked the action of the weapon, and the clip, and stuck it in his waistband. Putting the extra clip in his side pocket, he went over to the door, opened it, and stood watching the street for several minutes. Then he walked to his car and drove back to his lodgings.

Trez Chez was across the street from the Don's building, and Baby Joe went there every afternoon and sat at a seat where he could see into the lobby. Although at first he felt conspicuous among the vacuous and vain clientele of that neon poodle parlor he did not look it, and after a day he did not feel it either. After a while the regulars tried to engage him in conversation, but he was aloof without being rude and soon they dismissed him as a boor and a dullard and left him alone. After three days and nights he stopped going to the bar and instead parked his car down the street and watched all through the night and into the morning. He did this three nights in a row, driving each day to the airport and renting a different car from a different company, and each night parking in a different place.

Except for the fact that the most-feared hoodlum in the state occupied the top floor, the building was an ordinary residential apartment block just like any other and had a rhythm to it, a sequence of events that kept repeating itself. Baby Joe studied the comings and goings, committing them to memory, observing each person with care, taking note of each car, slowly accumulating the knowledge that he was going to need. Who came and went, how many times, and at what hours. Who had a routine and who did not. How they behaved. Who had children. Who frequented the local establishments up and down the street. Who used the bar, and the café next door. After one week he had identified the people that worked for the Don and the people that did not, and knew most of what he needed to know. He was ready for the next step.

From a public phone he called the number the Don had given him, hanging up as soon as he heard the Don's voice so he knew the dog was in his kennel. Although the two heavies he'd had the little dance with in the car park of the Crown and Anchor came down occasionally—though never at the same time—he had not seen the Don himself, from which he concluded that he rarely, if ever, left the building. Not much of a life...unless you were blind?

He had spotted the surveillance cameras on his first visit to the Don. On the front entrance, over the elevator door in the lobby, one in the elevator, and a pan-and-tilt on the landing of the Don's floor. There were no monitors in reception, so he figured that they were probably somewhere on the Don's floor. He also figured that, unless Jerry Springer was on, Liberty and Stratosphere were not the kind of guys who could be relied upon to sit watching a TV screen all day, which meant at least one extra person to contend with at any given time.

There was a uniformed security man at the elevator door, and Baby Joe noticed that nonresidents and strangers were directed to the reception desk and that the receptionist always made a call before they were allowed into the elevator, and another, from a different phone, after they were in. Including those two, that was a minimum of five targets, not counting the man himself. He had not seen any other people when he had been there before, but presumably somebody had been watching the Don while Liberty and Stratosphere had been frolicking with him in the car park. That would be an unknown factor when he made his move, but from his observations the Don didn't like to have any more people around than necessary, and his visitors usually didn't stay very long.

Allowing for two other people, for caution's sake, that was seven to one. Long odds at these stakes. Maybe he would get the chance to bring them down a bit beforehand, if it worked out. The reception guy and the uniform wouldn't be a problem except on the way down, unless he was in there a long time, in which case it probably wouldn't matter anyway and he would be beyond caring...but he would have to figure a way to stop the reception guy from calling in reinforcements.

He had noticed that Liberty, who had met him in the lobby, had punched in a code that allowed the elevator to go to the Don's floor. He had not seen a metal detector, and his car keys had not sent any bells ringing, but that didn't mean there wasn't one. There was a security gate at the garage, which required a resident's passkey to open it, and he reasoned that if there were an elevator that went directly to the apartments from the garage it would be similarly protected, and likewise the fire stairs. He had considered ringing the management company, posing as a prospective occupant and asking for information, but figured that maybe the Don owned the building and did not want to risk him being tipped off that someone was sniffing around.

Baby Joe knew it was going to be tight. The only chance he had was to hit the Don's floor running and get the first shots off before anyone realized what was going down and prepared a civic reception for him, complete with a twenty-one-gun salute. He had taken down Liberty and Stratosphere before, but they had not been prepared then, and just because they couldn't fight didn't mean they couldn't shoot. He was going to need the code. Whoever was in the elevator was under the eye of the camera, which precluded getting in with one of the Don's people and either muscling the code out of him or forcing the guy to take him up. He needed to get through the door, past reception, and into the elevator without being made, ride it as far as it would go, and punch in the code at the last minute. He presumed that there would be some kind of signal that went off inside once the code was entered. Once he was in he would have to take it one play at a time, but at least he remembered the layout of the apartment. Not knowing the configuration of the opposing team made it difficult to plan a strategy, so his basic game plan was just to shoot everybody he saw and keep shooting them until they stopped trying to shoot him.

His new baldheaded biker look had been enough for him to move around town incognito and to stake out the Don's building but he doubted it would stand close scrutiny, and anyway he looked weird enough in himself to attract attention. Besides which, it made his balls itch like hell. He would need something better. Dressing as a woman would be best, but no amount of pancake and mascara could make his weathered mug look like anything but the wrong side of a Kronk gym speed bag, and people were liable to take notice of a dame who looked like she could skin a buffalo with a potato peeler. Where the fuck was Crispin when you needed him?

On the morning of the seventh day Baby Joe drove back to his suite at eight o'clock, and drank coffee and read the Revue Journal until nine-thirty. Then he called Stephane's Theatrical Makeup and Costumes and spoke for ten minutes to the person that answered. After he hung up he took a long, hot shower to wash away the discomfort of the night, put the Glock under his pillow, and went to sleep.

The heat turned the end of the airstrip into a simmering mirage, and Helmut Snurge could not make out the tin roof and white walls of the "airport building" until he had almost taxied the Cessna Stationair up to it. He killed the engine, removed the headset from his slick head, and turned around to his lone passenger.

"Welcome to Blue Billabong, and thank you for flying with Luftkrank."

"Fuck off, you kraut ponce. Luft Wank, more like. Ya call that a fucking landing?"

"What do you expect, with your fat arse in the back? The aircraft is not designed for it."

Amid further pleasantries, Stavros and Helmut crossed the scorching bare earth to the dilapidated shed that served as departure lounge, arrivals hall, and baggage claim at Blue Billabong Airport. Helmut was a small, dapper German with a penchant for French cologne, who kept his white uniform immaculately turned out even in the heat and dust of the outback, his short hair greased back and his pencil mustache neatly trimmed beneath his prominent nose. Helmut was pilot, chief engineer, booking agent, and mechanic of Luftkrank, not to mention barnstormer, crop sprayer, search and rescue, flying doctor, and general lifeline to the remote community of Blue Billabong. It was he who had brought Asia, Crispin, Mary Rose, Bjørn Eggen, and Wally up from Cairns, and he was just returning from taking Stavros on a dawn mercy mission, Mercy being a full-breasted and liberal-minded young woman who plied her trade in an establishment in Numbat Flats, the nearest town to Blue Billabong.

In the shade, in a chair tilted back against the wall, sat a fat aboriginal in a pair of shorts and an open shirt with all the buttons missing. He was surrounded by crushed and empty beer cans and next to him was an ice box, into which he reached as the pair approached.

"Ev you blokes got anythin to declare?" he asked, cracking the tin.

"Yeah," replied Stavros, "yer mother's got a fat arse and she smells like a dingo."

"And your sister is a lousy fuck," added Helmut.

"I wouldn't be talkin like thet to the bloke 'oose got the beers, if I was you two bludgers."

"Ah, good on ya, Bruce," said Stavros, pulling out two cans and handing one to Helmut. "What the fuck are you doin here, anyway?"

"I'm waitin' for Kylie Minogue to land in a parachute and give us a fucken blow job, ya plonker. I'm waitin for you two wankers, whadya fucken think?"

"Why?"

"Wal sent me. Says I was to bring you straight to the bar, soon as you landed."

"Did 'e say what for?"

"Na, mate, but 'e dint look too fucken 'eppy."

"Right then, let's be 'avin yer."

Bruce and Stavros each took one end of the cool box and carried it to the dusty pickup parked behind the shed, where all three of them squeezed into the front seat and set off along the flat red road, leaving a long cloud of dust hanging in the still air.

Norm was not by nature a talkative bloke, and under normal circumstances did not open his mouth from one day to the next. Of course, having two electrodes attached to your testicles and your bare feet in a zinc bucket full of ice water were not normal circumstances. If Norm had watched more Humphrey Bogart movies, or read more Raymond Chandler, he would have known that two strangers approaching you for a light in a darkened street normally precedes receiving a heavy concussive blow behind the ear with a lead sap. But since Norm had been remiss in his reading habits, this is exactly what had happened to him and after being rendered unconscious he had been bundled into the obligatory waiting car and driven to a gated mansion in a part of town he was not familiar with.

When he was awakened by a cascade of freezing water he found himself naked and tied to a steel chair with his feet in a bucket, looking at a man with an enormously long mustache and a long braid hanging from the back of an otherwise shaven head. The man sat in a wheelchair with a saline drip in his arm, the bag being suspended from a frame that stood next to the chair, and both his legs were heavily bandaged. Standing around him was a group of men who looked like pirates. Two were dark-skinned, and one of these had only one eye and the other a prosthetic arm. Of the others, one was very fat and one very tall and slender, with a badly scarred face, and the other stood at a peculiar angle and supported himself on a cane. There was another man, younger, with a ponytail, who didn't seem part of the group and who sported two impressive black eyes. Also in the room were four Vietnamese who were naked to the waist, and who were very still. One of them stepped up and filled the bucket that his feet were in with ice water.

Norm began to get the impression that he was in deep shit, an impression that was confirmed when another of the Asians clipped an electrode onto each of his balls, a process which was, in itself, so painful that the electric current which followed seemed almost gratuitous. When the rhinoceros had climbed off his chest, the industrial battery acid was removed from his veins, and the magnesium flares removed from his orifices, the one in the wheelchair spoke.

"You want babies better you speak, chop chop."

"What do you want? Why the fuck are you doing this to me? This is a mistake. You got the wrong bloke."

"No mistake. You take man on boat. Man look like black man, Vietnamese man, same same."

"Yeah. Shit, yeah. But I swear I didn't…"

"Never mind. Where he go?"

"Sydney."

"Have big gold Buddha with?"

"Yeah. Yeah. I sneaked it through customs for him."

"Where he now?"

"I don't know, he, aaaaaaiiieeeeeeeeeh."

When the anaconda slid from his chest and the scorpions stopped stinging his pecker, Norm said, "No. Please, no more, for Christ's sake. I'm telling you everything. He stayed with me for a coupla days. He said he was going to Cairns. There were others on the boat. A fat poofter and a sheila, two old fogies, a man and a woman, and an old boong."

"Also one man look same like these. Strong man. No so young, no too old?"

"No, nobody like that."

"Sure?"

"I'm sure."

"You see black suitcase?"

"Yeah. Yeah, I did. The bloke brought it round to my place, the day before he went to Cairns. He left it."

"You still have?"

"Yeah, but there was nothing inside. Only newspapers, aaaaaiiiiieeeyaa."

When the electric eel had crawled out from his lungs, and the jellyfish removed from his glans, Norm soldiered on, "I swear to God. I looked as soon as he left. Just papers. I remember 'im swearing 'is 'ead off the day 'e brought it. I'm telling you the truth. That's all I know, the bloke gave me a thousand bucks to 'elp 'im out. Please, mate, don't 'urt me no more. Let me go, I ain't done nuthin."

Norm dropped his head onto his chest, and began to sob.

Long Suc turned to the men standing around him. "What you think?"

Dugong Heartache answered. "I think he's on the level. If he had the loot, why would he have come back to this shithole?"

"But if case go Australia, dollars go Australia, I think."

"It's possible."

"So what you do?"

Dugong addressed Booby Flowers. "What do you say, Rocky?"

Booby was a changed man, all the wind taken from his sails by the roughing up, the incidents he had witnessed, and his conversation with the Don, not to mention his personal stereo having been trashed when that guy pistol-whipped him. He didn't understand how he could be held even partially responsible for something that was patently not his fault, but it seemed to him that the Don's words had implied negligence on his part. That was as worrying as it was unfair, since it also implied that he was destined to be providing sustenance for the denizens of the South China Sea shortly, if the situation wasn't rescued. The arrival of this crew of outlandish brigands had not done much to ease his mind, especially as they all looked at him the way a well-fed lioness looks at a zebra. Interested, but not hungry. Yet. When he answered Dugong Heartache, it was in the manner of a small boy addressing a gang of big kids who he fears are going to steal his pocket money.

"Well, it certainly sounds like the stuff has gone south. And probably the money, too. The stuff he'd have trouble getting out of the country by air, so it's probably still there. The money…who knows?"

"What about the shamus? This one says he wasn't on the boat."

"Could be anywhere, but if we find him my guess is we find the money."

"Looks like we go to the land down under, then, ladies."

# Chapter 23.

While the aforementioned conversation was taking place, some of the money in question was actually traveling at thirty kilometers an hour, bouncing along a rutted dirt road, wrapped in plastic bags and secreted in the side panels and spare wheels of a Volkswagon Combi. Monsoon was driving with excessive caution because of the value of his cargo, which—in addition to what he thought amounted to approximately nine and a half million dollars—included one recently-dissected Machine Gun Jelly Buddha packed in cardboard boxes, and two unconscious geriatrics, carefully bound and gagged and placed side by side on a mattress in the back.

Once again, Monsoon was amazed at yet another dramatic change in fortune in a series of twists and turns of Byzantine complexity, a story that had had more ups and downs than a Norfolk whore's drawers on a Saturday night with the Pacific fleet at anchor in the roads. Taking it from the very beginning it had been an incredible set of reversals and windfalls, culminating in him having *all* the beans, baby. Monsoon Parker was headed, via a meticulously plotted route of back roads and isolated tracks, across an entire continent to Sydney, Australia, to begin a life of fabulous wealth and unprecedented decadence, of unlimited beaver and booze for the rest of his natural, up to his little multiracial eyeballs in snatch and scotch.

And all due—apart from an occasional miracle of Golgotha proportions—to his own natural genius, the undeniable talent that had only been waiting for the right moment to mature and blossom and buy him a one-way ticket to Filthystinkingrichesville. And to think, when this dance began he had been worried about being able to pay that wop cocksucker a lousy grand, plus vig. He figured the journey would take him the best part of a month, but having been one second from eternity being thirty days from paradise didn't seem like such a bum deal. He was going to enjoy every turn of the wheels.

How many ifs make a multimillionaire? If he hadn't borrowed the grand from the Don, and if O'Neal hadn't missed the free throw, he wouldn't have been desperate enough to start looking in the case and find the MGJ. If the Don hadn't tried to muscle in on his play, he wouldn't have been here, holding the green. If Frankie Merang hadn't tried to give the Don the high, hard one, it wouldn't have panned out and he wouldn't be chauffeuring a Combi full of untold riches across the outback. If the Mick gumshoe had not horned in, he would be history; and if the Paddy doofus had not then, in a feat of barely credible hubris, gone back to the states to face almost certain annihilation, it would not have been so easy to get the famous folding stuff away from the rest of these suckers. If that little prick with the ponytail had not wanted another snuff pic for his collection, he would be in that big sports book in the sky instead of on the road to Millionaire's Row.

There was only one way to look at it. It was just something that was meant to be, and it was as simple as that. Of course, it had not been a cakewalk. There had been many tight moments and some disappointments, too, along the way. Like, for instance, the disappointment of finding out that, after he had gone to the trouble of sucker-punching the little fag room service guy at the old man's hotel and used his passkey to get into the room and rob the suitcase, it had been full of newspapers.

But this is where his resourcefulness and instincts had paid off. He could have let it go at that and been satisfied with the MGJ. But he figured that, since it was unlikely that the Don would try to get away with such a corny dime-novel stunt, the old man must have pulled the old switcheroony himself later on. Which meant they either suspected him, or that there was some double-dealing going on among that crew; but it also meant that the cash was still around, unless of course it was the Mick who had thrown them all a serious curve, hence his disappearance. Anyway, it would be worth a trip north to find out.

After giving his last grand from the money that the Don had given back to him to Norm, when he had landed in Sydney, all he had had in his pocket was chump change. Except for millions of dollars worth of drugs, of course. Taking a piece that was easy to detach, which turned out to be Buddha's celestial hooter, he had set about doing a little retail business in Sydney and had immediately lucked out again. He discovered that Sydney was another fruit can, the Aussie equivalent of San Francisco, and tapping into the gay scene he had soon gotten a small bushfire going—not to mention one small, unexplained explosion in a Bondi hotel room. The gay grapevine bore him such fruit with the fruits that he very quickly had enough dough to charter a plane to fly him and his stash to Cairns, and to buy the Combi when he got there. Not only that, but he had established a rabid and starving market to come back to, which would be made even better by cutting off the supply for a while and leaving the fags gagging for it.

When he had gotten to the Big Blue Billabong Hotel he had been pleasantly surprised to find everybody except the old broad completely shitfaced, and it had been a thing of simplicity to slip a mickey into her tea. With all of them out of their trees—or in Wally's case, *in* a tree—or else out for the count, he had been free to scout around in peace and it hadn't taken him long to find the cash, all neatly wrapped in plastic and shoved under the floorboards in the old man's cabin where the simple old bastard had hidden it. The old duffer should really start reading a better class of comic. He had checked a couple of the packages this time, just to make sure.

The money had been converted to Australian dollars, but a buck was a buck in any language, and since he now considered himself a permanent resident, even that was convenient. He had stashed the dough in the Combi, and gotten himself a bottle from the bar. Even that had been free; because everyone had been so fucked up, he had been able to just walk in and take it. Plus, he had spotted the Greg Norman fan who had smacked him when he first walked in lying under a table and given him a couple of decent clips in the kisser with a pool cue just to help his hangover along. Back in Mary Rose's room he had studied the map carefully, drawing several alternative routes onto it in red pen.

And then for the pièce de résistance. He had pulled the old man from off the porch where he was sleeping with some kind of sheepdog—which, fortunately again, was also passed out drunk—and had dragged him to the back of the Combi, hog-tied him, and given him a shot of heavy duty sedative. Enough to keep him out for twenty-four hours. He had repeated the process with the old lady and pulled away into the night with his cargo safely stowed and the cool night air coming through the open window of the Combi, toasting himself with whiskey.

And now, as he drove through the night energized by a scotch and adrenaline cocktail, he saw the red eyes of large animals reflected in the headlamps and large flying things ghosted past overhead and fluttered around the beams. And as the sky began to turn to pearl gray and a pink glow appeared in the east Monsoon pulled up under a stand of eucalyptus, checked his passengers, took a piss against the wheel, stretched out on the front seat, and slept for a couple of hours.

Waking in the gathering heat he breakfasted on whiskey, gave his guests their daily dose, and headed south. He would carry Bjørn Eggen and Mary Rose one more day, and then leave them in the first one-horsefly town that he came to. And speaking of flies, it would be a shame that he wouldn't be a fly on the wall when all the shit came down.

Naturally it would be assumed that these two old farts were in cahoots with him, and they wouldn't know what planet they were on for a couple a days after he gave them a parting shot apiece. There would be total confusion and the hounds would be on the wrong trail, especially when he called and left an anonymous message giving the exact location of the fugitives, located in exactly the wrong place, miles from where they were and in the opposite direction to where he was headed.

By the time they got that Gordian knot untangled he would be well away, and so well established in Sydney — so utterly protected by his wealth and influence — that no one would be able to touch him — neither the general, nor the wop, nor that Mick if he happened to show up again. Monsoon looked though the dusty windshield at the seemingly endless red track unwinding before him through stands of eucalyptus without limit under a vast and cloudless sky. It had been a tortuous trail for sure, but now the road was straight ahead in every sense of the word. He was home free, with the bacon, and nothing could stop him.

The engine exploded with a deafening bang, and a hissing cloud of steam billowed around the windows. The motor seized and died, and the vehicle skidded to a halt. Monsoon climbed out, coughing, and surveyed the black smoke pouring from the hood. Letting out a stream of vile invective, he gave the side of the car a vicious kick. He heard a loud snap and felt a sudden excruciating pain on the top of his foot. As he hopped up and down, yelping in pain, a bird, like a large kingfisher, began laughing at him from the bough of a eucalyptus tree.

The unusual sounds were getting on the Don's nerves, but he knew he would have to tolerate them for a while. And anyway they had not left the building for nearly two weeks, so a little stir-craziness was to be expected. In the good old days they would have gone to the mattresses, but it was unthinkable in his condition that he allow himself to be lead out into the world as helpless as a babe in arms. It had been so long since he had heard the Sicilian dialect that it sounded alien to him, a foreign language to a mind that had become accustomed to even thinking in English. He found he had to concentrate, to scrabble through the museum of his memory, picking through the bones for a forgotten phrase, a word unused for decades. He had expected to be comforted by the familiar, but instead he was unnerved by it. Wrong again. He had been wrong about so much recently. He was slipping. Perhaps it was time to retire, to give it up, to go gracefully back to his villa in the hills above Palermo. And do what? Sit drinking grappa and spitting out olive stones, listening to the reminiscences of a bunch of fucking goatherds?

A burst of coarse language and harsh laughter came from the room next door where the boys were playing cards and drinking red wine. Had he once been like that, been one of them? When? He tried to remember, tried to feel some historic link, some kinship, some common blood, but could not. He was of another country now, another culture, another century even. But they were good men. He knew that. Good, strong men. Fierce and loyal and dependable. Men of the old school, the old way of thinking, where honor was still worth something. They had already proved it by putting down one minor rebellion with reptilian ruthlessness. Things had been better since then, calmer, and he was making at least some progress with the debacle down under. But these were still difficult days.

And there was the Irishman to consider. Who is to say that he might not think that the best way to be safe from the serpent is to draw its teeth, as he himself might have thought in the days of his vigor? He was obviously a capable man and, if he had been held in higher esteem from the beginning, perhaps things might have transpired differently. There would be no more mistakes, and no more underestimation. Only vigilance. And in times like these, these men, these four men of honor from the Mediterranean—family, blood, men whom he had summoned to stand his corner—these were the kind of men you needed around you.

He had shown his teeth, and the other dogs were putting their tails back between their legs. It was getting better, back to normal, back to the

Pax Imbroglio. But, caution, ever caution. Something might still happen, and if it did Don Ignacio Imbroglio would be ready.

It was only a question of time. They all knew it. Right from the very first second they had been like two packs of dogs, bristling, sniffing, probing, sizing up, waiting only for the first sign of fear from either side, the first act of overt aggression, to send the fur flying and the blood dripping. They sat at opposite ends of the bar, the one group rowdy and bumptious, drinking heavily, the other silent, still, drinking sparingly. They had arrived from Sydney on the same plane, one group first class, loud and loaded, rolling into Cairns like the supporters of a victorious rugby team, the other economy, filing into the customs hall in silence. They had driven down in separate vehicles, the one group singing, arguing, roistering, stopping frequently at watering holes along the way. The other group had driven directly, speaking in low voices to each other, eating on the move, not stopping.

It was going to happen, for sure, but not yet. Not until they had completed the job at hand: a tacit agreement between two groups of professionals, worlds apart in their attitudes and conduct, but united in their commitment to getting it done.

Stavros was nervous. The Big Blue Billabong Hotel was so out of the way he was lucky if he saw one party of tourists a month, let alone two on the same day, and this mob didn't look like your average day-trippers. The one crew was missing more parts than a prison workshop, and the other mob must be a delegation from the Asian Trappist society, because they hadn't said a fucking word to each other since they arrived. Except for one young kid with a ponytail, who looked as if Spock had accidentally beamed him to the wrong planet, this lot had that look about them, that body language, that arrogance that spelled trouble. You could almost hear them ticking.

Something was definitely up. Something bad. He knew it. It had been on the cards since Captain Cook had gone missing. First Bjørn Eggen and Mary Rose, and now this. Stavros paced up and down behind the bar, cleaning the same glasses over and over again, emptying clean ashtrays, keeping an eye on the ancient fowling piece that he kept loaded under the counter. It was only loaded with birdshot, just enough to sting the local rowdies up the arse if they got out of hand, but this new mob were not to know that. Things were all right for the moment, and at least they were keeping the register ringing, but he wondered what would happen when the regulars started coming in later.

It had not been difficult for people with A.S.S.'s experience to follow the trail as far as the Big Blue Billabong Hotel. Clerks, car hire receptionists, airline booking agents, credit card employees—all could be persuaded to divulge information one way or another. There were ways. There were always ways, and the people they were looking for were not exactly inconspicuous. Beginning in Sydney Harbor, using Norm's information as a starting point, they had spread out through the city, lifting stones, greasing palms, peeking through keyholes and into closets, speaking to doormen, taxi cab companies, and maîtres d'hôtel until they had built up a fairly accurate picture of what had happened.

Bopping around Sydney peddling MGJ Monsoon had left a trail that might as well have been fluorescent pink footprints, and they had correctly assumed that he would not attempt to make the trip to Cairns by commercial airline and so were able to find the pilot whose plane he had chartered. Based on what they had learned from the Don about Crispin they guessed, again correctly, that he would be ready for a bit of pampering after the rigors of the sea voyage and so were able to place him at the InterContinental. Picking up the flight details had been a piece of cake. The trail had gone a bit cold at Cairns until they had learned from the pilot of Monsoon's charter plane that he had left the airport by taxi, and returned with a brand new Combi, that was not rented, to collect his cargo.

As an experienced pilot himself Dugong had been able bullshit his way into the pilot's good graces, and over a couple of cold ones at the local flying club the pilot revealed that a mate of his had recently flown a right weird-looking mob up to Blue Billabong, in the back of beyond. The dealership where Monsoon bought his Combi had not been too difficult to find, and a mechanic had helpfully told them that he had been asked for directions to a place called Blue Billabong. Since — apart from a few tin roof shacks, a gas station, a general store, and a school — the Big Blue Billabong Hotel was more or less the town of Blue Billabong, it was the end of the line.

The four Vietnamese, sent by Long Suc to hold up his end of the deal, had waited in a cheap hotel by the docks for A.S.S. to conduct their detective work and had then joined them on the trip up to Cairns. Neither party knew for sure, but each was fairly certain that they had been given conflicting instructions from their respective employers as to what to do with the fugitives when they were apprehended.

The agreement between Long Suc and the Don was fairly straightforward and reasonable. For example, they had agreed that if either only the money or only the drugs were located, each would be returned to its respective owner. If both were found, the deal was to proceed as originally planned. On the point of what to do with the refugees, the situation was similarly cordial and uncomplicated. Long Suc had no idea who Asia and Crispin were, and therefore exercised no claim to or interest in them, and the Don himself merely wanted them scratched off as one wishes to scratch off a scab that itches. Likewise, the general had no interest in the fate of Mary Rose, whereas the Don had been quite specific in his request that she be returned to the USA in order to be debriefed on the failure of her mission, not to mention de-eared, de-fingered, disemboweled, and decapitated.

The Don had conceded that the general's reason for wanting revenge against Monsoon should take precedence over his own, as all he had done to the Don was cost him ten million dollars and ten million dollars was replaceable, whereas new feet were difficult to come by. Plus, Monsoon had made off with the drugs.

The general similarly agreed that the Don had a prior claim to Baby Joe, because although he had killed lots of his men, whereas he had only shot a few of the Don's, the general had a lot more men, so proportionally it was about even, plus the money he had absconded with was technically still the Don's. Of course, no one knew at the time that, except for one, the Don's men had actually been killed by each other, a redneck hunting party, a small furry dog, an old lady, and an elephant. As a professional courtesy, the Don had graciously conceded that his cousin Scungulo had been the victim of some overly zealous bodyguarding practices.

These were, however, merely the terms formally agreed upon between the Don and the general during their protracted telephone negotiations. Each man's private opinion, and therefore the instruction he had given to his respective agents, was quite different. There was, for example, the complicated question of ownership. Since the object of the exercise had been to exchange the money for the drugs, according to the general's thinking, the money had actually been his at the time of the ambush, and therefore he was perfectly entitled to suspend Baby Joe from barbed wire threaded through his earlobes and have an spectacled cobra and a starving mongoose surgically implanted into his large intestine. It would naturally follow that, if only the money were found, it would belong to him, and the loss of the drugs, which the Don had tacitly purchased, would be, although unfortunate, the Don's problem. Unless of course only the drugs were located, in which case they would belong to him, as the original owner, and the loss of the cash would be, regrettably, the Don's problem.

The Don's thinking on the subject was remarkably similar in that it was an almost perfect mirror image of the general's. Similarly, the Don privately concluded that the drugs had actually belonged to him when the shooting started, and that therefore he would be perfectly within his rights to insert an industrial carpet steamer into Monsoon's anus.

Furthermore—and to end the argument once and for all—revenge was a Sicilian specialty, not to mention a sacred duty, and in cases of conflicting interest a Sicilian's claim takes precedence in all situations pertaining to vengeance. He had therefore given instruction that the Vietnamese should be persuaded to hand over custody of all captives. The general had issued similar orders, which was naturally guaranteed to result in the monumental clusterfuck that Stavros was anticipating as he kept a concerned eye on his guests while the regulars started to file in.

Stavros operated a strict policy concerning the divulgence of information. He absolutely and positively refused to divulge any information to one-eyed Egyptians. Which is why, when Magnoon Piastre was ordering another round and casually said, "Listen. We're looking for some friends of ours who are supposed to be in the area," and described the parties in question, Stavros replied, "Nah, mate, sorry. We ain't seen no strangers 'ere in weeks. Don't get many visitors way out 'ere. You blokes on 'oliday?"

"Yeah. Sightseeing. Looking at all the kangaroos. Have you got any rooms?"

"Nah, mate. Sorry. We're full. This is our busiest time of year. End of the shearin season. Place'll be packed to the rafters with shearers, fresh in from the stations. Be right lively then."

"Shame. Where's the next nearest hotel?"

"That'll be Numbat Flats. Just down the road."

"How far?"

"Ah, only three 'undred miles. Ye'll do 'er in six hours easy, mate."

Magnoon nodded, gathered up the drinks, and carried them back to the table.

"What did he say?" Dugong asked.

"He says they're not here. He's lying."

"'Ow can you know?" Gaspart said.

"He's Greek."

"Ah. Ça va," Gaspart said, nodding sagely.

"He knows something. Plus, he said there aren't any rooms, but there's nobody in this shitbox, you can tell."

"So what's the plan?" Curtains said.

"There are no vehicles outside," Vladimir said.

"Right, and we 'ave not pass zem on ze way. Zey 'ave eizer already left, are still 'ere someplace, or are in front of us."

"Well, we know they flew here, so they can't be far away," said Magnoon.

"I say we stake the place out for a coupla days," said Dugong, "and send the slopes ahead to see if they find anything."

"But what if they find them, and we're not there?" Vladimir said.

"Yeah, good point. You're right. We need to keep an eye on the dink fuckheads. Okay. How about we camp out for a day or two, back in the bush? Do a recce, get the lay of the land. Watch the road both ways, see if they show. Maybe one of us can scout up ahead."

"I've got a better idea," Magnoon offered. "Why don't I pull this fucking Greek's teeth out until he tells us?"

"*Non*. Bettair we wait. We pretend to leave, and zen camp in ze *forêt*. Zat way 'e will sink we 'ave gone. We can watch ze 'otel, in case 'e tries to send a message, or warn zem, non? I cut ze wire, a few miles down the track."

"One thing," said Vladimir. "A place like this might have a radio."

"Right again," said Dugong. "Someone find out. If so, we can tune ours in to the same wavelength. I'll go tell the chief zip what the plan is."

"When do we move out?" Magnoon asked.

"When we've had a few more drinks, you fucking raghead cyclops," said Dugong, moving off with a grin.

The shadow of the Cessna flitted across the tops of the trees and advanced across the red surface of the road like a crucifix in a horror movie. Except for Crispin, whose eyes were firmly closed, everybody stared intently at the earth rolling by underneath. The thermals rising from the baking earth pummeled the small plane, tossing it, dropping it with stomach-churning swoops and then catching it again with neck-jarring jerks. They were into their second day of searching and had been aloft since dawn following the roads, calculating the maximum distance the Combi could have traveled. They had eliminated the main road yesterday and were following a minor road south, adjusting their distance calculations to accommodate the condition of the road. They were tired and worried and, in Crispin's case, scared shitless.

Since they had made the discovery that Monsoon's Combi was gone, along with Bjørn Eggen, Mary Rose, and the money, suspicion had followed on the heels of shock, with concern third by a nose, alarm a couple of lengths back, and despondency bringing up the rear. At the turn, it was alarm by half a length from despondency, and then concern coming away down the stretch. They had endlessly reviewed the possible permutations of motive and method, running different scenarios through their minds, postulating connivance and complicity, kidnapping and caught napping, double crosses, triple crosses, and noughts and crosses, not wanting to think the unthinkable but not being quite able to discard the idea either.

The hours until the plane had arrived had seemed interminable, and tempers frayed as the tension increased. Wally had quickly explained the situation to Helmut, and everyone had piled into the truck and headed back to the airplane. The relief had been palpable as they took off—for everyone except Crispin, that is, who had quickly realized that he was going to die as Helmut banked the Cessna into a vertigo-inducing spiral. The first day they saw nothing but miles of empty roads unraveling below, interspersed with tiny settlements and the occasional road train dragging a huge red cloud in its wake. The gathering gloom of sunset matched the mood in the truck as they trundled back to the hotel, weary and disconsolate after their long and fruitless search.

They were up and away again with the sun, heading at right angles to the immense shadows which crept across the limitless expanse of bush below. Just before ten, sunlight flashed on glass, and Wally and Asia both cried out at once.

"There, there, down there."

"Under that fucken gum tree."

"It's all down there, you drongos, and which particular gum tree did you have in mind out of the approximately forty million that I can see?" said Helmut, who was understandably a little testy.

"Just in front of the shadow of the plane now," Asia said.

"Yah. I see it now. Hang on to your arses. We go down for a closer look."

Crispin's shriek rivaled the engine's whine as Helmut dropped the Cessna into a Stuka nosedive and swept over the treetops. Except for Crispin, they all clearly saw the white Volkswagen in the shadow of a large stand of trees. Helmut pulled up into the sun and came round in a tight circle, holding the pattern as they searched the area for signs of life.

"Can't we land?" Asia asked.

"No. I am afraid we have not sufficient clearance between the trees."

"What can we do, then?" asked Crispin, whose curiosity had overcome his terror now that the aircraft seemed to be flying on a more even keel.

"We'll head back. I can radio Stavros, and they can bring the truck."

"How long will that take?"

"On this road? Sunset, I should think."

"Fuck."

"I agree."

"Helmut," Wally said, "head this crate over to Jimmy's. You can put 'er down in the meadow."

"Good thinking, Wal."

Crispin closed his eyes again as the Cessna made another abrupt and alarming turn.

"I don't understand," Asia said.

"Our mate. Jimmy. Lives out in the bush. Can eat ashes and drink stones. Not to mention 'e could find a white flea on a polar bear's arse with 'is fucken eyes shut. We'll send 'im overland to track 'em down, and we'll 'ead back, and in the meantime 'Elmut can radio Stavros."

Helmut turned the plane directly towards the sun, and the cabin was filled with a blinding light.

"How can you see where you're going?" Crispin asked Helmut.

"I fucken can't."

As Jimmy was returning to his Holden with a small kangaroo swinging lifeless from his shoulder a strange smell drifted to him on the wind and he froze, seeming to disappear into the surrounding heat haze. He circled around, coming upon his camp from behind a low hill, and soundlessly on leathery feet advanced to its summit. Crouching in the tall sun-bleached grass, he peered between the dry blades. He saw a single-engine Cessna pulled up in the shade next to the tree, and beneath its wing three men and a woman sitting on camp chairs drinking his beer.

One of the men was as black and wiry as beef jerky; another slight, with a white shirt, and hair that shone in the sun; and the third was fat, florid, and soft, and appeared to have a pile of cotton candy stuck to his head. The woman had flaming copper hair tied with a green ribbon, and a spectacular figure. Jimmy grinned broadly and ghosted forward without a sound.

Wally grinned, similarly broadly, converting his parchment face into a passable impression of a happy Shar-Pei as he fastened his gums onto the rim of his can like a limpet clam clinging to a rock.

"Strewth!" he yelled in dismay as a six-foot length of fire-hardened eucalyptus zipped through his beer, knocking it from his grip.

"G'day, Wally, g'day, Helmut," said Jimmy as he bent to retrieve his spear, sliding the can from it with a harsh rasping noise.

"Jimmy, yer useless, sheep-shaggin barstad, you've ruined me bladdy breakfast."

Tossing Wally another can, Jimmy responded with a stream of Ngadjonji, of which an approximate translation would go something like, "Stop nicking me fucking beer, you short-arsed, wrinkled old cunt, and why the fuck has that fat poofter got a dead fucking sheep on top of his head, and who's the sheila with the big knockers and does she fuck, and who are these wankers anyway, and where's me fucking cockatoo, you thieving bastard."

"This big fella's Crispin," Wally replied in English, pulling the ring on his tin, and indicating Crispin with his thumb. "This lovely sheila's Asia, an' no she don't, least not with dingbats like you. An' I et yer fucken cockatoo, so kiss me arse."

Wally did his Shar-Pei impression again, fastened his limpet lips to the can, tilted his head back, and waited for his words to sink in.

Crispin, meanwhile, was frozen to his chair with his mouth open, observing the proceedings with a disconcerting mixture of dismay and desire. His short-lived euphoria with his bucolic surroundings had evaporated in direct proportion to the ferocity of the hangover, which was currently hammering hot rivets into his sinuses, and his near hysteria over the most recent calamity. Still shaken from the turbulent and terrifying flight, Helmut having maneuvered the plane so close to the tree tops that he swore he could see the whites of the koalas' eyes, and finding himself for the first time in his adult experience without a building in sight, in the company of an unintelligible savage, Crispin was on the point of wigging out.

The incident with the spear had almost finished him, and the sight of the lithe, ebony figure of Wombat Jimmy, with the sheen of the morning sun on his sweating skin and his formidable equipment swinging in the antipodean breeze, had unleashed an irresistible stream of ecstatic imagery in his brain that had him almost swooning, so long had it been since he had indulged in the pleasures of the flesh. And what on earth was that frightful beast? It looked like it had been unearthed from a compost heap, and smelled even worse than the time that Nigel had his little accident. And why did it keep looking at him like that?

Asia was studying Jimmy with similar sentiments, but shared none of Crispin's trepidation and would have enjoyed the excitement of the bumpy flight and appreciated Jimmy's display of marksmanship, had she not been so overwhelmed with worry about Baby Joe, and concern for Bjørn Eggen and Mary Rose, not to mention the money. Despite all, she couldn't resist making a fuss of Walkabout, whom she thought was just the most adorable creature. Walkabout reciprocated, and just to prove it he lifted his snout from the beer she had just poured for him long enough to sniff her gusset. He quickly decided in favor of the beer, but then Asia had been all morning in the cramped plane and the hot sun.

She was stroking his rank fur, gazing at Jimmy and fantasizing about what his huge clam digger would look like in its proud state, when he spoke to her.

"G'day, sheila. I'm Jimmy. Me wombat's called Walkabout."

Asia summoned the best smile she could muster under the circumstances. "We've been introduced. He's cute. I'm Asia."

Asia turned her smile up a couple of watts and extended her fingers. Jimmy grinned, showing his perfect teeth, but made no attempt to take her hand. Crispin roused himself from his catatonic state, struggled to his feet, and stepped towards Jimmy with his hand outstretched and an unctuous smile on his sweating face.

He was midway through his second step when Wally leapt from his chair with a speed belying his years, dived full length, and tackled Crispin behind the knees. With a cry of dismay, Crispin collapsed onto the hard earth like a giant jellyroll, his arms flung out theatrically, and the beer spilling from his can in a glistening arch. He smacked into the dirt with his face inches from Walkabout's rear end. Walkabout dutifully farted. Crispin struggled to an upright position, and, as he did so, planted his pudgy hand smack into one of Walkabout's recent efforts. He suffered complete composure meltdown.

"YOU TOOTHLESS OLD CUNT. WHAT THE FUCK DO YOU THINK YOU ARE PLAYING AT?"

Wally stood grinning, still holding his can, proud of the fact that he had made the tackle without spilling a single drop. He turned to Jimmy.

"Lissen 'ow 'e's jabbering to a bloke what just saved 'is fucken life, eh, Jimmy?"

Crispin was futilely trying to wipe his hand on the red earth, while simultaneously glaring at Asia, who, despite all her anxiety, had slid from her chair and was sitting on the dirt holding her knees together and howling.

"What the fuck is that old goat talking about?" continued Crispin. "Is he completely deranged or what?"

"Na, mate," said Jimmy, softly, "it's fair dinkum. Wally just saved your life for sure. You wanna thank 'im 'stead a cursin 'im."

"Thank him for saving me from what?" Crispin asked, suddenly unsure, his eyes flicking around nervously as if searching for some thereto-unrevealed nastiness lurking in among the leaves.

"Me shadow."

"Your what, now?"

"'Is shadow," interjected Wally. "If a white bloke steps on it, it's curtains fer sure. Kill 'im quicker than fucken taipan."

Wally snapped his horny fingers to illustrate his point. Asia had stopped laughing and was looking from Jimmy's face down to his shadow, which was looking all of a sudden blacker and somehow sinister on the baked earth, and back to his face again. Crispin's mouth was open.

"Yah. This is correct," Helmut confirmed, looking grave.

"That's why I'm fucken famous, mate. Learned it from old ones. Dreamtime fellas."

"You mean you're trying to tell me that a man can die just from stepping on your shadow?"

"Only white blokes. Don't work with black fellas like Wally."

"This is also correct," Helmut added.

"Why, that's the most preposterous crock of horseshit I've ever heard in my entire life," said Crispin as he wobbled to his feet, fuelled by his outrage. Gathering momentum, he continued, "You mean to tell me that I have risked my life flying halfway across this benighted desert, at the ass end of the world, in the company of an unhinged gibbon, in that fucking gossamer deathtrap, piloted by a pomade-smeared refugee from Baron Von Richtoven's flying fucking circus, to listen to some mumbo-jumbo, voodoo bullshit about killer shadows. You have got to be shitting me, my dusky friend."

The light went out of Jimmy's eyes. Without seeming to move, he was suddenly in between Crispin and the sun, his shadow stretched out before him like a poisoned blade. Crispin blanched and took a step back.

"Try it," said Jimmy, in a very quiet voice, barely louder than a whisper, the whisper of scales, snake scales on dry stones.

"Ya," said Helmut, "if you don't believe, step forward."

Jimmy advanced half a step towards Crispin, who retreated until his spine thumped into the trunk of the tree.

"Wally, do something," Asia said, suddenly alarmed.

"Eh, Jimmy," said Wally, "'ow we gonna get this fat barstad in the plane if 'e carkes it?"

Jimmy's face cracked into a smile, and the air of menace dissipated as quickly as it had appeared. "Yeah, Wal. Good thinking. Chuck us a fucken beer, mate."

As Wally bent for the beers, Crispin and Asia exchanged a long, meaningful stare.

"'Ere, Jimmy," Wally said, "some mates of ours are lost, out in the bush. We reckon they're in trouble. We seen the Combi, but we can't get the plane down. We want yer ter go an 'elp em."

"We still don't know they're lost," said Crispin icily, regaining some of his composure. "Maybe they just ran off with the money. After all, Bjørn Eggen is Monsoon's grandfather, and Mary Rose is a gangster. I mean, look what she did before."

"What she did was save our lives, Crispin, *if* you remember," Asia said sharply.

"Nah, mate, Bjørn Eggen wouldn't pull a stunt like that. Mary Rose neither. London to a brick, it's that useless drongo grandson of 'is up to 'is tricks again. We shoulda let ol' Penguin Brew heave 'im overboard." Wally turned to Jimmy. "Lissen, mate. These are old folks. It might not go too good for 'em out in the bush. We don't know what they've got in the way of water. I reckon you're about an hour's trek from 'ere. I ain't got the legs for it no more."

"Yeah. No worries, Wal," Jimmy said, picking up his weapons. "Which way?"

"Aim for those blue gums, then foller the line of the 'ills, till you get to the stream. Foller the shadows, then turn east when you get to the road."

"Whaddya want me to do with 'em when I find 'em, Wal?"

"Just see 'em right. Truck'll be 'ere 'round sundown, I reckon." Wally nodded, and turned to go.

"Please hurry," said Asia.

"She'll be right, sheila," Jimmy said, beaming his smile. "See ya, Walkabout."

**SHANE NORWOOD**

Jimmy ghosted off between the trees, running effortlessly, seeming to float away as his image disappeared into the mirage. Walkabout farted.

# Chapter 24.

The good news was he was a millionaire. The bad news was he was in the middle of a waterless plain under the anvil of the sun with a broken foot, two dehydrated geriatrics, and nothing to drink but half a bottle of whiskey. Monsoon was a city boy. If you wanted water, you turned on a fucking tap, and if you were too hot you put the A.C. on. When he had meticulously planned his transcontinental adventure, he had meticulously failed to understand that there are places on earth that require greater self-sufficiency than the ability to pull into a gas station. He had not taken into account that there were stretches on his trip where he could literally drive for days and see no more sign of human presence than a dead sheep on the side of the road. He had no water, other than what was left in the radiator, no food, no camping gear, and was not adequately equipped to spend even one day in the moisture-sucking Australian bush. In fact, he was not adequately equipped for a trip to the movies. In the grip of this new and alarming reality, Monsoon did what seemed to him to be the most sensible thing. He sat down in the shade of a gum tree and drank the rest of the whiskey.

In the back of the Combi, Mary Rose was in bad shape. She was seriously dehydrated, and her feet and hands were badly swollen from being bound. She was unconscious and as white as a sheet, and her breathing was very shallow, coming in fast little gasps. Bjørn Eggen was better, but not much. His rigorous outdoor life and the essential soundness of his body had stood him in good stead, but the intense baking heat in the back of the Combi was sapping his strength fast. The force of the sudden skidding halt of the vehicle slamming him up against the back of the driver's seat had roused him, and he looked at Mary Rose and knew instantly that she was in trouble. He was still drowsy from the drug, but had sweated much of it out of his system.

Whoever had tied him up had been an amateur, binding his hands in front of him with duct tape. Aching in every joint and feeling the weight of every one of his years, he battled to a sitting position and shuffled over to the spare wheel. After a couple of minutes chafing the tape against the threads of the bolts that held it in place he was able to free his hands, which had also swelled but not as badly as Mary Rose's. Freeing his feet, he moved over to her and loosened her bonds. Her skin was clammy and he could barely feel her pulse, and when he lifted her eyelids her eyes were rolled back in her head. She needed water. Fast. Opening the back door and sliding out, his cramped legs buckled under him and he fell to the earth, landing hard, tasting the bitter red soil. He heard an exclamation, and looking under the wheelbase saw a pair of outstretched legs.

Clambering to his feet, Bjørn Eggen heard a cry of pain as Monsoon tried to do the same, supporting himself against the trunk of the blue gum. Bjørn Eggen hobbled around the back of the van and saw his grandson leaning against the tree, favoring his right foot and holding an empty whiskey bottle. His rage overcame his pain and fatigue, and the years melted away as he strode across the distance between them, snarling like a fighting dog, and drove his bony fist onto the point of Monsoon's nose, breaking it.

Monsoon went down with a yelp, smacking his head into the tree and dropping the bottle, which bounced off the red soil but did not break. Monsoon was used to life kicking him in the teeth, and had almost come to expect it. What he did not expect was to be kicked in the balls by his own grandfather as he lay on the ground under a eucalyptus tree with a broken nose and a broken foot. He vomited up the whiskey and looked up through tear-filled eyes to see Bjørn Eggen standing over him brandishing a branch, and as he tried to curl up, squealing wordlessly, Bjørn Eggen began to thrash him.

"*Skitten liggende gris*! You focken dirty fockpig. I should focken kill you, so I should. You are no more the grandson for me. You hear it, *ja*? No more the focken grandson. I shit on you!" Exhausted and dizzy, Bjørn Eggen dropped the branch and leaned back against the hot metal of the Combi, breathing hard, as Monsoon lay curled in the fetal position, whimpering.

Recovering his breath, Bjørn Eggen gently lifted Mary Rose from the back of the van and placed her supine in the shade of the tree, and she seemed to him as light and as frail as a bird. Dragging out the mattress from the back, he carefully rolled her onto it and removed her clothes, not concerning himself with her modesty. Fortunately, and through no foresight of Monsoon's, the Combi had come equipped with a toolkit, and this Bjørn Eggen now lugged around to the engine, where he began to salvage what liquid he could. After half an hour, he had a container of windshield fluid, half a container of engine coolant, a whisky bottle full of discolored radiator fluid, and four hubcaps full of sump oil.

The engine coolant he poured over Mary Rose, leaving the moisture to evaporate from her skin, and she moaned and stirred but did not wake. He put the windshield fluid to his lips, and tasted it. It was soapy, but potable, and removing his shirt, he soaked it in the liquid, and held it over Mary Rose's lips, shepherding her as she unconsciously swallowed the precious drops. He repeated the process until she had swallowed perhaps a cup. He then poured the sump oil onto her and spread it evenly over her body, massaging it onto her swollen hands and feet.

Finally he spread the damp shirt over her nakedness, picked up the bottle of radiator fluid, and set out to climb a distant eminence to see if he could see any sign of life or water. As he passed the still-prostrate and whining Monsoon, he attempted to spit on him, but his mouth was too dry.

He had to rest several times as the sun rose in the sky and the heat began to pulverize him. Breathless, he reached a high point and looked around and sat down heavily as his spirits sank. It was a desolate wasteland of sparse grass dotted with slender gray trees for as far as the eye could see in any direction—no sign of human habitation, no smoke, no distant sparkle or congregation of birds or beasts to indicate the presence of water.

And then he heard the plane. He looked up and saw the distant speck heading towards him. He scrabbled in his pockets for matches but found none, and his eyes began to search for something to signal with as the plane approached. He wanted to yell but had no voice, and anyway it was much too far away. He could tell that it was following the line of the road, which meant that it might be searching for them, and he watched anxiously as it reached the point where the Combi was parked. With indescribable relief he watched it dip and then bank into a tight circle and hold it, and he began to scramble down the hill as fast as his ancient pins would allow.

As he approached the vehicle, he was surprised to see a column of smoke rise into the still air, and as he rounded an enormous boulder and the Combi came into view, he was even more surprised to see a lithe, naked black man squatting over a fire, cooking a large lizard.

As he approached the man looked up, with a beatific smile on his handsome face. "Ah, g'day, mate. Tucker's nearly ready. How d'ya like ya fucken goanna?"

Too bewildered to speak, Bjørn Eggen looked to where he had left Mary Rose. She was gone. Rising panic caused his voice to break into falsetto as he said, "Vhat haf you vith the lady done?"

"Ah, she's right, mate. I 'ad to move 'er. Sun come round, see? 'Ere, I'll show ya."

Bjørn Eggen followed the young man around a rocky outcrop and found Mary Rose laying in deep shade, under a simple shelter of gum branches. A small fire nearby sent up an aromatic cloud of smoke. There was a green compress on her forehead and beside her, some kind of embrocation or emollient in a gourd. Next to her was a Wellington boot or galosh of some description, and he could see that it was filled with water. Bjørn Eggen knelt beside her. She was still out, but her breathing was more regular, her pulse stronger, and she had lost her ghastly pallor and appeared now to be in a peaceful sleep. He looked up to see the young man proffering the boot.

"'Ere, Blue. Ya look like ya need this yerself. Go slow, mate. Take 'er easy."

Bjørn Eggen put his lips to the neck of the boot, and the tepid, rubber-tasting water was better than any beer he had ever tasted.

"From vhere haf come the vater?"

"You ev to know where to look, mate. The old sheila's 'ad a couple a sips, and I gin 'er some o' me special brew. She'll be right."

"I haf no idea how I should be thanking you, my friend," he said, putting the boot carefully down.

"No need, mate. We all ev to look out for each other, out 'ere. They call me Jimmy. Wombat Jimmy."

Bjørn Eggen stood, unsteadily, and offered his hand, observing how much Jimmy looked like a young Wally. "I am Bjørn Eggen, and my companion is Mary Rose. You are perhaps related to Wally, I think so, *ja*."

Jimmy's face split in half. "Dunno, mate. With that old bastard, who knows?"

"Ja, it is so. Vhat of the other one?"

"'E's up shit creek without a fucken paddle, mate. Crook foot, crook nose. Someone must've upended 'im."

"Ja. Is so. Vas me who haf him upended, as you say so."

"Why's that?"

"Vas him who haf done this terrible thing to us. Mary Rose haf maybe to be dying from him, I think."

"Ah, yeah? The dirty fucken mongrel. Good on yer, mate."

"Where to is he now?"

"Asleep in the Combi. I fix 'im up a bit, but 'e needs a doctor for that crook foot."

"Fock him. Vhat now vill ve do?"

"'Ang fire 'ere, I reckon. Wally reckons the truck will be 'ere bout sundown. You get a bit of rest. I'll wake you up when it's cooler, for your grub."

"Thank you again, my good friend."

Jimmy smiled at Bjørn Eggen, and went to attend to his goanna. The old man sat down and looked at Mary Rose. He put his hand on her forehead and found it cool and not clammy like before. He bent over awkwardly and kissed her, and then lay down beside her. The bare, baked earth was the deepest, softest, most comforting feather mattress in the world, and before he had completed his third breath he was sound asleep.

Wally could see the fire blazing and the sparks lifting into the moonless night for a long time before they arrived at where the Combi was. Not knowing what to expect, he had come prepared and had a pump-action over-and-under 12-gauge on his lap. Helmut was driving, and Stavros was in the back with his fowling piece, which he had reloaded with buckshot. Bruce, who had abandoned his wait for Kylie Minogue, sat next to him, armed with his traditional weapons and with a broad white band painted across his face. Wally slowed as they approached, but accelerated again when he saw Jimmy silhouetted against the blaze, waving them on.

"G'day," Jimmy said as they began to climb out of the truck. "You blokes stop for a beer on the way, or what? Eh, Bruce, corroboree's next month, ya fucken prawn."

"Fuck off, wombat fucker."

Wally strode straight over to where Bjørn Eggen sat by the fire. Mary Rose lay beside him awake but shivering, despite the heat.

"G'day, mate. 'Owareya?"

"I am fine, but Mary Rose haf not do so vell I think."

"What about this bladdy mongrel?"

Monsoon was huddled on the opposite side of the fire, staring into the flames, and did not look at Wally or acknowledge his presence.

"What happened, Bjørn Eggen?"

"This one haf the drugs to us given, and tied us up in the car. For vhy I do not know. The car haf the engine broken and we haf become stuck. If not for Jimmy, Mary Rose would be very bad, I think. Very bad, ja."

Wally knelt beside Mary Rose, and took her hand. She smiled weakly, and tried to speak, but could not.

"Vally? Vhy for have this one done this terrible thing?"

"The fucken wonga, mate. 'E nicked the wonga."

"A vonga is being vhat?"

"I'll explain later, mate."

Wally climbed into the back of the van, and banged around for a few minutes. Climbing out, he walked over to Monsoon and stood over him. "All right, you little shithead. Where is it?"

Monsoon stared steadfastly into the fire.

"He haf not to me anything said, since I am giving him the punch in the nose, *ja*."

"All right. 'Ere, Jimmy, find us a fucken funnel web, will ya?"

"No worries."

One second Jimmy was there, the next he was gone, leaving Monsoon staring at the place where he had been, wondering what a funnel web was, but knowing that whatever it was, it wouldn't be good.

Wally sat down next to Bjørn Eggen. Bruce and Stavros came over with a case of beer, and some bottled water. "We brung some chicken broth. We dint know what was up, but we come prepared."

"I will make some for the lady," Helmut said.

Wally handed Bruce a beer, and opened one for himself. Bjørn Eggen looked at him quizzically.

"I dunno whether you should be drinkin this in your state. You better 'av water, mate."

"Fock water. Give me a focken beer."

"Okay. Good on yer mate. Now, 'ere's the plan. The plane is still by Jimmy's. Mary Rose is in bad shape. She needs an 'ospital. We'll drive back to the plane, and 'Elmut can fly you and 'er to Cairns. Okay?"

"*Ja,* is very good."

Suddenly and silently, Jimmy was back. In his hand was a jar, and by the light of the fire something black could be seen scuttling inside of it. Wally took it from him, and carried it to where Monsoon sat. Stravros and Bruce joined him.

"All right, boys. This bladdy mongrel don't wanna talk to us. Maybe 'e'll talk to our mate in the jar 'ere."

Monsoon screamed as Bruce grabbed him from behind and pinioned him, while Stavros grabbed his pants and pulled them around his ankles, exposing his genitals. Wally held up the jar to the firelight, so that Monsoon could get a good look inside. He shook it, and the huge spider reared up. Monsoon re-iterated his scream, only louder.

"Right, ya fucken ratbag. If this beauty bites ya, ye'll be a fucken goner before ya can say fucken Alice. 'Urts too, mate. You got three seconds to tell me what you did with the wonga."

Monsoon stared at the jar, and at the black, evil thing inside. He was paralyzed by fear and indecision, caught between terror and avarice. Terror was screaming at him to speak, and avarice was screaming at terror to shut the fuck up. Wally tipped the jar and the spider tumbled out and began to crawl, slowly and inexorably, towards Monsoon's privates, its sleek black abdomen glinting in the firelight. Avarice screamed at terror to speak for Christ's sake.

"In the car, in the car, in the panels, in the spare wheel, get it away from me, kill it, let me go, stop it, stop it, aaaaaaah."

Wally bent down and picked up the spider, held it up to Jimmy, and tossed it into the bush. "That's not a bladdy funnel web, ya fucken gallah."

"Nah, mate," Jimmy said. "Couldn't fucken find one."

The two parallel lines of small fires, seeming in perspective to be drawn together at their farthest remove, were going out one by one, and they could just make out the receding tail lights of the Cessna among the stars that blazed in the firmament with a brightness and clarity unknown and inconceivable to any city-dweller. Bruce and Jimmy were stamping out the fires that had been used to guide Helmut's take off, extinguishing each carefully in turn to prevent a bush fire, which would be disastrous to the local wildlife population, not to mention Jimmy's beer supply.

Wally and Bruce and Crispin were doing enough damage to it already. They sat by a crackling fire of their own on the seats pulled out from the Holden, and Asia was stroking Walkabout's belly under the terms of their agreement, whereby she wouldn't stop rubbing his belly and he wouldn't start farting. Monsoon sat in the shadows on the opposite side of the fire, nursing a beer, his wounded pride, and his thoughts of vengeance.

"So, whaddya blokes wanna do?"

"Oh, dear," Crispin said, "I thought all this was over. I mean, we're already at the ends of the earth. How far do we have to go?"

"We could stay here," Asia suggested.

"For how long, Asia? Come on. Be real."

"So what do we do, then? Wally, what do you think?"

"Well. Stavros reckons these blokes 'ave moved on, but even if that's so, it don't mean they ain't comin back. Dingbat over 'ere 'ad what they were looken for stashed in the Combi. London to a fucken brick, they ain't just gonna kiss it goodbye. If we was to give it back to 'em, maybe they'd leave it at that."

"What about the money? You want to give that back?"

"Depends what your peace of mind is worth to ya, mate. I thought you'd be right enough out 'ere, but I was wrong. What are ya gonna do, keep runnin for the rest a yer lives?"

"But what if we give them everything and they still...?" Crispin let the words hang in the air.

Nobody spoke for a long time. Bruce and Jimmy came back and joined them, and they sat in silence staring into the crackling fire. Thin wisps of smoke marched out into the night, drifting up into the darkness. A bolt of brilliant green flashed across the sky.

"Everybody make a wish," Crispin said, plaintively.

"I wish Baby Joe was here," Asia said. "I wish I could speak to him. I wish I knew where he was."

"It doesn't work if you tell everybody," Crispin said.

# Chapter 25.

It was like a marriage slowly falling apart. Nothing you could put your finger on, no one specific thing, just a slow, steady decline until you woke up one morning and all respect had gone, all love, until there was just an empty shell, a charade that both parties played out until one of them summoned the will to end it.

It had started to slip after the problems with the Mick. The Don had never treated him the same after that. Again, nothing specific, just small subtle things, a distance and coldness that wasn't there before. And then all these Guineas show up, just because things were getting a little tight. What kind of a slap in the teeth was that, after all he had done for the man? Maybe the stories were true. Maybe he was losing it. Well, he'd better be careful. There was certain information that people would be grateful for. And it wasn't like he hadn't had any other offers. Maybe it was time to start thinking about taking one of them up. It was a shit life anyway. Hanging around all fucking day, taking shit, fetching and carrying, every once in a while a couple of hours to go out and grab a brewskie if he was a good boy. It had all been that Mick's fault. He had sucker-punched him. Caught him when he wasn't ready. Well, if he ever got the chance again, it would be different. Much different.

Stratosphere looked at his watch, shrugged, downed his bourbon, washed it down with his beer, and pushed through the swing doors. And now what the fuck? Some holy Joe, panhandling outside a bar. They had no business being outside a bar. In church, okay. Even in the street, the mall...but outside a bar, taking advantage of people that had had a few, no way. It just wasn't fucking right. And he was going to straighten him out.

The priest stepped out into Stratosphere's path as he walked towards him, and the orange and green light from the bar sign glinted on his spectacles as he held forth his bowl and said, "God bless the generous of heart."

Stratosphere grabbed him by the front of his smock, and spat into the bowl. "Stick that in your fucking collection, Father."

The accepted Christian doctrine, on such occasions, is to turn the other cheek, and, while this is no longer widely practiced, Stratosphere was still extremely surprised when the cleric responded by chopping him in the throat, pushing him into an alleyway, tripping him, embedding a switch blade into his groin, and twisting it.

"I want the code," the priest said.

Stratosphere wanted to struggle, to writhe away from the pain, but the shock and fear was stealing his will and his throat was being pushed into the ground and his air choked off and the blade was burrowing deeper. He managed to say, "What fucking code?"

"The code for the elevator. The top floor."

"I don't know what the fuck..."

The blade twisted.

"All right, all right. Eight three six four, and then back again."

"Eight three six four four six three eight?" The priest said.

"Yeah. Yeah."

"You know what happens if this number ain't right?"

"Yeah, I know. I know."

"Good. Thanks, sweetheart. I'll tell your girlfriend you said hello."

A realization flooded into Stratosphere's brain. He half-smiled. "The fucking Mick," he said, before the light went out.

Handyman Harris was in a hurry. Seemed like he was always in a hurry these days, ever since his wife left him. And for a fucking mathematician. How do you figure that out?

Take the kids to school, run his business, pick the kids up from school, take them to baseball practice, take them to piano lessons, bring them back again, feed them, spend some quality time with the little bastards, do the shopping, do the washing, do the cleaning, fix the car. Always something to do, always someplace to be, and never a minute to scratch your ass. It wasn't easy being in his line of work and taking care of a couple of kids. And he was going to have to move to a bigger place. The kids needed their own room, and they needed a garden, and they wanted a dog, and he didn't care what anybody said, it's just not fair to keep a dog cooped up in an apartment. Guaranteed it was cheap enough. They don't come much cheaper than free, and the security was great, but all those creepy guys around, and those cameras looking at you all the time? Uh-uh, no sir. He didn't want the kids to be around it.

That's what he kept telling himself, anyway, but that wasn't the correct starting price, and he knew it. The real reason was the man upstairs. You didn't spend fifty-odd years in Vegas without knowing a losing bet when you saw one. I mean, he heard the stories about what went on up there, just like everybody else. Something was happening. The guy just didn't carry the same weight. He was hearing things, comments, smart remarks, wisecracks that would've put you in traction before, and people were saying them now and getting away with it. He just had that feeling. The eagle was going to fall from its nest, and you didn't want to be standing underneath when that happened.

Handyman looked at his watch. Shit. He was late picking the kids up. One lousy beer, that's all he'd had time for, and he hadn't even been able to watch the end of the game. He grabbed his pool cue, went rushing out of the door, and ran smack into a preacher, nearly knocking him over.

"Oh, Father, forgive me. I wasn't looking where I was going. Are you okay?"

"I'm fine, my son. No harm done. No harm at all. Goodnight to you."

"Goodnight, Father, and sorry again."

Handyman dashed across the street and round the corner. It wasn't until he got to his apartment that he realized his wallet was gone. *Would you fucking believe it? A priest! You can't trust any bastard these days!*

It's not nice to be ignored. It is especially unpleasant when you feel that you are being ignored for prejudicial reasons. But when the heavyset African-American gentleman had been ignored when he had stopped into the bar for a drink, an hour ago, it had not bothered him at all. It had not even bothered him when people who came in after him had been served before him, something that most people find infuriating. Even when the bartender had been, not exactly rude, but certainly offhand, he had not been offended. In fact he had been pleased. So pleased that when he ordered his second drink, he made a point of smiling at the bartender, and even when this smile was not returned he had not been upset. And when he had had finished his second drink, although he made a point of not leaving a tip, he had smiled courteously before he left.

Thus, one hour later, he was neither surprised nor offended when the receptionist at Don Imbroglio's apartment building had made him feel about as welcome as a pork sausage at a Saudi wedding.

"Yeah?"

"Good evening. I'm here to see Mr. Harris."

"About what?"

"It's a personal matter."

"Listen, I need to know why you want to see him. It's my job, see."

"I see. Well, I spoke to him on the phone, a little earlier. I'm returning something that belongs to him."

"Wait."

The receptionist walked to the other end of the counter and picked up the phone. He spoke a few words, looked back at the African-American gentleman, and laughed. His good humor had evaporated by the time he hung up and returned.

"Second floor," he said, his face a mask.

The gentleman thanked him, and turned away.

"Hey."

"Yes?"

"The bag."

"My bag?"

"Yeah. The bag. You got to leave it here. Regulations."

"Oh, I see. Well, here you are, then."

The receptionist took the brown, doctor-style case from the man without comment. He watched him wait patiently for the elevator, chatting pleasantly with the security guard, and watched the doors close behind him, and then picked up a telephone, a different one than the one he had used before.

"Yeah. Some shine just went in to see Handyman. How the fuck should I know? I'm just telling ya, like I'm s'posed to. Yeah, yeah, up yours too, asshole."

Some people find watching television interesting, others find it boring. Eric found it tedious to an unimaginable degree, but that was only because he had to watch the same program eight hours a day, every day. It was called "People Walking In And Out Of Doors And People Getting In And Out Of Elevators." What made it even worse, most of the time these were the same people. And you had to watch the program, even if you had seen it many, many times before, because if you didn't the boss got really angry, and really bad things happened when the boss got really angry. The only diversion was when you got to speak to that dipshit reception guy Klaus and rattle his cage, or the extremely rare occasions when something unexpected or surprising happened.

Like, for example, when a guy got into the elevator on the tenth floor, who had never even entered the building. The bald guy who kept his head bent, like there was something wrong with his neck.

Eric picked up the phone. "Hey, dipshit. How come you never rang me 'bout the dude on ten?"

"What fuckin' dude?"

"You s'posed to ring me every time someone we don't know gets in the elevator. Some turkey just got in on ten. Bald-headed guy."

"Listen, asshole. Having you as a camera operator is like having Britney Spears as a singing instructor. The only one been in or out for an hour is the nigger."

"Yeah, I seen him. He got off on two. But what about…?"

A noise, equally puzzling and alarming, cut short the conversation. Eric heard what sounded like an explosion at the other end of the line. He glanced back at the screen just in time to see the intruder fingering the code buttons. He banged on the alarm button, while simultaneously shouting "Fuck" into the receiver. Klaus wasn't listening. He had been distracted. Small thermite charges in doctor's bags will do that to you.

Never open the door to strangers, even if you have a gun in your hand. A wise policy, which Handyman Harris would have done well to heed, because when he opened his door with a .38 in his fist—with which, being fairly convinced he was being scammed, he intended to convince the stranger to give him back his wallet—the stranger karate-chopped him in the neck and knocked him out stone cold.

Baby Joe had correctly identified the fire escape as the chink in the armor. After he cold-cocked Handyman he pulled off the wig and the false stomach that held the Glock, his Heckler & Koch, and spare clips for both, and which concealed a lightweight bulletproof vest. He prepared himself and pushed through the fire doors at the end of the corridor.

He did not attempt to run up the staircase, as it is hardly ever a good idea to get involved in a gunfight with the mob when you are out of breath. Even so, he was breathing a little heavily by the time he came through the fire door on the tenth floor. He took deep breaths as he waited for the elevator, and had steadied himself by the time it arrived. Stepping through the opening doors he punched in the code and sat on the floor.

Baby Joe's fears about Liberty's ability as a marksman had been unfounded. He wasn't a much better shot than he was a pugilist. But even he could hit the back of an elevator at ten feet. But a strange thing was happening. As the bullets spewed from his gun it seemed to be getting heavier, instead of lighter. So heavy, in fact, that Liberty could no longer lift it, and had to drop it onto the carpet.

And then something even weirder happened. He saw this carnival clown, like a black and white minstrel with a black face and a white shiny bald head sitting on the floor of the elevator, shooting at him. Then he saw something even more disturbing.

Nothing at all.

As the slugs from Liberty's gun rattled into the steel wall above his head, Baby Joe measured three shots. The first one hit the big man in the stomach, the second just left of the heart, and the third went through the bridge of the nose, toppling him forward like a felled redwood.

Baby Joe was up and running, all light and speed and clarity, every detail as sharp as a razor, every sound a bell. A bespectacled figure came running from a side room, stopped, and tried to run back in. Two angry wasps from the Colt followed him and stung him to death. The barrels of Baby Joe's guns swung like black eyes and stared at the closed wooden doors, behind which was the Don. Baby Joe's own eyes stared too.

Closed. Why hadn't he expected that? He backed along the wall, away from the doors, towards the side room. He stuck the Glock around the doorframe, pumped three shots into the room at knee, gut, and eye level, and dived past the door, glancing in as he went. By the time he had rolled to his feet he knew that the room contained only a bank of cameras and their dead operator. Stepping over the body, Baby Joe moved up to the monitor, which still displayed the prostrate form of

Liberty. It was strange how you could tell that he was dead, and not just lying there, as if somehow dead people reflected light differently.

Baby Joe took the little joystick and tilted the camera until it focused on the Don's door, and panned back. It had been a cute move, but how long could he afford to wait? The phones would be red hot by now, and someone was already on the way and it probably wasn't the cops, although they might be coming too. Put yourself in the Don's place. What would a blind man do? He knows you don't know how many are in there. All he has to do is wait. And what if he's not blind, what if you were wrong about that? Like you were wrong about figuring the doors would be open. All these what-ifs can get you killed. Your move.

*Quiet again. My people must be down, or they would speak. Maybe him, too. How can I know? Does he watch on the camera? Is he that smart? If he is, then he knows I can wait. Does he know of these, these warhorses who chafe at the bit? These dogs. Shall I release them? Will he call my bluff? And die. He will die anyway. And what of the bomb? Does he have more? He is one man. I must finish this.*

"Pepe, Luigi, go. Carlo and Bruno, stay here."

Watching television. Dull program. Nothing happening. *Fuck this. Do something, or go.* He knew that.

Baby Joe started to move just as the doors burst open and a short swarthy man leaped out, blasting the empty space with a pump-action shotgun. Behind him another, taller, shooting with an automatic rifle. Behind them, the doors closing again. They ran down the corridor, shooting through the open doorway of the camera room. He was protected by the angle, but the noise was like every thunderstorm that ever raged, like giant waves booming onto the beach. He counted the blasts from the shotgun, one hand protecting his eyes, seeing the door and doorframe splintered, watching the plaster being shredded at chest height, glad it was absorbing the bullets and not letting them ricochet. The men moved out of range of the camera and as the angle narrowed the slugs from the automatic rifle began to hit the back wall of the room, but the shotgun fell silent. Baby Joe stuck the Colt around the door and emptied it in a fan pattern, aiming three feet off the ground. He watched the automatic ripping up the ceiling, meaning the barrel was up, and stepped round the door.

Luck or skill, it didn't matter. The short guy fumbling with a cartridge and the other lying on his back, shot through both legs. More ifs. If the man with the automatic had known enough to spread his shots and not shoot in the same place. If the guy with the shotgun had had another weapon. If the stillness of the shotgun had meant something else. Ifs will kill you. The automatic fell from the man's hand as a bullet from the Glock went through his temple. The cartridge tumbled from the other's hand as he attempted to aim the empty shotgun, with terror written on his face.

The Glock took it away.

*Silence again. Ours. His?* The story was written in sound. The shotgun stopped. A duet, pistol and rifle. The rifle stopped. The pistol spoke again. Once. And then silence. *Do you grow afraid, old man? Are you now afraid of the dark, which has been your house? How long has it been? Others will come. And find what? This is one man. If one man can do this, there will be nothing left anyway. It must be ended before. Does he know this?* Carlo and Bruno began to shout. He silenced them with a word. The word of Don Ignacio Imbroglio. He still had that. He would keep it.

"Carlo."

Baby Joe backed into the camera room, working by feel, watching the screen as he dropped the clip from the Heckler & Koch, the click sounding loud as he slipped the new one in. He dropped the half-empty Glock clip into his hand and slid it into his pocket, plugged in the full one, and pumped bullets into the chambers of both guns. The butt of the shotgun lay just outside the door, and he ducked down and grabbed it.

He heard voices — two men yelling, then a third. The Don. Then quiet again. Two more. At least two. Fuck. From where? He had watched. He had watched and still not seen. Had they already been there? Had he missed them? Had they come in the day, while he watched the nights? What difference did it make? There was there. Make them be not there. He watched the screen. Nothing. The man's ankle was in reach, and Baby Joe took ahold and hauled him backwards. Heavy. Dead weight. Watching the camera, he fumbled in the man's pockets. Three cartridges only. One outside on the floor. Too far. Leave it.

He slotted the three into the chamber, not taking his eyes from the screen. He glanced at his watch. Three minutes since the shooting, three minutes or three seconds, or three years. Too long. A lifetime if he didn't move. He put the pistols on the floor in the doorway, butts facing outwards. Evil symmetry, like sinister book ends. Checking the screen, checking the corridor with a flick of his head, he took up the shotgun, stepped out, and blasted the three cartridges into the big doors, high, low, and center. Releasing the scattergun and picking up the pistols all in one movement, he ran, following the explosions and smoke down the hall.

Something came rolling out of the doorway, something small like a toy, as if there should be a dog scampering after it. And then it became the biggest thing in the world. Bigger than the moon. A grenade. A fucking grenade! It was at his feet and he was in a confined space and he was going to die. They used to lie next to them. Impact, up and over. Superficial damage. Too close. Falling backwards, half thinking, half in blind rage, he kicked the grenade like soccer ball. A small bone in his foot snapped, but he did not feel it. A wind arose in the corridor, a sudden wild wind. A typhoon, filled with hot nails and razor blades. A demon lived inside it, a screeching demon with fiery sulfur breath and long bloody talons. The demon took him about the chest in its claws, and slammed him against the wall, and stole the air from his lungs and the sound from his ears. And then the demon and the wind went away and he could see what they had done.

They had torn away the doors, and scattered wood and plaster and blood, and they had taken away time, so that everything happened in slow motion, and they had spirited away noise, so that the world moved in silence, and a pall of smoke from the demon's breath still hung in the air. And through these gray wreaths he could see a man trying to stand and he tried to raise his raise his right hand to shoot this man but he could not. Ponderously, as if he were moving underwater, he lifted his left hand and aimed the Heckler & Koch and pulled the trigger. He felt the gun kick, but no sound came from it. The man stopped trying to stand up, and instead lay down and lay still.

Baby Joe tried to lift himself up, but his right arm would not work. He rolled onto his knees and got his back against the wall. Letting the H & K drop from his left hand he reached across and took up the Glock, which lay beside him. The fingers of his right hand dripped red and his trousers were wet. Pushing his back against the wall, he levered himself up and tried to take a step forward, but his vision blurred and he had to lean back against the wall. He vomited down the front of his vest. He rested there a moment, breathing heavily, trying to stop the room from whirling around, trying to extinguish the flares and fairy lights that danced in his head.

The demon brought the sound back, sending it roaring down the corridor like a train in a tunnel, shaking him, calling him back. Steadying himself, Baby Joe stepped into the chaos of the room. Here, too, the wind and the demon had played together. Shattered glass sparkled like frost in the deep carpet, broken furniture lay strewn about, and the monster had clawed deep grooves in the walls and ceiling. One man lay in the doorway and another by the Don's overturned desk.

The breeze blew through the broken windows, billowing the curtains, and between their shredded veils Baby Joe could see Don Ignacio Imbroglio standing on the balcony, looking out over the city as if in contemplation of some great mystery.

# Chapter 26.

Stavros had only been partially lying when he had told the members of A.S.S. that the Big Blue Billabong was full on account of all the sheep shearers. He had told them that because he wanted them to think that the place would be full of wild and woolly Aussies, who could deck a camel with either hand and buy it a drink afterwards. Actually, the Big Blue Billabong was going to be full on account of the busload of hookers that were coming up for the Saturday bash, wild and woolly sheilas who could deck a camel with either hand and buy it a drink afterwards. A band from Cairns was flying in, too, a raucous and violent rock-and-roll outfit with a great local following, the appropriately-named Vulture Skull Hangover. All of which meant that the hotel was going to be full to the rafters with every swinging dick within a two hundred mile radius who had the price of a pint and a piece of tail, and many who didn't.

Crispin and Asia had decided to return to Blue Billabong with the others and see what happened. What else were they going to do? Crispin had just about given up anyway, and his pompadour was hanging over his forehead in a sorry remnant of the pomp of its glory days, as if it too had wilted under the constant strain. All the shocks and nasty surprises, never knowing from one minute from the next what was going to happen, always something jumping out at you like on one of those hokey old Coney Island ghost trains. Ironically, for all his despair he looked better than he had in years. His trials and tribulations had taken a few pounds off him, and exposure to the southern sun had banished the pallor of his air-conditioned Vegas nightlife existence.

Asia looked absolutely magnificent, with that special wide-eyed fragile beauty that sadness seems to lend to women. Not having been in a position, especially in recent days, to give the best of attention to her toiletries, she did present a somewhat primitive appearance, but rather than suffer from it, it had bestowed upon her the advantage that the wild rose enjoys over the cultured. Sick with worry about Baby Joe and desperate to hear from him, something inside of her yet sustained her confidence, her belief that everything would be all right and that one day he would walk through a door, or around a corner, and tell her that it was done. That it was over.

She was aware that it was, perhaps, the strength of her desire overcoming her reason, but she was also aware of how much she needed to believe it and to have something to cling to. She also questioned whether, deep down, it was Baby Joe the Man or Baby Joe the Savior that she missed. If it was his rough-hewn charm and pragmatism, and the sense of security he gave her that she wanted, or if it was what he represented: the knowledge that she could resume her life. A life where nothing nasty was hiding under the bed or in the wardrobe. A life where you could turn out the light and the darkness was a comforting blanket and not a black screen on which to project your worst nightmares.

One thing was for sure. When this was over, no matter how it turned out she was never going back to those city lights and that life. At first it had seemed like a good deal. A few moments of discomfort, some brief unpleasantness in exchange for a world of things, things that she had never had; and if the occasional bout of self-loathing occurred it could always be drowned in whiskey and too-loud laughter. But she knew better now. If nothing else, this insane game of hide-and-seek had taught her that some things that are given away can never be recovered, and that a dead end is just that. Dead. End.

Wally had been unusually subdued on the way back and had disappeared somewhere as soon as they pulled up in front of the hotel, leaving Stavros and Bruce to unload the money and the Machine Gun Jelly, which had been loaded into the back of the pickup. The lifeless Combi had been abandoned, to become a koala-shit-covered home for spiders, snakes, bats, bugs, and whatever peripatetic creature wandered by looking for a place to sleep.

On the pretext that they might need another hand if things got hairy, Jimmy and Walkabout had come along for the ride, when actually the only hairy thing Jimmy had in mind lived inside a pair of polyester knickers and came out to play every time it saw a ten dollar bill or a crate of Castlemaine XXXX on the back seat of a Combi. Although Jimmy was a good man in a tight spot, which was another reason why he had come along.

Being one, Walkabout knew all about hairy things, and anyway, anywhere Jimmy went Walkabout went, especially if there was a chance of loads of beer and an uninhibited fart.

Once the truck was unloaded and the cargo secured Stavros set about making preparations for the night, which included giving strict instructions to the extra staff he had hired, removing all the windows, and reloading the fowling piece with birdshot. His people informed him that the people who had been looking for them had not returned and, somewhat reassured, Asia and Crispin decided to make an early start of Saturday and went to the bar.

Monsoon, who had spent the most miserable of nights and the most arduous of days being bounced around in the back of a truck with his former riches within a fingertip's reach, if he had been able to reach out a fingertip, was locked in the cellar. Nobody being quite sure what to do with him, and with everybody being preoccupied with more serious concerns, it had been decided to let him stew for a while, although a local physician had been summoned to attend to his nose and his foot. Even the physician, however, would have conceded that the term "physician" was stretching it a bit, his medical experience being limited to puncturing kedge-gutted sheep and shoving his forearm up gastric cows' rectums.

Monsoon was in a state of total and absolute demoralization and had capitulated totally to the capricious whims of the gods of cruelty and misfortune, who had obviously singled him out for special attention. He was in such pain—from his swollen nose and his throbbing foot, and from the unbearable loss of his fortune—that the bottle of whiskey that he had been given in lieu of anesthetic was doing nothing to alleviate it. Against the backdrop of the darkened cellar, visions taunted him relentlessly. All the women that he was going to fuck, all the cars that he was going to drive, all the lobsters and steaks he was going to eat. Monsoon at the races in a silk suit; Monsoon in the Salon Privé, sticking C-notes down the waitresses' bosoms; Monsoon in a ringside seat at the fights, rubbing elbows with the elite; Monsoon the cigar-smoking drug king of Australia, with a beauty queen on either arm and a wad in his pocket that would choke a humpback whale.

And in his vision all the characters—buxom, raven-haired beauties, head waiters, concierges, drug-dependent lackeys, bent jockeys, groveling toadying sycophants, dodgy shysters, politicians on the take, bribable police chiefs, mansion salesmen, limo dealers—all gathered and joined hands and began dancing around him in a circle, laughing, singing in mocking, childish voices, "Monsoon's lost his money. Monsoon's lost his money. Monsoon's lost his money."

Over and over again. Monsoon squeezed his eyes shut, cupped his hands over his ears, rolled into a ball, and begin to whine.

Can nightmares exist in permanent night? Is that possible? If they are heard, and not seen, what do they sound like? Will it be harder to die, being dark already? If there is an after, will it be dark there, too? *Are you afraid now? No. Of what? Too late for questions. What matters now why, or how, or if? If will kill you.*

The Don reached into his top pocket and, pulling out a cigar, moistened it with his lips and bit off the tip. He took his diamond-encrusted lighter from his pocket, diamonds that shone for no one, and held the flame to the tobacco, inhaling deeply. Smiling, he tossed the lighter over the balcony wall, seeing it glittering in his mind's eye as it hung at its apex before flashing down to the ground below. Would somebody be lucky? Luckier than he?

He sucked on his cigar, drawing the rich smoke deep into his lungs.

"What about the old lady?"

"She will be going nowair. Eizer we catch 'er latair, or pairhaps we do not 'ave to bozzair at all, *n'est-ce pas?*"

"Frog Features is right for a change. She might croak without our help, and anyway we can pick her up on the way back."

"The Don wanted her alive."

"Then he better get Jesus down here. Resurrections are out of my jurisdiction."

"*Mais*, you Baptistes 'ave preferential treatment, non?"

"Lissen, garlic breath…"

"Before you two start, when do we go?"

"As soon as Magnoon starts shooting."

"I'll go see if he's ready."

Curtains Calhoun climbed the small hill behind the encampment and lay down on the cool grass next to Magnoon Piastre. Below, the lights of the hotel competed with the headlights of the convoy of vehicles that continued to arrive from both directions. Magnoon was scanning through a pair of night vision binoculars with one arm draped over the stock of a .44 Ruger rifle. Curtains took the glasses from him and focused on the windows of the long bar. The place was rocking and rolling, and a band was in full flight.

Right at the end of the bar, nearest the bandstand, a very attractive redheaded girl sat next to a fat guy with some kind of weird fuzzy beret on. The faint sound of whistling and clapping rose up from the parking lot, and Curtains swung the glasses around to where an appreciative crowd of men of mixed race was watching a parade of garishly dressed women climb down the steps of a bus. He focused back on the girl.

"That must be them, right?"

"No. It's Abbott and Costello in drag." Magnoon said.

"Jaysus. What a fucking shame."

"What is?"

"The girl, man. She's a peach."

"Yeah, pity."

"Want the glasses back?" Curtains asked.

"No. I can use the scope."

"How many can you see?"

"Only two."

"What are you going to do?"

"I don't know. What does everybody think?"

"I'll go and find out."

Curtains went back down into the camp, and Magnoon picked up the rifle and peered through the night scope.

A.S.S., having tuned their radio to the hotel frequency, had followed events from the discovery of the Combi onwards, and had elected to move in; neglecting, of course, to give full details of the operation to their Vietnamese colleagues, who had taken up position on the same ridge a hundred meters further down. Eavesdropping on the arrangements concerning the evening's entertainment, they had also decided to take advantage of confusion, in every sense of the word. But business before pleasure, although in their case it was all pretty much one and the same.

Magnoon heard Curtains coming back up the hill and said over his shoulder, "And so?"

"Take the two you can see."

"And then?"

"We'll take care of it."

Magnoon settled himself behind the sight, snuggling the butt comfortably into his shoulder and resting his cheek on the smooth, warm stock. He pushed the sight snugly into his good eye. It felt like it belonged there. A trade tailor-made for a Cyclops. He lined the sight up to the first target, bringing the crosshairs to bear on the cheekbone, and then swung it onto the second. The barrel moved no more than an eighth of an inch.

"Everybody ready?"

"Yeah."

"Okay. Goodnight, sweethearts."

*Babam.* Two shots sounding like one. Two heads flying backwards. Two souls shocked out of their bodies. Just like that.

"Not bad."

"Shit. I could have hit them from here with a fucking pea shooter," said Magnoon, picking up his rifle.

Stupid, stupid. Weak and stupid. Think, man. Think. Pop pop pop like champagne. Click. Lucky, lucky. Nails being hammered into him. Falling backwards. Into the wall. Lucky again. If you fall down you die. The man standing up. With a blade. Coming. This other. Bleeding but not dead. Didn't check. Stupid, stupid. Time for one shot. Staggers, but does not fall. Too close. Grab the wrist. Gun slams against the wall. Knife goes in. Cold, but not pain. Feel the blade dig into the wall. Gun falls. Bring up the knee. Drop the head, bang bang bang like a woodpecker. Wrist free, grab the knife with your teeth. Slide it from your own flesh. Sticky. He bends for the gun. See the veins in his neck. Sweep the legs. Down he goes. Hand still grips. No tendons cut. Lucky lucky lucky. He kneels. Hand to the gun. Drop down. Knee onto the hand. Hear the fingers break. Kneel before each other. Facing. Two penitents. Last rites. Bring the blade up under the chin. Into the brain. The eyes go wide.

And then out.

A hundred meters away, the Vietnamese were having a similar conversation to the A.S.S. crew.

"They lie about everything."

"We should kill them."

"No. The general does not want trouble with the Americans. He wants to do business with them. But we can still teach them a lesson."

"I agree. But first the business."

"This is what we must do. You see what is happening here tonight. The Americans will want the women and the drink. They will want to listen to their rock and roll. They will not be serious. It will be a game to them, like before. That is why we will win, like before. They will drink and become foolish. We will go down in darkness and take the dark one and the drugs."

"And what of the money?"

"I think the money is in the black bags."

"I agree. I think the Americans know, but they do not want to tell us. I think they heard it on the radio, and they know."

"If the money is in the black bags, where is the one who stole it?"

"I do not know. Maybe the others have done something to him."

"Maybe so. But the general will be angry."

"He will not be angry when we bring him the drugs and the money and the black one."

"But the drugs belong to the Americans."

"Yes."

"The general cannot do business with the Americans if he takes their drugs and their money."

"He will not keep the drugs. He will give them to the boss of the Americans. The boss of the Americans will owe him a favor. It will be good for business. And it will make these ones look foolish."

"And us good?"

"And us good."

"When will we go?"

"Later, when all are drunk. We will take the spark plugs and distributor caps from the Americans' car. Also we will put sand in the tanks, block the exhaust pipes, and puncture the tires."

"Will that stop them?"

They all looked at the one who had just spoken.

"Sorry."

"We will take the black one and cut the tendons in his ankles so he cannot try to escape. One will do this. The others will find the money and the drugs. I saw them carry them into the big house. They will not be difficult to find."

"What if someone tries to stop us?"

"Do only what is necessary. Do not hurt anyone unless you have to."

"What if it is the Americans?"

"Then you may do what is not necessary. But do not kill them unless you have to."

"There is one thing."

"What?"

"These are not Americans."

"Who do they work for?"

"Americans."

"Then they are Americans."

"No. They are French."

"That is even worse. Rest now. I will wake everyone when it is time to…"

Two sharp cracking reports from a rifle cut short the speech, two shots so close in succession to one another that they sounded like one shot.

A cloud of cigar smoke. A soft breeze. A man enjoying his evening. Below, the sirens singing. Calling him onto the rocks. A noise behind.

"Mr. Young, I presume?"

Baby Joe swaying, gagging, holding it back. Black spots before his eyes.

"Don Imbroglio."

"You are a remarkable man, Mr. Young. A remarkable man, and a great deal of trouble. Under different circumstances, perhaps…Who knows?"

Getting weaker. Do it. Do it now. Step forward.

"Isn't this the part where I'm supposed to say, 'I'll pay you anything'? Not much point when you already have ten million dollars of my money."

Talking, talking. Don't listen. Finish it. The throat. No anger any more. No rage. Fire out. Just something to do. Something necessary. A simple thing. Do it. One more step.

"You know, Mr. Young, you are the only one who ever realized. If we had more time, I should have liked to ask you how you did that."

Raise the knife. Smell the smoke. Watch the tip glow.

"What? No grand speeches, Mr. Young?"

"You know."

"Mr. Young, I know a great deal more than you can possibly imagine."

The cigar spinning against the sky, end over end, glowing. The Don walking forward. Climbing. Follow? No. Watch. Watching the Don lying across the wall. His shiny shoes tilted into the air. And he was gone. Tumbling soundless into a darkness deeper still. Looking over the wall. Down below. Weird angles. Like a swastika. Blue lights. Turning to go. Dizzy. Sat down. Too late. Fell down. Back against the wall. Legs out straight. Tasting the blood. Hearing the breath. Bubbles. Watching the blood run into the carpet. Life was supposed to pass before my eyes. Where was it? No life. Only cold. Cold and dark. Darkness.

Baby Joe Young closed his eyes and slid sideways, leaving a bright red smear on the wall behind him.

And lay still.

# Chapter 27.

Vulture Skull Hangover was sounding pretty good, or at least they were to anyone who thought the LA Riots were entertaining. The band, led by the bass player Noni "Goat Bollocks" Kamehameha—a 400-pound Tongan who played the upright bass strung round his neck like a guitar—had originally been a Sydney heavy metal crew called Dildo Skyline and had been going pretty good until one night the lead singer had had this brilliant idea. Instead of biting the heads off rats and chickens like Ozzie Osbourne, he had brought a twelve-foot Siberian Tiger onstage and let it bite his head off. Apparently no one had informed the tiger that it was supposed to be an act, so that turned out to be the final performance of Dildo Skyline. The new lead singer—the self-styled Anna Rexia, an emaciated ghoul in a moth-eaten feather boa—was ripping up the stage like a peacock on amphetamines, trying to get the audience's attention. Unfortunately for Anna, as far as this particular audience was concerned she didn't have the correct equipment for the job.

Stavros was having a hard time again. One eye on the till, one eye on the clock, and one eye on Asia's tits was just not a mathematical practicality. At least he probably wouldn't have to worry about fights for a while. For one thing, until the crowd thinned out later there just wasn't enough room for a decent swing, and for another no one was going to risk missing out on getting some by getting crocked before the ladies showed up. But he didn't like it when the bus was late. You could feel that incendiary cocktail of testosterone and alcohol building up, and you knew that some bright spark out there was just dying to set it off. And with Captain Cook gone missing, there was no telling what could happen.

An unanticipated movement behind him made him jump, and he reached for the fowling piece.

"Shootin yer fucken mates now, are ya, ya mongrel?"

"Wally. Where the fuck 'ave you been hidin?"

"Went to fix the fucken phone line."

"What was wrong with the fucken phone line?"

"Some dirty stirrer cut it."

"Strewth. What does that mean?"

"It means I 'ad to go an' fix the fucker."

"I know that, ya bladdy nong. I mean, what does it mean?"

"It means it's gonna be a fucken bonza Saturday night. 'Ere, cop for this." Wally stuck a radio receiver on the bar.

"What is it?"

"It's a fucken nuclear submarine, what does it look like?"

"Looks like a fucken radio."

"Must be a fucken radio then, ey?"

"But waddya gonna do with it?"

"Oh, I dunno. I thought I might shove it up me arse and sing 'Walzing Matilda.' Whaddya reckon?"

"Nah, Wal. Fair dinkum. What's it for? We got the band."

"Lissen. I'll tell ya all about it later. Just stick it behind the bar, and don't let any barstad touch it, okay?"

"If you say so, Wal, but I still… ah, rippa. The fucken sheilas are 'ere."

As he spoke, a covey of painted harlots sashayed into the room to a rousing cheer and a barrage of flying hats. They were smiling and leering, winking, blowing kisses and sticking out their tongues, the immense Amazon in the vanguard driving a wedge through the packed press by main force. A suffocating bouquet of cheap perfumes bloomed around them as they pushed through to the makeshift stage, where the Amazon took the microphone. She was at least six-four and wearing a pink Basque, fishnet stockings that looked like real fish nets, enough war paint for a Comanche raiding party, and false eyelashes so long they were clearing more smoke than the ceiling fans.

"G'day, mates," she said, in a very creditable impression of Isaac Hayes, "are ya ready to root yer fucken socks off?"

A second salvo of tossed hats greeted her comment, accompanied by a primordial roar of yells, yodels, grunts, and whistles, with a couple of animal noises thrown in. She held up her hand for silence. No one argued with her.

"Right," she said, "mosta you blokes been 'ere before, but for those who 'aven't I'll go through the rules. Ya get ten minutes. If ya go over, ya pay extra. Short arm inspection and frangers obligatory. No fucken rough stuff. Dirt box engineering by prior permission only. No smoking in the fucken saddle. It's gonna be a long fucken night, so we'd best get to it. If any a you drongos've got any wonga left, you can buy us all a drink later. If we like ya, we might even buy you one, but don't 'old ya fucken breath. Now, I'm Loretta, and I'll be in number one. If ya prefer the dark side of the fucken moon, Rita's in number two. For anyone who likes 'is fruit ripe, Sandra's in three. For all you ex-navy boys, Jenny's in four, and, if you think you've got enough meat in your sandwich, Marilyn's in five. Now I know it ain't romance, boys, but it beats the old five knuckle shuffle. Good on yer."

Loretta handed the mike back to Anna and led the ladies around behind the bar and out the back door. The first fight broke out immediately as everyone headed for the doors at once.

"Strewth, 'ere we go," said Stavros, reaching for the fowling piece.

On the dark ridge above the hotel lights were flashing and, drowned out by the band and unheard by the rowdy mob below, small popping sounds like distant fireworks made faint echoes in the hills beyond.

Magnoon Piastre's fingers moved ever so lightly, barely touching the trigger, and two Vietnamese heads snapped back, the men dead before they even heard the shots. The other two reacted instantly, instinctively fleeing down the dark side of the hill into the sheltering night, away from the lights. It was a mistake, not that it would have made much difference. One got twenty yards before a measured burst from Dugong Heartache's semi-automatic trepanned him. The second did little better. He managed to reach the bottom of the hill and secret himself in a pile of leaf litter at the base of a tree. He listened to his quick heartbeat, and to the faint rustle of leaves, and his eyes searched the starlight, and too late he heard that other sound which was Vladimir Pizda's machete cutting the night air.

They buried the bodies in a shallow depression and hid them with light covering of leaves and soil.

"Somsing will dig zeze up before ze morning."

"So what? We'll be long gone by then."

"Now what?"

"Time for a little R and R. Let's join the party."

"*Bonne idée*. Ah am ready for a drink."

"And me. Who gets to take care of the girl?"

"We cut the deck. Aces high. Lowest card gets to do the fat one."

"I wanna fuck her before we waste her."

"Ah wish to fuck hair aftair we waste hair."

They were laughing as they trudged back up to the ridge, walking slowly on account of Gaspart Descourt's bum pin.

Things had quieted down somewhat, both in the bar and in the cabins behind. Most of the punters who had come for the girls were either spent, or else their money was. Loretta was standing outside the cabin with a beach towel stretched around her, enjoying a cigarette and a break when she saw a dark figure approach.

"Come back in ten minutes, mate. I'm 'avin a break."

"It's me, Wal."

"Jesus, Wal. I don't think I can 'endle that after the night I've 'ed."

"Nah, Lol. It ain't that. I need you to 'elp me. It might sound like I've lost me fucken apples, but I need ya to do exactly like I say. Come inside while I tell ya." Wally ushered Loretta into the cabin, looking around carefully before he followed her in, and closed the door behind them.

## SHANE NORWOOD

Lately, Crispin's moods had had more swings than Battery Park, but he was definitely on the up tonight. He was letting it all hang out, and even if he didn't have as much to hang out as he once had it was still pretty spectacular. After a few bottles the Australian sparkling wine that he was guzzling like it was going out of fashion had begun to taste like Bollinger, and when Anna had let him sing a couple it had been just like the sweet remembered days of old, with his adoring public rapt at his every word. The fact that half of them were so far gone that they couldn't even see him, that most of them couldn't understand a word he was saying, and that a peculiar-looking group of cripples in the corner kept making sheep noises, did not deter him in the least. He was a fucking *star*, baby, and fuck 'em if they couldn't appreciate him.

Asia was sitting outside on the veranda looking at the brilliant stars, distorted by the tears that were welling uncontrollably in her eyes. Seeing the prostitutes had upset her, and in her present despairing state she couldn't help herself. That was it, really, wasn't it? That is what she had really been doing. Five-grand-a-night suites and four-poster beds and room service bubbly didn't change the fact that what she had been doing was no different to what those girls back there were doing. No different at all. In fact, worse. At least they were honest. At least they weren't running around making excuses for what they were, pretending to be something else. She might just as well get up and go back there and help them. But she knew she wasn't that tough. She was out here crying, wondering what was going to happen. Well, fuck it. She was going back inside, and getting drunk. And if those fucking spastics in the corner didn't stop staring at her and giggling like a bunch of retards, she was going over there and straightening them out.

He had stiffened when they first walked in, and had nodded to Bruce, who had gone to fetch Jimmy and Wally, and he had counted the locals who were still in any condition to help out if any shit started. But after a couple of hours nothing had happened. They had just sat in the corner, drinking and minding their own. They had seen Asia and

Crispin, but so far they had not approached them, nor had they said anything to him. They kept sending the kid with the ponytail to the bar, as if they didn't want to speak to him. Obviously they were just waiting until the place emptied out. It was already starting to wind down, and the band was packing up. Wally had told him not to worry, but he couldn't help it. And where were those Asians? Stavros looked around the room. Maybe fifty people left. Some guy asleep on the floor, Bruce sweeping up broken glass, a game of darts at the back, TV flickering with no sound on, light looking too yellow, fans spinning slowly over it all, winding it tighter and tighter. Better change the shells in the scattergun.

They say time is a great healer. But we're not all afforded that luxury, and in a pinch a bottle of rotgut scotch and a sense of injustice will help some. Monsoon had roused himself, if not to a fit of righteous anger at least to the point where he was considering how he might escape his current predicament, beginning with how he was going to get the fuck out of this cellar. The whisky had not killed the pain entirely, but it was badly wounded and not expected to survive, and he was at least able to manage a decent hobble without yelping in pain every time he put his foot down.

The cellar in the Big Blue Billabong had been designed to keep things in, with a view to preventing people from the outside taking things out as opposed to preventing people from the inside taking themselves out, and Monsoon quickly spotted the weakness in the system. The doors were locked from the inside, and with the ingenious use of a tin lid folded in quarters and hammered flat he was able to unscrew the two hinges.

Outside the air was warm compared to the dungeon he had just been in, and he limped over to the shadow of the hotel. Peering round the edge of the building onto the veranda, he saw a fat man lying unconscious on the boards with a full beer beside him. Things were looking up. Monsoon grabbed the beer and sat down with his back to the wall, resting his foot and turning his thoughts to how he was going to retrieve his money and his drugs, steal a car, and head south after setting fire to this fucking shitheap hotel and everyone in it.

He heard footsteps on the veranda and leaned back into the shadows. A stream of urine arched through the air, glowing in the light, and spattered onto the ground next to him. He was being splashed, but he didn't dare move for fear of attracting attention. He heard the sound of a zipper and scuffling shoes and risked a peek to see who it had been. What the fuck? The little dipshit with the ponytail. Now what? He needed to get a better vantage point to see what was going on. Helping himself with the wall, he got to his feet and hobbled around the back of the building.

"Hey, baby. Why'ncha come 'n sit with us? You too, Krispy Kreme."

It was starting. Dugong Heartache had ambled over to the bar where Asia and Crispin were sitting. Stavros had been right. They had been waiting. Apart from them, there weren't more than half a dozen people left in the bar, and they were all out of the game. Stavros quickly strode through to the office, where he found Wally on the phone.

"Wal."

Wally held a hand up, and kept talking. "You sure you got it straight? Yeah. One hour? And don't forget. Right to the very end. The full version. Yeah, I know that. Lissen, Wayne, this is fucken important, mate. Life an' fucken death. Don't fuck it up, all right? Bonza. One hour. Too fucken right, mate. Yeah, you too. Good on yer."

As soon as he hung up, Stavros said, "Wal, we got a problem. Those fucken raspberry ripples are startin something."

"Yeah. I know."

"One of 'em's talking to Asia. You should've let me tell 'er an Crispin that those were the guys."

"Nah, mate. No point in scarin 'em for nothin."

"Fuck me, Wal. It ain't nothin. I betta get Bruce an' Jimmy."

"I told 'em to stand back."

"What the fuck d'ya do that for, ya drongo?"

"I got it covered, Stav."

"So what are we gonna do, Wal?"

"Give em a fucken drink."

"Do what? 'Ev you gone fucken loopy, or what?"

"Nah, mate. Trust me. It's sorted. Get us a tray, and seven glasses."

Back at the bar Asia suddenly understood and looked around, but there was nobody in sight. No Wally, no Stavros, no Jimmy, no Bruce. She looked at Crispin. He shrugged.

"Okay," she said.

They followed Dugong back to the table. The man with one eye stood up, and with exaggerated courtesy offered her a chair. She sat down, with a mocking curtsy.

"Pull up a chair, Slim," the one with red hair said to Crispin.

Crispin sat next to the one with the missing hand and the dark Mongoloid eyes that stared at him over cheekbones like marble. He looked at Crispin like he wanted to eat him, and not in any connotation of the word that Crispin would have been comfortable with.

"*Enchanté, mademoiselle,*" the one with the artificial leg said, bowing his head.

"*Vous et français, monsieur?*" Asia asked.

"*Mon Dieu, non. Je suis Belgique, mademoiselle. Sacre bleu. Français. Merde.*"

Dugong Heartache was about to speak again when Stavros emerged, bearing a tray with seven beers and seven shot glasses on it.

"Gentlemen," he said, "since you've bin such good customers, an' since yer the last dogs to die, so to speak, I'd like to offer ya one on the 'ouse."

Asia and Crispin looked at Stavros, but he avoided their eyes.

"What is this shit?" Curtains was curious to know.

"Ah, local speciality, mate, fucken dingo killer. Rippa stuff. Get it down yer. Good on yer." Stavros set a shot and a beer in front of everyone except Asia.

"Don't I get one?" Asia said, taking the opportunity to catch his eye and give him a meaningful look. Stavros's easy smile told her nothing.

"Nah. We don't give it to sheilas. Too much for 'em. What'll you 'ave instead?"

"Is that so?" she said, miffed despite the gravity of the situation. "Some of that sparkly wine stuff, then,"

"Glass a bubbles comin' up."

The men were all looking at each other as Stavros walked away.

The one with the red hair picked his glass up and sniffed it. "Smells like brandy to me."

"What do you think?"

"Out here? These fucking primates? Nah."

"Gaspart?"

"Ah doubt zey 'ave ze sophistication. But you nevair know. Give it to zis one."

Vladimir took a shot glass and handed it to Booby, who had not spoken the whole evening, and except when dispatched for more drinks had just sat there, withdrawn inside himself, listening to his music in his head. Waiting. Waiting for the whole thing to end, to get away from these insane people. To get home. Expressionless, not really understanding what was going on, he chugged down the drink. The others stared at him.

"So?" Curtains said.

"So what?"

"So what is it, asshole?"

"Tastes like brandy."

"Give the doughnut some."

Magnoon handed Crispin a glass. He snatched it rudely. He was getting a bit fed up at the way he was being spoken to by these people, even if they were cripples, and if it didn't stop they were going to get the sharp end of his tongue. He tossed it back.

"Brandy. Big deal. I believe the landlord has lemonade available if this is not to your taste."

"Ooh, careful boys, the puppy bites," said Dugong, raising his glass.

"Fuck it," Magnoon said, knocking his back.

The others followed suit.

"So," said Dugong, "now that we're all acquainted, where's the fucking…"

"Hi, boys…"

They all looked round as Loretta led Rita, Sandra, Jenny, and Marilyn across the floor. "Mind if we join you blokes? We've 'ad a rough night."

"I'll say," said Rita. "My minge feels like a fucken welder's glove."

"At least it's only your minge, luv," said Marilyn. "I'll be lucky if I can shit before fucken Wednesday."

The girls began to shriek like harpies and set about pulling up chairs. The members of A.S.S. exchanged glances.

Gaspart shrugged. *"Pourquoi pas, mes amis.* Life is short, non?"

"Yeah, it can wait. What can we offer you ladies?" Dugong said.

"Champagne, a course, ya fucken drongo. Don't think we're cheap just 'cos we're fucken cheap."

More squeals of laughter.

Stavros brought the champagne over, and then more, and there were toasts, and dirty jokes traded, and the girls began bombarding Crispin and Asia with questions about Las Vegas, and they began to relax. But gradually the men from A.S.S. withdrew from the conversation, becoming quieter and quieter, until they were just sitting, staring at the others, and glancing at each other.

Dugong Heartache said quietly, "Okay."

There was a startling crash as the table went over. Vladimir elbowed Crispin in the eye, knocking him backwards off his chair. The peculiarly musical sound of six women screaming simultaneously echoed through the now-almost-empty room, as the five men each produced guns from behind their backs.

Thereafter, it was all done quietly and very efficiently. Gaspart herded the terrified girls and the few remaining customers into a corner. The one man who protested was knocked unconscious with a backhand swing of a gun butt. Vladimir took Asia and Crispin, who already had a large swelling above his eye, into the opposite corner and made them kneel on the floor, facing the wall. Curtains and Magnoon vaulted the bar and came back dragging Wally and Stavros by their collars, with guns held to their heads. They were pulled to the same corner as Asia and Crispin and made to kneel beside them, but facing back into the room.

"Now listen." Dugong pulled up a chair and spun it round, sitting with his chest resting against the back in his best B-movie gangster style. "These two are gone."

Crispin whimpered, and Magnoon hit him on the back of the head with his gun. He raised his hands to his head, and began to sob.

"As I was saying," Dugong continued, "these two are history. You, I oughta shoot you for fucking lying to me. But I won't, if you do the right thing. You, I heard ya on the radio, so I know you know what's going on. I know about the old dame, and she's gone too. Now, it don't matter to me whether I shoot you or not. But if you don't tell me in five seconds where the money and drugs are, you and your pal are dead meat. Now you know we're gonna find it anyway, even if we have to demolish this shitpile, so why don't you be a smart guy, and tell me."

Wally took a deep breath. "Sorry, Stav. It's in the office. Under the floorboards."

"Vladimir."

There ensued a period of what was, for the captives, unbearable tension, and for the captors light entertainment, the silence broken only by the whimpers and sniffles from Crispin and the girls in the corner, and the sound of furniture being moved.

Vladimir came back. "Bingo."

"Good boy," Dugong said to Wally. "Now, all we need is for your pal and fat boy here to help us load up, and for you to tell us where the other one is, and we'll be on our way."

"He's in the cellar. Behind the hotel. Locked in."

"Keys."

Wally handed over the keys, and Vladimir and Curtains went to look. Supervised by Magnoon, Crispin and Stavros were made to start ferrying the bags and boxes from the office and into the A.S.S. Land Rover. Dugong Heartache stood in the middle of the room, holding his beer in one hand and his gun in the other, smiling.

"You know," he said to Asia, "you're a real looker. Maybe if you was to be nice to me an' the boys, it might go a little easier for ya."

Asia didn't answer. Dugong shrugged and took a swallow of his beer. Vladimir and Curtains came back.

"Nada. But the door's been unscrewed from the inside."

Dugong looked at Wally, who was as surprised as he was. "He must have got out. We left him locked in."

"Well, now we have a problem, see, because…WHAT THE FUCK?"

Wally followed Dugong's eyes to the opposite corner of the room and smiled. Gaspart Descourt had dropped his gun, dropped his trousers, bent Loretta over a barstool, and was rogering her with such vigor that his prosthetic leg had fallen off.

"You frog-eating asswipe, what the fuck do you think you're…?"

Magnoon Piastre sprinted across the room, rugby-tackled Rita, ripped off her underwear, and began climbing into her as if he were trying to stab her to death with his dick, all the while braying like a sunstruck mule.

"What the fuck is going on here? Has everybody gone completely fucking nuts? Vladimir…?"

Vladimir wasn't listening. Vladimir was too busy driving his throbbing member into Marilyn's recess. The force and rapidity of his strokes were shunting her across the floor like a giant mop, and he was shuffling forward frantically trying to stay in situ.

Dugong was about to yell when something bumped him in the back, and he swung round, gun poised at the ready, only to drop it to his side in amazement as he saw Curtains wheelbarrowing Jenny across the room, with her legs on his shoulders and his wang embedded in her at an angle that appeared almost impossible, not to mention downright painful. Even more amazing was the sight that greeted him in the window. Crispin had been transformed from a whining suet pudding into two hundred and fifty pounds of humping machine, and had Booby Flowers bent over the windowsill, sticking it to him with a force that was threatening to bring the wall down. And Booby was loving it, which was the only non-surprising aspect of the whole scenario.

Dugong turned around in absolute confusion, pointing his gun at everybody in turn, feeling he ought to shoot somebody but not knowing quite who to shoot. When he saw Sandra slinking across the floor towards him, he decided she would be as good as anyone, and he leveled the weapon at her chest. But then a funny thing happened. He couldn't pull the trigger. It seemed to be stuck, and not only that, but the gun was getting hot. So hot, in fact, that he was compelled to drop it. And then he himself began to get hot. So hot that he had to take his clothes off. So hot that Sandra also had to take her clothes off. And then this kind of orange mist descended over his eyes, and he looked down and was startled to see this enormous orange snake staring at him, until he realized it was his pecker, only twice as big as it had ever been before. A sound came out of his throat that he did not recognize, and the next thing he was sliding on his ass towards Sandra like a buck naked hockey player. He neatly kicked her ankles out from under her and as she came down skillfully caught her and impaled her on his sword, and commenced to bang the living shit out of her.

Asia, recognizing the symptoms, turned to look at the grinning Wally.

"Why, you sly old goat. You slipped them a Machine Gun Jelly mickey."

"Too fucken right, sheila. Now let's get all these people out of 'ere smartish. Stavros, yer useless prick, don't jus' stand there like a fucken stunned mullet. 'Elp me get these people out."

Just then, they heard the sound of an engine starting up and revving, and loud music playing. All three ran outside and saw the A.S.S. Land Rover pulling away, and a black hand extended out of the driver's seat window, flipping them the bird.

"Monsoon! Wally, he's getting away with the money!" Asia screamed.

"The fucken dirty bastard," Stavros commented.

"Don't worry about that drongo. 'Elp me with these people."

Asia looked at Wally, then at Stavros, then at the receding red lights of the Land Rover. Wally and Stavros were already on their way inside when she looked back. Taking a last long look at the fast-disappearing car, she followed.

Inside it was like the end-of-shooting party at a Fellini film. Things were being done to people in attitudes and positions that defied belief.

Jimmy and Bruce came bounding in, and stood open-mouthed in total astonishment. Asia, knowing what an enervating evening the girls had already had, looked on sympathetically as they were being reamed from anus to Venus and back.

"Jimmy, Bruce, tip these two poofters out of the window, will ya. We gotta get 'em into the fucken freezer," Wally said.

"Ya what?"

"Ya got to take 'em down the fucken basement and lock 'em in the freezer, mate."

"What the...?"

"I ain't got time ter fucken explain now, yer pair a drongos. Get a fucken move on, willya?"

Shaking their heads, Jimmy and Bruce approached the problem. Crispin was lost to the world and grunting like a bear with its dick stuck in a beehive, while Booby was sounding like a trumpet in a maternity ward. They decided it was a simple question of mechanics, and grabbing one of Crispin's legs apiece they upended him, tipping him over the windowsill with Booby still attached. The pair crashed to the ground under the window. Booby, perhaps fortunately, was knocked unconscious in the fall, but Crispin continued to whale away.

Bruce tried tapping him on the shoulder, but Crispin rogered on regardless. Jimmy tried tapping him on the back of the head with a three-foot hardwood log, which got his attention. They unplugged Crispin, who was, unbelieveably, still air thrusting even though he was knocked spark out, and Bruce lugged Booby down into the cellar while Jimmy went for a wheelbarrow. Between the two of them they managed to load Crispin, carefully avoiding his still-waving wand, and wheeled him down the ramp. They stashed the two of them against a crate of frozen emu burgers and levered the door closed.

The few remaining customers were gawking like rubberneckers at a train crash, the trauma of having been kidnapped by a gang of gun-wielding paraplegics completely forgotten. Aided by Bruce and Jimmy, Stavros shepherded them out into the night.

Asia looked for Wally and saw his woolly head appear from behind the bar. He was holding a transistor radio. Asia looked at him in blank incomprehension. The entire room was reenacting the rape of the Sabine women, and Wally wanted to listen to the radio.

"Wally, what are you doing?"

"Listenin' to me favorite program."

Wally clicked the switch, and turned the volume up full, just in time to hear a smooth voice say, "…and if you're on the roads, cobbers, watch out for roos. And now a very special request for me mates down at the Big Blue Billabong Hotel, Wally and Stavros. I love this one, and I know you do, too. It's from Sergeant Pepper's Lonely Hearts Club Band, and it's 'A Day in the Life.'"

*I saw the news today, oh boy…*

"Okay, boys!" Wally shouted.

Jimmy rushed forward and grabbed Sandra's legs, pulling her off Dugong Heartache and out of the door. Dugong stared about in confusion while his dick continued to twitch like a diviner's wand. Then he spotted something across the room.

*A crowd of people stood and stared…*

Bruce got Magnoon Piastre in a full nelson and lifted him bodily off Rita, who slid out from under him and dived out of the nearest window. When Bruce released him Magnoon immediately attempted to dive out of the window after her, but in mid-flight someone grabbed his ankles and he stalled and came down, cracking his chin on the windowsill and knocking himself stupid. As he struggled to rise something hit him on the back of the head, knocking him flat again, and he felt himself being pressed down. Before he could react, Dugong Heartache was aboard him, pumping away and banging Magnoon's head into the floorboards in time with his thrusts.

*The English army had just won the war...*

Wally was battling to pry Jenny loose from Curtains Calhoun, who had by this time done at least fifty laps of the floor and was foaming at the mouth. Stavros came to her aid, body-slamming Curtains to the ground and then wrist-locking him while Wally wrenched her free and helped her to the door. As soon as he was released Curtains wailed like an alley cat with a boot up its ass, and pounced.

*Woke up, got out of bed, dragged a comb across my head...*

Loretta stood up with Gaspart Descourt still desperately clinging to her and humping away in a frenzy. Despite her strength she could not dislodge him, so reaching down she picked up his false leg from the floor and began clubbing him around the back of the head. At the third impact it registered, and he released his hold and slid to the floor, but as she started to walk away he grabbed her ankle. As she turned round to stab Gaspart with her stiletto heel, Curtains landed on his back, got him in a chokehold, and began nailing him to the floor. Still he refused to release Loretta's ankle, and she made for the door dragging both of them behind her. Only when Jimmy jumped on his wrist did he finally let go.

*Four thousand holes in Blackburn, Lancashire...*

Vladimir had finally shunted Marilyn up against the skirting board, and she was vainly trying to lock her fingers into his close-cropped hair when Asia exploded a bottle onto the back his skull. Marilyn then lifted her thighs abruptly and cracked his head into the wall. Dazed by this double whammy he went limp long enough for Asia to drag him off Marilyn, and holding hands the two girls hightailed it out the door. Vladimir stood up, looking bewildered, pointing his dingus this way and that as if it could tell him the way to go. His eyes fell on the flabby ass of

Dugong Heartache, who by now had rendered Magnoon Piastre insensible by banging his head into the floor, but who was still pounding away. Vladimir gave a Cossack war cry and bayonet-charged Dugong.

*Now they know how many holes it takes…*

Wally stood in the doorway, holding a beer, his customary grin restored to full wattage, watching the bum fight at the Both Ways Corral until the final chords rang out. Then he turned and walked across the veranda to where the others were standing. They stood in silence, waiting, hearing only the banging and squealing and groaning from inside. And then…

BOOM!

No more nuts. Bye-bye balls, auf Wiedersehen wieners, and you can kiss your A.S.S. goodbye.

# Chapter 28.

There was always fucking something! It could never just go completely right, could it? A whole continent to cross, and now the radio was fucked. It had been all right a second ago, and then it just went dead. Shit. Oh well. Soon he would be able to buy himself a whole fucking radio station if he wanted one, never mind a fucking radio. He checked his rearview mirror for the fiftieth time. Nothing. Still, he hadn't expected there would be since he had had the good sense to knobble all the other cars in the parking lot before he set off. Nah, he was home free. The just rewards for talent. Might as well stop and take a leak.

Monsoon pulled over and climbed out. Moths gathered around the headlights as he stood with his dick in his hand and a smile on his face, listening to the satisfying splash. Then Lennox Lewis and Sonny Liston both punched him in the solar plexus at the same time. Whirling fireballs came billowing out of the windows like angry ghosts and carried him into the sky and deposited him in the branches of a eucalyptus tree from where, looking down, he could see the rising column of flame and smoke that had been his dreams.

It was actually quite pretty, really. He heard a scratching sound beside him and looking around saw a koala staring at him, with the light of the fire reflected in its startled eyes.

"What the fuck are you looking at?" he said, just before he passed out.

Sparks began to float into the night sky like electric moths, and the percussive sound of exploding bottles reached Asia and the ladies where they sat in the back of the pickup parked across the road, watching the fire beginning to climb up the shingled roof of the hotel.

Crispin and Booby, both prostrated by their exertions now that the drug had worn off, were completely unable to move and seriously chilled out. The reason they were unable to move and seriously chilled out was because their naked buttocks were frozen to the floor of the deep freeze, where they had been thoughtfully placed so that the lead lining would protect their MGJ-impregnated nuts from the sonic waves.

Wally, Stavros, Jimmy, and Bruce came staggering across the veranda, each carrying something. Wally the cash register, Jimmy and Bruce cases of beer, and Stavros some kind of furry animal with smoke coming from it. They were grimy with soot and smelling of smoke from their fight with the fires started by the explosions, a battle they had lost, compelling them to beat a hasty retreat and concede the Big Blue Billabong Hotel to the flames that were beginning to engulf it.

They set the crates down in a semicircle and sat on them, staring at the orange curtains of fire.

"Ah, well. Saves the bladdy funerals."

"Ah, yeah. An' the questions."

"Too right."

A series of soft pops and hisses echoed the ones emanating from the fire as Wally opened beers and handed them round. Asia climbed down from the truck and sat with her back against Wally's knees. The light from the fire illuminated their sweaty and begrimed faces as they gazed at the inferno.

"Here's to ya," said Stavros, holding up his bottle.

"Yeah. See ya," said Wally.

"I 'ope she don't spread to the bush," Bruce said.

"Nah, mate. We're lucky. Wind's in the right direction."

"Wher'd'ya find Captain Cook?"

"Ah, some fucken dingbat had stuffed 'im down the chimney. One a the blasts musta shifted 'im."

"Is 'e right?"

"Yeah. No worries. 'Is fur's a bit singed, but apart from that 'e's good as new."

"That's a fucken relief."

They lapsed into silence, drinking beer and watching as the front facing of the building collapsed and the roof came down, sending a sinuous tower of sparks snaking into the darkness.

"There she goes, Wal."

"Yep."

"How long d'ya reckon to put her back up?"

"Reckon we should wait 'til the fire goes out first, Stav."

Asia was finding it difficult to understand their attitude. They were sitting round watching their own hotel burn down, drinking and chatting like it was some bonfire. She half expected one of them to walk over and stick a couple of potatoes into the fire. They appeared to be more concerned about the stuffed koala than the building.

"Didya check the wonga in the register, Wal?"

"Yeah, Stav."

"Good night?"

"Yeah. Rippa."

In the distance they could see a faint glow and a thin orange line rising into the air.

"Looks like another fire down the road, Wal."

"Yeah. Reckon it's that fucken nong Monsoon. Stupid barstad must've 'ad the radio on."

"D'ya wanna go an' look?"

"Yeah. Might as well. Soon as I finish me beer."

The first hint of blue was in the eastern sky as Wally, Stavros, and Asia stood around the blackened shell of the burnt-out Land Rover, feeling the heat on their faces. There was no sign of a body in the front.

"Whaddya reckon happened to the dingbat, Wal?"

"Dunno."

"Reckon 'e got out?"

"Dunno, mate, but the fucken dingo's'll be 'avin their meat well done if 'e didn't."

Looking at the faintly glimmering embers, Asia felt sick.

Ashes. Mary Rose in hospital. Nigel dead. Maybe Monsoon, too. All those others. Wally's hotel gone up in flames. And Baby Joe? And for what? For ashes. She began to cry. Wally put his arm around her.

"Don't waste yer tears on that one, sheila. 'Sides, maybe 'e scarpered?"

"I'm not crying for him, Wally."

"What then?"

"For everything. For all of this. For all the trouble we've caused. And now you've lost your hotel on top of everything. It's all our fault."

"Don't be a bleeding clip, sheila. It's nobody's fault. Shit 'appens. The hotel was insured, and anyway, Stav could do with a break."

"Too bladdy right."

"You're just being kind, I know. Even if we still had the money, we could put things right, but now that's gone up in smoke too."

"No it 'asn't."

"But I saw them loading it into this Land Rover."

"Nah. You mighta seen 'em stickin something in 'ere, but it wasn't the wonga."

"I don't understand."

"The money is in a safe deposit vault, back in Sydney. You don't think we'd be fucken stupid enough to be runnin round with ten million fucken dollars in cash, do ya?"

"But I thought…"

"Nah. We knew Monsoon might try something after Bjørn Eggen saw him looking at the case back in the hotel. We put these packets together to pull his pisser. A couple had some Aussie bills in 'em to make it look good."

"But why didn't you tell us?"

"Well, Asia. The truth is we weren't dead sure about Mary Rose, either. We wanted 'er to think we 'ad the wonga with us, to see if she would try anything. That's why it didn't look too good when she first went missing."

"Did Baby Joe know about this?"

"It was 'is fucken idea. Now come on, let's go an' see about finding a place to kip that's still fucken standin."

Under different circumstances it would have been idyllic. The sun was a low scarlet orb on the horizon, and the distant rock glowed magenta. Jimmy lay against the warm steel of the Holden, looking out over a meadow where the setting sun tinged the tips of the sparse grass blood red, and a small herd of wallabies bent to their grazing. Walkabout was laid across his thighs with his paws in the air, and Jimmy gently stroked the animal's belly as he regarded the bright sparkle of the distant plane.

Bjørn Eggen sat in a camp chair in front of his tent, smoking a pipe and drinking beer. Mary Rose attended to her pots, which were suspended over a fragrant fire of eucalyptus branches, peering into them over the tops of her spectacles. She had made a full recovery, and had even put on a little weight. Bjørn Eggen was also restored to full vigor, and days spent striding through the bush with Jimmy, observing all the new things with the enthusiasm of a child, had bronzed his formerly pallid Nordic face.

Crispin and Booby had set up their tent at some distance from the others out of a sense of delicacy, and now lay dozing in afternoon heat. The episode with the Machine Gun Jelly had been a revelation to Booby Flowers and had started him on the first steps of a voyage of self-discovery, with Crispin as his willing guide. It was not so much a case of him getting in touch with his feminine side as Crispin touching his masculine inside, and although at first it had felt strange he was slipping increasingly easily and comfortably into it. And so was Crispin. The only difficult part was cultivating his mustache, which steadfastly refused to grow despite every encouragement.

Asia was wandering through the bush at the edge of the encampment, absorbed, as had become usual, in her own thoughts. She had only been persuaded to stay after great efforts by the others, and contested the wisdom of that decision with herself on a daily basis. She had almost despaired of hearing from Baby Joe, as had they all, and shared the same unspoken fear that cast its cold shadow over them, intensified a hundred times in her case. Thoughts of him pursued her through her days and nights and followed her into sleep, where dreams of him haunted the edges of her consciousness. It disturbed her that in her dreams she could never see his face clearly, and that even awake she could not quite summon an image of him into her mind. She felt that she needed him and missed him more than ever, and worried that she had lost him before she ever actually truly had him, but at the same time she felt the memory of him fading from her, no matter how hard she tried to cling to it.

In case there were any more surprises they had decided to build a camp out at Jimmy's place while they waited for news of Baby Joe, one way or another. Nothing had been heard from him, or about him, and Helmut had been sent on a mission to Cairns to try and get some information, to check the news and the internet, to check anything that might give them a clue as to what was happening, but he had returned empty-handed.

It was Helmut who was now approaching, zooming in low over the tree tops, making a pass over the camp and dipping his wings before banking down and gliding to a showy landing on the makeshift runway. He waved as he stepped from the cockpit, and from the other side, Wally ducked past the still-spinning prop. Helmut walked to the back of the Cessna, opened the door, and dropped down the small step. All waking eyes were on the plane as Helmut reached inside and took hold of a pair of crutches, and Wally held out his hand and assisted a heavily bandaged man down onto the red earth.

A distant kookaburra answered Asia's loud scream as it rang across the meadow and echoed in the far hills. The last of the sun burnished her wild hair, flying behind her like the uncombed tail of a red mare as she galloped across the grass and through the trees to the airstrip. The man, limping forward on his crutches, stopped as she raced up to him, panting from her mad sprint.

The man before her looked so frail and wan, so aged, that she feared to hold him, and instead stood before him and raised her hand to his cheek with tears streaming down her face. The man smiled at her and something of what he had been shone through, and as she looked into the pained but undimmed eyes of Baby Joe Young, she knew.

It was over.

The rock glowed blood red, so that even at this distance you could almost feel the warmth of the stone. Like its celestial twin, the pulsating half-sun stood on the rim of the world, lighting their faces with its fading glow. Except for Jimmy, they sat in the camp chairs under the eucalyptus, listening to the chattering of kookaburras and watching the sunlight on the long grass of the meadow and tinting the russet fur of the wallabies.

Asia sat on the ground with Walkabout laid across her thighs, leaning her back against Baby Joe's bandaged legs. Bjørn Eggen had his pipe in one hand and a beer in the other, and Mary Rose sat with her hand resting on his arm. Crispin and Booby sat a little way back, holding hands and whispering to each other. Helmut sat next to Bjørn Eggen with his feet resting on a crate, and beside him Woolloomooloo Wally sat with a beer clamped to his mouth, smiling at no one in particular, looking as ancient and unfathomable as Australia herself. Jimmy stood on a nearby boulder, leaning on his spear and facing the vanishing sun, his face turned to ancient amber by the dying light.

A fire crackled in front of them, and the smell of roasting meat mingled with the scent of the burning gum. Peace and contentment was upon them and they luxuriated in the silence, until finally Asia said, "You know we can never go back, don't you?"

They all looked at her.

Baby Joe moved his arm in an expansive circle along the horizon, saying with a gesture that could not be properly articulated in words. "Now, why the fuck would we want to do that?"

The laughter rang out loud and without reserve, startling a crew of roosting budgerigars into flight from the branches overhead. The birds circled, twittering, and headed off through the deepening twilight to find a more peaceful perching place.

Walkabout farted.


The End.

# Epilogue.

It had not been so much a case of lack of evidence as of lack of interest. By all reckoning, Baby Joe Young's life should have been over that day. The paramedic who brought him back from the brink of eternity had not given him one chance in a thousand; but then, every once in a while a thousand-to-one shot comes in, even in Las Vegas. By the time the surgeon had finished pulling bits of metal out of him, he had enough lead to roof a church and enough iron to shoe a horse, and given the amount of stitches used any tailor worth his salt could have knocked up a pretty decent raincoat. Remarkably, none of the blades, bullets, and bits of fragmentation grenade that had pierced him had hit anything that might have proved inconvenient later on, but he had required enough plasma to keep every wino on the North Side happy for a week. It was loss of blood that nearly killed him, and a couple of times he was looking at the big white light, but something inside him refused to go, and Baby Joe dragged himself back to the world of pain.

And thereafter, his recovery was swift. He was gimping to the head when medical wisdom said he should have been sitting in a wheelchair with his dick in some nurse's hand—not that he would have objected to that, especially—and was in physical therapy when he should have been bed-bound and wondering how he was going to get at the itch under the cast on his broken arm that was driving him round the bend. In short, his journey from the trauma unit pissing out blood to the men's room at the Whale Lounge pissing out Guinness was remarkably short.

Of course, as soon as he was well enough to speak the boys in blue had been extremely interested in what he had to say. The Don's apartment had looked like Kuwait City Center when the police arrived, and such was the destruction and mayhem that there had been absolutely no way to recreate what had happened other than to notice that there had been a serious difference of opinion. The one witness who was still in a position to shed any light on the subject was bleeding worse than the Turin Shroud, and among the many theories formulated as to what had happened, the one about a middle-aged man single-handedly assaulting an apartment containing more firepower than a South Central crack den and annihilating almost as many Italians as Mount Vesuvius did not receive much consideration.

Not surprisingly Baby Joe also avoided this version of events in his testimony, instead maintaining that he had merely been the victim of some unfortunate timing, being in the Don's office on legitimate business when the St. Valentine's Day Massacre reenactment society had burst in and started spraying lead. Some minor aspects of the case—such as forensic evidence, fingerprints, bullet matches, angles of entry, powder burns, etcetera—were not exactly overlooked, but given the apparent obviousness of what had happened and the evident state of deceasedness of most of the perps, were not examined as diligently as they might have been. The one witness that came forward kept saying something about some mysterious, black, fat man.

Three days after Baby Joe got out of the hospital, and the day before his flight to Australia, he was sitting in his customary seat in the Whale when a senior vice squad dick with whom he had a nodding acquaintance walked up to him, handed him a brown paper package, patted him on the back, and told him he might want to consider taking a long vacation. Inside the package was the videotape from the Don's security camera.

Case closed. God Bless America.

Baby Joe never fully recovered from the events of that day. Eventually his body healed, although he was left with a slight limp and his left arm would not extend properly, but in his mind he was never the same. Some part of him had died in that building, some fire in him extinguished, replaced by the absolute knowledge of his own mortality and a bizarre kind of postcoital depression that remained with him, a pervading sorrow like a cool mist that he could see through but never quite lift. The Don's last act, and his final words, would live with him until the day he died.

He moved to Northern Queensland, and with his share of the money built a house on the beach and bought the boat that he had always wanted. Asia went with him, and they sat on their veranda each evening watching the birds flying towards the setting sun and the light fading on the sea that Baby Joe knew, inevitably, he must one day watch alone.

Asia was happy. She gave half of her money to her mother and bought a small souvenir shop close to where they lived. She was very popular and soon made many friends in the community. She closed her shop at five o'clock every day and went to a small bar on the waterfront, where she could have a glass of wine and watch Baby Joe's boat sailing home though the surf outside the reef.

And each night, as they lay in each other's arms, she clung to him too tightly, as if to restrain the fleeing moment. But who may contain the wind?

Bjørn Eggen took Mary Rose back to the Arctic Circle. She loved it immediately and Bjørn Eggen was extremely happy, even though she made him stop carrying dead fish in his pockets.

He felt sufficiently re-invigorated to get himself a new dog team, and it was on his sled that he carried Mary Rose Christiansson across the sunlit snow and back to his house by the lake on the summer's evening they were wed in the Gjudbumsenningbjerg chapel.

Wrapped up in furs, with their breath rising in white clouds, they walked the dogs through the forest, and in the evenings they sat by the fire and drank aquavit all through the twilight.

Wally and Stavros rebuilt the Big Blue Billabong Hotel and reinstalled the somewhat-scorched Captain Cook to his rightful place, and life continued as before. Except something in the land, a voice from the dreamtime, was speaking to Woolloomooloo Wally, telling him it was time to become Birring Barga again.

He gave Wal's Outback and the boat to his eldest children and he shipped his wife and her sisters, and as many of the kids as could be identified, back to Blue Billabong. In later years this resulted in some very interesting genetic combinations among the population in the surrounding area. Rodney had to be retired from show business, having discovered that it was much more fun sitting on people's heads than stealing their cameras. She was introduced to a wild herd in the highlands, where she fielded advances from amorous bulls and kept a watchful eye on the occasional tourists that visited the region, just in case the opportunity to sit on one of them presented itself.

As the years went by Wally left the running of the New Big Blue Billabong more and more to Stavros and spent more and more time in the bush with Jimmy and Walkabout, where he listened to the voices of the land and the wind in the trees and the birds and the animals, and stood on the painted rocks at dawn, singing the old songs and waiting for the dreamtime.

Crispin flourished in the land down under. He and Booby moved to Sydney together, but it didn't work out and Booby went back to the States. Crispin bought a beautiful apartment with a spectacular view overlooking the harbor and, even though he didn't need to, went back to work, getting a regular gig at a swish little club in Kings Cross, and was soon the darling of the swinging scene.

Feeling that he needed something more relevant to his new home, he changed his name to Ned Jelly. Besides, Crispin Capricorn was such a dreadfully silly name. Crispin—or rather, Ned—furnished his new apartment with the same opulence and style that he had his Vegas apartment, except that the new one had wooden floors, no white carpets, and no Japanese lacquered tables.

He had bought him himself a new Bichon Frise puppy, a cuddly little fur ball bitch that he called Dolly Doo, and he wasn't taking any chances.

Booby was the reason that things didn't work out between him and Crispin. Having discovered his new sexuality he wanted to explore it to the full and didn't want to be restricted. He moved to San Francisco, changed his name to Booty Florette, and took to wearing the dresses he swiped from the chic boutique where he got a job as a window dresser. His nights were spent sinking ever deeper into the steaming sexual swampland of the bathhouses.

It wasn't the best time to be doing it. The inveitable happened. He started to waste away. Eventually he became too weak to work or go out and was confined to his apartment. He bought of copy of *Women and Men* by Joseph McElroy. He became deeply absorbed in it. The book has 1192 pages. One late summer's afternoon, as he lay on his camp bed under the window, he reached the bottom of page 1191. As he turned the leaf to page 1192, he turned his toes up and he croaked.

Long Suc went into rapid decline. How are you going to kick ass with no fucking feet? Actually, loss of face cost him more, and within a year he had been pushed out by more vigorous competition. Taking his considerable fortune, and what was left of his dignity, he moved to the Thai border, where he opened a very successful cathouse and spent his twilight years smoking opium and having his dick sucked and his ego massaged by girls young enough to be his granddaughters.

Not a bad result when you consider what traditionally happens to the bad guys in stories such as this.

Handyman Harris was compelled by circumstances to find new accommodation, ending up in the suburbs with a small garden and a dog for his kids. He also made other radical changes to his lifestyle.

For example, whenever he shot pool he insisted that the phone be disconnected, he never opened the door to strangers, and every time he saw a man of the cloth he religiously crossed to the other side of the street.

Hazy Doyle was overjoyed to discover the fifty grand that Baby Joe had left him under the Buddha, especially as he had run out of papers at the time. It was only the unpleasant taste that saved his windfall from going up in smoke. Not everyone is changed by success, and Hazy never let his riches go to his head, largely because he could never remember from one minute to the next that he was rich.

He continued to surf the Milky Way by day and tune in to the groovy intergalactic transmissions, and at night dead people continued to fight each other in his dreams, and once a year a guy he knew, a buddy from the war, climbed in through his window and gave him a beer that he never opened.

Of the other peripheral characters the reader may be curious about:

Norm—he of the electric appendage—retired from the sea and moved to Fremantle, where he became a night watchman at an ice cream factory, spending his free time watching cricket and rugby, having a few tinnies with his mates, and on the occasional Saturday night plugging himself into a twelve-volt battery just for old time's sake.

Bruce eventually surrendered to a sense of futility and abandoned his wait for Kylie Minogue to parachute from the sky and give him a blowjob. He is currently waiting for Beyonce Knowles to parachute from the sky and give him a blowjob.

Penguin Brew eventually ran the Wollongong aground in broad daylight on a reef in the Society Islands, with a cargo of soap powder. When he sobered up in a Papeete jailhouse three days later, he came to the conclusion that it was time for the sailor to come home from the sea. He retired to his house in Manly and became a common sight in subsequent years, rolling along the littoral from alehouse to alehouse, telling outrageous sea fables to anyone who would buy him a measure of the amber nectar.

Helmut, whilst heading back to Cairns after the three-day opening bash for the New Big Blue Billabong Hotel, carrying the wife of a prominent media mogul and a Rolf Harris impersonator, and somewhat the worse for wear, became disoriented, ran out of gas, and had to ditch in the Torres Strait. Helmut survived completely unscathed, but of the mogul's wife and the Rolf Harris impersonator, neither hide nor hair were ever seen again, although recently a Canadian anthropologist claims to have heard a canoe-load of Torres Strait Islanders enthusiastically singing "Tie Me Kangaroo Down, Sport." The media mogul was so grateful that he gave Helmut a new plane and made him his personal pilot. Helmut still gets letters from Rolf Harris fans.

The two young men who had been hired by Monsoon to pretend to be officers in the Marines, and who turned out to be trainee grade-school teachers from Wisconsin, were disappointed when no one showed up after so much meticulous preparation. They were even more disappointed when they were arrested and sentenced to five years apiece for impersonating military personnel.

Vulture Skull Hangover disbanded after Anna accidentally perforated her duodenum with an electric chrome dildo onstage at a private gig and gave herself a two thousand-volt enema. The surviving members are currently looking for a new lead singer.

Loretta and her crew went to New Zealand for a well-earned vacation with the money that Wally gave them for their help. Except for Marilyn, they returned well rested and resumed their former activities. They can be found any Saturday night at the New Big Blue Billabong Hotel, Queensland. Marilyn met a young ski instructor from America called Davy Dupree, fell in love, and ended up living in Brian Head, Utah.

Almost a year to the day after the events described, two tipsy college girls from Phoenix, Arizona, in town for the weekend, were blowing their allowance on the dollar blackjack tables in Binion's Horseshoe, in downtown Vegas. During the shuffle they were speculating about a small, dark figure sitting at the bar behind them, staring into a glass of bourbon and a half-empty schooner of beer.

"It's him, for sure."

"It can't be, Alice. Just look at his clothes. He's wearing rags. And he smells."

"I'll bet he's incognito. He doesn't want to be recognized."

"Are you out to lunch, or what?"

"No. I'm serious. It's him."

"No more martinis for you, girlfriend."

"Okay, I'll prove it. I'm going to ask him." Alice straightened her skirt, fussed with her blond hair, and strolled over to where the man sat. He looked up as she approached, and Alice looked into his big, sad brown eyes.

"Excuse me," she said, "but are you Tiger Woods?"

The man turned away from her, hung his head, and wept into his beer. As Alice walked away, embarrassed, the man was banging his head on the bar.

Finis.

# About the Author

A line in Ulysses reads, "Only the sacred pint can unbind the tongue of Dedalus." Shane Norwood firmly believes this, just as he believes that it would be foolish in the extreme to argue with James Joyce. For this reason he has dedicated himself to the diligent consumption of copious amounts of booze before sitting down to write, in an effort to emulate the great ones. How successful this experiment turns out to be remains to be seen, but in the meantime it can be safely said that Shane Norwood seriously enjoys his writing.

Shane is a devoted family man who keeps food on the tables by walking around in circles in Chile masquerading as a casino manager, and occasionally pretending to be Robert Mitchum. Shane was born in a steel town in the north of England in 1955. Shane has five children. He is engaged in a breeding competition with his eldest daughter who is currently winning six to five. Although his soul knows it is English because of the larceny that lurks therein, the rest of him is no longer sure. One daughter is American, one is from Kenya, one son is from South Africa, two sons are from Chile, his wife is from Argentina, his horse is an Arab, and his dog is Italian. At one time Shane was a fisherman in Hawaii. In his heart he still is, although he hopes that, pretty soon, he will also be able to think of himself as a writer.

# Credits

This book is a work of art produced by Shannon & Elm, an imprint of The Zharmae Publishing Press.

Sara Bangs
Editor-in-Chief

Tony Kuoch
Cover Art & Design

Eric Tate
Copy Editor

Amanda Kreklau
Proofreader

Andrew Call
Reviewer

Allyson Schnabel
Managing Editor

Travis Robert Grundy
Publisher

The Zharmae Publishing Press
Spokane | May 2014